Nothing Good Happens After 2am

Niamh Hargan is a writer and lawyer. Born and raised in Northern Ireland, Niamh is now based primarily in Scotland. *Nothing Good Happens After 2 a.m.* is her third novel.

Also by Niamh Hargan

Twelve Days in May
The Break-Up Clause

Nothing Good Happens After 2am

NIAMH HARGAN

HarperCollins*Publishers*

HarperCollins*Publishers* Ltd
1 London Bridge Street,
London SE1 9GF
www.harpercollins.co.uk

HarperCollins*Publishers*
Macken House, 39/40 Mayor Street Upper
Dublin 1, D01 C9W8, Ireland

Published by HarperCollins*Publishers* 2026

1

A catalogue record for this book is available from the British Library

ISBN: 978-0-00-870058-4 (HB)
ISBN: 978-0-00-870059-1 (TPB)

This novel is entirely a work of fiction. The names, characters and incidents portrayed in it are the work of the author's imagination. Any resemblance to actual persons, living or dead, events or localities is entirely coincidental.

Set in Sabon LT Std by HarperCollins*Publishers* India

Printed and bound in the UK using 100% Renewable
Electricity at CPI Group (UK) Ltd

This book contains FSC™ certified paper and other controlled sources to ensure responsible forest management.

For more information visit: www.harpercollins.co.uk/green

Prologue

1 January 2025

The new year was only a few hours old by the time Robbie turned the corner onto Epworth Street. It was cold but bright, the sort of early morning that London in January so rarely provided, and all was quiet. Across the city, those who hadn't decamped to whatever other place they were from originally would be sleeping off hangovers for several hours to come. There was a time Robbie would have been doing the exact same thing.

As it was, he found himself on a deadline. Even across the festive season, every moment he hadn't been working had been ruined by the guilt of not working, and his desk – a nondescript corner of a nondescript office in Holborn – was calling to him.

Before that, though, this little pilgrimage. This stupid, sentimental thing.

He walked across the street, right up to a squat building of yellowed London stock brick. He took in its familiar narrow doorway, attempted to peer through the single window to the left. Quite why, he didn't know. There was, notoriously, nothing to see here. A purple velvet curtain, now thick with dust, concealed every centimetre of what was inside. And of course, there was no sign above the door. The whole 'no sign' thing had been a big deal, back in the day.

Still. Those who knew where to look had always found exactly what Robbie's eyes settled upon next. It was still there, below the number on the door, the paint faded but visible.

Half a heart melted into half a skull, the whole image no bigger than a handprint, and it made things so obvious, really. A say-what-you-see situation.

Love and Death.

Robbie almost did speak the name aloud. How ridiculous. He tamped down the urge and exhaled a little laugh instead, watching his own breath appear in the cold air in front of him.

That logo had been his idea, as it happened. Not in specific design but in notion. 'I think we just need to give people *something*,' he'd implored Otto, all those years ago. A breadcrumb, a promise, some little whisper of *yes – you made it; you've come to the right place.*

After all, Shoreditch had felt like such a schlep to get to back then – positioned, as it was, right inside a Venn diagram of the unsavoury and, much worse, the unexciting. Plus, nobody had maps on their phones by which to navigate themselves in those days; they didn't carry whole communities of strangers around in their pockets.

When he thought of his youth and early adulthood in those terms – thought of how vastly everything seemed to have changed in the blink of an eye – it always made Robbie feel positively geriatric. A part of him knew that was crazy talk. He knew that there were some upsides to an urban, contemporary existence, and one of them was that, at least among all the other almost-42-year-olds he knew, the general consensus seemed now to be that 42 was *young*, actually.

Young-ish.

He hadn't been feeling young lately, though. He definitely didn't feel it this morning, looking at the facade of Love and Death. What was it that journalist had called the place? *The most influential bar of the century.* Now *there* was a sentence to make a man feel ancient.

The journalist's name was Esther, and Robbie had spoken to her reluctantly, via Zoom, just before Christmas. She was putting together a 'long read', she'd said. Something of an 'oral history'. On account of the upcoming anniversary and all.

'Did you always want to be a bartender?' she'd asked him, by way of opening gambit.

Robbie had just chuckled, reclining a little in his desk chair. He'd booked out a meeting room specifically, prepared himself an underwhelming coffee from the fancy machine.

'I don't know if anybody grows up wanting to be a bartender, do they?'

He sure hadn't. Even if he *had*, he wouldn't have used that term – it was one of the many things that Otto had brought with him across the Atlantic and, by sheer force of personality, managed to transpose onto London's nascent craft cocktail scene.

'So, then, what prompted you to get into the industry?' Esther had continued.

'Uh . . .'

Robbie had found himself faltering. He supposed that what had prompted him to get into the industry, if he wound that tape all the way back, was Anna-Claire. Ironic, really, given how things panned out. But not an irony he'd felt remotely like sharing with a head and shoulders on his computer screen.

'Oh, you know. Just kind of . . . fell into it, I suppose.'

'Always the way,' Esther had replied, her voice still warm and buoyant. Evidently, this was not her first rodeo. A taciturn subject hadn't seemed to faze her in the least. 'So, take me back to the beginning. If you can remember that far! I'm just pulling up some photos of the opening night right now, in fact – looks like quite the party.'

Robbie hadn't needed to see the pictures to know exactly the ones she was talking about. At one point in his life, he'd all but studied them. New Year's Eve, 1999. Absinthe and rum captured mid-pour behind the bar. People twirling, clinking glasses, kissing one another on the lips. For static images, there was just such a sense of *movement* to them, such a sense of life. A new millennium was beckoning, and the small crowd of hand-selected guests at a tiny Shoreditch speakeasy didn't seem to feel one iota of fear, about Y2K or anything else. They were in feathers and sequins, bow ties and braces, drunk on the idea of something spectacular ahead. The very next night, apparently, Otto had instituted his notorious photography ban. Those pictures now felt all the more precious, all the more iconic, as a result.

'What do you remember most about those early days?' Esther had prompted then, and Robbie had realized with a start that he'd let himself get lost in thought. Nostalgic, suddenly, for a night he hadn't even been present at, swept right back up in the lore and the legend of Love and Death. Hadn't that always been part of the problem, really?

He'd cleared his throat a little, tried his best to refocus on the screen before him, tried to sound casual in his response.

'I showed up five years in, so I couldn't tell you,' he'd answered, and who could say why he'd added what he did next. 'You'd need to ask El.'

Apart from anything else – apart from the strangeness of her name on his lips – he'd quickly realized that his statement wasn't even entirely accurate. Time was funny that way. These days, he seemed to find it harder and harder to really trust his own memory.

He'd hurried to course-correct: 'Although, actually, she didn't start herself 'til . . . I don't know. 2002 or 2003 maybe. She was Otto's first hire. Before that, it was just Otto himself behind the bar. Solo.'

Robbie couldn't recall what Esther said in response, or indeed what he said himself for the remainder of their allotted thirty minutes together, beyond it being as little as humanly possible.

However, standing on Epworth Street now, he was all too aware that the article was due to be published today. Up and down the country, it would soon be spread across kitchen tables, to say nothing of the clicks that would follow around the world. Probably many thousands of eyeballs, all told.

He remained unsure whether his own would be among them.

Still, he found he was glad that he had come here this morning. It felt right, having done some small thing to mark the birthday of this place. Not to mention, of course, its deathday.

With that thought, Robbie reached out to trace his fingers across the symbol on the door, that little heart-skull. It was an instinctive act, and he watched his own hand as though it belonged to someone else. Thoroughly embarrassing behaviour on his part, no doubt, but along with that awareness – along with the melancholy that suddenly threatened to overwhelm him – there was undeniably a certain enjoyment to all of this, too. A certain sense of the cinematic, somehow.

Even as he turned to walk away, Robbie couldn't help but pause at the corner, twist his neck to give the street one final glance.

And that – the very last moment available – was when he saw her.

A woman with a dark pixie cut, her whole body dwarfed by a bright cerise Puffa coat, walked towards the bar from the other direction.

Robbie's breath hitched in his chest, his brain struggling to put the pieces together. Partially that was for obvious reasons: she looked different, and he hadn't been expecting her. Plus, there was the other thing: that initial half-second's worth of surprise that he used to feel quite frequently, upon seeing her in the daylight.

After all, he'd seen this woman so often in silhouette; all the way back to when she was really just a girl, he'd stood beside her in the flicker of streetlights or candlelight or the sepia lowlights of some bar or other. Was it any wonder that she'd come to exist that way in his mind's eye?

At least, mostly she did. There were a few notable exceptions.

From the other end of the street, she spotted him now, too, literally stopping in her tracks when she did. She stared across at him, agog, her lips parting slightly.

It's you, her expression said, and he watched the very second that it shifted into something more droll, something slightly self-deprecating. *Of course it's you.*

We must stop meeting like this.

Of all the gin joints in all the towns in all the world, etc.

Robbie let himself follow her gaze back towards Love and Death. It was not what it once was. He and this stranger were not what they once were, either.

But they were here, together, after all this time. They'd each woken up this morning, in their separate beds, and had found themselves compelled to make the exact same journey.

Didn't that count for something? In the deepest, most vulnerable and least trustworthy parts of his own mind, Robbie thought it had to count for something.

Part One

Chapter One

The third time Robbie ever came to Love and Death was at the beginning of summer 2005. It was 3 a.m. on a Wednesday morning. Or was that still considered Tuesday night – in spirit if not in fact? Either way, leaving his flat stone cold sober in the wee hours, everything in Robbie's body told him that he should rightfully be heading to an airport, not a secret cocktail bar in East London. However, it had become a needs-must situation.

By then, he'd at least learned how to easily identify the correct street, the correct building. He'd discovered that, in a nod to the old American Prohibition-era speakeasies, admittance required all prospective customers to ring the doorbell and then give a password. Or rather, in this case, a passphrase: 'Saint Bibiana, pray for me.'

(He'd had time to research that one by then, too. Bibiana, he'd learned, was the patron saint of hangovers.)

Robbie didn't have to think too hard to come up with any number of people in his life who would balk at such an utterance. It was sacrilegious. Much worse than that, there was the suspicious ring of Catholicism about it. Nonetheless, when a disembodied greeting came from the intercom at Love and Death that night, Robbie couldn't say the words fast enough.

The next thing he knew, a buzzing sound rang out, and he was able to push the door open, show himself inside.

That was new. It felt like progress, compared with his two

prior attempts. Equally, however, the change was disconcerting. The jitters in his stomach ramped up a notch, and he could no longer tell if they were the good sort or the bad.

When he stepped into the warm, dark cocoon of Love and Death, he barely registered the smoky scent of incense or the jazz music still playing quietly. Certainly, he did not notice any bodies beyond the one right in his line of vision.

Because sitting on a stool at the bar – sitting *right there* – a low-ball glass in front of him, was a lean, straight-backed figure. Robbie found it impossible, at least in the current lighting, to estimate the man's age, but he had an ostentatious handlebar moustache, and he wore a perfectly tailored bottle-green three-piece suit. Somehow, these facts in combination were enough for Robbie to know: here was Otto Kettinger – the person he'd been looking for.

Third time lucky.

For a beat, Robbie just stood there, mouth slightly agape, as though in the presence of a deity. Then, he rushed to shake himself out of it, stepping forwards and extending a hand.

'I'm Robert,' he said, because, back then, everyone called him Robert. He called himself that.

'Well, hi,' Otto drawled, meeting his handshake. There was something cartoonish about the drawl, the way there often seemed to be when an American was out of context (in other words, out of America). He took in every inch of Robbie, not bothering to hide the quizzical expression on his face – exaggerating it, if anything. 'What can I do for you?' he asked.

Robbie took a deep breath. This was it. The moment.

'I'd like to work here,' he replied. Politely, but confidently. He'd had some practice in this domain, after all. If he hadn't learned to push through – taught himself to believe that he was just as deserving, just as capable, just as good as other people – he probably would never have left Belfast.

Before him, Otto immediately lost interest. 'Sorry, kid. I'm not hiring,' he said, and it was strange how the very air in the room seemed to change. Just seconds ago, Robbie had been able to *feel* Otto's curiosity, the force and the fizz of it. Now, the flatness of its absence was equally obvious.

'I don't want paying, if that helps,' he rushed to add. 'I understand that you wouldn't . . . that is, I've heard you only offer actual *jobs* to people if they've come by personal recommendation. Plus, I've already got a job. Or, come September, I do.'

'Is that so?'

Robbie nodded. 'At Citibank. It's like a grad scheme thing, you know? I've just finished a history and economics degree. At Oxford.'

People normally had some sort of reaction to that information, whether it was positive or negative, whether it was one they expressed or one they rushed to conceal.

From Otto, however, there was nothing. He took a lingering sip from the amber liquid in his glass. 'Well, alright. And so, cocktails come into this whole thing where?'

Otto set his glass down again on the bar, leaned back a little, as though to regard Robbie anew. 'Let me guess. You knocked up some Mojitos for a bunch of dorks, and they liked 'em, huh? Look, I got nothing against hobbyists, kid. I mean, I *kind of* do, but whatever. Point is, I wish you well with the economics or whatnot. You want some place to hang for the summer, drink some drinks, meet some girls – cool. Good for you. But this ain't it.'

'What?' Robbie spluttered in response. 'No! That's not . . . I mean . . .' He found himself trailing off helplessly. Nothing of Otto's assessment was anywhere close to the truth. He should have made that obvious from the outset, he thought, cursing himself internally. He'd started this all wrong. He pushed his glasses – plain, rectangular frames – up his nose a little, out of habit.

'I've been working at The Randolph Hotel,' he began again. And suddenly, the issue seemed no longer to be that he couldn't find the words, but rather that he had far too many of them, tumbling out of his mouth almost of their own volition. 'It's a hotel in Oxford, like a five-star kind of place? I just mention that so you know that the customers are . . . y'know, let's say they're kinda fussy about their drinks. Anyway, I needed to save up to buy my girlfriend an engagement ring – we're actually getting married at the end of August, so I'm definitely, uh . . . off the market, so to speak. When I applied for the job at The Randolph, it really *was* just a way to make some money for the ring. I didn't know anything about drinks – as in, zero. But then I started behind the bar and . . . have you ever just felt . . . I don't know, like kind of *obsessed* with something?'

Otto said nothing for a moment, just regarded Robbie. 'I have.'

'I don't think I ever had, before then,' Robbie replied earnestly. 'They trained me from nothing at The Randolph, and pretty soon, I was working all the hours I could, just because I loved being there so much.'

In the end, he'd had enough in savings not just to buy Anna-Claire's little diamond but to see him through the summer after his final exams, too. And so, like many a 21-year-old before him, and many that would come after him, Robbie had set off for the big city with a dream.

That was a month ago. Since then, he'd been making his way around London's cocktail bars, for research purposes. There had turned out to be surprisingly few places of any great note to get through. Intently, Robbie had studied the ways that different places did things. He'd sampled from their menus and tried to figure out the ratios of ingredients. He'd struck up random conversations with bar staff like – it had to be said – a bit of a weirdo. Through all this, it had quickly become clear that across the city, there was one name on everyone's lips: Otto Kettinger. The Yank. Inventor of the Clementine, the Ludlow and – of course – the Cecilia, to name but a few. In the American Bar at The Savoy, the barman had told Robbie that those who were *part of the scene* asked for the Cecilia more than for any other drink.

There'd been something delicious about the sense of initiation that came with all of it: the tidbits of information collected slowly, both in real life and via various arcane corners of the internet; the mangled, conflicting instructions he'd received from different sources as to how to find Love and Death; the knowledge that even looking for it in the first place required *knowing someone who knew someone.*

Mercifully, he managed to convey all of this to Otto only in abbreviated form.

'Anyway, I have this summer before I start at Citi,' he continued. 'Practically everyone I know is in Indonesia right now. But I don't want to scuba dive or sunbathe. I don't want to build Habitat for Humanity houses, to be absolutely honest with you, or repopulate the rainforest or whatever. What I want to do, more than anything, is just perfect my Vieux Carré.'

For a second, Otto seemed to take that in. 'What kind of rye are you using?' he asked then.

'Rittenhouse.'

Otto clicked his tongue against his teeth. 'There's your problem. Try Sazerac. And don't be scared of the Bénédictine liqueur. Lot of people chicken out after five mils, but trust me, you're going to want to do ten. Really gives you that earthiness.'

Robbie gulped, trying to commit every word to memory. 'Okay. Got it.'

'So, what do you like about it? Making drinks,' Otto prodded then.

What didn't Robbie like about it? He struggled even to know where to start. He had some sense of the question, though, as a test. And if he said so himself, he was pretty good at tests.

'I like the history of it. I've been reading this book, *The Bon-Vivant's Companion* by Jerry Thomas. Do you know it?'

A hint of a smile tugged at Otto's lips. 'I sure do.'

'I mean, pretty crazy, isn't it? When I found out that book was first published in *1862*, my mind was pretty much blown. I've been doing all the digging I can into the whole history of cocktails. I couldn't believe how much, like, social history is built into every single drink.'

Robbie paused for breath, powered now by sheer enthusiasm. 'I love how cocktails connect us with the past that way – and they connect us with each other in the present, too, obviously. Making good drinks is kind of like playing an instrument or speaking a language. It brings people together. Except those other things require natural born talent. Whereas with drinks, a lot of the time, it's actually just maths. Science. I suppose maybe that's what I like about it most, in the end. Any given cocktail in the world . . . okay, I might have to get it wrong and get it wrong and get it wrong, but all the while, I know that eventually, I can get it *exactly* right, forever.'

He stopped, suddenly aware that he seemed to have been talking for some time. For a moment, the silence felt very loud indeed.

And then, from somewhere, a crash. At the other end of the bar, a girl was lifting a tray from the glasswasher, plonking it on the draining board with a clatter that might – uncharitably, but accurately – have been deemed deliberate.

'Sorry!' she said, as soon as Otto and Robbie turned towards her. She didn't *sound* particularly sorry.

It was then that Robbie realized he actually knew this girl. Or at least, he knew her to see – that's how people would have put it back in Belfast. He still often, in his own mind, put things the way people did back in Belfast. The girl was tall and slender, a dark-brown fringe all but covering dark-brown eyes, her hair falling practically to waist-length. Robbie recognized her because, on not one but two previous occasions, she'd been the person to send him packing from Love and Death.

14

Chapter Two

The first time, he'd come before the bar opened.

After he'd buzzed and spoken the magic words into the intercom, the door had cracked just enough for the girl's head and torso to appear in the gap.

She'd been wearing a loose, minimally present top that he'd wondered whether she might have crocheted herself. It had that look about it.

'He's not here,' the girl had said, after Robbie had asked for Otto.

'Oh. Do you know when he might be around?' Robbie had replied.

'I don't.'

'You don't,' Robbie had repeated, enunciating the words slowly. His delivery, he'd thought, made it clear that he was awaiting further explanation. However, in the silence that followed, the girl offered him zero. Zilch. Nada.

'It's just I'd really love to have a quick word with him, if that's possible,' he'd continued, undeterred.

Alas, she'd been even less deterred.

'Otto . . . he likes to keep quite a close circle, you know? He's very private. But thanks anyway for your interest,' she'd said.

And, with that, she'd promptly shut the door in his face.

*

The second time around, Robbie had come to Love and Death during service. After a twenty-minute wait on Epworth Street, the doorman had eventually ushered him inside, directed him towards a seat at the bar. Robbie's eyes had darted around, taking in every detail hungrily. Or thirstily – maybe that was the more appropriate term.

The space felt sultry and intimate, with room for around thirty patrons in total. Sumptuous velvet upholstery and tasselled lamp-shades made a shabby London side street feel like a little piece of what he imagined Havana or New Orleans to be. The perimeter was lined with booths, and in the middle, half a dozen candlelit tables were dotted around. The real showstopper, though, was the bar itself. Robbie had never seen such an array of drinks as he took in along the back wall. They'd been immediately fascinating to him, not so much in their volume as in their variety – their rarity. Overhead, a bronze semicircle surrounded the bar, filament bulbs positioned all the way along it, jutting from both the top and the underside of the structure. And on the ceiling, an elaborate Art Deco mirror reflected the light, casting all of Love and Death in a warm golden glow.

Less than ideally, the girl that Robbie had encountered previously was working behind the bar. Another person was there that night, too – a muscular young man with dreadlocks to his shoulders. Immediately, Robbie was disappointed to note that this guy didn't match any description he'd heard of the mysterious owner of the place. Nonetheless, of the two options presently available, he knew which person he'd prefer to serve him.

Alas, within moments, the girl made a beeline for him, her expression shifting quickly into recognition.

An interaction of a frustratingly similar flavour to their previous one had followed, though she had at least concluded matters this time by offering him a drink. And Robbie had figured, what the hell? Why not try to salvage the expedition? He might as well have something to show for his twenty-minute wait.

As it happened, what he'd got was the best Pisco Sour he imagined he might ever find outside of Peru.

He looked over at its maker now, giving her a little wave.

'Hi,' he offered.

She said nothing, just raised both of her eyebrows, tilting her chin upwards a little in greeting.

'That's Eloise,' Otto filled in.

'Just El is fine,' she corrected immediately, and in the glance between them that followed, Robbie had the sense of an old exchange here, something of an inside joke. Evidently, Otto knew how to elicit a response from her when he wanted one.

'El here's my girl Friday,' he continued.

'And every other day,' she muttered. She couldn't seem to help the affection creeping into her voice, though, fighting to show itself on her face.

Otto smiled, too. 'So whaddya reckon, El? Could we use a barback around here this summer?'

She shrugged. 'Not really.'

Otto leaned towards her in a conspiratorial sort of fashion, lowering his voice. 'I know, right? If we needed one, we'd have one. But what can I say? I kinda like this kid.'

From his spot less than a metre away, Robbie couldn't figure out whether or not he was supposed to have heard this. Or even if he was supposed to act like he hadn't.

In any case, Otto soon turned towards him once more. 'Do you know what a barback is?' he continued, before throwing his hands up dramatically. 'Ugh, what am I saying? Of course you don't! Baseball, barbacks, and cheese in a can – three things your fine country is just going to have to embrace sooner or later, and if you ask me, it should be sooner.' He paused, took another luxurious sip from his drink. 'A barback, in simple terms, is a bartender's assistant. I started as a barback myself, many moons ago, and let me tell you, I ain't ever learned more than I did that year. For you – I don't know – you might even think it's a step down from whatever you been doing at your fancy-schmancy hotel. I mean, it won't be, but you might *think* it is. We're talking slicing twists, cleaning glasses' – he gestured towards the ice wells – 'keeping these babies nice and topped up. If there's one thing I *will not compromise on* here at Love and Death, it's the ice programme.'

Robbie nodded readily, like he agreed nothing could be worse than a subpar ice programme. He wasn't entirely sure anything they'd done with ice at The Randolph could have been considered a *programme*.

'. . . You're telling me you wanna do all that for probably the last real summer you'll ever have in your life, Robbie?' Otto asked.

Just like that, Robert was Robbie. And in fact, he was only too delighted to be.

In the years to come, he'd retell the story of this moment, compare it to the one in which he learned that he – a boy born and raised in the shadow of the shipyard in East Belfast – had been admitted to the University of Oxford. He'd play it for laughs, and people would indeed laugh in response every single time. But in some sense, the analogy was a true one.

Robbie took in the scope of the opportunity before him and found he didn't mind at all that he would obviously have to become a little different in order to avail of it.

'Late nights, long hours?' Otto continued. 'For, in your case, *literally no money?*'

His voice rose with each new question, and Robbie felt an energy stirring inside him, felt the intensity of the older man's gaze. El, too, was looking intently at him.

Then, with a smile spreading across his face, he uttered the words that would – at least arguably – ruin the rest of his life: 'When can I start?'

Chapter Three

Eloise Tippett had always been a night owl. By the age of 17, she was working in a shitty bar full of shittier men, and even as she ushered them out the door at closing time – *you don't have to go home, but you can't stay here* – she'd known that she herself would definitely not be going home. The night was young, and so was El; she was all too ready to set about making some bad decisions.

At 22, she lived in a three-bedroom house in Hackney Wick, occupied at all times by between five and seven people. It was a fluid sort of situation, total acceptance of which was the main condition of residence. There seemed always to be someone in the first throes of romance (loudly), while another was in the midst of a protracted break-up (loudly). One housemate had recently taken up the Atkins diet on the very same week that another had committed suddenly and passionately to vegetarianism. The whole place was full of rickety, threadbare furniture and the clutter of other people's lives, a dehumidifier in the living room fighting a losing battle against rising damp. From behind the sofa, a large, discarded placard had found what appeared to be a permanent home. *WAR CRIMINAL*, it read, above a close-up photo, and El often felt that George W. Bush's blue eyes were following her wherever she went.

She didn't love that. But she loved almost everything else about the place.

Her parents, of course, would have hated it – her father in particular. And while El had just about ceased doing things specifically *because* her father would not have approved of them, she certainly still considered it a big bonus.

She was clattering around her bedroom at 4 p.m. when Kat woke, bleary-eyed. She took in El's appearance for a second, all confusion, watching as El pushed at least ten gold bangles up over her wrist.

'Are you on a clopen?' she asked.

'Mmm,' El replied.

Kat's face contorted in sympathy. Closing the bar one night, then opening it again the very next, was the shortest of straws. It meant clean-up duties *and* prepping duties, and little time between shifts to do anything but sleep. Kat understood; she worked at a bar in Soho herself, and El liked that the two of them shared a broadly similar schedule. She liked having sex that didn't come with a side of ego-management or a sliver of fear. Their relationship had, by now, gone on for a year, and El had moved into Kat's house-share, but still she considered it a fairly casual thing between the two of them.

'How was last night?' Kat murmured.

El paused, her mouth frozen, in any case, for the application of a dark burgundy lipstick. Even if only in her own mind, she had to admit that last night had turned out to be one of her more unusual shifts. And she'd been there the evening James Blunt came in.

Aside from Otto, there were a total of seven people working at Love and Death. Leon and Cormac handled the door on alternate nights. And behind the bar, the rotation included herself and four others. All of them were required to operate under certain rules. There was a certain way things were to be done.

Number 1. Within ninety seconds of a customer's behind meeting its allotted seat, he or she was to be offered that month's menu – a lean dozen drinks, ever changing, with classic cocktails available on request. The menu was to be accompanied, always, by a miniature glass of something Champagne-adjacent, *compliments of your host*. (El sometimes wondered whether anything she produced for the entire remainder of a person's night at Love and Death came close to beating the delight of that first free mouthful of fizz.)

Number 2. Absolutely no food of any description. Cocktail garnishes aside, not so much as a cashew nut crossed the bar on Otto's watch, and woe betide the customer who complained within his earshot.

Number 3. No star-fucking. On the occasions that a celebrity showed up, staff members were under strict instructions to treat them like any other patrons. Not better, and not worse. Lining one's pocket via a quick phone call to the paps, as happened routinely at any number of other London hotspots, was a sackable offence. (There was nothing, of course, to stop El keeping her own mental tally of the famous faces she'd served thus far: beyond Blunt, there was also Keira Knightley, and, on a separate occasion, Alan Rickman. She'd quickly developed a hope of collecting the entire cast of *Love Actually*, purely for the pithiness of the anecdote.)

Number 4. No guitar-driven music. Otto's judgement on what constituted guitar-*driven* was final, if often contested, and carried out on a song-by-song basis.

Number 5. No jeans.

Number 6. *Absolutely* no sportswear.

Number 7. No drugs.

Number 8. No cameras.

Number 9. No mobile phones.

And, on top of all that, there was one more thing:

Number 10. Otto was never, ever to be identified.

There were times he identified himself, of course. Very much so. There were times, of his own particular choosing, when he was all flamboyance, when he commanded the entire bar like it was his living room and everyone present had been personally invited to his birthday party.

Equally, however, there were nights – there could be whole weeks – where he wanted to see and speak to nobody. With the exception, sometimes, of El. If the problem was a creative one, if he was mixing ingredients like some sort of mad scientist, she was often the only person he seemed able to tolerate. Or perhaps it was that *she* was better able than most to tolerate *him* when he was in one of his moods.

It was a funny thing, really. El knew that she was Otto's protégée. But somewhere along the way, she seemed to have become his protector, too. More and more, over the last few months, people had been coming into Love and Death looking for *him*, wanting a sighting of *him*, wanting to be served by *him*. That had to be a lot of pressure, El thought.

It was also, sometimes, very evidently a lot of fun. She'd watched on many a night while Otto sat with his nose buried in a book, his lips twitching with amusement as people enquired as to his whereabouts. She'd heard him have lengthy conversations with unsuspecting customers, delightedly tossing out increasingly outlandish theories about the owner of this place.

Was his desire for anonymity really all about privacy, then? About a certain intensity that just didn't always mix with meeting other people's needs? Or was it something more calculated than that? Did Otto know that, in the end, there was nothing more appealing than elusiveness?

El couldn't always say for sure. But one way or another, in giving Robbie Saunders the heave-ho – twice – she had only been doing exactly what Otto wanted of her. It really had been nothing personal.

Robbie's outright refusal to take no for an answer . . . *that* felt a little personal.

Part of El was not surprised – or at least, she knew that she *shouldn't have been* surprised. She'd met plenty of guys like Robbie in her life, after all. The phrase 'Oxbridge prick' sprung quite naturally to mind.

In her bedroom, El could see her girlfriend reflected in the mirror now, and briefly she considered offering up all of this: the whole story, a real answer. She was short on time, though. And Kat, even when half-asleep, often wanted to discuss the underlying psychological root of El's woes in a level of depth that El herself really did not.

So, back to the basic question: how was work last night?

'It was alright, yeah,' she replied. 'Good. No rest for the wicked, eh?'

And then, with a final, quick swipe of black eyeliner – she was entirely convinced that the less time spent, the better the result – she was out the door again.

It was like that, in those days. She sometimes felt she spent more time at Love and Death than she did away from it. However, she wasn't complaining. Houses, she thought, were one thing. Before the age of 12, El had lived in Chicago and Geneva and Doha. She'd lived in Birmingham, Alabama and Birmingham, England. There were cities – entire countries – that she didn't even remember. She'd slept and eaten and watched TV in at least a dozen houses.

Home, though?

El wasn't entirely sure how or when it had happened, but somehow, when she conjured up the concept, the only place that came to mind was an unmarked door on Epworth Street.

Chapter Four

By the time El got there, Marcus was already in motion behind the bar, biceps flexing as he hauled and shovelled ice. Slightly annoyingly, Robbie had beaten her to it, as well. But then, time-keeping had never been El's strongest suit.

Generally, she began each shift in the little kitchen that they all referred to, generically, as 'the back'. This evening, however, she let herself linger by the side door she'd just slipped through, let herself observe the two men before her. They could not, visually, have been more different. Marcus, resplendent in dreads and a loose silk shirt, versus Robbie's beige chinos and crisp short-sleeved number. He was brandishing a notebook and pen, and appeared to be already expounding on some topic or other. There was, she thought, a degree of entitlement there – a degree of arrogance.

'I actually have kind of a list,' El could hear him saying. 'Just in my head, you know? Of the people I'd consider to be really *leading* the industry at the moment. The greatest living drinks creators.'

El rolled her eyes.

There followed a series of names – including Otto's, of course, plus various others that El would have claimed sounded familiar. Some really *did* sound familiar. Sasha Petraske, Dick Bradsell, Dale DeGroff . . . she was sure they were indeed all very good at whipping up a Martini, and top blokes to boot.

She couldn't seem to help what tumbled out of her mouth next. 'How many of them are women?' she called out loftily.

Both Marcus and Robbie turned to meet her voice.

'What?' Robbie asked, confused.

'On your list. How many of them are women?'

There was, she felt, an obvious mischievousness to the enquiry, to the lilt in her tone. She was still young enough that the lack of female representation in her industry – at the creative level, the *history-making* level – didn't make her sincerely angry. It didn't seem like something that was actually destined to affect *her*, a woman. It was just a fun jibe to toss out here and there, when the opportunity arose.

Across the bar, Robbie seemed to think about the question for a second. When it was obvious he could come up with nothing – with no one – El took the win.

'Interesting, isn't it?' she proclaimed blithely, and with that, she swept off into the back, letting the door swing behind her.

The hour or so that followed was the same whirl of activity that it always was. There were lemons and limes to be juiced, of course, but also guavas, cranberries, papayas – whatever other weird and wonderful fruits Otto had managed to source in a given week. The proceeds then had to be double-strained and decanted into glass bottles. Pouring spouts were attached to said bottles. Finally, the bottles were placed in the fridge, ready to be brought out to the bar as needed during service. It was a straight-forward, if time-consuming and repetitive, process.

As was her routine, El put on some music and got to work. It occurred to her that if Robbie would soon be taking some of these tasks off her plate, that was at least something to be grateful for. They worked on a two-day 'use-by' system at Love and Death, and El sometimes had nightmares that involved being consumed by a tsunami of ever-multiplying volumes of juices and syrups.

'Alright, Emmeline Pankhurst,' Marcus said, by way of greeting, when he came in to collect something or other.

El just chucked a tomato at him, and he caught it neatly.

'You've met our new recruit, I see,' she said.

'Yeah. Otto's here now, giving him the spiel. Interesting fella, ain't he?' Marcus said cheerfully. 'Sort of intense.'

Not for the first time, El remarked internally on Marcus's total lack of grandiosity, his natural disinterest in drama. Both were rarities in their line of work. She would know. Didn't she have, herself, strong tendencies towards grandiosity? Didn't she have a *huge* interest in drama? She adored revealing news to people, passing on tidbits of gossip.

To that end:

'He's just here temporarily,' she told Marcus. 'He's going to be an *investment banker* in September, if you can believe that. Or an accountant or something along that line – I don't know exactly. At Citibank. He went to Oxford.'

Sadly, Marcus took all this news entirely in stride. 'Oh right. That explains it then, don't it?' he said. 'Explains the outfit, anyway.' And, with an armful of Tupperware boxes now balanced under his chin, he disappeared as quickly as he'd arrived.

On autopilot, El returned to her own task, feeling more than a little dissatisfied. Of course, generally speaking, she prided herself on a level of looseness – a certain degree of laissez-faire, a capacity to go with the flow, and so on. What was the point in having been schlepped all over the world as a kid if she couldn't at least say that for herself? Per her own regular declaration, she took people as she found them.

She also called things as she saw them, though. That was another favourite phrase. And the bizarreness, the slight injustice, of Robbie's sudden presence at Love and Death – however temporary – felt undeniable to her.

Of its own accord, her mind darted to the dozen or so CVs,

including some from the city's most coveted talent, that she'd personally watched Otto toss right in the wastepaper bin. She couldn't help but think that at a minimum, any one of those applicants would have promised to stick around for more than three months.

As opening time approached, El re-emerged from the back, this time with half a dozen glass bottles clasped carefully between both hands. The soulful strains of Tracy Chapman were drifting out over the sound system now. Further down the bar, with Robbie hovering beside him, Marcus was topping up the canisters that held an array of different garnishes. Otto was settled at a table, ostensibly absorbed in a hardback novel, his eyes darting upwards every minute or so to take in all the details.

El looked around her with a pleased, anticipatory sort of feeling. This part was what she always imagined it might be like backstage at a theatre, before the curtain went up: everyone gathering their props, taking their places, awaiting their public.

She was making final preparations at her little station when Robbie sidled up to her. The notebook, she saw, was still firmly in hand.

'El,' he started. 'Look, I feel like maybe we might have got off on the wrong foot. I know it's probably weird for you to suddenly have a new person around, and I know you might not necessarily want me here, but I j—'

Instinctively, El held up a hand to stop him. It irritated her that – on top of everything else – this guy would presume to know her feelings, that he would presume his own capacity to influence them. It irritated her that he was correct on both counts. A heart-to-heart, though? Just because he'd decided they should have one? And right now, of all times? No.

'Robbie,' she said, all frankness. 'I don't care that you're here. I've been in this game a long time, okay? People come and go.

You're *definitely* going to come and go. You've literally said exactly that. This is a jolly for you, even if it isn't for the rest of us. And, I mean, *yes*, I'm sure it would be nice, being able to live without an income for a whole summer. *No*, if you asked me to guess, I probably wouldn't bet that your drinks will set the world on fire. But at the end of the day, you're not even going to be making any drinks here, are you? So, whatever.' She gave him a smile and held out both arms, before dipping down into a bit of a bow. '*Welcome.*'

What she was expecting in response to this, when she straightened, she did not know. Might he be pissed off? Intimidated? Charmed by her, in some way even he couldn't totally explain? El would have been fine with any of those options. Together, they represented the typical range of human reaction that she tended to elicit. As it was, from Robbie, she got . . . nothing.

He just studied her for a moment, and the steadiness of his gaze made her uneasy. She returned to her drinks station and, for lack of anything else to do, began to line up her cocktail shakers with totally uncharacteristic precision.

Then, at last, he spoke again. 'So, you've worked in a lot of different bars before this, then, have you?' he enquired conversationally.

El found herself a little thrown by the delivery. 'Yep,' she replied. Five, by her count.

Wordlessly, Robbie seemed to take that in.

'What?' she prompted.

He offered a little shrug. 'Nothing. It's just weird you aren't better at getting along with people, that's all.'

He said this like it was a fact, like it was the most neutral observation in the world. From his spot further down the bar, Marcus snorted out a laugh. El elected to ignore him. She had more than enough to deal with right now, so flabbergasted was she by what struck her as the worst insult she could possibly imagine – far further below the belt than anything she'd just tossed out herself.

'I'm *excellent* at getting along with people,' she told Robbie.

Again, he said nothing. But this time, in the tiny raise of his eyebrow, the tilt of his head, he said everything.

Over by the door, Cormac was showing the first customers inside now. One after another, three sets of couples emerged through the thick velvet curtain – taking in the space, getting settled, discussing whether it was how they'd imagined it would be or not.

El looked towards them pointedly, then back to Robbie, a sudden glint in her eye. 'Watch me.'

Chapter Five

What Robbie remembered later, about that first shift, was the scramble of it. The nervousness, the uncertainty. The frustration of being close to the action, but not quite *in it* the way he really wanted to be. The realization (brand new to him) that, somehow, all of those feelings could combine to create what he could only, overall, call a positive thing – what he could only call a thrill.

And, yes, he remembered El, too. In his memory, she was in constant motion. That night, she was wearing a light, unwieldy sort of thing that ended mid-thigh – he thought it might be described as kimono – with a pair of chunky knee-length boots. For almost eight hours straight, she seemed to be everywhere at once. She was magnetic, unpredictable, like a whirlwind.

She threw her head back and laughed with abandon, and it was impossible to ignore the way her long hair rippled down her spine as she did.

Her body moved instinctively to the music, and those glimpses of bare skin – of pale slender legs where her dress ended and before her boots began – couldn't be ignored, either.

She mixed ingredients with ease, added the final touches with a flourish, snuck the occasional shot herself along the way. She flirted, as far as Robbie could see, with absolutely everybody.

Four conversations at once seemed like exactly the number she needed to have, just to keep things interesting for herself. 'Okay, so here's my question,' was her frequent starting point. And after that, it was context-specific, it ran the gamut:

'What's South Africa *like*, then? I've actually never been.'

'Are we saying Scientology is like Kabbalah? As in, kooky but harmless? Or are we saying it's like *wow, these people should be in jail*?'

'And do you reckon you have a type, as such? I do know this guy – he's one of my housemates – who's actually just been broken up with, so he could be an option. Nice face, good height, not an arsehole. You'd potentially need to be quite into playing *Gran Turismo* on the PS2, is the only thing.'

Watching her was a bit like watching a performance, Robbie thought. Not in the sense that anything about it was insincere. Quite the opposite. Like all the best performers, El was entirely sincere. She was entirely present. She was funny and attentive, and there was a spontaneity in her, a lack of self-consciousness that Robbie suspected might easily be mistaken for a lack of self-awareness.

The thing about El Tippett is that she just doesn't see the effect she has on people.

He could almost hear that phrase, looking at her.

He could imagine it being a part of the appeal, even – the notion that she had *no clue how talented she was, no idea how beautiful.*

In fact, what turned out to be most intriguing to him was the opposite of all that. He lingered in the periphery of the bar as she twirled a bottle of grenadine, licking a splash of it from her index finger, and the reality was so incredibly clear to him. Hadn't she all but confirmed it herself? Here, in this little bubble, El knew exactly the power she wielded. She loved it.

And, at least on that first night, all but unable to tear his eyes away from her, Robbie had to admit: he loved it, too.

*

After the first night, a few additional facts about El also became fairly clear fairly quickly.

For one thing, she was messy. Even if it hadn't been a key part of Robbie's job to essentially clean up after her, he would have noticed that. It struck him as incredibly sloppy, the way she might shove a bottle of gin back among the vodka bottles if she was distracted. As for the typical state of her workstation, the sheer frequency of the spills and smashes that happened on her watch . . . Robbie couldn't help his instinctive response to such things. They scratched at something deeply embedded within him: the belief that there was value in being careful, the sense that there was a proper way to go about things.

How she got away with it was a mystery to him.

Generally speaking, Otto's standards turned out to be every bit as high as Robbie had expected them to be.

'That cannot happen again, am I clear?' he told one of the other bartenders, during Robbie's second week.

Said bartender, Tom, had served a Bramble with just a slight error in the ratio of liquid to crushed ice. Maybe the crème de mûre hadn't quite been perfect, either. When it had gone out, Robbie had privately thought it looked a little watery. The customer hadn't complained, though. Five hours after the fact, it was 3 a.m. in the morning, and Robbie had forgotten all about it.

Otto, on the other hand, evidently had not. His stare was unyielding, his tone sharp as a knife, and the bottom dropped out of Robbie's stomach in sheer sympathy. The implication – that Tom was now one more screw-up away from finding himself unemployed – was all the louder for not having been directly spoken.

Meanwhile, for El's errors and omissions, what remonstration came *her* way?

'My God, El*oise*, you have to stop charging around this bar like a baby elephant,' Otto said to her, more than once.

Or: 'I *cannot* talk to you again about the garnishes on those Black Demures, kid. I know you think you're getting it right, but you're not: you're getting it *almost* right.'

In other words, Otto didn't give her an entirely free pass. However, as far as Robbie could see, he came pretty damn close. His aggravation with her seemed always to be laced undeniably with affection.

'Can I ask you about those Clover Clubs?' Robbie asked El, on their fifth or sixth shift together.

It was early on a Tuesday, and the place was dead. Robbie supposed maybe this was a built-in risk factor, with a secret bar. That particular evening, the customers barely outnumbered the staff. Cormac on the door, El and Aziz behind the bar, plus Robbie, made four of them.

'Sure,' she replied. Aziz had ducked into the back for something, she had little choice but to engage.

'I noticed you went for about thirty mils of sugar syrup,' Robbie continued.

She offered no response, and Robbie was once again conscious that he – *he*, who generally got along with more or less everyone – had yet to have a single interaction with this girl that he'd characterize as pleasant. He knew for certain that if he proceeded down his current line of questioning, this wasn't going to be the first. And yet, he could not seem to help himself. What was that about?

'It's just the Bible gives fifteen, I think,' he said.

'The Bible', Robbie had learned, was what everyone called Love and Death's internal recipe book. It contained the preferred house style for all the classics, plus the methods, ingredients and quantities for any original concoctions. He'd already memorized its contents from front to back.

El just looked at him. Briefly, her eyes flickered downwards, to the hardback he had tucked beside the cash register. It made sense, he thought, to bring something to occupy himself during quiet periods on shift. This evening's choice was *The Savoy Cocktail Book* – published in 1930 but still, in Robbie's opinion, a treasure trove of information; a delicious glimpse inside a version of London he sometimes suspected might suit him better than the present one.

'I'm not a big reader,' El said dryly. Then, she nodded over towards her customers, two women in their late twenties or early thirties. They were, at that very moment, clinking glasses happily at their table. 'Anyway, I knew they'd want them sweeter,' she said.

And that, Robbie decided right then and there, was bullshit. He would have respected her more if she'd just admitted the mistake. Maybe he didn't do a great job of keeping his feelings off his face, because El stared at him, as though awaiting his comeback.

'What?' she asked then.

'Nothing,' Robbie shrugged. 'Otto obviously just really trusts you, that's all.'

For a moment, El flushed with pleasure. Then, her expression hardened. 'I'm not fucking him, by the way. Just in case you were thinking that.'

Robbie blinked. 'I wasn't thinking that.'

'People often seem to, so.' She paused for another moment, her chin tilting up in defiance. 'I just wanted to make that clear.'

'Cool,' he said quietly. The thought might, in fact, have crossed his mind.

Chapter Six

The truth was that El had never, not once, had to wonder about Otto's motives. And that was no small thing. After all, when she had first laid eyes on him, if there was any set of people she generally didn't like, didn't trust, it was older men.

A psychologist would have said *daddy issues*.

El said *bar work*.

On the afternoon in question, she had been at Old Street tube station. Specifically, she'd jumped the barrier, been spotted by a member of the station staff, made a run for it, and been caught nonetheless.

The man's hands were large. They made her feel pinned down, like an insect, and immediately, the panic rose in her. Something about his snarling face, the roughness of his grip, suggested this might be a tricky one to wangle out of. To say nothing, of course, of the fact that El was very evidently in the wrong here. She'd just – it came as a slight shock to realize – committed a minor *crime*. All at once, she wasn't sure how well *I've seen tons of people get away with this* would stand up as a defence. Or, for that matter, *I'm completely and utterly skint*.

Nonetheless, she gave as good as she got. It seemed the only thing to do, in the circumstances: try to wriggle free of the station attendant, make her own voice louder and bolshier than his, assert herself as a *piece of work* – the sort of psycho it really would be much easier to simply wash his hands of.

The tussle continued as throngs of other commuters passed by, all focused resolutely on getting wherever they were going. El didn't blame them. What were cities made for, if not minding your own business?

Still. For all the many friends she'd collected in London, for all the house parties she could reliably liven up, she was suddenly struck by her fundamental aloneness here. She couldn't deny that it felt like a reprieve when a voice came from behind her, loud and authoritative.

'Alright, let's simmer down over here, huh?'

Both El and the TfL man stilled, though he kept her firmly within his grasp.

'Who are you, her dad?' he asked, all sarcasm. And his doubts were probably merited. When El really looked at her rescuer – Otto – she could see he was younger than his dapper attire first suggested. Maybe forty-ish.

Nevertheless, he didn't miss a beat.

'As a matter of fact, I am,' he replied smoothly. 'So I'll thank you to take your hands off of her. She was just messing around.'

'Where's her ticket then?' the attendant demanded harshly. He loosened his grip a little, though.

Otto glanced over at El, as if – by some miracle – she might be able to produce one. Silently, she conveyed that she could not.

Something about his expression in response, about the quick flash of amusement she imagined she could see hidden in there, was incredibly calming to El. It made her feel, at once, that this whole thing was essentially a scrape – an *escapade* rather than a crisis. It made her feel that the two of them were in it together.

'We realized on the train that she'd lost it,' Otto said. 'We were joking that she'd have to make a run for it at the other end. Kid was just trying to make me laugh, is all.'

The attendant cocked an eyebrow, unconvinced. Otto produced a ten-pound note and tucked it into the attendant's top pocket.

'How about you keep the change and I don't report you for manhandling a teenage girl for no reason, huh, pal?'

He tossed the threat out with a casual sort of confidence, and for a long moment, it hung there in the silence, nobody saying or doing anything. El felt the seconds tick by, as though they were in a Mexican standoff right here in Islington. She could practically see the cogs turning in the station attendant's head, as he weighed up whether this was really worth it. What he now had before him, after all, was a complainer of the worst and most experienced sort: an American.

Eventually, with a huff, he released El and turned away from them. 'Look after your stuff next time, princess,' he spat out as he walked away, evidently determined to have the last word.

In the circumstances, El was happy to give it to him.

Standing opposite her, Otto just smiled – he had the twinkliest eyes she'd ever seen – and then, faster than she could even register it, he was on his way, too.

For a moment, El stood, frozen, struggling to compute everything that had just happened. Then, she hurried after him.

'Hey! Why did you do that?' she asked, once she'd caught up. They were out of the station now, on Old Street, and he slowed to a stop.

He just shrugged. 'Power to the people, right? What age are you – 18, 19?'

'19.'

'I might have jumped a few turnstiles myself when I was 19.'

With another little smile, with a conclusory sort of nod, he commenced walking again. A second later – there was nothing else for it – El did the same.

She gestured vaguely in the distance. 'I . . . I'm going this way, too,' she said awkwardly.

Again, he just nodded affably. That was what ended up being most intriguing to El: the fact that this guy – the extremely smooth, stylish American gentleman who'd just come to her rescue – seemed to want nothing more from her. Their paces were perfectly in step now, and yet he was clearly content to walk in total silence until they went their separate ways. Naturally, nothing could have made her feel more like talking.

'Do you live around here?' she asked him.

'Work,' he replied. '*And* live, I guess. *What's the difference?* is what it feels like, most days,' he added, with a little chuckle.

El didn't know what he meant by that one – not yet.

'Not today though, eh?'

'What do you mean?'

She nodded down towards the plastic bag he was carrying. The logo of the V&A Museum was printed prominently across it. 'Have you been at that tiaras exhibit?' she prompted.

He seemed to regard her anew, as if reassessing her somehow. 'What are you, an art student? Or a fashion student?'

As it happened, neither was an uncommon assumption. El wasn't sure what it was about her.

'Oh no. I'm not any kind of student. I'm just a barmaid. So you could say I chat for a living. Or eavesdrop for a living. I haven't actually been to the tiaras thing myself – I just had customers in talking about it a few weeks ago. You'd be surprised the conversations that go on in a third-rate boozer in Dalston.'

A smile tugged at his lips. 'I bet.'

'Maybe I will go, though,' she continued. 'To the exhibit, I mean. I do actually quite like fashion. And,' – here, she had the decency to blush – 'I like free things to do in London.'

He chuckled. 'Otto Kettinger,' he offered then.

'Eloise Tippett,' she replied, because he was a proper adult. It felt like she should give him her full name.

After that, she wasn't sure how it happened, but as they walked together, she found herself telling this man her whole life story: about her parents and her friends, about the person she currently fancied and the person who fancied her (they were not the same). With Otto interjecting gently here and there, everything seemed to spill out – all the bits of being 19 that felt like freedom and fun, all the bits that felt like confusion and chaos.

'So, what are you thinking, about the future?' he asked her.

And it was funny – that was, at its heart, the very thing her father had demanded, incessantly, for about as long as El could remember. Something about the way Otto asked the question, though, didn't put her hackles up in the same way at all.

'I don't know, exactly. I actually kinda like bar work. Bits of it, anyway.'

It felt like an admission, like the sort of thing nobody said. However – as with everything else she'd thrown at him in the previous fifteen minutes – Otto didn't seem to find it the least bit weird.

'What do you like about it?'

'Well, it's three o'clock on a Wednesday and I'm bumming around, talking to you, having just got away with a minor crime,' she joked.

'A civil infraction, at most,' he countered, smiling along. Somehow, though, it was clear he was still awaiting her real answer. He didn't plan on letting her off that easily.

'I like that it's sociable,' she said. 'And it's creative, too, kind of. Or, maybe that's not the right word – I don't know. But you have to think on your feet. Like the other day, this woman wanted a rosé, and we didn't have any – I mean, not a drop; the delivery hadn't come. Anyway, she was making a whole ruckus – where she thought she was, I don't know. The Burton Arms isn't The Ritz; it's more *take what you get and be grateful*. But anyway, I went into the back and put a tiny bit of Merlot into some Chardonnay, gave it a bit of a stir . . . She said it was nicer than Blossom Hill.'

Otto seemed to choke on nothing but air. 'Now *that* I think is probably a crime,' he exclaimed. His horror quickly gave way to something else, though. A curiosity, an interest in her that seemed different to the kind she was used to fielding from random men.

'You guys do any cocktails at this place?' he asked then. 'The Burton Arms.'

'Cocktails? Nope.'

'I think maybe you'd do well with cocktails,' he told her.

And there it was. Inside one sentence, the beginning of the rest of El's life.

Chapter Seven

She took the job at Love and Death because of Otto, and because she thought of jobs – in general – as inherently temporary commitments. That was the thing about bar work. It was always easy enough to pick up some more of it elsewhere.

'Do you really reckon you can do better than this?' one of her former employers had memorably asked her, all incredulity, the day she'd handed in her notice.

'Maybe not. But finding an *equally* shitty job will be *no problem*!' she'd tossed back.

And, within the week, she'd been proven entirely right.

Love and Death was nothing like any of the other places, though. From the beginning, Otto was nothing like any of the other bosses.

For a fortnight, he put her through her paces. No customers, just him and her, before opening hours. He told her the names of all the glasses and the names of the cocktails that belonged in them. He said that what she should be aiming for, in any single drink, was *balance* – that perfect mix of sweet and sour, with every element distinguishable but none overpowering. He told her the quantities, to the millilitre, that would help her achieve this.

The first thing she ever made, per Otto's instructions, was a Daiquiri. She thought it tasted pretty good until she tasted his version of the very same thing.

'I don't understand! I followed the recipe exactly!' she said. Immediately, though, even she suspected that might not be true. After all, she often thought she'd *looked everywhere* for an item that someone else could come along and locate inside ten seconds flat. She frequently walked blithely onto trains going in entirely the wrong direction, no matter how many times she'd sworn it would never happen again. Put simply, even her very best efforts at efficiency, at thoroughness, often fell short. She winced.

Over and over, every drink she produced for Otto seemed to end in a wince – or rather, in two of them. His and hers.

By the end of that fortnight, she knew she would soon be sacked. And it was a shame, because there was something about stepping through that velvet curtain at Love and Death every night. The place had a sense of secrecy, a kind of sexiness that made her insides fizz.

There wasn't that thread of danger, though – the way there often could be, in other parts of El's life, when she was chasing a similar feeling. Instead, at Love and Death, she also found a certain *comfort* in the physical space. It was akin to the ease she'd felt around Otto himself on that first day they'd met. It made her feel, totally illogically, that she had somehow landed exactly where she was supposed to, that this was meant to be.

'Okay, El,' Otto said, at the beginning of their third week together. He'd adopted a no-nonsense tone of voice, the sort that would be ideal for telling a person, swiftly, that things just weren't working out. 'How about this? Make me a French 75.'

El froze, like a deer in the headlights. Her brain was swimming with all the numbers, all the new vocabulary that had been thrown at her lately. 'I don't remember the—'

'Forget about that,' he interrupted. 'You know what it should taste like at this point. You know basically what's in it – I hope. Just go with your instincts. It has to look good, and it has to taste good. That's it. Simple.'

Another person would surely have laughed out loud. What had Otto been doing, these past weeks, if not underlining the true complexity of mixing cocktails?

For El, however, it was as though something clicked immediately into place. Suddenly, this *did* seem simple. She got to work, losing all sense of time passing, losing the awareness of Otto watching her every move. Everything disappeared beyond the task in front of her. When she'd shaken her mixture for a few seconds, she prised open the shaker and – the same way she'd seen Otto do – scooped a bit of liquid up with the tip of a straw. She tasted it, thought about it, added a bit more lime juice.

When at last a concoction that pleased her was in the coupe glass, she pushed it towards Otto.

'Well, it's not quite like how I make 'em,' Otto said, after a sip, and her heart sank. He was looking at her, though, with that same curiosity she'd seen before. 'It might be better,' he added quietly.

Instinctively, El lunged towards him and threw her arms around him, letting out a squeal of excitement. She could feel him seize up a little against her, and she froze, too. Suddenly, she feared she'd breezed past one too many boundaries. When she stepped back, though, he didn't seem annoyed.

He patted her on the shoulder in a slightly awkward fashion. It struck her as adorable. Paternal. It tugged at something soft and ignored inside of her.

'You nailed it, kid.'

'So I can stay?' she asked. She could hear the hope in her own voice, the vulnerability. In other circumstances, she'd have been utterly mortified by both. 'Stay working here, I mean.'

'Of course you can stay,' he replied. It was as though he hadn't been countenancing the alternative at all.

El brightened instantly, took on a wheedling tone, just for fun. For the distraction of it, maybe. 'Even though I didn't know what samphire was, never mind the fact that it could be pickled?' she asked.

Otto merely rolled his eyes.

'Even though, the other day, you told me I was "spunky" and I laughed for fifteen minutes?'

He couldn't seem to help replying this time, a little peevishly. 'Like I said, that's a *perfectly normal* adjective in the US.'

'Even though you actually *know for sure* I have a history of trying to run from the law?'

'Alright, alright! Enough. Let's move on to Highballs and Collinses today, Eloise – before I change my mind.'

For a long time after that, it was just the two of them behind the bar at Love and Death. Long hours, close quarters.

When eventually Aziz came along to join them, his very presence – the very fact that a new hire was both necessary and possible – represented a mark of success. And El liked Aziz. She and Otto had chosen him together. She knew that they were, in a way, at the beginning of something. But undeniably, it felt a little like the end of something, too.

'Things are gonna be different, eh?' she said. 'When it's not just you and me behind here.'

Otto just shrugged. 'We'll see how he works out. Either way, it's still going to be you and me, kid. At this point, we're family.'

Chapter Eight

'Do you fancying coming out tonight, after work?' El asked Robbie. 'It's industry night at Salazar.'

She asked him because that was what she'd undoubtedly do if it were any other colleague standing three feet away from her. To treat Robbie differently to how she treated other people – to let him *make her* different, and for that to be seen by those around them – seemed oddly like it ceded some sort of power to him. Moreover – and this was critical – she entirely assumed that he wouldn't come.

'What do you mean?' Robbie asked. 'What's an industry night?'

'Oh. There are various places that stay open after hours, exclusively for people in the bar trade. Mostly in Soho or West London rather than out this direction, obviously.'

'Aren't you knackered by the time we finish up here? I'm asleep the minute my head hits the pillow.'

'Well, let's just say we figure out some ways to keep the pep in our step.'

If Robbie understood her meaning, he didn't show it. 'It does sound kind of cool,' he offered instead. He pushed his glasses upwards on his nose. 'Getting to network with people from other bars, find out how other people are doing things, and so on.'

'Mmm. I mean it's not really a *learning opportunity* or anything. It's more just, you know . . . for fun.'

Increasingly, El doubted that Robbie was familiar with the concept.

For all the ways in which she and he had bumped up against each other in their encounters thus far, she'd had to cast a particular version of him from her mind pretty quickly. The theory of him as a guy who was destined for bigger and better things – and knew it all too well – who was doing this job short-term, for a lark, and surely couldn't much care about it . . . that had simply become an impossible theory to subscribe to.

On the contrary, Robbie seemed to care an incredible, extraordinary amount, and he didn't mind who knew it. He asked endless questions, took copious notes. His trusty notebook was, by now, filled with pages of even handwriting. He sometimes flipped through them in what El considered a needless performance of urgency.

We get it: you're a gold star swot, she felt like saying, but managed not to.

She knew no one else like him. Her life, through no explicit design on her part, was now populated mainly by artists, musicians, as-yet-undecided layabouts . . . the sorts of 20-somethings who either worked in or frequented the new bars popping up all over town. In other words, her life was populated by *cool* people.

Robbie Saunders was *not* a cool person. The strange thing was that he didn't seem to realize it. Or, if he did, he didn't care. He was quiet, but he wasn't shy. If he had something to say, he said it. Hadn't she learned that, to her cost, a time or two already?

'Does Otto go?' he continued. 'To industry drinks?'

El cocked an eyebrow. 'What do you think?'

Of course Otto never came along. He had to protect the mystique. Not that he put it that way. It was a younger man's game, he said instead – oh, he could tell a tale or two from industry nights back in New York! In London, however, he left it to his staff to find the places to spend their tips and wind down. Or, as the case sometimes was, to spend their tips and keep the party going.

El went out after almost every shift, and typically didn't return home until sunrise, her high heels dangling from two fingers as she walked.

That night, she was nothing short of staggered when Robbie decided to join her and Marcus at Salazar on Greek Street. It had once explicitly been billed to El as a 'cocaine and get laid' spot.

On arrival, she wasted no time in handling the first portion of that particular twofer, and soon her thoughts turned naturally to the second. She was pretty sure Kat was making her way here tonight, too. This place was where they'd first met, as it happened. She cast her eyes around as she made her way back from the bathroom, spotting countless familiar faces as she went. Many of her closest friends and enemies seemed to be in attendance. It was an incestuous business, bartending. A Franz Ferdinand song was playing loudly, and across a crowd of other bodies, someone passed her a shot with a grin. El grinned right back and downed it. She felt the bass guitar of the music become her heartbeat, and thought she must surely have the very best job in the whole world.

There were no cocktails served after hours – who wanted more work after work? It was spirits or beer only, for the industry crowd. Or, lately, a third option had grown in popularity:

'I have to say, ten out ten for marketing on these things,' Marcus said, approaching with Robbie in tow, his hands wrapped around three Jägerbombs. 'I've never tasted anything worse – I told Otto about them, and he looked like he was in genuine distress. He made me threaten the Jägermeister rep with some sort of cease and desist.' Marcus passed a glass over to Robbie. 'Get this down you, mate.'

'I've, uh . . . I've actually never had one,' Robbie admitted.

'Does the job, I'll tell you.'

Robbie just smiled, a little bashfully. 'Would you believe me if I told you I've never really drunk to *get* drunk?'

'That's interesting,' El found herself chiming in blithely. 'I *only* really drink to get drunk!'

It wasn't even true, but she heard it come out of her mouth, nonetheless. It made Marcus laugh, and Robbie chuckled along as well.

There was something about the way he looked at her as he did, though – as if he just didn't quite understand why she would reduce their whole lives and livelihoods to its lowest common denominator like that. As if he knew that she didn't really mean it – as if he could see right through her, right to all the many hours she'd spent, across those first weeks and months with Otto, practising and perfecting the thing she loved best.

It reminded her of the conversation she'd had with Robbie last week – the one where, for some reason, she'd voluntarily raised the notion of her and Otto having an affair. It was as though, in her attempt to be assertive then, and her attempt to be funny just now, she'd managed only to make herself vulnerable somehow.

She pushed the recollection away. This was a party, after all. And hadn't she always had an aversion to the melancholy? Gazing at herself in the mirror, pressing one plaintive key on the piano, all that shit girls did in films . . . it wasn't for El. She wanted to lean, instead, into the glamour and the grime of life – they were, in her mind, one and the same. She wished Robbie would just go ahead and let her.

Averting her eyes from his, El grabbed the Jägerbomb with her name on it and tipped it right back.

*

Not long after that night, El would recall it and actually feel some nostalgia for the before times – the period in which all Robbie really did was hang around, *noticing* things.

Forty-eight hours later, she, Jamie, and Otto were all behind the bar, practically tripping over one another. Robbie darted between them to top up supplies and rinse glasses. It was sweaty and delicious, the sort of unexpectedly busy Saturday night that El lived for – the sort of night where she didn't have to think, she could just *do*, where Love and Death felt like the centre of the world.

'Can I have a Cosmo, a Cecilia, a Ramos Gin Fizz, and a Corpse Reviver,' she could hear a customer asking Jamie, to the left of her at the bar.

Cumulatively, there were probably twenty different ingredients involved there. Twenty different quantities to recall (or, in her case, to roughly recall) from memory, all to be combined into something beautiful and delivered with a smile inside ten minutes maximum. She took in the slight look of panic in Jamie's eyes, saw the colour that had already risen rapidly in his cheeks. El generally rated his drinks, and thought he wouldn't be the worst guy in the world if he could only accept that she simply did not watch football. He'd never been much good at coping with volume, though.

With three Palomas of her own already underway, a sympathetic glance was about all she could offer him. Otto, too, was otherwise engaged, crouching down to view his creation at eye level, adding honey-cardamom syrup one millilitre at a time.

'I could make one of them.' Robbie's voice piped up, seemingly out of nowhere. 'The Ramos Gin Fizz maybe? Or whichever one.'

Immediately, the significance of the offer was clear. It was almost startlingly bold, in fact. The Ramos Gin Fizz was known by bartenders everywhere as the most difficult and labour-intensive drink in the cocktail universe.

Needless to say, Jamie was only too thrilled at the thought of sidestepping it. He looked over towards Otto and repeated the offer hopefully, waiting for permission or refusal.

Beside him, El felt her awareness shift in a way it rarely did on nights like this, when she was in the flow. Even as she busied herself salting the rims of her own glasses, her whole focus was suddenly on Otto – on the nod she could perceive out of the corner of her eye.

'Let me taste it before it goes,' he said quietly.

And with that, Robbie got moving. First, he separated the egg whites, adding them to his cocktail shaker. Precise quantities of orange blossom water, lemon juice, and lime juice all followed. Next: simple syrup, London dry gin, a tiny pinch of salt. Robbie did five or ten seconds of a dry shake, like that. Then came the addition of ice – not too much, of course, to avoid over-dilution. Six to eight *full minutes* of shaking, then the shaker was prised open once again, this time to add the cream. Another few seconds' shake, just to integrate. The goal, effectively, was to whip the cream and egg white into a light, airy cloud – almost a meringue – that would eventually rise up over the rim of the glass and stand firm on its own.

El could sense the whole process happening rather than see it, could feel the tension in her own body as Robbie *at last* finished shaking. He added a little soda water to the glass and then – carefully, carefully – poured his mixture in. The glass went in the fridge for two more long minutes. When it came back out, Robbie poked a small hole in the viscous surface of the concoction, added a bit more soda water, and watched the drink rise. Like magic.

The final product was elegant, unshowy, belying all the patience and skill that had just gone into it. Robbie slid the glass over towards Otto, his hand slightly shaking, as though he were a chef on the day of a Michelin inspection.

Otto grabbed a straw, pinching the top of it and catching a little of the drink in the bottom.

He raised it to his lips, swallowed, considered. He quirked an eyebrow, repeated the process.

El was outright staring by then – they all were: she, Jamie, Robbie, even the customers sitting at the bar. When, at long last, Otto smiled his approval, El swore she saw it as if in slow motion. It was that very same smile she always wanted from him, the one she so rarely saw anyone else get.

Robbie had been at Love and Death for less than a month.

Chapter Nine

Needless to say – it was a tale as old as time – one drink led to another.

After Robbie made that first cocktail at Love and Death, he never really stopped making them. At least, not altogether. His official status didn't change. On quieter nights, he reverted to being a barback only. On busier ones, however, it became a given that he'd be drafted in.

El was sometimes irritated by this, sometimes grateful for it. In any case, it was the summer, and she was 22 years old. She had plenty of other things to be getting on with.

She danced to 'Mr Brightside' and got high on ecstasy and tried valiantly to believe that Brighton on a warm-ish day was just as good as the Costas Bravo, Blanca or Sol.

She went to see *Mr. & Mrs. Smith* four times in the cinema, unable to figure out who was more attractive, Brad or Angelina.

She decided, on a whim, to get a tattoo. Three little birds, stamped in black ink along the outer edge of her wrist, became quite the conversation piece for a week or so in Love and Death.

'What do they symbolize?' asked curious colleagues and regulars alike.

El just tossed the question right back at them, taking great enjoyment in hearing everyone's guesses. She confirmed none but denied none either.

Live 8 brought 200,000 people to Hyde Park in early July, and El wasn't totally certain how the whole thing was going to benefit the people of Africa, but that was for someone else to figure out. For her personally, it meant adding Chris Martin and Gwyneth Paltrow to the list of famous faces she'd served (a Pegu Club for him, and an Aviation for her).

She met Kat's parents, albeit only accidentally, when they all ended up at the same pub for lunch one weekday afternoon. Afterwards, she and Kat walked through Trafalgar Square together, the place thronged with revellers celebrating London's winning Olympic bid. El had been only dimly aware that this was on the cards at all, and 'Twenty Twelve' felt very far away indeed. Nonetheless, there was something intoxicating about the way things felt suddenly so joyful in the city, so possible.

'They really liked you,' Kat murmured later that night, curling into El in bed.

'Who did?'

'My mum and dad!'

'I really liked them, too,' El replied easily, and who could have predicted that this information would prove such a turn-on?

Kat's hand crept under El's T-shirt and upwards, her mouth suddenly warm and insistent on El's neck. El let out a giggle, feeling her whole body loosen with an anticipatory sort of pleasure – a glorious end to a glorious day.

The next morning, London was bombed. El slept through all of it – she missed the panic and the confusion, the period of the unknown. By the time she awoke and turned on the television, things were brutally, undeniably *known*. Four terrorist attacks had come almost simultaneously during the morning rush hour, targeting commuters on the city's public transport.

'Should we just close?' Jamie asked worriedly, even as they

went through the motions of preparing to open Love and Death that night. 'Can't imagine we'll have too many customers.'

The enquiry was directed at Otto, but Robbie was the one who replied first. El remembered that.

'We will,' he said quietly but with certainty. 'Trust me. The place'll be packed.'

And, as it turned out, he was just right. They had a line out the door.

Two weeks later, it happened again. More bombs, more horror and disbelief. Robbie didn't let any of it in – not the way other people seemed to. He knew better than that. He didn't think much at all about how many bombs he'd seen before in his life (none), or how many times he'd seen the aftermath of a bomb (a handful), or how many bomb scares had interrupted his daily existence since childhood (an endless, relentless amount, until a bomb scare no longer scared him one bit). He, too, had other things on his mind.

He wrote and rewrote his wedding speech, that summer. He spent hours on the phone to Anna-Claire, who was back in Belfast. It had seemed to make sense, that she would wait until after they were married to join him in London. For starters, they couldn't live together before then. And of course, she'd had her own summer plans mapped out months in advance: eight weeks leading a youth scheme with her church, plus a series of afternoon teas with various permutations of female friends and relatives, in celebration of the upcoming nuptials and all.

Robbie loved that his fiancée was the type of girl – woman; should he be saying woman? – who was always busy. He loved that she knew her own mind, that she had a certain ambition behind that wholesome exterior – a certain focus about creating the precise kind of life she wanted for herself. It wouldn't have worked at all for her to spend the summer hanging around doing nothing, while he pursued an obsession that had come as a surprise to them both. Not his Anna-Claire, who liked to have a date book full of appointments but also to be in bed by eleven.

None of that meant he hadn't missed her, though, while they'd been apart.

In the middle of August, he flew to Belfast for a long weekend, and the delight of seeing her again – to say nothing of the swirl of last-minute tux fittings and cake tastings – meant he didn't have to think too much about how thoroughly strange it was to be back there. Without any clear reason for it, he just seemed to feel ever so slightly tense.

'What will we have to talk about after the wedding's over?' Anna-Claire asked him, when they realized they'd spent an entire car journey – all the way from the airport out to her family home – discussing nothing else.

They both laughed, because they knew that, really, they'd never run out of things to talk about.

'Sometimes I still can't believe how lucky I got, you know?' he murmured. 'With you.'

He looked across at her from the passenger seat, the car now parked in her parents' driveway. Blue eyes, blonde bob curling under her chin, she was as pretty and fresh-faced as he'd ever seen her.

'I know. Me too.'

And the best bit was, they hadn't even really had to try. The two of them had bonded in their very first month at Pembroke College, on account of being the only two Northern Irish undergraduates in that year's intake. In those early days, Robbie suspected he might have welcomed *any* kind of Northern Irish, so surrounded was he by Tarquins and Crispins. But, extra fortuitously, he and Anna-Claire had turned out to be the same kind.

'I'm from Hillsborough,' she'd told him, at a freshers' week bop, and of itself that made the situation fairly clear.

Then, across the couch from him in the JCR the next day, she'd made a casual reference to her membership of the Girls' Brigade.

She'd offered an equally casual enquiry about where he went to school.

These were the ways Northern Irish people got the measure of one another. Robbie had seen the English students do a version of the same dance, though for them it appeared mainly to be about placing one another economically.

Across the sea, Ulster folk weren't altogether above that either. (Already, from their brief interactions, Robbie suspected Anna-Claire had been a piano-lessons kid, that her home in Hillsborough might bear little resemblance to his own terrace in East Belfast.) That stuff wasn't what really mattered, though, in Northern Ireland. It wasn't what united or divided people.

A few more interactions had followed, quickly and inevitably, in the dining hall or the quad or the library. Robbie and Anna-Claire began to look for one another, to perceive one another as a friendly face. Traipsing through the porter's lodge together on the third week of term, their conversation had stalled as they reached the point where their paths diverged.

She hesitated, then stepped forwards to hug him goodbye.

'I'm pleased you're here, Robert,' she'd told him shyly.

Robbie watched this girl tug a baby-pink T-shirt down to meet her denim skirt, he noted the slight flush of her cheeks, and he felt a whole new world of possibility open up.

University life hadn't thus far proven to be quite the intellectual haven for geeks he'd thought it would be. There still seemed to be plenty of occasions on which he didn't know quite the right thing to do or say or wear. Inside one sentence, though, this girl made it all feel okay. She made him feel like *he* was okay. Or, maybe, even better than that.

*

From there, the relationship had progressed in a way that was thrilling, of course, but that also had a certain straightforwardness to it. Robbie and Anna-Claire hadn't had to work to avoid all the drama and discord that was on full display among scores of other newly formed Pembroke couples. Robbie supposed that was the thing about finding the person you were really and truly meant to be with: it was *easy*. He and Anna-Claire just liked each other, and then they liked each other more, and then yet more again, until eventually they had come to seem like an obvious, immovable part of one another's lives.

Now, there was less than a month to go before they would be man and wife.

On the last day of his trip back to Belfast, they took a drive out to the coast and sat together on the steps near Portstewart Promenade. Afternoon turned to evening with the Atlantic Ocean out ahead of them, the remnants of fish suppers at their feet.

Anna-Claire nodded towards the families in their eyesight. At a little play park, children were hopped up on sugar and the notion of being out late, parents hovering nearby to rescue or reprimand as the need arose.

'Can you believe that's going to be us?' she murmured.

Robbie thought suddenly of the life he'd made in London this summer. He thought of Love and Death, and the feeling he still got every time he walked through the door of the place. It was about the drinks, but it was also – much to his own huge surprise – not about the drinks at all.

Yes, he could feel himself getting better, quicker, more consistent behind the bar, and he loved that.

He also loved Otto, though – loved pleasing him, loved feeling that Otto no longer merely tolerated his presence, but seemed to actually *want* him there.

He loved Jamie and Marcus, Tom and Aziz – the way they made him one of the lads. Even El . . . He certainly wouldn't say he loved her, but there was something undeniably compelling about her, something that kept a person coming back for more.

At the end of every shift, when all the customers had left, Robbie knew that he had just experienced a night – a particular combination of people and place and all five senses – that would never come again. And what was more, he knew – as he allowed a beer or a whiskey to be passed his way – that it wasn't even over yet.

One late night after another, by increments so small he'd hardly noticed them, he'd developed a certain appreciation for that tell-tale looseness in his limbs, in his tongue. If anything, he had begun to wonder why he'd resisted it for so long. What had he been afraid of?

Drugs of any sort were still out of the question, as far as he was concerned. However, he was a lot less shocked by the sight of an empty baggie than his new friends seemed to assume he might be. What, he wondered, did they think went on in the hallowed institutions of their fine country? It had always struck him as ironic, actually – what he was sure Oxford's undergrads would have perceived as seedy and sad and criminal on the street that Robbie had grown up on, they seemed to find in themselves to be good clean fun. A jolly.

At industry nights this summer, he'd seen a slightly different attitude yet again. Whipping up all those liquid intoxicants, on a professional basis, seemed to create an assuredness around drugs – here were people who thought they could handle themselves. Mostly, Robbie had to acknowledge that they *could*. He'd never seen anyone overdo it to the point of being frightening or burdensome. What was it El had said that time, about boosting her energy? If he ever suspected she'd had a line or two, that seemed to manifest only in her being even more the life of the party than usual.

In any case, all of it seemed a world away, here in Portstewart, with a tableau of Northern Irish family life playing out before him.

He let his gaze linger on the swings – the very same ones that he'd played on himself as a child and that he knew his fiancée had, too. It felt like a scene from the past and a scene from the future all at once.

He wrapped one arm around Anna-Claire, pulling her close to him.

'I can't wait for that to be us,' he told her, and he meant it. Then, after a beat, 'Maybe not *quite* yet, though.'

'No,' she agreed contently. 'Not quite yet.'

They'd discussed that one already, agreed upon it easily. Parenthood, they'd decided, could be postponed just a little – it seemed only sensible to get a few more of their ducks in a row first. They had a plan.

As far as Robbie was concerned, reneging on a plan was up there with being late, skipping queues, and the overall concept of 'winging it'. These were things he simply did not do.

And yet.

Staring out at the sunset – there could be something incredibly clarifying about a sunset – the prospect that they might, ever so slightly, *alter* the plan . . .

Not in the interests of getting somewhere faster, or of ticking the next thing off an imaginary list . . .

Just for the fun of it.

For the first time in Robbie's life, that prospect crossed his mind.

Chapter Ten

El had no idea how it happened, that she and Robbie Saunders ended up sitting alone together in a booth at Love and Death in the early hours of the morning.

It was the very end of August, and they'd thrown an impromptu stag party for Robbie in the bar. A stag party slash leaving party, El figured, because the guests didn't have to be male. They didn't even have to know Robbie all that well – who *did* know him all that well, after only twelve weeks? To have encountered him at some industry thing across the summer and/or to be on texting terms with another of Love and Death's employees . . . that was enough.

Otto wasn't typically one for 'hosting the competition', as he called it, after hours. Of course, he adored a lock-in, but preferably one populated by his personal invitees: beautiful, sophisticated types for whom discretion was paramount, for whom East London had an appealing sense of the gritty and underground. Or interesting up-and-comers, Shoreditch locals who'd visited frequently enough for Otto to have taken a shine to them. Several nights a week, he was more than happy to keep the bar open as late as friends and regulars wanted him to. Drinking, dancing, discussing, dreaming – as if he'd ever have called time on any of that.

By contrast, a bunch of post-shift bartenders? The idea of

providing little more than a place for them to get drunk or get high, then eventually get off with each other? That held very little appeal for Otto Kettinger.

In honour of Robbie's upcoming nuptials, though, he'd decided to make an exception. Predictably, he'd also decided to do an exceptional job of it. He'd shooed everyone else out from behind the bar and was doing the serving himself, batting away attempts at payment. He'd relinquished control of the playlist – *finally*, some indie rock in this place – and turned the charm up to a hundred, telling one grand New York tale after another to eager young bartenders. Every one of them, El knew, would ditch their current job in a heartbeat to come and work here. Who wouldn't, when Otto was in this mode?

At one point, the whole gang had pinned Robbie to a chair and trooped in circles around it. 'I'm Getting Married in the Morning', they'd sung-shouted tunelessly, as he downed a pint like a pro. There followed a litany of relationship advice from people who would not begin to consider marriage for another fifteen years.

Robbie took it all on board, nodding sagely even when Tom said, 'Sometimes, mate, I honestly think the best thing is just to pretend you haven't heard what she's said to you. Just pretend you haven't heard it and go for a run. Saves so many arguments, I'm telling you.'

By 5.30 a.m., the crowd had thinned, and the music had been turned down a little. But still, a few groups lingered at various tables, talking nonsense amid sticky surfaces and empty glasses.

Sitting opposite El, in the booth, Robbie seemed to clock their new situation at the very same moment she did. Jamie had been there with them – relaying the triumphs and even greater triumphs of Chelsea F.C.'s season thus far – until suddenly, for some reason or none, he wasn't there any longer. For the first time all summer, it was just Robbie and El. No diluting agent.

They each cast around for something to say to one another and, perhaps not unexpectedly, she got in there first.

'So. You and . . . Anna-Claire, is it?'

Robbie nodded.

'You're young to be getting married.'

'S'pose so,' he replied. 'I mean, to be fair, it's not that weird where we're from.'

'Anna-Claire's Irish, too, is she?'

'Northern Irish,' Robbie corrected reflexively.

'What's the difference?'

'Northern Irish is British. Or' – even this small concession would, he knew, be considered traitorous in some quarters – 'it *can* be British.'

'For you, it's British.'

'Uh huh.'

El took that in for a moment, reached for her drink. 'Seems like kind of a shit-hole over there, if you don't mind me saying,' she added conversationally.

At times – nice days on the north coast notwithstanding – this was precisely Robbie's view of the place. However, as it turned out, he *did* mind her saying. 'Yeah well. London's also kind of a shit-hole, so.'

'I couldn't agree more,' she answered frankly, not missing a beat. 'Who'd live here if they could help it?'

Robbie snorted. He knew El didn't really mean that; it was just one of those things she tossed out there, designed to surprise a person – disarm them. It worked.

'Have you been in London your whole life?' he asked.

'Wow. S'pose I must finally sound like a local. My 12-year-old self would be thrilled.'

He looked at her blankly.

'Both my parents are American. I was born over there, but we moved around a lot when I was little. As in, like . . . *a lot*. We settled here just as I started secondary school. My dad was, like, weirdly into the whole English public school system – or the idea of it, at least. Do you know how many promotions he sacrificed so that his daughter could have a world-class education? 'Cause if you don't, he'll tell you.'

It was the most he'd ever heard her say about herself, and maybe she was surprised by it, too – by the acerbity in that last bit, especially. She was breezing on past it faster than he could figure out a response. 'Anyway. Are you close to your family?'

'Hang on . . . let's stick with you for a second. What school did you *go to*, exactly?'

When she said the name, Robbie recognized it immediately. He'd been to university with more than a few of its alumni.

'*Oh*,' he replied, as a wholly unforeseen picture began to form rapidly in his mind.

'What?'

'Nothing.'

'Ugh. *What?*'

'Well, it's just ironic, isn't it? That all this time you've acted like I was born with a silver spoon in my mouth – don't deny it; you have – when in fact, of the two of us . . .' He let the sentence peter out, with an exaggerated shrug.

Immediately, El's whole face animated, her voice rising hotly. 'I'll have you know I haven't taken a fucking penny from my parents since I was sevente—'

'Alright, alright,' he interjected. And then – he knew it was a risk, but he just couldn't help himself: 'Rich girls are always so sensitive about it.'

His lips twitched with amusement. El said nothing, though. For a moment, Robbie cursed himself, sure she was going to get right up and leave. Instead, she let out a huff of irritation. But even as she did, she couldn't seem to stop the corners of her own mouth edging upwards a little.

It felt like nothing short of a triumph.

'Look, El, I really don't care,' he continued blithely, finishing off the last sip of his whiskey, letting it embolden him all the more. 'You're posh, fine; you're not posh, fine; you are, and you don't want to be, fine. It's mental, how obsessed British people are with class.'

'*British* people are?'

'Mmm-hmm.'

'But, Robbie, didn't you just tell me *you* were British?'

And didn't she have him there? How strange, for her to have hit upon the precise disconnect that he himself had been wrestling with – had been trying by turns to ignore or explain or outright deny – ever since he arrived on this island.

'Touché,' he said, and El smirked at him.

She nodded towards his empty rocks glass. ''Nother one?'

Robbie couldn't remember how many he'd had already. He was drunk, and she was, too. That was the only reason the two of them were here, having this conversation. But in any case, he found he wanted to keep having it.

'Why not?'

'So, are you religious?' El asked him, when she returned to the table. She had a bottle of Jameson in one hand and a bottle of Merlot in the other. The tattoo on her wrist caught his attention as she topped up both of their glasses.

'Wow, this is getting deep,' he joked.

'Oh, you love it.'

'Have you paid for these? Free bar's closed, I reckon.'

El ignored the question, just reached for a languorous sip from her drink. He watched the birds on her wrist again, watched her fingers clasped around the glass, chipped nail polish and all.

Red wine wasn't the drink of choice for many other 22-year-olds, Robbie thought idly. It had stained her lips a little. It suited her, though, in the way that she seemed to be able to make things – her Seventies clothes, the smell of cigarette smoke – suit her. With a start, he realized that her glass was back on the table now. He might have been staring at her for a moment too long. Any amount of time, in fact, was too long.

If she noticed, she didn't show it. She was probably, he realized, just used to attracting a little extra attention. Extra probably felt like a normal amount.

'Are *you* religious?' he asked her then.

'God, no. Anyway. I asked you first.'

'Uh . . . yeah. I suppose I am.'

'What kind of religious?'

'What do you mean?'

'Well, I don't think you're a practising Sikh.' She snorted. 'What kind of Christian? Isn't that the whole thing over there, in *Northern* Ireland? That you have to be one kind or the other? Don't think I don't notice when you try to change the subject, Robbie.'

'Don't think I don't notice when *you* do,' he tossed back.

They stared each other down, at an impasse – but one that felt warmer, somehow, than it usually did between them.

In truth, Robbie hated it when people in England didn't ask about Northern Ireland, didn't seem to know or care to know anything about it. However, he found he hated it just as much when they asked. He hated trying to explain it – trying, in essence, to explain *himself*. He appreciated that this put others in somewhat of a no-win situation. Sometimes, that felt like Northern Ireland all round: a no-win situation.

'I'm a *Protestant* Christian,' he said eventually.

'Anna-Claire, too?'

'Yep.'

'And so what does that mean?'

What sprung most immediately to Robbie's mind, in response,

were all the things that being Protestant meant that he was *not*. He wasn't sure it was supposed to be that way, really. In any case, El didn't hang around for his response.

'Like, are you saying you've never . . .' She let her sentence trail off meaningfully. 'Are you waiting for marriage and all that?'

Robbie flushed slightly, bracing for impact. 'Yeah.'

El just shrugged, raising her wine glass to her lips again. 'That's cool.'

Robbie let out a half-laugh. 'You think?'

As had been made clear to him between ages 12 and 21, that was not what most people thought. Not remotely. He'd been all set to defend, deny, pivot, pretend.

'I mean, cool's probably the wrong word,' El amended, with another shrug. 'I suppose I don't think it's *cool*. Or, like, *uncool*. I think it's fine, is what I'm saying. Whatever.'

'Yeah? You don't think I'm doomed to just be forever behind the curve at this point?' He could hear the vulnerability in his own voice, and he cursed it.

For a moment, El just looked at him. There was the sense of an *assessment* about it, as though she were taking in every bit of him, thinking of him, suddenly, in a very particular context.

'Well, let me put it to you this way, Robbie,' she said then. 'By all accounts, eighteen months ago, you didn't know your arse from your Espresso Martinis. I'd say you're a fast learner.'

She raised one eyebrow, the hint of a sly smile playing about her lips, and Robbie was obviously extremely, extremely drunk – more so even than he'd realized. Because suddenly, with their eyes locked on one another's, it felt as though the air changed around them. Just fractionally, fleetingly.

Or, he might have imagined that entirely.

In any case, it ceased to matter to him one bit that El could never so much as make a Margarita the same way twice. She was a marvellous bartender, he thought, and a marvellous person, and he wished – suddenly, and with more intensity than he was used to feeling – that they'd been able to have this type of conversation earlier. What he wanted, now, was no less than to understand everything about her. Maybe even to have her understand everything about him, too.

The next thing he knew, El's friend Kat – Robbie had met Kat, by then, on one night out or another – was upon them, squeezing into the booth beside El.

She leaned down, nuzzling El's bare shoulder. 'Hey babe, I'm flagging,' she said.

El smiled affectionately. 'Lightweight. That's okay, though.' She pressed a sloppy kiss to the other girl's lips. 'I'll see you at home?'

Robbie was stunned, scrambling furiously to catch up to the reality before him. Nonetheless, even *he* could tell, in the pause that followed, that El hadn't given anything close to the response that Kat had been hoping for.

'Great,' she chirped tersely, and then – as quickly as she'd arrived – she was gone.

In her mind, El gave Robbie sixty seconds to bring it up. He took ten, maximum.

'I didn't know that you two were . . .'

'What?' she asked, like a dare.

Unrelatedly, she realized in that moment that her feet were throbbing. Without a second thought, she slipped them out of her high heels and settled them on Robbie's side of the booth. It was wholly a matter of comfort – she stayed a very respectable distance from his thigh – but still. He stared down at her legs as though they were aliens that had landed beside him, then looked back up at her with that same expression still on his face.

El bit back a laugh. 'What?' she repeated.

'. . . Nothing,' he replied then.

'Do you reckon I'm going to hell?' she prodded, all mischief. She liked to grab these moments where she could.

Of course, it wasn't always possible. There was the time she and Kat had been forced to get off the tube three stops early because a group of guys had started to crowd them, paw at them. El had hated feeling afraid, and more than that, she had hated that those men *knew* she was afraid. They'd got just what they wanted. All her chutzpah, all her usual *sass* and *sparkle* had dissipated to nothing in that moment. As soon as she and Kat had closed the door on what was, back then, only Kat's house, El had burst right into tears.

Then there was the time on the South Bank, when a woman not much older than El and Kat themselves had seen them kissing and had said loudly to her friend, 'Fucking disgusting, innit. Dykes.'

If El set that sort of thing aside, though (and granted, it did sometimes feel like such a huge, unfair amount to have to set aside), she often quite enjoyed the capacity her relationship had to surprise others. She felt vaguely ashamed of this fact, but it was true. She liked being able to slightly throw people off-kilter. *And what of it?* felt like a very natural question for her to be asking the world at large.

Opposite her now, Robbie looked at her with all the sudden, wide-eyed sincerity of the inebriated. 'El, I don't think you're going to hell,' he said, and then he smiled delightedly. 'That rhymed!'

El could only smile back in response. So much for this guy not drinking to get drunk.

For the umpteenth time, she was struck by the contradictions in him, by how difficult she found him to pin down. There were occasions he seemed so much younger than her, in the way that people who'd been to university often did. On any array of subjects related to Love and Death, related to the bar trade in general, he knew so much less than her. But then, there were ways in which he felt much older than her, too. So much more settled and sorted. So much cleverer.

Within days of his arrival at Love and Death, she'd felt sure she knew everything about him – or everything that mattered, anyway. Tonight, it seemed that the opposite was true. It seemed she'd somehow gone three months and yet learned almost nothing that mattered about Robbie Saunders.

'It's been nice having you here this summer, Robbie,' she said. Admittedly, she probably could not have cited any specific examples of having had a good time *with him*. But she'd certainly had some very good times in which he was also present. She was feeling magnanimous.

'Has it, aye?' he replied dryly.

'It has!' she said staunchly, both of them laughing a little now. 'You're . . . a very interesting person.'

'Well, good news,' Robbie replied. 'You're not quite rid of me yet, as it turns out.'

El set her wine glass on the table with a sudden clatter. She pulled her feet back down to the ground, sat up a little straighter. There was a level of drunkenness that could always be reversed immediately, should the circumstances require it.

'What?'

'I'm staying,' Robbie said happily.

'What do you mean?'

'Just for a year. Anna-Claire's doing her PGCE at King's, so we decided that while she's doing that . . .' He trailed off, as though the rest were obvious. 'I was kind of freaked out about even raising the idea with her, if I'm honest, but she was amazing. Like, *of course* she was. And Citi has agreed to defer my place until next September, so it couldn't have worked out better, really.'

'Hang on. You're going to continue working here – unpaid – for a whole 'nother year?' El was still struggling to compute. She felt like a moron, like the kid in class who just didn't quite get it. She did not enjoy feeling that way one bit. It was too familiar.

'Oh no, paid,' he replied. 'I'll be a bartender now, officially. Otto's offered me a proper job.'

'When did this happen?'

'Just last night.'

A fresh development, then. Nevertheless, it stung a little, to know that Otto hadn't shared it right away. El felt utterly dazed.

'Right. Great,' she mumbled.

In a flash, every single one of her previous thoughts – all that introspection and generosity of spirit – was gone. Vanished. But when Robbie offered her his glass, she clinked her own against it anyway. What else was there to do?

Part Two

Chapter Eleven

Nobody had asked Otto Kettinger to come to London. Nobody had offered him a job he couldn't turn down, begged him to come and show the Brits how it was done. He'd never even had much interest in visiting until he found himself aboard a one-way flight in the fall of 1999. It was, by that point, mostly a question of getting out of New York. The desire to get away from New York was overwhelming – matched only, in fact, by the desire he'd once felt to move there.

Absolutely nothing about his birthplace in rural Pennsylvania had held any appeal for him, and that included, for the most part, every member of his family. As quickly after turning 18 as Otto could manage it, before he'd even graduated high school, he was on the Greyhound out of there. When he arrived into the Port Authority Bus Terminal on Manhattan's 8th Avenue, it was January – objectively one of the worst months in the city – and he soon saw that everything being reported on the regional news station his parents had favoured was entirely true. This place *was* dirty and crime-ridden and quite literally rat-infested. The crack and Aids epidemics were indeed playing out in full view.

All these difficulties were especially obvious where Otto ended up living, on the Alphabet streets of the East Village. It sometimes seemed like the entire neighbourhood was just sirens and park-bench memorials, people in various uniforms sweeping in to accomplish some dire assignment or other and then getting the hell out. But what did it matter to Otto? He had an important task ahead of him. Of course he did. Why else did anyone up and move to New York City, if not to fall in love?

Naturally enough, he initially assumed the whole endeavour would involve another person. One single person, just out there waiting for him, poised to make the rest of his life mean something.

Thus, for a year or so, he committed himself to sleeping with every girl that he possibly could. Then, as a matter of thoroughness, of *ruling out*, he turned towards boys. For obvious reasons, he had to be a little more careful there. However, he conducted enough preliminary research to know that the full experience, so to speak, would definitely not have been worth dying for.

Sex, in all the many iterations he'd sought it out, had been *fine*. The issue was not, as he'd previously assumed, that every single person in his hometown was so entirely uncharismatic. Instead, if anything, the issue turned out to be him. The pursuit of sex simply did not motivate Otto in the way it seemed to motivate others, and nor had he found the experience of it to be any great shakes. Certainly, it was nothing in comparison to standing, dazzled, in front of the *Water Lilies* at the Metropolitan Museum of Art. It couldn't hold a candle to the feeling that he got when watching the New York City Ballet, or crammed into a mosh pit of punk rockers at CBGB, or listening to the Philharmonic at Lincoln Center, or taking in an Off-Off-Broadway play, or swallowing the first bite of crème brûlée at Lutèce . . .

For his first couple of years in the city, he experienced these things by being available to do them at the least popular – and therefore cheapest possible – times of the week. And, thereafter, the trick was making friends. One thing he'd always been able to do was talk to people. 'You got the gift of the gab alright,' his sixth-grade teacher had told him, back in Pennsylvania, in a way that made it clear this was not a compliment.

In lobbies and laundromats, galleries and grocery stores – mostly just to amuse himself – Otto struck up conversations. Ushers, interns, assistants . . . each new buddy seemed to lead to another, almost all of them living, like him, below 14th Street. In the fullness of time, many of these kids would rise through the ranks as painters, writers, chefs, festival programmers – they'd move uptown and begin to shape the output of the places they worked. They would, eventually, become part of Manhattan's beloved and cantankerous artistic elite, tweeting outrageous things and getting away with it on account of old age. Back then, it was enough for Otto that they could sneak him into side doors, for free, and then meet him for a drink afterwards.

He quickly had a full schedule, and it was with this whole scene – high culture, pop culture, the New Yorkers who conjured it all from nothing – that Otto fell in love. Deeply, completely, head over heels. *Sunday in the Park with George*, when it burst onto Broadway in 1984, obsessed him. His roommate Sarah, who ran a 'screenwriters' society' out of the apartment and bussed tables at The Odeon, obsessed him. Andy Warhol, in general, obsessed him.

It turned out that a life full of passion, pleasure, and giddy infatuation, did not require sex. If anything, Otto suspected that his disinterest in sex might have been the secret. To at least some degree, he felt like it was what *gave him* everything else.

For one thing, it opened up a lot of his time. For another, it lent him an air of mystery; his friends were so unable to fathom a life of chosen celibacy that they assumed Otto must surely be having all sorts of discreet, sophisticated affairs. And, finally, it made for a far greater capacity to preserve each new connection he formed. The simple reality, he found, was this: not fucking people, trying to fuck them, or trying to discontinue fucking them, vastly less-ened a guy's capacity to piss other people off.

For almost a full decade, Otto's job – at a thoroughly nondescript bar on Delancey Street – was the least interesting thing about his life. It could have been any job. If a coffee shop or a pharmacy had called him back before the manager of Cat's Eye, Otto had no doubt he'd have gone to work at one of those places instead, and enjoyed it comparably. 'Whatever,' he'd say, when people asked what he did for a living. 'It sucks, obviously, but it's fine for right now.' He would sometimes talk of 'working on a novel' that never quite got beyond the talking stage. He took a pottery class, every Thursday for four years, and despaired of all the misshapen vases he ended up with as a result.

Then, in 1992, came the Cecilia.

Otto always kept the specific details of its creation to him-self, no matter who asked. In broad terms, there was a no-reason house party at his place: people crowded dangerously on the fire escape, music blasting from a boom box practically all the way to Tompkins Square Park. There was his new pal Cecilia, who didn't drink beer. There was a bodega nearby that opened twenty-four hours.

And the rest, as they said, was history.

In retrospect, the recipe itself was almost embarrassingly simple: mashed up strawberries and raspberries, a dash of grape-fruit juice from a carton, a generous pinch of granulated sugar, plus cheap Cava. It wasn't rocket science. Every ingredient was chosen on the basis of nothing more than instinct and availability. But somehow, accidentally, Otto had landed on what he would eventually learn was the perfect combo, if you wanted a cocktail to really travel. The Cecilia was balanced, it was palatable to a lot of drinkers, and it was easily replicable, with everyday ingre-dients, in a lot of bars. The holy grail.

He started making it at his own workplace, first of all. People who didn't know him personally at Cat's Eye saw all those who *did* know him personally downing this fizzy pink delight, and they wanted to get involved. They started asking for it at other places nearby. When a couple of other bartenders and managers came into Cat's Eye to enquire about it, Otto got a kick out of giving them a demo. Slowly, the whole thing began to take on a bit of a life of its own.

He wouldn't have wanted to overstate the matter. It was still, ultimately, a drink known only by a small section of lower Manhattanites who were just beginning to be considered cool, just beginning to think of themselves as *well-connected*.

However, as it turned out, that was more than enough for the *New York Times* to give it a few inches of space. Saturday edition, May 9, 1993. *Crisp, delicate and oh-so-drinkable, prepare for the summer of Cecilia*, they wrote. Otto felt he'd happily get the words engraved on his headstone. He practically skipped into Cat's Eye that night, and they got one last shift out of him – he remembered that – before they fired him just after closing time. A bartender who outshone the bar? Evidently, it wasn't quite what the management there had in mind. They continued to serve the Cecilia long after he left, though – he remembered that, too.

Word swiftly got around – Otto made absolutely sure it did – about how he'd been screwed over, how his considerable, *Times*-rated talents were now in want of a new home. Then, just like that, came the Rainbow Room.

It had been making the papers, too, and plenty. Positioned on the sixty-fifth floor of 30 Rockefeller Plaza, it was an enormous, Art Deco bar and restaurant. Inside, head bartender Dale DeGroff had been almost single-handedly leading a cocktail revival in the city.

As well as resurrecting the classic pre-Prohibition drinks that had fallen out of fashion, he'd been coming up with his own inventions. Fresh ingredients, apparently, were his whole thing. He couldn't abide the synthetic, bought-in juices and syrups that had become the norm. On Dale's watch, out were beachy, get-smashed-fast concoctions, and in were sleek, serious drinks. A 'second golden age of cocktails' was upon the people of New York, allegedly, and mostly thanks to one man behind one bar.

For his part, Otto didn't entirely know when the first golden age of cocktails had been. The 1920s, he guessed?

He was objectively unqualified to work at the Rainbow Room.

Nonetheless, he took the job when it was offered to him, then scrambled to figure out the answer to one key question: did he actually, *really*, *truly* give a shit about making drinks?

What he discovered, night by night at the Rainbow Room, was that he did.

There would have been no way to survive there if he didn't. It was fucking hard work. Late nights, long hours, off-the-charts expectations. However, Otto took to high-class bartending like a duck to water. The creation of a perfect cocktail tapped into his natural curiosity, his natural penchant for glamour. He loved it in the same way he loved fashion or sculpture or watching four weird Serbians tap dancing in a black box theatre. Except he wasn't a spectator any longer. He was, suddenly, the show.

It was as though the whole thing had been destined. So many of his friends, he began to see, would soon have outgrown him, had he stayed a nothing bartender at a nothing bar. As it was, he had an invite to the best party in town every night. People came to him for gossip and introductions, for hot tips and free therapy, for jaw-dropping views of the Empire State Building and a cocktail with a good strong kick. All those years he'd spent cultivating his social skills, cultivating his faith in his own personal taste . . . it was clear now that not a second of that had been wasted time.

Of course, it didn't take too long at his new workplace before Otto gave the Cecilia something of a refresh. The strawberries and raspberries began to be described as *muddled*; the grapefruit juice was painstakingly squeezed and de-pulped. The pinch of granulated sugar became exactly fifteen millilitres of sugar syrup, the Cava switched for Champagne. A sprig of thyme made its way into the mix as a garnish. That was the recipe that ended up being written down, made to last longer than anything he could shake and serve with a smile.

He had his reasons for the cynicism that eventually began to take hold – about the city, about the whole scene in New York. It terrified him, to sense the weariness in himself – and much worse, to see the staleness of his creations. Time, then, for a new challenge. Naturally, as soon as Otto began to contemplate an exit from the Rainbow Room, he thought of the Volkov Brothers.

They'd approached him in late '98 – two almost identical guys with Irish-red hair, Italian-American accents, a Russian last name, and a fortune of indistinct origin. Otto had enough of a profile to draw the cool crowd now, they'd said. Would he have any interest in opening up his own place? If so, they wanted to be the lucky ones to help him do it. They'd be silent investors. *Quiet as fucking church mice* – that was the phrase that had been used.

At the time, Otto hadn't been interested. Nonetheless, after that meeting, the Volkovs had followed up with an *email*, of all things. Months later, and with some difficulty, Otto retrieved it on a PC at the New York Public Library. He was a hunt-and-peck typist, totally disinterested in the internet, even though everybody said it was the future. He couldn't imagine ever needing to ask Jeeves anything.

Anywhere you want, the brothers had written, at the end of their message. *Just name your spot and we're in.*

It was the sort of offer that almost nobody got in their whole lives, and – reflecting on it seriously for the first time – Otto's mind was a complete blank.

Where could he go, outside New York? For whatever reason, no other American cities even crossed his mind. As for the American non-cities, of course they were even less of an option. If his Pennsylvania upbringing had taught him anything, it was that he was not made for rural life or anything close to it. Even crossing the bridge into Brooklyn always made him feel a little queasy.

Paris, then? Florence? Barcelona? These were all notionally appealing to him. He just wasn't sure how appealing he himself would be, outside the framework of the English language. By now, Otto believed entirely that creating cocktails was the thing he was always meant to have done with his life, that his legacy would be in liquid form. But still, he put at least fifty per cent of his success in the industry down to a natural capacity for a little verbal flourish. The *gift of the gab*.

With that in mind, options narrowed down rapidly. Almost all of Europe was effectively out, given the language barrier. Not quite all of it, though. And hadn't Otto, at one point, made it his life's central mission to own a Vivienne Westwood T-shirt – the *GOD SAVE THE QUEEN* one, with the Sex Pistols lyrics printed on it? Hadn't he, just a week previously, seen *Notting Hill* at the Quad Cinema in the Village?

How about London? he typed onto the computer screen, just to see what it would look like.

Then he halted, deleted each character carefully. Questions, when you wanted someone to give you a lot of money, were not the thing. Instinctively, he understood that this next phase of his life – even more than anything that had come before – would require him to project certainty. To project a *vision*.

He shrugged both his shoulders back and gave his head a shake, index fingers poised.

I've been thinking about your offer, he typed. *And I know exactly where I want to do it.*

Chapter Twelve

London had turned out to be nothing like he'd thought it would be.

The food was worse than expected; the weather was better. People were far less polite than Hugh Grant had led him to believe. They were far more polite than Johnny Rotten had led him to believe.

As for cocktails, the scene that had gone past 'burgeoning' and was proceeding apace towards 'flourishing' in Manhattan seemed barely to exist at all in London, when first Otto arrived in late '99. There were the hotel bars, of course – Otto acknowledged that it was possible to get a half-decent Martini in The Savoy or The Connaught. A handful of buzzy new restaurants also offered a small cocktail menu.

Cocktails didn't seem to stand alone, though, the way they had begun to back in New York. They existed to complement some other experience – an expensive hotel stay or an expensive meal – but they were not the main event. The majority of Brits, to the extent they thought about cocktails at all, apparently did so mainly in association with foreign holidays. They could conjure the image of something boozy and colourful, presented to them, poolside, in Italy or Spain. On the home front, though? Not so much. Long Island Iced Tea, served by the pitcher in American-style chain bars, seemed often to be as good as it got.

Although it wasn't for Otto – a foreigner – to say aloud, the prevailing culture around drinks in Britain struck him as functional and depressing. Why were last orders being called so *early*? Where was the glamour here? Where was the fun, the flair, the element of surprise?

Enter the Cosmopolitan.

In fact, it wasn't the newfangled thing that most people imagined. Madonna had been photographed holding one at the Rainbow Room all the way back in the mid-Nineties, causing a surge in orders for a little while thereafter. It had seemed crazy, at the time, the influence that a photo could have.

But, television, baby. There was, evidently, nothing like it.

When Carrie Bradshaw declared the Cosmopolitan her favourite drink, when four fictional characters started downing them every episode, the impact was very real. Popularity within a certain venue, or even a certain city, turned out to be meagre success compared with the global reach of *Sex and the City*.

For Otto, running a new bar single-handedly in a new country, it was briefly a godsend.

The show introduced an audience of millions to the notion of *going out for cocktails*. Moreover, it helped combat a fairly significant barrier to entry, as far as large swathes of the British public were concerned: most people simply didn't know what to order.

Suddenly, they'd heard of this drink – that was step one. Then, they liked it – step two. They liked how it tasted, and also what it represented. Freedom. Femininity. Success.

The issue, in the years since then, had become prising it from them.

And no one could say Otto Kettinger hadn't been doing his darnedest.

At Love and Death, he'd invented endless cocktails, come up with endless names designed to intrigue or amuse.

Pop My Cherry.

The Side Piece.

Blue Murder.

The Pear Necessity.

Once El came along, the two of them could spend hours tossing names back and forth.

Shortly thereafter – and supported, in this area, by much vaguer interest from El – he'd begun a 'farm to glass' programme, sourcing all the fresh herbs, plants, and fruits he could from London's surrounding counties. He'd imported elegant, mouth-blown glassware from halfway across the world. He'd painstakingly perfected the baking of fine chocolate wafers with which to top a sweet, coffee-based drink. He had, at one point, spent weeks fermenting bananas in the small hours of the morning.

All of this, he did in the pursuit of excitement, of newness, of *wonder* – his own, but mostly other people's. In a way, the whole thing felt altruistic to him. Fighting for the cause kept him, quite literally, awake at night.

Still, by the time Otto was approaching his sixth year in business, many of his customers, more often than he would have liked, bypassed the drinks he loved best, the ones he was proudest of. Instead, they often fell back on old favourites. A Margarita, perhaps, or a Sex on the Beach. Most of all, the Cosmopolitan.

I feel like I'm being sucked dry! he wrote in a letter to a friend back in the US. His best friend, really. They hadn't moved to emails. There was a certain romance, Otto and Cece both felt, to ink and paper. It was how they'd always done it.

Seriously. Am I losing my mojo? Just this constant pressure to be generating, you know? Of course, I don't let any of the staff see it – not at all – but it's stressful, it's exhausting, it's expensive . . . remind me why I do this, again?

Oh, don't be so dramatic, Otto, came her response, a few weeks later. *First of all, you know you say some version of this every two years, right? Second of all, this is a matter of basic management. You aren't a one-man-band anymore. How many times have you sung El's praises to me? And your new guy – the one you like – he must have settled in by now, right? Do you really think you're the only one who can have a good idea? If you ask me, you need to put those kids to work!*

So it was that, in late January 2006, the entire staff of Love and Death assembled. They perched on stools around the bar, a sense of anticipation bubbling. It was the middle of the afternoon, and they were never summoned en masse this way. They'd been waiting thirty minutes already for something to happen.

'Do you reckon we're in for a bollocking?' Tom asked.

'A bollocking about what?'

'Could be anything, couldn't it?'

'Speak for yourself,' Aziz replied. 'I've been the model employee!'

'It's been quiet since Christmas, though,' Robbie chimed in. 'And Otto's been . . .'

El shot him a dirty look. 'He's been *fine*,' she said staunchly.

'Well, I'm just saying—'

Robbie cut himself off, all conversation halting as, at last, Otto emerged. He was, as ever, in a three-piece suit, and he carried with him some unknown item. Whatever it was, it required both hands and was covered by a sheath of silk fabric. Everyone whooped and hollered at the sight, as much in relief as in excitement. That twinkle in Otto's eye augured well.

He smiled enigmatically as he set the offering down on the bar.

'I have two words for you!' he declared, once the group had quietened again. 'Cocktail flights!'

Around the bar, this announcement was greeted by silence.

'Alright, I'll bite,' Robbie said. 'What's a flight?'

Otto beamed. 'I'm thrilled you asked, Robbie. Really, I am.

Because as you may have noticed, I've prepared for something of an unveiling. Behold . . . this month's flight.'

With a flourish, he removed the fabric from the mystery item. Underneath were three drinks, unfamiliar to everyone, each one served in a miniature glass. The bases of the glasses slotted into perfectly fitted grooves on a little wooden tray.

'Three for the price of one,' Otto declared. 'We'll offer a new flight of cocktails every month. I want us to really push it – people are much more likely to branch out if they know they're ordering a smaller glass. Essentially, what we're giving them here is some built-in back-up options.'

He paused for breath. 'And here's the other thing. Guess who's going to be coming up with the drinks for the flights? You are. Or should I say, *we* are. Every second week, all those who want to come along are invited to a little something I like to call "cocktail jam".'

This time it was El who asked, 'What's that?'

'Well, think of it like how a band jams, but with drinks. I want you to bring something we don't currently serve here at Love and Death. It could be a twist on a classic or – even better – something totally new that you've come up with yourself. Either way, be prepared for feedback. Whoever's presenting will give us all the basic recipe, and the wider group will riff off of that – maybe it's about incorporating a different idea or a different ingredient, or making a tweak to the quantities. How can we figure out a way, together, to make each drink the very best it can be? That's the question.'

'So it's like peer review,' Robbie said.

'You could put it that way,' Otto replied mildly. Evidently, he didn't plan to ever put it that way.

'And is this, uh . . . compulsory?' Tom chimed in.

For a moment, Otto just looked at Tom. 'No,' he said lightly. 'It's not compulsory.'

'I mean, I . . . obviously I'm happy to do it,' Tom rushed to add, and Otto smiled graciously in response. It didn't quite reach his eyes.

'Anyhow!' Otto continued. He crouched down and, from somewhere, produced several trays full of drinks – they were the same cocktails as were on the flight, enough for everybody to try one of each. 'I figured, what's a drink if you don't get to taste it, right? Pass these around.'

Hands duly reached over one another in a flurry, glasses crowd-surfing along the bar.

'We *cannot* allow ourselves to get complacent, folks,' Otto continued, over the hubbub. 'It's a new year, and I've decided: this is the year of invention. I want us to be – well, I happen to think we already are, but I want us to *stay* – the most innovative cocktail bar in this city. The culture starts *here*. It is what we say it is. Okay?' He held his own drink aloft in a toast. 'Down with the Cosmo!'

Chapter Thirteen

If there was one thing Robbie and El probably did not need in their workplace, it was a means by which they could openly criticize and be contrasted against one another.

Already, from the moment Robbie had arrived back to Love and Death after his honeymoon, the two of them had reverted to a predictable dynamic.

The difficulties between them were, in short, the very same ones that had been obvious within their first week working together. Where he was cautious, she was reckless. Where he was studied, she was spontaneous. It was, at this point, impossible for others at Love and Death not to notice the vast differences in their approach to the same basic activities. Now armed with some level of job security, didn't Robbie give as good as he got?

'You can't blame the tube all the time,' he told El, when she once again waltzed into Love and Death twenty minutes late, cursing TfL.

'Why not?' she replied, shrugging off her coat. 'The tube is always so shit.'

'Well, exactly. But we all have to be on it. That makes it a neutral factor. It's just something everyone has to navigate, like . . . I don't know, cooking dinner. You couldn't show up late for work four times in a row and say, "Oh, it's just I had to make dinner."'

Even as he proclaimed this, he suspected that if El were the sort of girl to ever make herself a proper meal for dinner, that was exactly what she'd say.

'Well, sorry we can't all live in Kensington, Robbie,' she huffed.

Robbie rolled his eyes. It was true that he and Anna-Claire had fallen on their feet, accommodation-wise, thanks to a university pal. That was Oxford for you. Robbie hadn't stopped being shocked by the sheer amount of property to which many people in their early twenties seemed to have access. But in the circumstances – the circumstances being a flat off Holland Park Avenue belonging to someone's parents, with rent so cheap as to be almost free – he wasn't complaining.

In any case, how this was relevant to the issue at hand, he had no idea.

'If anything, I actually have a longer commute than most people, *because of* living west,' he said.

El let out an exaggerated sigh.

'How long until you go to work at Citi, again, Robbie? Would you think about starting a bit early? We can never have too many bankers in the world – that's what I always say.'

The very day after Otto announced cocktail jam, El got to work. She just couldn't seem to stop herself; her brain was bursting with ideas. By the time Kat rose for the day, El was already ensconced in their tiny galley kitchen, busy in a swirl of ingredients. Their housemate Moss was in there, too, trying valiantly to reclaim some space to make his Super Noodles. Another recent addition to the household, a stray cat they'd named Tina by collective vote, skulked about underfoot.

Kat hovered in the doorframe, took in the scene. 'What's happening here?' she asked.

El turned to look at her. 'What do you mean?'

'You're awake, for one thing. It's only noon.'

'Oh well, you know. Best part of the day and all that.'

Kat just snorted.

'This was Otto's idea, was it?' she asked, once El had explained her current mission.

'Obviously.'

'Sounds like he's perked up a bit then.'

El tensed slightly. She wished she hadn't said anything, not even to Kat, about Otto's recent melancholy. Wasn't it her job to coax him out of those funks? For reasons she could not exactly explain, ever since Robbie had decided to stick around, she wanted to prove her loyalty to Otto all the more.

'A bit. You know how it is. There's always a bit of a lull after Christmas. It's been rough on him.'

Kat offered only a hum of generalized agreement.

'Plus, he has SAD,' El continued.

'What?'

'Seasonal affective disorder. As in, like, the darkness in autumn and winter makes him depressed.'

'That's not a *disorder*,' Kat scoffed. 'If that's a disorder, then every person in Britain has it.'

El just shrugged. Rifling through the cupboards now, she was only half listening anyway. 'Well, maybe every person in Britain *does* have it.' Her eyes landed on something. 'Do you think a melted Milky Way would taste nice?'

Meanwhile, on the other side of town, Robbie poured coffee from a cafetière into two cups, and the simple act felt soothing and grown-up. Though it was Saturday, Anna-Claire sat hunched over a textbook at the dining-room table, with the radio on low in the background.

She glanced up when he delivered her cup. 'Mmm, thank you.'

He dropped a kiss on her lips. 'You're welcome,' he said. 'I'll not disturb you.'

They smiled at one another as he left her to work, then flopped onto the couch. Everything about this flat was comfortable and in good taste, chosen by a landlord who'd intended the place, initially, as his own city bolthole. Robbie's younger self could never have imagined living in a place like this. His younger self could never have imagined the ways in which, inside these four walls, a whole new world had opened up to him: low-fat yoghurts in the fridge, and a shower tray so littered with products that Robbie could barely find room for his feet; waking with another person, and going to sleep with them; learning their habits, their foibles and irritants. It was intimacy as he'd never known it before. And then there was the sex.

As far as Robbie was concerned, things in that domain had started off pretty damn good, and – through a process of trial and error that was more methodical, that involved more communication and comedy than he would have expected – they were only getting better. Overall, he couldn't think of anything less fun than going through that process with someone he didn't really know, didn't really trust, didn't really love. He had no regrets.

On the sofa now, he sipped his coffee and picked up his novel. Of its own accord, though, his mind drifted. What, he wondered, might he bring to the first cocktail jam? He'd think about it for a week or so first, he decided – weigh up a few options, do some research before committing to anything.

As ever, it was hard not to get swept along with Otto's enthusiasm for this new initiative, hard not to be seduced by his delivery of the whole thing. He really did have a touch of Willy Wonka about him sometimes, Robbie thought.

If he were being brutally honest, though, a few other things had also occurred to him.

Firstly, these flights of cocktails would be labour intensive. Secondly, they would be costly. If the former had struck anyone else in the room yesterday, he was certain the latter hadn't. He very much included Otto in that assessment. Nobody at Love and Death, least of all its owner, seemed to spend any time contemplating the question that came increasingly to Robbie's mind: how on earth was this place making any real money?

There were the running costs, the staff costs, not to mention the costs of all the ingredients – only the best for Otto. His refusal to cut corners meant that even on busy nights, Robbie wouldn't have been surprised to find they were making a loss.

'You know, he sometimes has me turn people away?' Cormac had told Robbie once. 'As in, even when there's space inside.'

Robbie had been nothing short of gobsmacked. Nonetheless, he'd attempted to see the logic. 'Artificial scarcity, I suppose?' he'd replied. 'Oldest trick in the big book of economics?'

The doorman hadn't been remotely convinced. 'Can you imagine literally any pub in Ireland being at that kind of craic? I don't get it. Does Otto want to be popular, or does he want to be unpopular? Because if you want to be popular, you – I don't know – hire a PR. You get a few students to stand and hand out flyers on Oxford Street. You *put a sign outside your fecking business*. At a minimum, you let people in when they schlep all the way here, and then you let them order whatever the hell they want.'

Robbie had been unable to stop himself laughing aloud. Put in such a way, all of that – the exact opposite of Otto's philosophy – was very hard to argue with. He liked Cormac a lot.

Back when he first arrived, there'd been something about the other man's thick Waterford brogue that had instinctively made Robbie wary. He felt strange about admitting that, even to himself, but it was true. As the months had gone by, though, he'd come to look forward to their fleeting interactions. There was something about hearing certain familiar turns of phrase, something about Cormac's willingness to call a spade a spade, that Robbie now actually found quite comforting.

'Whatcha thinking about over there?' Anna-Claire asked him then.

With a start, Robbie realized he was staring into space, ignoring his book altogether.

He considered a true response, but none of it was important, really – not when his wife was deep in study mode. And in truth, he probably already talked more about work than any one person could be expected to bear.

'Oh,' he said. 'Nothing. Nothing important.'

Chapter Fourteen

A fortnight later, the first cocktail jam came and went. Then the next, and the one after that. As winter melted into spring, the twice-monthly meetings became a key feature of life at Love and Death: gearing up for them, debriefing after them. The space between them seemed to gallop past.

Upon his very first sip of any given drink, Robbie found it almost impossible to tell how Otto was going to respond to it. Mercurial – that was the word for him. That was one word for him.

On his good days, he was the best teacher, the most encyclopedic and empathetic mentor. He had the most insightful suggestions, all shared generously. It felt like a pleasure to come in before the bar opened to the public, unpaid, just to hear him talk. On his good days, he adored not just the result but the process.

'Oh, this is awful! It's just awful!' he'd say giddily. 'I love it. You know why? Because at least I haven't tasted this before.'

His criticisms would be sardonic, served with a wink. 'Wow. This is like something one of your *carpeted pubs* would serve.'

On his less good days, though . . .

Robbie once watched Otto take a single mouthful of someone's effort and pour it – pour all that time and expense – straight down the sink.

'Why show up if you're not even going to bother showing up?'
he'd ask.

He could be dismissive, like that – cutting. At times, he could
skate very, very close to outright humiliating people.

He was, by and large, easier on El than on anyone.

'I suppose it makes sense,' Marcus said, when Robbie observed
as much. 'I mean, she's always helped Otto out with his creations.
She just seems to have a knack for knowing what will work. Half
the specials in the time I've been here, I'd say she's had a hand in.'

This was news to Robbie. In a flash, it was clear to him why
El had always got the sort of latitude she did, in terms of her
disorganization, her spillages, her fondness for a free pour. All
along – in a way that was perhaps more peripheral, more private
than cocktail jam now rendered it – she'd been bringing something to the party that none of the rest of them had been. And as
it turned out, that wasn't good looks or personality: it was talent.

That wasn't to say that Otto liked everything she came up
with.

'A swing and a miss, kid,' he'd tell her, at least half the time.

El's number one gift – maybe even more than anything to do
with her creative capacities – was that she didn't seem to *mind*
missing. She had another swing lined right up.

Few of them, as it happened, were to Robbie's personal taste.
El typically went big: glasses rimmed with salt she'd dyed a mixture of jewel tones, or topped with a cloud of candy floss; glasses
she quite literally set on fire in front of everyone's very eyes.

She liked to tell a story with her drinks, it seemed. Without fail,
she'd preface the presentation of them with some elaborate tale
or other. 'Picture this,' she'd start, and who could predict what
magic carpet ride they'd all be dragged on from there?

It all seemed a little gimmicky, to Robbie.

'I just don't think everyone necessarily wants to beat their way
through a cloud of dry ice before they get a sip of their drink,'

he'd say, as El's latest creation was unveiled to *oohs* and *ahhs* from their colleagues.

'I just don't think everyone necessarily wants to sit through a history lesson before they get a sip of their drink,' she'd toss back.

And on and on it went.

It was true that, for his part, Robbie stuck exclusively to resurrecting obscure drinks from the past. He loved the idea of bringing something long forgotten to a whole new generation. He loved sourcing the authentic ingredients, assembling them painstakingly, explaining the genesis of the thing to his peers. Understated elegance – that's what he was going for. A touch of *class*.

Otto respected that – supported it, encouraged it, complimented it, even. But he didn't *delight* in it – not the way he did with El. Week after week at cocktail jam, Robbie could see the writing on the wall.

And some deeply ungenerous part of him, a part he was slightly ashamed of, didn't like it one bit.

Intellect and diligence had simply never let him down like this before. Hadn't he always been top of the class? Hadn't he relished that, relied on it, all but pinned his entire identity upon it?

He had to figure out a way to get there, he decided. It was as simple as that.

For El, too, the whole thing was a revelation.

It was true that she'd always helped out, here and there, with the menu at Love and Death. She'd suggested names to Otto, or concepts. She'd thrown a few ingredients together – just as a starting point, just as an idea – and let him make adjustments as he saw fit. Sometimes, in the past, he'd barely made any at all before he put a drink on the menu.

She had enjoyed all that, but she also hadn't thought much of it. If she had any skill as an inventor, she'd considered it akin to her capacity to chat to a stranger, or to pick up an ugly dress at

Brick Lane Market and, a week later, have a skirt and top that people stopped her on the street to compliment. Fun, for sure, but not a big deal really. Nothing particularly remarkable.

There was something about the format of cocktail jam, though – something about taking *ownership* of what she presented. Very swiftly, El found herself hooked. Here, she realized, was something she could actually be the *best* at. And it turned out to be something *valuable*. Who knew? She sure hadn't.

Now that she was taking drinks-making seriously, acting not merely on impulse, there was a lot to weigh up. Her own taste. What she knew of Otto's taste. What she knew of the public's taste.

Otto, for example, disliked vodka. It added nothing to a cocktail, he said, in terms of either flavour or presentation.

The public, for example, disliked gin. Outside the familiar context of a G&T, it was unfashionable – that was the long and short of it.

What else? By and large, women were afraid of whiskey and dark rum. Men were afraid of everything else.

'Something that isn't pink,' they'd say, sometimes, and wait for El to laugh. On occasion, she'd had men ask her to put something served in a delicate coupe into a different glass. Often, faced with an unfamiliar scenario and the risk of looking girly, they just ordered a measure of hard liquor and had done with it. 'I don't think I've ever seen one that big,' El felt like saying, pornily, every time she produced a whiskey neat.

When it came to her own inventions, she found she didn't give a shit about converting men to the things women liked. Conversely, the idea of a woman hopping up on a barstool and ordering something dark and strong . . . that struck her as cool. Sexy. Powerful.

She worked on something for weeks – months, even – with precisely that woman in mind. She brought it to cocktail jam over and over. There was always something not quite right about it, though. The vision in her head never exactly matched what was in the glass.

'Hazard of the profession, I'm afraid,' Otto replied, when she told him that. 'But keep chipping away at it, won't you? You'll get there.'

El added more bitters, and then the particular whiskey she'd chosen didn't seem quite right. She changed the whiskey, and suddenly she needed less orange liqueur. She switched one sugar cube for two, just to see what it tasted like; she took half a cube away again.

It was probably the first time in her life she'd ever really stuck at something.

How irritating, to realize that her father, her teachers in school . . . they had all been right: perseverance *did* seem to be quite an important feature of success.

How irritating to realize that Robbie Saunders, too, had been right about a thing or two. An extra five mils here or there *did* change up the drinking experience.

More and more, she could see how much Otto valued Robbie's precision, his consistency, his encyclopedic knowledge of drinks.

'Hey, Robbie,' he'd say. 'Remind me what's in the Horsefeather, again? Ginger beer or ginger ale?'

'I promise I'm leaving you in the safest possible hands,' El heard him tell a customer, another time. 'This guy always delivers.'

She watched, too, as Robbie sought out new ways to integrate himself, to make up for (what she considered) his entirely uninspired drinks.

Always, it was: 'We're getting a lot from that supplier – I could give them a ring and see if they can do us a better deal?'

Or: 'I figured it might be worth digging a bit more into our average pour cost, for these new specials. Industry average is between 18 and 24 per cent, apparently. Shall I go ahead and do that?'

Otto greeted every such suggestion with nothing but enthusiasm, and El found herself wanting, suddenly, to be a little more like Robbie.

At heart, she still believed that bartending was essentially an instinctive thing, a personalized thing – that it really was much more art than science (or, for that matter, maths). But was there any harm in trying to make herself the full package?

She began taking more care over each drink, making more effort to do things exactly how the Bible said. She even found herself – truly, she could hardly believe what was becoming of her – surfing the internet in the afternoons, trying to retain some of the references Robbie already had at his fingertips. None of it came naturally to her. Quickly, she could see all the extra effort that must have gone into him getting every single one of the compliments he did from Otto.

How strange, to realize that for all their many differences, in a certain core way, she and Robbie Saunders seemed to be exactly the same. Loath as El was to admit it, he had an intensity to him that she recognized. She could see clearly what Robbie would do for Otto's attention, for his approval. It was the same thing she'd do herself – whatever it took.

And yet, between the two of them, she couldn't help but think she'd ended up with an extra burden, somehow. The burden of continuing, on some level, to pretend she didn't care all that much. That she was a devil-may-care, fun-time girl, that any of her successes were the result of sheer force of personality on her part, stumbled into by luck and charm and natural talent. Not grafted and grasped for. Not wanted, desperately.

One evening, shortly after Easter, El was dashing around the house in a whirlwind when Kat arrived back, brandishing a plastic bag.

'Okay! A Chinese feast awaits!'

El halted, winced. 'Bad news. I actually have to go into work. Tom's just been sacked.'

Kat knew Tom, too, of course, and her face fell in sympathy. 'Oh no!'

'I know. I mean, honestly, it was probably a long time coming, but still.'

'Do you absolutely *have* to go in, though? Can't you get out of it? I mean, I've just got us all this food. I was sort of thinking we could get cosy, have a bit of . . . *alone* time.'

The implication passed El by entirely. 'If I don't go in, then Robbie definitely will, and—' She cut herself off. It felt vulnerable to even go there. 'Whatever. Look, I'm sorry – I've told Otto I'll do it now.'

She paused, took in Kat's pouting face. Increasingly, it was becoming clear that she and Kat had the same job and yet they had very different jobs. Kat had no great love for bar work. She had a love for making jewellery out of glazed polymer clay, and doing so in the daylight hours. Alas, this had proved – so far – to be economically unviable. Hence, her job at the Golden Lion on Dean Street, serving pints to office workers and tourists across five shifts a week. Outside said shifts, though, she never seemed to give the place – or anyone in it – a second thought.

'You're not too cross with me, are you?' El said, her tone wheedling now. She wrapped her arms around her girlfriend and kissed her. She brought her absolute A-star game to the task, sweeping her tongue against Kat's lips, dipping one hand slightly below the back of her jeans, breathing, 'I promise I'll make it up to you,' against her skin.

It worked.

'I . . . I understand,' Kat confirmed, a little breathlessly, once they'd parted. Perhaps she still didn't look *hugely* pleased. But it was more than good enough for El to consider one problem sorted for now.

She continued her quick sweep around the house, gathering her things in a hurry, doing what she could with her appearance. She was tired, though.

She'd worked last night, and the night before. That was to say nothing of the extra time she'd been putting in at home, researching and experimenting with new concoctions.

And so, a bump or two before this shift, just to help stay on her toes. It wasn't about being high. It was about being *alert*. Without it, she knew she'd just feel so exhausted all night. She'd revert to old mistakes – the sorts that Robbie would absolutely never make.

It was the first time El had ever done a drug by herself.

In truth, she didn't love the idea of it. But she did it, that night. She might have done it a few nights after that, too.

Chapter Fifteen

Mostly, both Robbie and El looked back at the brief sensation they'd had that night before he got married – that strange mixture of intrigue and understanding – as a drunken, fleeting thing.

Of course, there were moments when that was harder to do. Very occasionally. Moments when they weren't bickering, weren't rubbing each other the wrong way.

The first time Anna-Claire came into Love and Death – that was a good example.

Getting her there had undeniably been a bit of an effort. She was just so busy since moving to London, commencing her postgrad, reconnecting with various networks of friends from school and university. If she didn't have studying, she had lesson planning. If she wasn't at her Young Women's Fellowship, then she was at swing dancing.

Robbie continued to love this about his wife: that she was such a doer, that her interests were, in certain ways, different from his. He didn't mind a bit that cocktails weren't high on her list. Why would they be? She wasn't a big drinker, in general. She disliked the loudness of bars and being around drunk people. Even the beverages he'd whipped up for her at home had been greeted with an enthusiasm born more of love for him than love for anything he could possibly pour into a Collins glass.

Her visit to Love and Death, Robbie knew, was in that same

spirit – the spirit of being supportive of an interest they did not need to share.

Was there, perhaps, the slightest hint of reluctance on her part to come? Had his tales of this place – of Otto, of the famous faces that sometimes appeared after midnight, of El and the trays of flaming cocktails she'd balance on one hand – had all of that built up into a picture that his wife found somewhat intimidating? Did she not entirely want to meet the version of her husband who sometimes stayed out late and woke up with a thumping headache of his own creation? If those things were true, Robbie and Anna-Claire never discussed them.

The night she decided to drop in – early doors, on a Wednesday – it was himself and El behind the bar. That wouldn't have been Robbie's dream scenario. Jamie, Marcus, even Tom's replacement whom he barely knew . . . he'd have taken anyone over El, he realized. There was just some instinctive thread of resistance in him to the idea of his wife and El Tippett in the same space. He couldn't explain that, exactly, but it was how he felt.

'Do people ever call you AC?' El began jauntily, as Anna-Claire hopped up onto a stool at the bar that night.

'Uh . . . no,' Anna-Claire replied, and Robbie had the sense of watching two very different animals. It was like putting a pony and a tiger in a field together and seeing how they got on. He had the urge to jump in, to attempt some bridging of the gap.

However, as it turned out, there was no need. Almost before his very eyes, El seemed to shape shift. She did the thing she did, with all her customers. She set about making his wife feel right at home.

'It's kind of overwhelming, isn't it?' she said, with a nod towards the menu.

'Gosh! It is!' Anna-Claire replied. 'I suppose I might have a . . . Cosmopolitan?'

Robbie winced, hating himself for the vague sense of second-ary embarrassment that rose up in him.

El just smiled. 'A perfect choice,' she said, with just the same sort of reassurance that Robbie imagined Anna-Claire would project in the classroom. 'Or you could try a Cecilia? It's like a fruity, fizzy sort of thing. Very light. Otto actually invented that one – so you could tell people you've had it *almost* right from the source.'

'Alright then, yes. That sounds lovely,' Anna-Claire said. The relief of a choice made was obvious.

'Coming right up. Robbie tells us you're training to be a teacher. Very proud husband, this one. So, how's it going? I don't know how you're doing it. Pretty rewarding, though, I imagine?'

It was just the encouragement Anna-Claire needed, and even as El started to move around the bar, reaching easily for ingredients, she continued nodding along at intervals, offering a question or a laugh here and there.

Somewhere in the midst, Robbie caught her eye for a second.

Thank you, his look said.

Don't mention it, hers replied.

Another time, Robbie was on his way into work. As soon as he turned onto Epworth Street, he could hear the sound of raised voices. It was El, he realized, and an older gentleman – both of them were animated and gesticulating, clearly in the full flow of an argument.

Robbie coughed deliberately, and the moment she saw him, El clammed up. In turn, the man glanced backwards, clocking that they now had company.

He turned back to El, stepping closer to her, saying something in a low voice. All the while, El stood stony-faced, almost delib-erately, defiantly detached now. Robbie had never seen her that way. She looked, suddenly, very young.

Robbie wasn't sure what to do – whether to step in or step

away – when suddenly the man turned again. This time, he strode right down the street and out of sight, without so much as a nod in Robbie's direction.

'Are you okay?' Robbie asked El, once he was within talking distance.

El tilted her chin up. 'I'm fine.'

'Who was that guy?'

'No one.'

'Was he a dealer?' Robbie asked. It was just the first thing that came to mind. He'd been at enough industry nights with El to see that she'd stepped things up a little in that domain lately. 'Are you in some kind of trouble?'

She let out a mirthless laugh. 'No. That was my dad.'

Robbie couldn't rule out the possibility that his jaw dropped in surprise.

'We're not close,' she added then.

That much, Robbie thought, had been obvious. 'Was he . . . abusive?' Robbie asked carefully. 'When you were growing up?'

El frowned. 'What? No. He was just an arsehole.'

Robbie found himself utterly at a loss for what to do with that information. 'Do you, uh . . . do you want to talk about it?'

El sighed. 'Do you get along with your parents, Robbie?'

'Yeah. I mean, you know. More or less.'

'Okay. Do you have brothers and sisters?'

'One brother. Younger. He's an apprentice joiner.'

'And do you get along with him?'

'Well, we're quite different.'

'But . . . ?' she prompted.

'But, yeah. Basically, we get on alright.'

'Then no,' she said, sounding more tired than he'd ever heard her. 'I don't want to talk about this with you.'

Robbie found he couldn't blame her one bit. 'I'm sorry,' he said.

'What are you sorry for?'

'I'm sorry that whatever just happened . . . happened. I'm sorry that I saw it.'

She just nodded. Together, they made their way into Love and Death. Another shift awaited, whether they liked it or not – another bunch of strangers to whom they would give everything they had, for one night only.

'Are you alright, El?' Marcus asked, as soon as they'd pushed through the curtain. 'You look a bit . . . not yourself.'

Robbie clocked it when El froze in response, clearly unnerved to find herself seen – twice – in a way she didn't want to be.

'We've both just been screamed at by a streaker on City Road,' he jumped in. 'It was really quite shocking.'

Marcus burst into laughter, and El couldn't seem to help smiling along too. She glanced over at him.

Thank you, her look said.

Don't mention it, his replied.

Chapter Sixteen

In June, a guy came into the bar in a sports jacket and sunglasses. He was the first through the door at 6 p.m. and made a beeline for Otto. He seemed to know exactly who he was looking for.

'I'm Marvin C. Johnson,' he said, extending a handshake. 'I'm a location scout on *BST*.'

Immediately, El's ears pricked up. She was a little curious, sure. But she was also ready to run interference. Every part of her expected that Otto was poised to duck out, pass this problem to her. That was how they did it.

Thus, she felt more than a little discombobulated when, instead, Otto simply accepted Marvin's handshake.

'Otto Kettinger,' he said, and the slow, curious drawl of his voice reminded El suddenly of the first night Robbie came into Love and Death – almost exactly a year ago now. 'You're going to have to take those glasses off if you're going to even think about having a conversation with me,' Otto added.

Marvin duly did. 'Force of habit,' he said, with a little laugh. 'I've been spending a lot of time out in LA recently . . .'

He let the phrase linger meaningfully, all but begging to be asked the details. Evidently, this guy – with his cockney accent and slicked-back hair – was not an LA native. In other circumstances, if El had been asked to guess at the nature of his involvement in the film and television industry, her thoughts would have turned immediately towards a haul of DVDs in the boot of his car, offered at a very reasonable price.

When Otto said nothing, El jumped in.

'So, should we have heard of . . . *BST*?' she asked.

'You will do soon,' Marvin replied confidently. '*BST* as in "British Summer Time". Good title, eh? Think sexy young professionals in the capital, contemporary stories for the times we live in – London like you've never seen it before. *Britain* like you've never seen it before. None of this twee, home-counties bullshit. But not your *Trainspotting* bleak-as-fuck thing either. We're keeping it sleek, keeping it fun, keeping it *authentic* . . . The city is really going to be a character in itself, you know? That's absolutely paramount for us.'

'Right,' El said. It was a lot of information and yet somehow also no information at all. 'Well . . . brilliant.'

For a long moment, all four of them just stood together in silence. Otto, Marvin C. Johnson, El, and Robbie – of course Robbie was there, too. El felt increasingly like he was everywhere she looked, all the time – in her workplace, on her nights out, inside her brain. In theory, his new date for leaving Love and Death was right around the corner. She hadn't heard him say the word 'Citibank' in a while, though – and there was a time when it had seemed to be every second word out of his mouth. She hadn't enjoyed the constant namechecks, but their reduction now struck her as somehow more ominous.

Meanwhile, Marvin's eyes darted around appraisingly. He gave a tiny nod, almost as if to himself. 'Well, I'll get right to it, folks. I'm liking what I'm seeing here. I'm wondering how you'd feel about the bar being used as a filming location for our first episode?'

'I don't think so,' Otto replied immediately.

Marvin looked nothing short of gobsmacked. 'Oh.'

Evidently, people said no to him very infrequently.

'Well, that's a shame. This lush, speakeasy-style thing is exactly what the director had in mind. Somewhere we can put our cast and it'll have that real intimate vibe, you know?'

'Mmm,' Otto replied noncommittally.

'Plus, think of the publicity.'

'That's exactly what I'm thinking of. Like you said, we have a very intimate space here at Love and Death, and we're inclined to keep it that way. How did you even find out about us?'

'I'm a location scout, ain't I? People say to me all the time, "Marv, you've got eyes everywhere." We'd put everything back just how we found it, if that's what you're worried about. And of course we can offer a very generous *remuneration package*.' He said the phrase like he'd recently learned it. 'So, what d'you reckon? Is there any way we could work something out? I'd be happy to have our lawyer get something across to you. Easiest money you'll ever make, I'm telling you, mate.'

For a long moment, Otto said nothing. He clicked his tongue against his teeth, his eyes narrowing in what appeared – staggeringly – to be consideration. 'No lawyers,' he declared then. 'But why don't you send me your proposal? We'll see.'

Later, in a quiet moment on shift, El watched as Otto sidled up to Robbie.

'If that guy *does* send something over . . . you feel like taking a look at it?' he asked.

'Okay. Sure. I mean, I'm not a lawyer, obviously. But I'm happy to have a read if it's helpful.'

'Gotta use that Oxford education somehow, huh?' Otto replied, and together, they both chuckled lightly.

Behind them, El let four glasses tumble into the dump sink with a crash.

'Jeez, El*oise*!' Otto exclaimed, turning to look at her. 'You okay back there?'

The warmth in his tone – the total ignorance to her feelings that it suggested – almost hurt El more than anything else. Suddenly, she knew in her bones that Robbie wasn't going anywhere come September. She wasn't entirely sure Robbie himself knew that. His wife, she would bet, certainly didn't.

'Oh, I'm fine!' she replied, all too brightly. 'Absolutely fine!'

'Can you believe he's even considering it?' Robbie asked El, later that night. 'I mean, Love and Death – the bar without even a sign outside – on television?'

They were clearing up after closing, wiping down surfaces, gathering items to be refrigerated or thrown out. They could do it like clockwork now. El always found it peculiar, being so physically in sync with a person who often threw her so wildly off her stride in other ways.

She shrugged, avoiding Robbie's eye. It had been a long night. She knew she would need a pick-me-up if she wanted to make it to the club after this. She might, in fact, need a pick-me-up regardless. She felt a little twitchy, desperate suddenly for some privacy and a smooth surface.

Moments ago, she had checked the rota for the next month. Otto had given more Friday and Saturday shifts to Robbie than he'd given to anyone else – including her. Everyone knew those were the best shifts. They had the best tips, but much more than that, from her point of view, they were the most *fun*. They offered the most opportunity to shine. They were, frankly, the shifts she perceived as hers.

It was hard to swallow the sting of it, and all the more so in Robbie's presence. She scrubbed vigorously at a drip tray, thought again of the blow tucked away in her handbag.

'That's Otto for you,' she replied flatly. 'Who knows why he does anything, really?'

*

The next evening, El had been planning to bring a brand-new drink to cocktail jam. Instead, she brought the one she hadn't been able to let go of – the one she'd presented at least five times already, the difficult child she loved the most.

This time, though, she decided not to care about what Otto liked (much less what Robbie, or any of the rest of them, liked). She decided not to care, even, about what her customers would probably like. *Fuck it*, she thought, as she mixed the drink that evening according to her personal taste and nothing else. She might have been a little buzzed.

When she looked at it in the glass – just amber liquid, a sleek cuboid of ice, and an orange twist to garnish – it was, even visually, so different from her usual style. Taste-wise, it certainly wasn't at all like the sweet and fruity drinks that were currently most pop-ular. This was the kind of thing she could imagine a businessman drinking in the Fifties, tie loosened after a hard day at the office. Or maybe, in some fantasy world, a 20-something girl in the Noughties. A girl who'd *had it* with trying to please other people, who found she'd lost interest in colourful, playful drinks . . . who just wanted something that packed a punch.

'Our old friend, back again!' Otto said, when he saw her offering. 'And you're doing maple syrup this time – interesting. Actually, what are you calling this one? I don't think we have a name yet, do we?'

El paused. She'd never even thought about it.

Beside her, though – just *waiting* to toss in his two cents, no doubt – she could sense Robbie's presence. With his eyes on her, the answer seemed to arrive in a flash, as though heaven-sent.

Amusement twitching at her lips, she fought the urge to look to her left, kept her focus on Otto instead. 'The Citi Slicker,' she replied. And, for good measure, she spelled it out. 'That's C-I-T-I.'

Otto just chuckled. At the time, that seemed like all there was to it.

Chapter Seventeen

'Breakfast in bed!' El proclaimed, hopping back in beside Kat on the morning of their anniversary, tray balanced precariously on the duvet. Despite a brutal come down from the night before, she was rising above it valiantly.

Meanwhile, Kat wriggled upwards to a sitting position. She was unreasonably beautiful, even first thing in the morning, and a beaming smile spread across her face. Not for the first time, El thought that her girlfriend could easily be a model, if the jewellery design didn't pan out.

'Two years, eh?' Kat said happily, reaching for a bite of toast and jam.

'I know, I can't believe it,' El replied. 'How lucky are we? Finding a friend we get to shag.'

Kat frowned. 'Is that how you see me?' she asked, after a moment. 'As a friend you get to shag?'

'Yep,' El declared. It struck her as charming, whimsical, romantic.

If Kat's elation, on the other hand, seemed to have faded fast, El was none the wiser. She simply did not notice.

A few days later, El was heading for an after-hours drink with Marcus and Jamie when she spotted Kat waiting outside the bar on Dean Street. She smiled, pulling her girlfriend in for a quick kiss in greeting. They were in Soho, after all, and surrounded by friends. It felt safe.

Immediately, though, she could sense that something was up. Even she couldn't have missed it, this time. The tension seemed to be radiating off Kat.

'I want to go home,' Kat said.

'What, now?' El replied, all confusion. 'Are you alright?'

'Does that matter to you? Like, *really*?' Kat asked, her eyes narrowing. It felt like a rhetorical question. And then came the kicker: 'We need to talk.'

The intake of breath from those around them was audible.

'Good luck, mate,' Jamie muttered, as he and Marcus hurried away, shuffling into the bar with mumbled goodbyes.

El couldn't help but chuckle grimly in response. It was a bad move. Kat was still very much not smiling.

Left alone with her, El felt ambushed, irritated. 'So, what? You want to just . . . get the night bus?'

In this, one of the financial and cultural centres of the world, the tubes stopped running shortly after midnight. El surmounted the issue, mainly, by staying out so late as to catch the first early morning tube home.

Kat offered nothing in response, and El sighed with impatience.

'Let's just . . .' El ran through the list of recreational options available at 3 a.m. It was a short list. 'Let's go and eat something fried.'

At ChickenQuicken, they sat opposite one another at a chipped formica table, each with a red plastic basket of chicken and chips before them. They'd caught the place during a relatively civilized window, before the clubs closed. Behind the counter, the staff were having a raucous good time, hollering to one another over vats of sizzling grease, grime music blasting. Compared to what El was now fairly sure lay ahead of her – the type of thing she termed in her own head a *concussion discussion* – she would have been only too delighted to grab a hairnet and join them. As it was, she took a bite of her chicken tender, elbows on the table, and accepted her fate.

'Alright, babe. I suppose we should just get to it then, shall we?'

'Okay,' Kat agreed solemnly.

There followed a protracted silence.

El half-frowned, half-chuckled in confusion. 'Well, no, you . . . *you* have to tell *me*,' she clarified. 'I was having a fine night until you arrived with your knickers in a twist.'

Kat huffed out a sound of sheer disbelief. 'Well, if that doesn't just say it all. You think this is a bolt from the blue, and I think it's been a long time coming.'

El openly groaned now, putting her head in her hands, letting her face contort in horror. Truly, this was her worst possible version of a fight. She would take screaming and slamming doors over this, any day. 'I don't know what you want from me here, Kat. Can you tell me what you want?'

'Right now? Or in general?'

'Either.'

At last, she seemed to have given her girlfriend the opening she needed to really let loose.

'At this point? For starters, I'd like you to ease up on the blow.'

Whatever El might have been expecting, it was not that. Her eyebrows shot upwards. It was true that she indulged more now than she used to – and, in ways that didn't always feel particularly indulgent, often just necessary. Still, she was utterly insulted.

'Jesus, Kat. Who am I talking to here? Robbie fucking Saunders? As a matter of fact, even he's never *berated* me about my *drug use*. And you've been known to enjoy a party favour or two yourself, I might add.'

'Less than you,' Kat replied.

'I didn't realize we were keeping a tally. And I don't appreciate the implication that I'm some kind of junkie. Am I high right now?'

'I'm sure you would be, if I hadn't stopped you going into that bar!'

'I'm sure I would be, too,' El couldn't help but fire back, deadpan. The undertone – that in fact she would much *rather* be high than be here, having this conversation – was, she hoped, obvious. 'What else?'

'I'd like you to stop going into work when you aren't even on shift,' Kat continued. 'I'd like you to look at me like I'm the only person you could ever even *think* about being with. I'd just like . . . I don't know how to say it! I just want it to be *even* between us. Do you know how many times I looked at my mobile tonight, wondering if maybe you'd checked in? Too many – that's what I decided, at long fucking last. I'm actually a catch, you know! Plenty of girls would be psyched to get a text from *me*!'

Kat paused for breath, then huffed out a heavy sigh, as though admitting a sort of defeat. 'But unfortunately, I'm crazy about you, El. You know that I am. I miss you when you're not around, and I wonder what you're thinking, and I obsess over what you want and how to give it to you. And sometimes, I just . . . don't think you do any of that with me.'

Her eyes were wide now, her voice a little wobbly, and El found herself softening.

'Obsession isn't healthy,' she said gently.

Alas, it didn't seem to have any comforting effect.

'That's rich, coming from you,' Kat snapped back.

'What's that supposed to mean?'

'It means you're obsessed with Love and Death and everyone fucking in it. Some people more than others.'

'Again, what's *that* supposed to mean?'

'It means you flirt with all of them, or you let them flirt with you! Robbie! Marcus! And Otto . . . well, let's be honest, El: you'd be on your knees for Otto in ten seconds if he so much as asked.'

El felt the accusations like a series of full-body blows. She didn't know which part to take issue with first. Her relationship with Otto – once the most solid thing in her life – often felt on shaky ground these days. But to have it debased in such a way felt so spiteful, so viscerally wrong. As for the very idea that she fancied Marcus or *Robbie* . . .

It all came down to the same issue. The issue of men. Of her having ever kissed a man in the past, slept with a man in the past – of the possibility she might want to at some point in the future.

'Oh my God, Kat, I can't have this fight again. I'm sorry you don't think I'm a proper lesbian.'

'Tell me I'm wrong.'

El wasn't entirely sure what Kat was referring to anymore. Nonetheless, her response came instinctively. 'You're wrong,' she said.

For a long moment, the pair just looked at one another, tension pulsing between them.

Then, Kat sighed heavily, began again. 'Look, it's not like I'm saying I want to go and live in the countryside and grow our own veg or whatever. Okay? I don't fancy being the only Asian *and* the only gay in the village, thanks. I want to live in Hackney and make things and meet people. I want to party and have a good time *with you*. But this whole past year, I've been waiting for you to just . . . I don't know! I mean, I introduced you to my parents!'

'Well, you didn't really,' El countered. 'I mean, you did, but only because we happened to bump into them at the pub.' She cast her mind back, then amended for clarity. 'Twice.'

'Oh, for fuck's sake, El! They were there, and we were there – twice – because I made sure of it! A blind man could have seen that!'

El was sincerely stunned. 'So, what?' she asked, after a moment. 'You want to meet my parents, is that it? Because my mother fucked off back to America five years ago, and my father – sorry, I don't mean to put too fine a point on this, babe – would despise you. For absolutely no reason. I suppose we could call round, and the two of you could hash it out. Is Eloise far too gay, or is she not quite gay enough?'

Kat let out another huff of frustration. 'This is not about your parents, it's . . .' She trailed off helplessly.

What El wanted, mostly, was for this to be over. She reached across the table for her girlfriend's hand, adopting a conciliatory murmur. 'Look. It's late, we're tired. I think you just—'

'No!' Kat snatched her hand back. 'You always do this! You make me feel like I'm insecure for no reason!'

El cocked an eyebrow. 'I mean . . . could that be because you're insecure for no reason?'

'You're doing it again!'

El had no clue where to go from there. She ate a few chips. They were undercooked; sadly, even the ketchup couldn't mask it.

'Can you picture your life without me?' Kat asked then. Under the harsh fluorescent light, her typically flawless skin looked blotchy and stressed. 'Can you imagine being happy without me? Be honest.'

El paused. Those questions didn't strike her as the most immediately pertinent ones. Did she want to end her relationship with Kat, tonight or in general? Was she in any way unhappy with Kat? She could easily have answered *no* to those. And that felt, to her, like enough.

Was it really necessary that she also pine for Kat every second they were apart? Should she be unable to countenance any other way to exist than the precise one she'd hit upon by accident? Was that what being in love was supposed to be? El didn't know.

She considered herself, in many ways, an excellent girlfriend. As well as being faithful, she was curious and easy-going. She took an interest in Kat's interests (certainly, she had more polymer clay jewellery now than she ever thought she'd possess in a lifetime). She'd made friends with Kat's friends. She was unselfconscious and unselfish in bed.

And in return for all that – not even in return for it, merely sitting alongside it – she otherwise proceeded doing pretty much what she wanted, when she wanted, with her own life. She sincerely did not consider that unreasonable.

She returned, in her mind, to what Kat had asked her:

Can you picture your life without me? Can you imagine being happy without me?

'Well . . . I mean, yes,' she said. Her response was brutal in its simplicity. Some part of her felt defiant about the brutality of it. *Don't ask the questions if you don't want to hear the answers,* she felt like saying.

Before her, the air seemed to go out of Kat. 'Well, that's it then, isn't it?'

El still didn't altogether understand why it had to be, but suddenly – from the look on Kat's face – she understood for certain that it was. This whole conversation was indeed over, although not in quite the way she'd wanted it to be.

Kat was welling up, fat tears sliding down her cheeks, and El felt emotion catch suddenly at the back of her own throat. Two years – and three days – was a long time. It was the longest she'd ever been with anybody. She hadn't seen this coming in any way whatsoever. The surroundings also created an undeniably depressing backdrop. She wished they'd been able to break up on Hampstead Heath or outside an arthouse cinema. It mattered how things ended, she thought, every bit as much as how they began.

*

They got the night bus home together, sitting side by side as the N55 wound its way through Bloomsbury and Clerkenwell, along Old Street, then up Hackney Road. A few rows in front of them, two friends were sharing a pair of earphones, the faint strains of a Girls Aloud song audible. Further up ahead, a man was having a full, if slurred, conversation with his reflection in the window. Another woman was discreetly vomiting into a brown paper McDonald's bag.

Kat and El watched the whole scene unfold in silence, until they were almost at their stop.

'Otto warned me you'd never be happy with me, you know,' Kat said then. 'As in, long-term. I can't believe that fucker was right on the money.'

'What?'

'A few months after we first got together. I was hanging around waiting for you one night at Love and Death – big surprise – and he's like, "The thing about El is: she'll never be satisfied with one thing for too long." He said it like that, all paternalistic. He says, "She's the same as me that way. She's built for a change. For a challenge." Like, fine, just go ahead and *tell me* my relationship's doomed to failure, Otto, that's *great*! Thanks for the heads up!'

El's face contorted, displeased. Why would Otto interfere like that? It made no sense to her. She didn't like it one bit.

However, there didn't seem much point in getting into it with Kat now.

'You'll have to move out,' Kat added, after another moment. She pressed away more tears with the heels of her hands. 'It's okay if it takes you a week or two to find somewhere else.'

Huh.

El took that in for a second, then cocked her head quizzically. 'I mean . . . do I *have* to move out?'

She loved that house, no matter its temperamental plumbing and questionable decor. And surely the whole point of a living situation such as theirs – the communal aspect of things, the progressiveness of it all – was that, after an unavoidable period of transition, they'd quite easily be able to cope with the slight change in dynamic that now presented itself. What was this, really, if not an opportunity to subvert some societal expectations?

Alas, Kat was evidently not feeling at her most subversive. She let out a laugh, but it sounded more weary than joyful. 'Fucking Christ! El! We've just broken up. *I have broken up with you.* Yes, that means you'll have to move out of my house.'

Chapter Eighteen

All at once, through this unfortunate series of fiascos that weren't her fault at all, El's entire life seemed to be falling apart! She said so herself, with what she deemed very convincing merriment, to all and sundry in basement bars and dodgy clubs.

After all, who liked being unceremoniously dumped? Who liked a constant threat of being leapfrogged, undermined, forgotten, at work?

In some ways, perhaps the situation at Love and Death was bound to come to a head sooner rather than later. In others, it was hard to say how long things might have gone on just as they were, had it not been for the fucking TV show.

On the day *BST* was being filmed, El was one of the last to arrive at the bar. Across the previous four weeks, she had gone from a person who was notoriously, acceptably, charmingly late, to a person who operated on two modes – so very late as to be outright offensive, or absent altogether (although, in her defence, that was only the one time).

Otto was, she knew, starting to lose patience with her. 'Are you okay?' he'd asked her, in a quiet moment. It was after the no-show.

She'd looked back at him blankly.

'Look. Your life is your life, El,' he'd continued. 'Your business is your business. But I'm giving you one opportunity – this is it; it's happening *right now* – to tell me if anything is seriously wrong.'

A part of El had wanted to tell him that, yes, everything *was* seriously wrong – to spill it all out, the same way she'd done on the first day they met. The greater part of her had known that things were different now.

Thus, instead, she'd shaken her head, every bit the sullen teenager.

'Alright. Well, in that case, you'd better shape up, kid. It's shape up or ship out.'

El had let out a bitter half-laugh. So much, she'd thought, for *family*.

Since things had ended with Kat, she'd been bouncing around, by necessity. Friends with free sofas had become her best friends. Friends with free sofas who might want to do a line (or two or three) had become her bestest friends.

In truth, the grime was feeling a little less glamorous than it used to. Everything had begun to feel, more than anything else, *exhausting*.

When she got into Love and Death that evening, the place had already become a television set. There were lights, boom-mics, people everywhere. Everyone seemed to be incredibly busy, but when El looked more closely, no one seemed to be *doing* anything much. Over in the corner, three women she presumed to be the actresses were standing around, make-up artists dabbing ineffectually at their faces.

Notwithstanding the present scramble of activity, El headed straight towards the bar. It seemed fine for her to sort herself a quick drink. After all, wasn't she essentially a spectator here? This was like a live cinema experience, or a West End show come to East London for one night only. Refreshments were surely part of it.

En route, she accidentally bumped into a chair, and some piece of equipment tumbled to the ground.

'Eek!' she said, with a giggle.

The whole thing caused a bit of a clatter, sure. It drew a few glances. What appeared to El to be a sixth former dressed head to toe in black came dashing over as though an infant child had just been pushed from a balcony. Ultimately, though, it could have happened to anybody. It was no big deal.

Behind her, Marcus grabbed her arm. 'What you doing?' he hissed.

'I want to make myself a drink!'

Marcus tugged her away from the bar. 'You can do that back here – there's plenty in the stockroom.'

She tried to shrug him off, but he wasn't to be shrugged. He all but dragged her into the back kitchen, ignoring her yelp along the way.

'What the fuck is wrong with you?' he said, once they were out of view of the TV crew. He tried to laugh a little as he said it, and something about that laugh made El feel suddenly awful.

The thing was that she and Marcus were friends. They'd known one another, by now, for years. They had fun together, usually. He was up for a little bending of rules, usually. In a flash, though, El could see the position she seemed to have put him in now. He was the school kid who didn't want to be a square, didn't want to lose his mate – but didn't want to get in trouble either, who couldn't help but feel things were suddenly going a tad too far. She hated the sensation that came over her at this realization, and she pushed it away.

'I'm fine,' she replied, her voice coming out fractious and agitated, even to her own ears.

'Just go home. Sleep it off – I'll cover for you. Fuck, I won't *have* to cover for you, will I? You're not even supposed to be here.'

Very few people, in fact, were supposed to be there. In reality, it appeared that absolutely everybody who worked at Love and Death had shown up and was now crammed into the back kitchen. Cormac – bold as brass – had even brought his girlfriend.

There was a circular window towards the top of the door, and El peered through it into the bar, staring across at the actresses again. Disappointingly, she didn't recognize any of them. But nonetheless, she was here now. She didn't plan to miss the show if she could help it.

As far as Robbie was concerned, the whole evening started off fine.

Otto was on top form, greeting everyone from exec producers to runners effusively, like they were old friends. He even turned a blind eye to all the staff who'd showed up uninvited.

'Scoundrels, all of you! Get in the back, and make sure you're seen and not heard!' he hissed. He had that twinkle in his eye, though.

Over the past few weeks, and despite a staggering number of emails and phone calls from the *BST* production team, it remained unclear to everyone at Love and Death what the actual plot of this television show was going to be. The producers' communication seemed to be all adjectives – *glossy! provocative! modern!* – and no verbs.

What Robbie had gathered, thus far today, was that the scene at hand involved three very good-looking actresses. They'd be sitting at the bar, saying something about empowerment and demonstrating said empowerment with a clink of three cocktail glasses. That close-up of the glasses was to be the very last shot of the episode, apparently. He couldn't imagine the whole thing would take more than fifteen or twenty minutes to film, tops.

Afterwards, the cast and crew were going to stick around, celebrate getting their first episode in the can with some drinks at Love and Death. 'Two birds, one stone – I love it,' location manager Marvin had declared, when he'd come for the final walkthrough the previous week.

Robbie was busy whipping up three prop drinks for the actresses when El showed up. Immediately, it was clear that she'd gone past the point he'd seen her at before – in other words, past the point of plausible deniability – and a sense of dread washed over him.

Out of the corner of his eye, he could see Marcus trying to manage the situation, trying to sweep El off out of sight. She looked outright terrible.

Generally speaking, there was no better person to pull off a smudged eyeshadow, a dress draped off one shoulder, than El. But the devil was in the details. She was thinner than she used to be, Robbie noticed. She'd developed a slight twitchiness where previously there had been looseness, a bug-eyed expression on her face where once there'd only been mischief. Looking at her now, it didn't seem to Robbie that there was anything rock and roll about it any longer. It was actually a little frightening.

Meanwhile, Otto just wanted this all to be over.

When Marvin C. Johnson – a wheeler-dealer, if Otto had ever seen one – had first come into the bar, of course Otto had been disinclined even to entertain his proposal. But then, he'd thought back to the Volkov Brothers – to his initial meeting with them, to the way he'd exchanged email addresses with them just to humour them. And then, eventually and unexpectedly, the day had come that he'd wanted to get in touch.

Had that been the best idea, in the end? He supposed he didn't know. It wasn't the end yet. Lately, they'd certainly proved a little louder than he'd thought silent investors would be.

Hence the appeal of Marvin's formal offer, when it duly arrived with lots of zeroes on the end of it.

That was why Otto was doing all this, really. He was doing it for the money. Crude and prosaic, but true. In any case, there was no going back now.

Moments before filming began, a man with a walkie-talkie approached. Jake. Or Jack.

'Change of plan,' Jake said. (Otto was going to go with Jake.) He was the assistant producer, apparently. 'So, you know we asked you for something fun that the girls could drink? And you suggested the Cecilia?'

Otto nodded.

'Slight problem with that. I wouldn't even call it a problem, as such. A hiccup, let's say. I mean, obviously the drink is *delicious* – top work there, mate, absolutely. It's just the whole *Sex and the City* thing, you know? The Cosmo thing. Our DP's concerned the Cecilia's too similar.'

It was idiocy on a level that Otto hardly knew what to do with. 'It's nothing like a Cosmopolitan, except insofar as they're both pink,' he said.

Jake shrugged apologetically. 'We're working in a visual medium here. So, what else have you got for me? We're happy to adjust the script, make sure you get a bit of a namecheck in there, of course. What are all the cool kids drinking these days?'

Otto certainly knew what he wanted them to be drinking, in the very near future.

When he hopped behind the bar, Robbie was there to hand him what he needed, almost before he even realized he needed it. Five minutes later, he presented the final product to Jake in a coupe glass. It was yellow in colour, with a drizzle of spiced honey syrup and a dusting of bee pollen on top of its creamy egg-white head.

'It's a new one. The Cordelia. Actually it's *so* new I'm still tweaking it.'

'Looks great. Let's just have Kate try it to make sure she likes it, and then we'll get moving.'

'Who the hell is Kate?'

Jake nodded towards one of the actresses, his voice falling to a hush. 'Kate Carroll. She's our lead. I mean, it's very much an ensemble show, obviously. Very much. But, you know. *Of* that ensemble . . . she's the lead.'

'Alright. Well, what does it matter if she likes it?'

'If the show takes off, random people are going to be sending her one in every bar she goes to for the rest of time,' Jake replied. 'So she says. She's read an interview with Sarah Jessica Parker, and apparently it happens. Anyway. She says she has to be able to drink it.'

Otto didn't for a moment think this show was going to take off. Nonetheless, he watched as Jake disappeared with the drink into a huddle of cast and crew.

When he returned, it was with a wince on his face. 'Bad news, my man. It's not for her.'

Otto bristled. 'What doesn't she like about it?'

The logical part of him knew it was bad form, to interrogate like that. There was a time he never would have dreamed of doing so. Increasingly, though, he found it hard to resist. What if people were sometimes just plain wrong? What if they needed to be encouraged to expand their palates? Hadn't that been the whole philosophy behind what he'd declared (he'd admit, perhaps a little bombastically) the *year of innovation*? A good cocktail was a complex thing, and experience had shown him that some people had to be taught how to understand it.

Or . . . on the other hand: what if the Cordelia simply wasn't a very good drink? What if he should have gone with a simple lemon wheel to garnish? He'd overcomplicated things with the bee pollen, perhaps. What if he still hadn't come up with anything, in the *past decade and a half*, that could best the Cecilia? In truth, perhaps much of the *year of innovation* had just been about pushing away that fear, about striving to get his own mojo back.

And now, here he was, having somehow allowed his cocktail bar to become a television *circus* . . .

Contrary to popular belief, Otto Kettinger wasn't above the occasional moment of utterly crippling self-doubt. He was, in the end, human.

Before him, assistant producer Jake just shrugged. 'I don't know. No accounting for taste, eh?'

As well as being a truism, it was just plain true. Suddenly, it felt to Otto like the most horrifying thing, to have the fundamental success or failure of his *whole life* determined in such a way.

When a loud voice interjected from somewhere behind him, it actually felt like a relief at first. It really did.

'How about this?' El called out, but she didn't stop at Otto and Jake. She swept right past them and over to Kate Carroll directly, a rocks glass outstretched in her hand. It was half full. 'Excuse my lipstick.'

Kate, to her credit, *did* excuse it. Without missing a beat, she grabbed the glass and took a sip. As she did, it felt as though everyone in the whole place sucked in a breath, awaiting her verdict. Of course, for most of them, it really wasn't an existential thing. They just wanted to get this show on the road, get their jobs done.

Kate swilled the liquid around in her mouth, swallowed it, took a moment to consider. Otto supposed she would probably have been in the wrong line of work, had she not been able to meet the drama of the moment, and maximize it.

'Oh, wow,' she said. 'This is great. I love this.' She took another sip. 'What's this one called?'

'The Citi Slicker,' El replied. There was nothing a single person in Love and Death could have done to stop her.

'Fun. I like that it has that masculine vibe, you know? Works for the characters.'

'Yeah. Who *are* the characters, by the way? We've been trying to figure that one out.'

'Well, they're all a lot of different things, I suppose. Very multi-faceted, and . . .' Abruptly, Kate Carroll seemed to realize she was not on camera and lose interest. 'Stockbrokers, basically. Sexy stockbrokers.'

She took another sip from the drink, nodding decisively. 'Let's go with this,' she declared.

And so, they did.

Hours passed. Hours and hours. More hours than anyone, in the future, watching three minutes of screen time, would ever be able to contemplate. El didn't care. She was on cloud nine.

As soon as filming finished, it was 'Crazy' by Gnarls Barkley on blast, and Citi Slickers all round. Citi Slickers and beers. Crew guys, as it turned out, liked what they liked. Everyone else, though? Turned out everyone else liked what *El* liked – the thing she'd created and believed in, even when nobody else at Love and Death had especially seemed to. She hopped around the party, feeling like her old self again – feeling young and gorgeous and alive.

What was it people said? You had to have the rain to get the rainbow – or something like that. Yes, life had been challenging lately. Yes, she might have been a little sad, a little stressed, a little flaky. But hadn't she proven herself, with that actress, when the moment arrived? She wasn't even the slightest bit concerned by where she might sleep tonight. Increasingly, it seemed like nobody would be going to bed at all.

At almost 2 a.m., she was still behind the bar, albeit exclusively to serve herself.

She wondered what this next drink was going to be. She let herself pluck ingredients according to whim, feeling, in her bones, the rightness of everything – knowing that she was meant to be in *this* place, doing *this* thing, forever. It had been like that, tonight: the particular concoction of booze and other miscellany that she'd decided upon meant her mind had felt like an accordion, expanding and contracting. One moment, she was spacey and sloppy, her sense of time and place hazy; the next, she was hyperaware, taking to people at a mile a minute.

At the other side of the bar, and a few feet to El's left, Kate Carroll lingered with Otto and Robbie. Robbie was perched on a stool, his back to the bar, the other two standing at either side of him.

'I gotta tell you, I really loved those Citi Slickers,' Kate was saying.

El, near enough to overhear but not quite near enough to be immediately observed, grinned.

'I can tell,' Otto teased in response. It was true that Kate was slurring just a tiny bit now. She and Otto seemed to have made fast friends.

'So, you're responsible for those, huh?' Kate asked.

'Guilty,' Otto said.

El stopped in her tracks. Later, replaying the whole thing, she'd think that was an interesting choice of word. *Guilty.*

'This guy right here was actually the inspiration,' Otto continued. 'For the name at least.'

'Oh wow, really?'

'I mean . . . I suppose in a manner of speaking, yeah,' Robbie replied, as El's heartbeat sped up. Her hands still seemed to be moving of their own accord, combining things in a cocktail shaker, but all the while, it felt like her heart was about to explode out of her chest.

'Robbie was straight out of Oxford, headed off to Canary Wharf himself before he met me,' Otto said proudly. 'Can you believe it? He actually had a job offer at *Citi*bank! Now look at him. My second in command.'

After that, there were no two ways about it. El lost her fucking mind.

'What?' she said sharply, loud enough to carry.

Robbie swivelled around on his stool, Otto and Kate turning to look at her, too.

'I'm sorry,' she said. 'What was that, Otto? *You* came up with the Citi Slicker?'

He had the decency, at least, to look a little chagrined. 'No, I—'

El slammed her shaker on the bar, cutting him off. 'This is bullshit! You know, all this time, I thought you wanted a . . . a partner. But you didn't, did you? You wanted a sidekick.'

'El, that's not—'

She didn't want to hear it. 'No! You've been *manipulating* me, *leeching* ideas from me for years! That's the truth of it, Otto. Show me *one* drink you've come up with, in the past four years, without input from me. You can't. And, you know, I didn't even think that was a problem? I've *defended* you. I've protected you. And what thanks do I get?' She gestured towards Robbie. 'First you replaced me, and now you're trying to actually *steal* from me. Oh! *And* you told my girlfriend that I didn't really love her!'

'I didn't tell her that,' Otto replied calmly. He took her by the elbow. 'Come outside. We can talk about this.'

She shrugged him off, his tone driving her crazy. Crazier. That word Kat had used came back to her – *paternalistic*. What a difference there was between that and paternal. It had taken her far, far too long to see it.

'Kat was the *love of my life*!' she continued, undeterred. 'And you sabotaged it! Why would you do that? Was it just that you liked it, when I made you absolutely everything? I'm sure you did. Fucking men.'

'Alright, El,' Robbie interjected quietly. As though, at this point, it made any difference. As though, at this point, everyone else in the bar wasn't staring at them like the only thing missing was the popcorn. 'Let's just . . . simmer down, okay?'

She leaped on him. 'You! You do *not* tell me to simmer down. You ruined everything, you fucking anally retentive virgin!'

For what felt like a long moment, there was total silence in Love and Death.

'What the fuck?' Robbie said then.

It was the first time El had ever heard him swear. It seemed like he was realizing, in real time, how very satisfying it could feel.

'This is . . . *not on*,' he continued in a low voice, all barely concealed fury. Still perched atop his stool, his hands now gripped the bar. 'I know you think you're special, El. Everybody here is aware you think you're *super-duper special*. But, I mean, look at yourself. You're a half-dressed cokehead with daddy issues.'

El felt the fury spread through her body like liquid, white hot and galvanizing. She reached for her cocktail shaker, prised it open, and even in the moment, a part of her knew that what she was about to do was very wrong – what a waste of a perfectly good drink.

And yet.

She looked down at her concoction. The liquid was viscous and vivid, just as it should be. She poured it, ice and all, right into Robbie's lap.

Part Three

Chapter Nineteen

El, like a lot of only children, was smart. Not book smart – that was for sure. But perceptive. Mature. A *real live wire*. That was what people said.

All her curiosity and confidence only went so far, though. A clever child was still a child.

Thus, it was quite a long time before El could answer the question that had perplexed her as far back as she could remember. She would hear her parents fight, and – much more frequently – she'd hear the silence between them. It seemed like the silence went on for days sometimes. Theirs was not a household marked by explosive anger so much as by the total absence of laughter. Lying in bed at night, El would tally up the facts she knew about her mother and father individually, their likes and dislikes, their flaws and attributes, and she would wonder: *why on earth are these two people together?*

Why they *got* together, she never exactly worked out. She never asked her parents about their first date or what drew them to one another, about who asked who out and whether it had been a long time coming. Those things felt, in an instinctive, unspoken sort of way, like they were off limits. None of her business. Her father had been sent to her mother's hometown of Atlanta, Georgia, for work, and the two had met by chance at Piedmont Park, and the rest was history. That was about as much as El ever knew.

As to why her parents were *still* together, however – she'd figured that one out eventually. They were still together, she'd realized with some considerable surprise, because of *her*. They were *sticking it out for her sake*.

This idea, when it first struck her, aged 13, seemed so preposterous as to be almost laughable, and it stayed that way for the next five years. Then, like clockwork, when El turned 18, her parents filed for divorce. Job done. Perhaps not particularly well done – El was, after all, by then a barmaid who had recently dropped out of a very expensive school, all but forced herself to take up smoking, and moved into the first of what would become a series of squats in Haggerston. But at least Darleen and Daniel Tippett could say they had given it their best shot. The old college try. And, freed of their legal obligation to their only offspring, they wasted no time in cutting one another adrift, too. Darleen was on the first plane to LAX as soon as the paperwork was signed.

Plenty of people would have stopped there. Los Angeles, with its proximity to fame and the ocean, was practically catnip to those wanting a new life, perhaps a whole new self.

Darleen, however, had other ideas. Hopping into a rental car and heading inland, she arrived at her intended destination within less than an hour: Anaheim, California. Home of the Mighty Ducks, no fewer than twelve craft breweries, and Disneyland.

El's journey some five years later felt much more like an exile than an escape. When she got to her mother's condo – jet-lagged, sad, and with no pharmaceutical assistance available to her – she went straight to bed and stayed there for eighteen hours.

When she woke, she moseyed into the kitchen-living-room in her pyjamas, feeling like a visitor. She supposed she was, in fact, a visitor. This was not a home she'd ever lived in. It wasn't one she'd even spent any time in, or seen any photographs of, or taken any interest in whatsoever.

Sun streamed in from the little balcony, and she cast her eyes around, absorbing all the details she'd ignored the previous night. There was nothing remarkable about the shell of this place. Everything – the flooring, the kitchen units, the sofa – was white. *A blank canvas*, she could imagine some keen-as-mustard estate agent saying; *plenty of scope to put your own stamp on it.*

As for the particular stamp her mother had gone for, though . . .

There were flower-shaped cushions dotted liberally around the living room, with a bold striped rug under the coffee table. On the kitchen counter, a few novelty mugs sat alongside a mishmash of crockery. Magazine cutouts were pinned haphazardly to the fridge door by magnets shaped like Disney cartoon characters.

It was all just so *colourful*.

That was the first slightly weird thing.

Darleen pushed a plate of chopped melon across the kitchen island towards El. 'So!' she proclaimed, sounding peppier than El had ever heard her – that was the second slightly weird thing.

El hopped up onto a stool. 'So,' she repeated.

For a moment, silence. Then, her mother spoke again. 'So whatcha doing here, sugar?'

Sugar?

Undoubtedly, that was the third weird thing. There was no qualifying it any longer.

El lifted a piece of melon to her lips, then dropped it again. Now that she thought about it, she hadn't eaten much of anything since she left London. She just couldn't summon the enthusiasm. Her head was pounding.

And perhaps, if she'd had a different kind of mother, this was the point at which she could have confided the whole thing. She could have said that mere days ago, she had parted ways with her employer, following a drug-induced rant (because yes, she sometimes used drugs, in a normal enough sort of way). She could have revealed that she had recently been made homeless by her girlfriend (because, yes, she had had a girlfriend). She could have explained how, after Love and Death, any other cocktail bar in London would have felt like a colossal step down – like nothing less than a humiliation. Added to that, taking a job at any other cocktail bar in London would have required her to stay, inevitably, in the orbit of Love and Death. The idea of continuing to hear every morsel of gossip about the place, of watching from the sidelines, seeing now-former colleagues at industry drinks . . . El hadn't been able to bear the thought.

Equally intolerable was the knowledge that if she stayed in London, all the details of *her* life would inevitably make their way back to Love and Death – to Otto and Robbie – in perpetuity. The incestuousness of the whole scene had seemed suddenly much more pernicious than it ever had before. The very morning after *the incident*, she could well imagine that the rumour mill would be working on overdrive already, recasting her as the villain rather than the wronged party.

And of course, El traditionally wasn't one to shy away from a bit of controversy. She had welcomed it, even, in the past. But somehow this was different. She'd known – known by the dead feeling behind her, yes, by the tight ball of something unnamed in her gut – that she simply didn't have the stamina either to ride this one out or to embrace it.

No. Three days after the *BST* party, El had woken from a fitful sleep and realized what she needed to do.

She needed to disappear.

In fairness, sitting now at a kitchen island in a strange apartment in a strange city, El acknowledged that perhaps the mother to whom any daughter could reveal all of this was a rare one indeed. But it was equally fair to say that Darleen had always been particularly far from being such a mother. El wasn't inclined to treat this technicolour imposter version any differently to the one she'd grown up with.

An answer, though.

Some sort of answer was required of her. What was she doing here, in Anaheim?

'Suppose I missed you,' El said, and she thought the sliver of irony – the facial expression and tone of voice that fell just short of sincerity – was obvious.

However, her mother merely smiled. 'Well, aren't you sweet,' she said, and swiftly – like this was all very normal, like El dropped round for a long nap and some watermelon every other week – she began to busy herself around the kitchen. She lifted dishes from here and there, distributing them to the sink or to the cupboards.

El watched it all happen. She wondered where on earth to go from here, what to say next.

In the end, she didn't say anything at all. She didn't have the energy.

For the days and weeks that followed, El watched reruns of *The X-Files* and worked her way through family-sized bags of crisps. She slept late into the day, only sometimes making it out of the clothes she considered pyjamas and into those she considered loungewear. She picked at her skin and wished, desperately, for cocaine. Had she known anyone at all whom she could call to try to score, she absolutely would have called them. As it was, she had no option but to ride out the sweats and the shivers, the headaches and the nausea. It was terrifying, to note those symptoms in herself, to know what she'd have to call them if she could ever have faced saying the word aloud. *Withdrawal.*

Why, she wondered, did this place have to be so aggressively *bright* all day long?

Each morning, while her mother donned a purple T-shirt and headed off to work at Mickey's Toontown, El played and replayed certain interactions in her head. She cursed Otto and Robbie and Kat and the *whole fucking lot of them.*

By the time New Year's Eve 2006 rolled around, she was in bed (not asleep, but trying to be) by 10.30 p.m. It was agonizing to know that, halfway across the world, Love and Death was continuing on without her. She wondered if Robbie had indeed stuck around, as she'd suspected he would. Or perhaps he was in a suit and tie somewhere by now, a real Citi Slicker. Somehow, she doubted it.

In any case, every night, the doors were still opening at the place she'd once considered home. Drinks were being dreamed up, and customers were being served, and little by little, the culture of a city was shifting. It would, El imagined, be as though she'd never been there at all.

Of course, she'd had a barrage of texts from London friends when she first got to Anaheim, ranging from the curious to the amused, from the frustrated to the concerned.

Nothing from Otto, though.

A part of her – a part she would have denied vociferously and convincingly – had really thought there would be. For a while, that had felt like what she was doing here, really: just giving him a chance to miss her, a chance to embrace the spirit of forgiveness, perhaps, but also the spirit of contrition.

You made some mistakes, kid, he'd say when he called her up, *but, hell, so did I.*

That it hadn't happened confirmed one thing, well and truly. El didn't know Otto like she used to. Perhaps she'd never really known him the way she'd thought she did. Certainly, towards the end, she had lost the ability she'd once had to predict him, to influence him, to sync her desires to his and vice versa.

That loss was so much more acute than the separation from Kat. (The vague recollection of having called Kat the *love of her life*, that last night at Love and Death, now seemed entirely ludicrous.)

Apart from anything else, El could easily imagine a time – at some point in the future, when Kat had a new and better girl-friend – where the two of them might be friends of sorts. Friend*ly*.

She and Otto wouldn't be like that.

On the contrary, with each day and week and month that passed, it seemed increasingly likely that El would never see or hear from him again in her life.

He'd sacked her in front of everyone, that night.

'Go home, kid,' he'd said quietly, as liquid pooled in Robbie's lap. 'You're done here.'

She'd laughed. She could feel the chemicals in her bloodstream, the slight sense of mania within herself. 'Oh, come on, it's early. I'm just getting started.'

'No,' he'd repeated tersely. 'You're *done*.' He'd looked at her intently for another moment, anger and disappointment throbbing between the two of them, going in both directions. 'You're fired, El.'

It was quick and painful. There was no room for doubt.

When she thought about it these days, she didn't feel much of anything.

Then, one wholly unremarkable Friday, El was lolling in front of the television, midway through something she considered a *background watch*, when her mother arrived home from work.

'Great news!' Darleen trilled. It had become almost normal by now, this relentless cheer from her.

El just raised an eyebrow, her question asked in the silence.

'I got ya a job!' her mother continued.

It was enough to prompt verbal response. Immediately. 'Oh my God. What?'

'Today. At The Park.'

'Christ! You got me a job at Disneyland?'

'I sure did.'

'Doing what? Children don't like me. And, I mean, who can blame them? Mother! What possessed you?'

Darleen waved away the concern. 'No, silly! It's a position at one of the bars. The Tipsy Parrot. I saw a sign in the window – me and some of the girls drop in there after our shift sometimes; it's a fun spot. Anyhow, when I told the manager about you, she done went right ahead and took that sign *down*, just right there in front of my eyes! You start tomorrow. Is this a good omen for the new year or what?'

For a long moment, El said nothing.

Her mother sat down beside her on the sofa, her voice quieter now. 'Sugar, I know it's hard,' she said. 'Good Lord do I know. But you gotta try. Okay? You have to *try*.'

It was as close as they had ever come to an acknowledgement of how things were before. El would have liked to claim that this was the catalyst, for her – the memory of the years in which Darleen, far from all her present colour and movement, had seemed instead to exist, listless, in greyscale. El would have liked to say that, suddenly, she could see that former version of her mother in the present version of herself, and she didn't like it one bit. Perhaps that would have made sense, for her to have realized she was on the brink and been seized by a desire to claw herself back.

In reality, though, it wasn't that at all. It was what Darleen said next, nudging her shoulder against El's: 'Also, at this point, it's shit or get off the pot, honey.'

El frowned. 'What does that mean?'

'It means it's been months. You get yourself a job, or you get yourself out of my condo.'

El started at The Tipsy Parrot the very next day.

Chapter Twenty

Back when El was 18 years old and on her third job already, she'd worked at a chain bar. There had been frozen food and ugly upholstery, and mild sexual harassment as a matter of course. The weeks were punctuated by karaoke, pub quizzes, drinks promotions on football Saturdays. Plus, of course, stag and hen parties. Honesty compelled El to admit that the latter were the greater of the two evils. She would watch ten women arrive, trussed up in boas and sparkly tops, and she'd know – as sure as she knew her own name – that she would be on her hands and knees at three o'clock in the morning, scraping those feathers and sequins off the floor. That was, of course, to say nothing of the interim. The volume. The pitch. If it made her a bad feminist to hate it, then fine. El was certain, in any case, that she *was* a bad feminist.

The Tipsy Parrot seemed like the sort of place a hen party might come. Or a *bachelorette party*, El supposed she should say here.

It was a tiki bar positioned in the middle of Adventureland – one of what El had learned were eight themed 'lands' within Disneyland as a whole. The *Indiana Jones* ride was one of its star attractions. Another was a cruise ride, on which travellers could ostensibly visit locations as disparate as Cambodia, India, and the Congo, all within eight minutes flat.

As for the bar itself, when El had asked Diane, her new

manager, about the specific theme of the place, Diane had replied, 'When you think about it, really, who doesn't love Hawaii?'

The same woman, in El's induction session, had outlined a few key job responsibilities: 'You gotta be fast, you gotta be honest, and you gotta keep it a party in here,' she'd said. 'Can you do that?'

The last one in particular, El had never in her life felt less able to do. But she'd thought of Darleen, of the lingering threat of eviction from a place she didn't even want to live.

'Absolutely!' she'd said.

And she must have been convincing enough, because Diane had wasted no time in letting her loose.

El looked around at the neon colour scheme now. She took in the wicker tables and chairs, the sheer *volume* of decorative parrots. The whole place was pattern on pattern, stuff on stuff. Even the drinks seemed to come only in various garish hues, most of them complete with a mini umbrella or some similar accoutrement. Every person – whether staff member or customer – who'd ever set foot through the door at Love and Death would have despised it here.

In the far corner, one of El's new colleagues was currently delivering a round of drinks to two couples – they looked to be in their fifties, all kitted out in large Disney sweatshirts, plus shorts and sandals. The bartender was laughing her head off right along with them (*yucking it up*, El now knew her mother would say), unloading bright blue concoctions in hurricane glasses from her tray onto their table.

'Hey, so I'm Frankie,' the girl said, when she got back behind the bar. 'Frankie Magliano.'

She had olive skin and green eyes, wavy brown hair reaching just past her chin, and not a scrap of make-up on her face. El had, in fact, noticed her as soon as she came through the door. Obviously. This girl was a knockout.

144

'El Tippett,' she replied, with a little wave.

'How's your first day going? I know it can be . . . a lot.'

El barely heard the question, didn't respond to it.

'I guess it could always be worse though, right?' the other girl chirped. 'Always something to be grateful for.'

El looked around, desolate, like a war correspondent surveying a wasteland. The last thing she needed right now was an upbeat American, no matter how good-looking. The thought of her mother awaiting her at home, absolutely nothing but pep in that woman's step, was bad enough.

'I don't know what that possibly could be,' she said wearily.

Frankie cocked her head. 'Well, have you ever been to Disney World *Orlando*?'

'No.'

'Trust me,' Frankly said wryly. 'This could be worse.'

El couldn't help it: she let out a quick burst of laughter. The sound of it, the sensation, actually shocked her a little. She – who'd always existed with such a readiness to be entertained, who'd taken that approach to life *deliberately* – hadn't properly laughed in so long.

'I mean, obviously the uniforms . . . suck,' Frankie continued, pulling uncomfortably at the hem of her T-shirt. 'I can't even pretend any different on that one.'

El looked down at herself. 'I . . . actually kind of love the uniform,' she found herself admitting. 'Like, I would choose to wear this.'

'You would choose to wear a hula skirt and a crop top?'

Lately, El hadn't chosen to wear anything non-elasticated. But from what she remembered of herself, before? 'I really would.'

And when Frankie laughed, it made El laugh again, too.

'Guess I'm just more of a "jeans and a sweater" girl myself. So, what brings you here, huh? Aside from the fashion opportunities, obviously.'

El paused, wondering how to broach it all, before realizing she didn't have to. 'My mother lives here,' she said, and left it at that. 'What about you?'

'Oh, I grew up in Anaheim. I'm saving to move to LA, though. I want to be an actress. Clichéd, I know.'

In someone El already disliked, this would indeed have seemed a cliché. But in someone she already liked, it was interesting. And – El realized then – she *did* like this girl. She liked this feeling of getting to know a new person. She had simply forgotten that she did.

'Are you any good?' she asked. Maybe it was a bit of a test, to see if Frankie took offence at her bluntness.

'I don't know.' Frankie nodded towards the table she'd just been serving. 'Did you buy that I thought that guy over there in the baseball cap was the next Adam Sandler?'

'One hundred per cent.'

Frankie shrugged, all innocence, an *I couldn't possibly comment*.

Another smile twitched at El's lips.

'So, I have two Mai Tais for table six next,' Frankie added after a moment. 'Would you wanna make 'em, and I'll just be here in case you need anything? Or you could just watch me do it this time – that's cool, too.'

El couldn't remember the specific quantities involved in a Mai Tai (if she'd ever known them, specifically). She wondered, though, whether she'd retained the ability to fix a drink, if necessary, at the end; to figure out, by taste alone, what adjustments were needed.

It felt like a long while since she'd been behind a bar. She let her gaze scan across the set-up, taking it in this time not as a mere observer but as a professional. Suddenly, her fingers practically itched with the urge to get going.

'I'll make them,' El replied. 'I want to.'

How strange, after all this time, to realize that it was true.

*

Very quickly, it became clear to El that the differences between her old job and her new one were much more than merely aesthetic. For starters, every single person who worked at The Tipsy Parrot was a woman. At Love and Death, El had thought very little about the all-male staff (herself, of course, aside). At times, she'd prided herself on being one of the boys. On other occasions, maybe a part of her had even liked it a little – that sense of herself as special, as having evidently been the only girl Otto deemed up to snuff. She'd never especially wished for more female company behind the bar.

It turned out to be kind of nice, though – hearing the chatter of the other women around her at work, the specifically female nature of their compliments to her. *Girl, you gotta tell me how you get your hair so smooth; ohmygod look how pretty you have made that Daiquiri!* Little by little, they began to build up El's social stamina again.

And the lack of ego. Wasn't that something? Every bartender at The Tipsy Parrot had only one key measure of success: did the customer leave happy?

Of course, the customer had been sacrosanct at Love and Death, too, but in a slightly different sort of way.

'You know who are the most important people in an art gallery?' El could remember Otto saying, once. 'The people who've paid for a ticket. Not because of the money. But because what does the art matter, really, if nobody sees it? We can't do any of this if nobody comes to drink here. Remember that.'

If it occurred to anyone in the room, back then, that Otto wanted a certain type of person to come and drink there – that he wanted them to be having a great time inside the specific circumstances he'd designed and deemed optimal – then nobody mentioned it.

Within a month at The Tipsy Parrot, the thought certainly occurred to El. In the cold light of day, Otto's proclamation started to seem more than a little grandiose. Absolutely nobody in her new environment believed they were making art in a glass. They were just working for tips and trying to have some fun along the way. And what was wrong with that? El, for all her faults, was no snob.

The first time she saw the store cupboard, chock full of boxes of 'citrus mix', her brain had flashed back to the hours and hours she'd spent at Love and Death, juicing all those lemons and limes. Truthfully, she felt nothing but sheer relief. Cutting certain corners – perhaps as a general philosophical matter, and certainly at this particular point in her life . . . that turned out to suit her just fine.

'Maybe I should learn to drive,' El said to her mother casually as they hopped out of her car after another day at Disneyland.

Darleen struggled to hide a smile, and El pounced.

'Don't be smug! This doesn't mean anything. It doesn't mean I'm staying here. It doesn't mean I like it.'

'No, of course not. I get that. You just want to invest some time and money in being able to get around the place more easily. I understand.'

El rolled her eyes.

'You could call Ted!' Darleen suggested.

El looked at her mother blankly.

'Ted Tarrent! Trust Ted Tarrent!'

Somewhere, in the recesses of her mind, this slogan felt familiar. 'Is that the guy whose face is on the benches?'

It was a marketing strategy, this side of the pond, that still perplexed El. To the extent a bench was going to be associated with any person, she felt that person should be a dead one. To the extent a bench was going to have any secondary function, she felt it should be in facilitating a small cry while she was on her period. She wasn't there to find a lawyer or a wax therapist.

Nonetheless, a few short weeks later, El found herself in the driver's seat of a RAV4 with Ted Tarrent.

'Alrighty Eloise,' he said. He was eating pieces of chopped apple out of a plastic sandwich bag. 'Let me start by saying that 95 per cent of road users out there, if you'll excuse my French, are just plain doing it wrong. I'm here to help you become not only a competent driver but a *safe* one. I know it seems daunting right now. But don't you worry. I am in this with you all the way, for the long haul.'

El frowned. She wondered, precisely, how long a haul they were talking about. She didn't ask.

There was no such thing as industry drinks in Anaheim. But there were certainly a lot of *activities*. Mini golf. Slot machines. Bowling. There was a pleasing, the-more-the-merrier, cross-generational feel to it all. In truth, El *could* somewhat see why her mother liked working at what she called simply 'The Park.' It was so vast that it felt a bit like a city in itself. But not like a real city, where – at least in El's experience – it was a person's own responsibility to seek out and maintain a community, to find a specific alignment of interests, to embrace whatever horrendous sequence of public transportation was required. Here, instead, the community was just . . . literally whoever worked at The Park's various amenities and wanted to stick around after a shift. That was it.

People came and went, with no great performance about the whole thing. In the course of her first few months at The Tipsy Parrot, El saw one co-worker head off to college. She saw another return because she'd dropped out of college, then leave again to enrol in a hairdressing course. In the end, the line-up seemed to maintain a broadly similar feel, no matter the particular players. They were like the Sugababes of bar staff.

'So, what about you?' El asked Frankie, the day after someone's leaving drinks. 'When are you headed off to LA?'

'Mmm, I'm not sure yet,' Frankie replied vaguely. She seemed a little embarrassed. 'I mean, I do know it probably won't happen,' she clarified, a moment later. 'The whole acting thing, or whatever. But . . . I guess some part of me just wants to try anyway, you know? I got bitten by the bug in middle school, and I can't seem to get unbitten.'

'I can understand that,' El replied. 'I mean, not that I have any interest in being an actor myself. But I can understand wanting a stage. An audience.'

She looked down at herself then. She was essentially wearing a costume. Ahead of her this evening was the opportunity to dance and chat, to make elaborate, if arguably tacky, concoctions for people who'd be only too delighted to drink them.

And so, she thought, a stage? An audience?

She had them, she realized. She had them *back*. Perhaps not the way she would have wanted or expected – perhaps not in a way anybody else would have respected whatsoever.

But when had she ever cared a jot about that?

Chapter Twenty-One

All of Anna-Claire Saunders's problems, if she really thought about it, came down to one person.

And the irony was, she'd actually *liked* El.

When she'd met her, that first time, she couldn't help but think that Robbie had vastly misrepresented her. This wasn't necessarily a huge surprise. Couldn't all men – even the really lovely, intelligent ones, like her husband – be quite bad judges of character? Didn't all of them seem to miss obvious subtext all the time? Didn't they omit all sorts of crucial details from the stories they relayed about mutual friends, claiming they simply *hadn't thought to ask*?

After that first visit, Anna-Claire had gone into Love and Death two or three more times, always in the early evening, and she'd never found El to be anything but welcoming, respectful, competent – everything Anna-Claire would want in a waitress or barmaid.

Maybe – Anna-Claire felt a little bitchy even thinking this – El was little less *good-looking* than she'd anticipated. She didn't know how she'd generated the impression of some model-gorgeous goddess (Robbie hadn't conveyed it, at least not specifically). But honestly, there was a degree of relief (she couldn't specifically explain that one, either) in seeing this girl in the flesh, with her random clothes and her excessive eyeliner.

In any case, that was all irrelevant now.

The point was that El Tippett, no matter how nice, had ended up being the problem. *She* was the reason why Anna-Claire, for the very first time in her life, found herself entirely without a road map.

A mere six weeks after El disappeared, Robbie decided he wanted to decline his place on Citibank's graduate scheme. Not defer it any longer. *Decline* it.

'With El gone, Otto needs the help,' Robbie said.

He and Anna-Claire were sitting at a table in Borough Market at the time, having coffee and croissants. It was the first Saturday in forever that Robbie hadn't spent sleeping off the previous night's shift.

Anna-Claire felt herself freeze. She forced herself to stay calm, keep her tone of voice even. 'Can't he just hire someone else?'

'It's not as simple as that.'

This time, Anna-Claire allowed herself a little frown. She failed to see how it wasn't precisely as simple as that.

'He hasn't taken it well, since El left,' Robbie added.

'Didn't he sack her?'

She'd had the basic details from Robbie already, of course. And she'd been sincerely sorry to hear them. The knowledge that El had ended up a poor drug-addicted mess and was now off God knew where doing God knew what or with whom . . . Anna-Claire took absolutely no pleasure in that. If something about it did buoy her slightly . . . she still didn't think she'd call that *pleasure*. The whole thing simply felt like a cautionary tale. It said something, she thought, about being *too* freewheeling, *too* untethered from faith or family, from the things in life that really mattered.

'It's complicated,' Robbie said, polishing off the last bite of his croissant. 'Anyway, I just . . . I would feel bad to leave, at this point. If El was still there, it'd be a whole different ball game.'

Anna-Claire took that in. 'So, are you saying you want to stay there – out of sympathy, or whatever – just in*definitely*? For*ever*?'

Robbie cocked his head. 'Well, forever's a long time,' he said.

Anna-Claire didn't consider that much of an answer. She tried to imagine what her mother would have to say about all this – although in a few short hours, there'd be no need to imagine it; she planned to relay every detail of this conversation as soon as humanly possible.

In the meantime, she renewed her efforts to remain composed, even as the panic and dismay flooded over her like a wave. The problem was that she just had absolutely no practice with this – with things not going exactly as she'd thought they would.

After all, hadn't she grown up in a very nice family, in a very nice town? Hillsborough was twenty minutes and a world away from Belfast: close enough for trips to the big River Island but far enough not to be bombed or bothered by all those tricky Interface Issues. Anna-Claire had known how fortunate she was, to go to a good grammar school, and to get a glimpse of the Royals any time they visited Northern Ireland, and to have so many extracurricular activities within which to make likeminded friends and excel. Then, she'd headed off to The Mainland for university, wasting no time in finding the right sort of boy – one who ticked all the boxes, who saw the world just as she did. Everything was perfectly on track.

It was staggering, to have done everything by the book and yet somehow find herself here: with her husband saying he wanted to commit himself to poorly paid, dead-end work – to a job whose hours she considered both unsociable and far too sociable.

She picked at the last flakes of her own croissant, tried and failed to come up with some way to convey all this.

'Well, let's see how things go,' she offered instead.

She heard her own voice aloud, sounding so much calmer – so much more amenable – than she really felt. It was probably just as well. The time for her and Robbie's first fight probably wasn't here, in the middle of Borough Market. Had he known that, banked on it, when deciding how to break the news? It didn't seem out of the question.

In any case, they moseyed around a few more stalls together

that afternoon, picked up some overpriced chutney before making the journey home to their lovely flat.

Anna-Claire cursed El Tippett every single second of it.

At Love and Death, Otto refused to even mention El's name most nights.

For a while, of course, she'd been the subject on everyone else's lips. There'd been a sense of frenzy about it, everyone leaning into the mounting drama. Updates were regular, though they constituted no new information.

From Jamie: 'Kat has no idea where she might be either, apparently.'

From Marcus: 'She hasn't responded to any of my texts. Though in fairness, she hasn't responded to anyone's texts, so at least I know it ain't nothing personal.'

From Cormac: 'I overheard Otto ringing round all the hospitals.'

And wasn't that a sobering thought?

Robbie could barely stand the thought, actually.

Every snarky interaction he'd ever had with El had replayed in his brain, every secret sliver of vindication he'd felt as she'd begun to spiral out of control . . .

Looking back, he could see there were times he probably hadn't much helped matters when El was struggling.

But would she have welcomed any help, from him? Almost certainly, she would not have. On the contrary, hadn't she seemed, up to a point, to thrive on the ways they challenged one another?

Everyone was gathered at cocktail jam – Otto had all but lost interest in it, without El, but it still happened occasionally – when at last the text came through on Marcus's phone. Robbie leaned in to stare at the screen. The date showed that it had been months, by now, since Marcus's last attempt at contacting her.

> I'm all good, thanks. Just needed a change.
> Will be rooting for you, though xxx

Plenty of mystery remained – where was she, for one thing – but the tone of finality was undeniable. Over the hubbub of everyone else's analysis, Robbie watched as Otto took a deep breath in and out.

'Well, that's it, then,' he said quietly, almost as if to himself.

'What do you mean?' Robbie asked.

Otto just offered a small shrug. Robbie had never seen him look so . . . lost. 'She's alive. Beyond that . . . you don't think a person has the right to disappear? If I didn't, Robbie, I'd be one hell of a hypocrite.'

After that, Otto often sequestered himself in the back, working on new concoctions alone, while Robbie took the lead out front. He was a hard worker – he could absolutely say that for himself. He relished the opportunity to really prove his worth, just as much as he would have done at an investment bank. Some nights, he was sure he did the work of three people, producing drink after drink – each one perfect – and the rush of it was like nothing else.

He'd stayed at Love and Death because of that rush.

He'd stayed because he wanted to stay more than he wanted to go and work in a bank. It was as simple as that, really, though it wasn't what he'd told his wife.

He and Otto were, objectively speaking, proving to be a good team. And Love and Death was, objectively speaking, a much more even-keeled work environment without El around. There were times Robbie found it a huge relief to have the element of competition with her removed.

Other times, he felt that it hadn't gone away at all, that perhaps he was still – would always be – competing with her. Always losing to her. Because no matter his talents and dedication, Robbie just couldn't stop Otto from missing El – even if Otto never expressed it aloud.

It seemed that nobody could fill the specific gap she'd left. Gone were the days of El and Marcus dancing around the bar after closing, when they should have been wiping tables. Gone were the random pronouncements, the *what would you do if* questions on slow nights. Gone was the excitement – basic and prurient as it surely was – created simply by what El might be wearing on a given evening.

There were no two ways about it: without her, Love and Death was less chaotic – less unpredictable, less maddening in many ways. But it was a hell of a lot less fun, too.

In any event, life in London refused to stand still. Robbie became a fairly regular fixture on the industry scene. He and Anna-Claire spent whatever spare time they had ticking off the city's cultural offerings or seeing old university pals. By now, almost all of them had migrated from Oxford to London, too.

Robbie wasn't sure he truly fitted with that whole crowd, any more than he ever had. They were always welcoming to him; he liked them a lot in so many ways. They'd just grown up so differently from him, though. And the concerns of their current jobs were now so different from his, to boot. There were times that all parties involved seemed to feel the gap and didn't quite know what to do about it.

As for the various talks and 'small groups' that Anna-Claire attended in connection with church . . . those didn't quite constitute Robbie's dream social life either.

He'd been happy enough to accompany Anna-Claire when they were students. But outside the convenience of that setting, outside the associated free pizza and the chance to spend time with his new girlfriend, he found his enthusiasm much reduced.

Still, he began to think it might be good for him, to find some new activities of his own – ones that didn't revolve around making drinks, thinking about drinks, or drinking drinks.

'Me and a few lads are putting together a football side,' Cormac said to him, one night at work. 'As in, Gaelic football. Just for the craic, like – nothing serious. Practice would be Saturday mornings. Do you fancy it?'

Robbie hesitated. He had never considered himself an athletic person. He had never been picked first in PE – although of course, Gaelic games in particular were never on offer at *his* school. His adolescence had been football in the English sense of the term, plus rugby and cricket. Back then, the very idea of engaging voluntarily with the activities of the GAA – the Gaelic Athletic Association – would have struck him as utterly insane. Risky, on multiple levels.

Now, though, he found he perceived no real risk at all. The only thing that seemed insane was having his adult life dictated by how he had been in school. Wasn't he already, in all sorts of accidental ways, very different from the man he'd once anticipated turning into? More and more these days, he felt inclined to say yes to things, see where they took him.

'D'you know what? Count me in,' he replied.

It took less than five seconds for a bout of uncertainty to grip him.

'Although, you know I'm . . . that is, you know I'm not Catholic, yeah?'

He was pretty sure Cormac did know that, though they'd never discussed it.

And perhaps he was entirely correct, because Cormac didn't bat an eyelid. 'That's fine, yeah. You'll pick up the rules in no time. As long as you're happy enough to just do a quick confession with the team priest before you hit the pitch, it'll be grand.'

Robbie must have looked horror-struck.

'I'm messing with you!' Cormac said, breaking into a grin. 'I'll see you Saturday morning.'

Robbie grinned right back.

Chapter Twenty-Two

El was on the early shift, finishing at 6 p.m., and Darleen came in with a group of her friends from Mickey's Toontown. It seemed only polite, for El to join them when she clocked off – just for one drink, to be sociable.

By 8.30, somehow she and her mother were the only members of the gang still there, and Kayla – another bartender at The Tipsy Parrot – was delivering a fourth round of Piña Coladas to their table. She hovered for a moment and performed being on tenterhooks, awaiting El's verdict.

El played along, slurping a mouthful through the straw. 'Perfect,' she proclaimed, though really it was a tad too sweet. The previous effort had been a tad too boozy.

Bizarrely, having always been considered a little slapdash at Love and Death, she had come to be viewed as a master of quality control at The Tipsy Parrot. It really was all relative.

Here, she knew she had no particular reputation when it came to creativity with drinks. Why would she have had? She never invented anything, or so much as tried to – she was done with all that. Instead, she knew that her co-workers thought of her as careful, consistent, knowledgeable. Even Diane, the manager, often deferred to her.

The strangest thing was how other people's perception seemed to influence her perception of *herself*; how it influenced the way she behaved. She never got as granular as, say, Robbie Saunders. She never hovered over her fellow bartenders, assessing their creations down to the millilitre. But lately, she had been known to dispense the occasional bit of unrequested advice. Certainly, she cared increasingly about making sure that the drinks she sent out were right on the money. After all, didn't she have a reputation to live up to?

She sometimes wondered if that was what had happened, with her and Robbie – or one of the things that had happened, before he'd happily taken half the credit for something that was never his – if, maybe, the two of them had just become more and more entrenched in their respective roles at Love and Death, without ever meaning for it to happen; if perception, both internal and external, had become reality.

'You know what Joan Crawford said about a Piña Colada?' El offered then, to Kayla and her mother.

'What?'

'That it was even better than slapping Bette Davis in the face.'

The other two laughed in response, and El thought of Otto. She'd got that little tidbit from him. It was annoying – how often he still popped up in her brain, uninvited. Him and Robbie both.

'No Frankie tonight then?' Darleen asked, once Kayla had disappeared.

At this stage, El thought it was pretty obvious that Frankie wasn't working, but still, she glanced instinctively towards the bar. 'Nope, she never works Thursdays. Acting class.'

'The two of y'all seem to be getting along very well . . .'

Immediately, El got the picture. Her mother had just been searching for a segue. She kept her voice deliberately neutral in response. 'We are, yeah. Frankie's great.'

The two of them were definitely different in lots of ways. For one thing, Frankie's casual style was nothing like El's. Off the clock, the other girl wore denim shorts and a white T-shirt most days. She always chose some offbeat indie thing when they went to the cinema, while El preferred the biggest, broadest star vehicle available. Frankie was practical in ways that El was not; she existed in Anaheim with the confidence that came from a lifetime of local knowledge. Conversely, self-doubt could creep up on her quickly – far more quickly than it did for El.

As a pair, they found all the same things funny, though. That counted for everything.

The previous weekend, they'd gone out together for some driving practice. El's progress on that front had begun to feel like one step forwards, three steps back, and Frankie couldn't fathom that she was still having lessons.

'What are you doing?' Frankie had asked, as El hovered at the first junction, both hands on the steering wheel.

El had kept her gaze facing resolutely forwards, her eyes darting from left to right. 'I'm waiting for a gap.'

Frankie had exhaled in disbelief. 'What? There won't *be* a gap. You pull out, and people *make* a gap, because they have no choice.' She gave the centre console a few quick, no-nonsense taps. 'This is California, baby. You need to drive this car like it's stolen.'

Even in her terror, El had let out a quick burst of laughter. It felt like better advice than she'd got in months with Ted.

Opposite her mother in The Tipsy Parrot now, she couldn't help but smile at the memory.

'Are the two of you . . . ?' Again, Darleen trailed off meaningfully. It was the first time she had ever made any reference to El's romantic life in any form. It was weird. But it also felt good – like a tiny cracking open of something.

'Ugh. No, Mom.' El had used that term in her early childhood, lost it somewhere in adolescence. It came out of her mouth again now, instead of 'Mum,' without her noticing. Then, something else did, too. 'Are *you* dating anybody?'

'No, I am not!' Darleen exclaimed giddily.

'So, what it is it then?'

Her mother just looked at her blankly, and El huffed with mock impatience.

'Come on. We both know you haven't always been like this.'

'Like what?'

'Like the way you are here. All . . . happy.'

A smile spread across Darleen's face. She gestured around her vaguely. 'Well, that's the beauty of this place, sugar. It's magical. You must see it yourself now, right? The way people's eyes just light up when they even arrive in town, never mind get into The Park itself. You know my parents brought *me* here when I was little?'

El hadn't known that.

Darleen nodded. 'My eleventh birthday. Best weekend of my life probably.' She took another sip from her cocktail. 'Anyhow . . . I know people get all sniffy about "Disney adults" or whatever, but if there's something about being here that just makes people happy – and there ain't no denying that there *is* – then what's wrong with that, huh? Being here is just like . . . I don't know. It's a soft place to land, I guess. And the weather ain't half bad either.'

El nodded along. It was a sweet sentiment.

She just wasn't sure it altogether tracked, when she zipped through the first eighteen years of her life. Attempts to bolster her mother's mood during that period had included – but had not been limited to – talking therapy, cold-water swimming, hypnosis, yoga, attending an array of churches and motivational seminars, running, eating less meat, eating more meat, weaving pointless items – with a proper loom that took up half the living room – and (on her father's dime, of course) regular trips to hushed, fragrant places full of other well-heeled convalescents.

The best outcome, from any of it, had been a temporary bump in her mother's outlook – boosting her to what El had always thought of, in her own mind, as a five out of ten. Neutral. There could be weeks of that, or months sometimes. But it was never very long before Darleen dipped back down to her natural state: a one or a two out of ten. Nobody had ever said the word 'depression'.

In view of all that, it was . . . *something* to be asked to believe that a top-up of vitamin D and a quick visit to the Magic Kingdom would potentially have done the trick all along.

Fundamentally, El *didn't* believe that. How could she? Suddenly, it seemed all too obvious what had boosted her mother up to what was now at least an eight-point-five on an average day. It was not so much a question of additions to her life but subtractions.

'Were you really that miserable in London?' El found herself asking. 'Or, wherever – in all the other places we lived. Were you really that miserable with us?' She didn't like how it felt, hearing the question out loud. The baldness and the vulnerability of it. She rushed to fill the space around it. 'You can tell me. I get it. I'd be pretty miserable shacked up with a thicko kid *plus Dad* myself.' She forced out a laugh.

Her mother didn't join her. Instead, Darleen's expression softened. 'Oh, sugar. It was nothing to do with you or your father. Not really. I mean, I *am* happier here than I used to be. You're right about that. But you want to know what the best part is? It's knowing *I* made it happen. All by myself. For myself.' She offered a little smile. 'I didn't always think I had it in me, but it turns out I did. And I know it wasn't always easy, before. I know I had my down days here and there.'

It was like calling Hurricane Katrina a spot of bad weather. El couldn't help but bark out a quick laugh. There was just something so darkly comedic about it, about the moments that rushed towards her with visceral force.

Her 8-year-old self, realizing she didn't understand much of anything at her fourth new school – when had the other kids learned all this stuff? She'd done her best with her extra 'catch-up' homework at the kitchen table, her mother dead-eyed and exhausted in the living room, her father still at work.

Her 11-year-old self, sleeping over at a friend's house, crying at the contrast – in atmosphere, in everything. The parents had thought she was homesick, and El hadn't known how to explain that it was the exact opposite. She'd let them drive her home in her pyjamas at midnight and cried all the harder once she got into her own bed.

Her 13-year-old self, armed with a soapy flannel and the instruction from her father that this had *gone on long enough* – somehow or other, she must make sure her mother was washed; it was easier for her, she was a girl. By then, of course, school was a lost cause. She'd recently been enrolled at her seventh (and final) one, and had accepted once and for all that she was simply not smart enough for academics. Better, then, to declare no interest in the whole business – better to concentrate instead on winning friends, on finding all the joy she possibly could in the times she was out of her own house.

Her 16-year-old self, coming home bursting with excitement, unable to conceal it this time. 'I got a job, Mum! Like, a paying one. Two-fifty an hour, at the Rose and Crown, collecting glasses. Just part-time – for now.'

Her mother had struggled to summon a smile, never mind a congratulations or a question, or even some mild concern about whether that pub was really a suitable place for her daughter.

Things between them were so different now. So much better. And El was – in a legal, technical sense – all grown up. The things that happened in the past were over and done, unchangeable by any number of heart-to-hearts in a kitschy Disneyland bar. Still. Was it wrong to want some kind of acknowledgement of the past? Suddenly, El wanted that more than anything.

'I mean . . . I don't know if I would say "down days here and there,"' El replied. She tried to keep her voice light. 'I'd say it was like living with a ghost, and a lot of the time, the ghost kind of despises you.' She cocked her head. 'Would we call that a *ghoul*? That sounds about right, actually. Who knew all you needed was a big hug from Daffy Duck, eh?'

She forced another chuckle, but it came out sounding entirely mirthless. And, once again, Darleen wasn't laughing along. For what felt like a long moment, her mother just looked across at her.

'Wow,' she said quietly. 'You really are something, Eloise, you know that?'

It wasn't a compliment.

With that, she got up from the table and walked right out the door.

Left alone at The Tipsy Parrot, El immediately felt all the air go out of her, go out of everything about the evening. Had she been the one in the wrong, just now? The *only* one in the wrong? She really didn't know.

She downed a shot of vodka, then another, and for the first time in a long while, they didn't seem quite strong enough. It didn't take much to remember the euphoria, or the nothingness, that a powder or a pill could offer.

Even the possibility awakened something in her brain, a familiar anticipatory tingling in her synapses. By now, she probably knew someone who knew someone . . .

But, no. She fought to push the thoughts aside, gulping down a pint of water instead.

When she got home, neither she nor her mother made any move to discuss what happened. There were no apologies from either side.

But the next day, they each woke up, and they still lived together in that little condo. Day by day – somewhere between *do you have any whites to go in this wash?* and *I picked up salad for lunch* – they got to work on a silent repair job.

That, El supposed, was family.

Chapter Twenty-Three

The man (the next man) who would change El's life arrived alone and sat at the bar. Right off the bat, he conveyed an extremely *not from around here* impression. For starters, he was wearing an expensive-looking suit, complete with shiny shoes and shiner cufflinks. The open collar of his buttoned-down shirt seemed to be this guy's only nod to the fact that he was currently at a theme park and not in some nefarious boardroom.

He ordered off-menu – that was the other thing. A gin Martini – cold, dry, with a twist. It was the first time in memory that El had served a clear liquid, without some sort of monstrous garnish, since she arrived at The Tipsy Parrot.

'Can I get you anything else?' she asked him, when he'd drained his drink.

This time, he picked up the menu and selected something from it. She got to work and was settling the cocktail down in front of him in a flash.

'One Suffering Bastard, as requested,' she said, with a smile.

He smiled back at her. 'Gotta love that accent,' he offered then. 'What's an English rose like you doing in a place like this?'

It wasn't the most interesting way to be flirted with – not by a long shot. But El was in a good mood; she was willing to lower her standards slightly. It was a quiet, in-between time of day, 4.30 p.m. or so. There were just two other couples in the bar, sitting at

165

tables, minding their own business. In other words, they offered her no mileage at all. Meanwhile, here was a person – any person, and actually somewhat of an intriguing one – with whom she could shoot the breeze.

'You know, I first came for the arts and culture,' she said, 'but really why I've stuck around is the great health care and the low incidents of drive-by shootings.'

'Really?' the man asked dubiously.

El snorted. 'No. Not really. How about you – what brings you to The Park?'

She called it that now. The Park. Just like her mother did.

'Schools are on fall break, so I brought my daughter and a bunch of her friends. She's nearly 12, but she's still a huge Disney nut. Good excuse to spend some time together, you know?'

It struck El that if there were one thing this man seemed very definitely *not* to be doing right now, it was spending time with his daughter.

However, she wasn't there to judge. She had never subscribed to the notion that a bartender's job was to be fawning. Not to judge, though . . . for the most part, she thought that was fair enough. She thought most people deserved a place like that they could go to, outside of the confessional box.

'Sounds fun,' she said.

'This is good,' he said, lowering the Suffering Bastard from his lips and looking at the glass, as if appraising it anew. 'It's *really* good.'

'Glad you like it.'

'I had to see if that Martini you whipped up before was a fluke, you know?'

El just smiled in response.

'Did you put something extra in that one? It tasted a little different, but in a good way.'

'A tiny bit of lychee syrup,' she said.

Her customer seemed to take that in. 'Where else have you worked?' he asked her, after a moment.

'Oh, y'know. Various different places.' And then, she couldn't help it: she wanted someone to be impressed by her again – like, *really, properly impressed*. For some reason, she suspected that before her right now might be just the man for that job. 'I worked at this bar in London for a while,' she said. 'Love and Death.'

It felt almost strange, to say the name aloud. Lots of days, she barely thought of it at all anymore.

Right on cue, the man's expression shifted into recognition. 'Oh wow. O-*kay*. No wonder you know what you're doing.' He held out his hand. 'I'm Paul Daly. I'm the owner of The Avalon.' He said this like he expected recognition from *her*.

She met his offered handshake and decided not to fake it. 'Sorry. I'm not really up on the whole drinks scene over here. I mean . . .' She scanned the surroundings with an open palm. 'Obviously.'

Paul seemed to take no offence. 'It's a rooftop bar, in West Hollywood, just off the Strip. Views to die for.'

El nodded. She did at least have the vaguest notion of where he was talking about. She'd seen *Pretty Woman*.

'We're not the Chateau or the Polo Lounge *yet*, but I like to think our menu's actually a little fresher. A little more fun, you know?' He tilted his glass towards her. 'How 'bout you come fix the good folks of Los Angeles some of these fine beverages, huh?'

El just laughed.

'I'm serious.'

This time, El stopped what she was doing, regarded him closely. Her brow furrowed. 'Are you . . . what's happening here? Are you coming on to me? Are you messing with me? Are you offering me a job?'

'The last one,' Paul said. 'Definitely the last one.'

It took a lot to fluster El. And yet, all at once, she heard herself become the bumbling, ever-so-polite Englishwoman. 'Well, that's very kind of you, but really, I . . .'

She stopped herself, unable to figure out the end of that sentence. But what? *But I'm not really looking for anything right now? But I'm happy where I am?* Were those things true?

Paul approached her unease with all the expansive bonhomie of the wealthy and powerful. 'You have to think about it, I get it,' he said, and he shifted in his chair. 'I gotta get back to Destiny right now, anyhow – that's my daughter. But I'll swing by again tomorrow – how's about that? See if you've made up your mind.'

'Wait!' El said. 'Are you seriously just offering me a job on your fancy-pants rooftop in LA? You don't want me to – I don't know – do a trial shift?'

Standing now, Paul took a last decisive sip from his drink – it was still half full – and then placed the glass back down on the bar. 'You just did one.'

Of course, El couldn't help it. There was a computer in Diane's office, and people used it all the time. Diane had explicitly instructed her staff to 'just go on ahead and feel free, girls, whenever y'all need to check your email or MySpace. I know how it is.'

El didn't have MySpace – or the slightest interest in getting it.

However, she found she *did* have more than a passing curiosity about The Avalon. With the office door open and one eye still on the bar outside, she typed the name into Google. She skipped right to the image results.

'Wow,' she murmured, out loud, when she saw the place.

The bar itself, sleek and beautiful as it was, actually felt like the least of it. The whole space was huge, with sunset views for days and that classic marker of Californian confidence – no roof whatsoever.

Perfectly coiffed greenery had been imported from somewhere and appeared now as though it naturally sprouted from the wooden floorboards. Cream leather furniture was dotted around, all of it slightly larger than it needed to be, slightly lower to the ground than it needed to be. Overhead, strings of bare bulbs criss-crossed the whole place, striking El as incredibly chic in their simplicity. There was a pool, too – albeit one that, from the photos, looked more decorative than functional. It was a place around which attractive people could congregate and stay dry.

The whole set-up looked, frankly, like an incredibly good time. It looked like a place El would very much like to have a drink.

Later that night, in celebration of having at last passed her driving test, El went to an early bird dinner with her mother and Ted. They made for an odd trio, and El wondered if this was a standard part of Ted's services. In any case, she'd become vastly less fussy about the specific details of her social life. A Chinese-style buffet, at which she brought the average age down by twenty-five years, was absolutely fine by her.

'You see, Eloise?' Ted said, as they toasted her success with three Diet Cokes. 'What did I tell you? Slow and steady does it. I can rest easy in my bed at night, knowing you're out there using your turn signal, checking your blind spot, and what else . . . ?'

'Avoiding distraction,' El filled in dutifully, and Ted laughed delightedly, as though she'd told a wonderful joke.

'She's going to be great,' Darleen said proudly. 'My girl.'

El just didn't see it coming, how nice that felt to hear. It was stupid, she was sure, but she felt like she might be about to cry. She supposed she'd just never had much success to celebrate before, in the way of passing things. Nor, of course, had she had a mother much inclined towards celebration.

A few weeks previously, El had gone to her mother's en-suite bathroom in search of tweezers. What she'd found instead had surprised her and had also made total sense. She'd waited two days to broach it, at what she'd thought would be a good time:

specifically, during the commercial break of *Desperate Housewives*. Apart from the fact that watching *Desperate Housewives* tended to represent Darleen Tippett at her absolute happiest and most relaxed, drugs were always being advertised on television here. El had felt sure she'd get some kind of semi-natural way into the topic. And, indeed, so she had.

'Hey, Mom? Why didn't you tell me about the Zoloft?' she'd asked gently, at the tail end of the side effects for some diabetes medication or other.

On the opposite side of the couch, her mother's expression had frozen.

'I . . . came across them,' El added. 'Googled it.'

She'd felt sure she was about to be in for an earful about minding her own business.

Instead, Darleen had looked away. 'I don't know what you're talking about,' she'd said, all nonchalance.

And, El could have pressed the matter. It was on the tip of her tongue: *Well, I saw them in your bathroom cabinet, with your name on them. Either you're on anti-depressants or you're selling them all around Disneyland, which would be hilarious. Which is it?*

Or, option B – an option that would once have never crossed her mind – she could just . . . let this lie.

It had been easy, in the end, to claim some misunderstanding on her own part, to change the subject, keep the peace.

Looking across at her mother now, El swallowed the emotion that threatened to rise up in her. Darleen Tippett was imperfect. She always had been, and she was still. In many ways, she had not been a very good mother. But she wasn't a bad *person*. And hadn't she been willing to tolerate – hadn't she been largely quite *enthusiastic* about – her adult daughter's presence in her home for over a year?

El reached for a spring roll, chomping through it in three easy bites. It tasted better than expected, actually. This *whole experience*, in Anaheim, had turned out to be so much better than she could have ever expected.

That said, she allowed herself to cast her eyes around the restaurant. Not in judgement, just in honest observation. A good portion of the local population did appear to have moved here specifically with a view to dying here. El was extremely, *extremely* sure that she didn't want to die here. And there was one clear way to make sure that didn't happen.

She needed, quite simply, to stop living here.

The next day, when Paul sidled back up to the bar at The Tipsy Parrot, just as he'd promised he would, El wasted no time.

'Can Frankie come, too?' she asked. 'To LA, I mean. To work at The Avalon.'

'Who's Frankie?'

El nodded over towards her friend. She was, at that moment, bent over a table, sweeping up Dorito dust from its surface. Perhaps sensing the eyes on her, she turned briefly towards El and Paul, flashing them a quick, brilliant smile.

'She's a good bartender,' El rushed to add. It was true-ish. And then, she brought out the big guns. 'I . . . I won't take the job unless you also have one for h—'

'Honey,' Paul interrupted. 'It's LA. A girl who looks like that can always hitch a ride.'

Two weeks later – with farewells to her mother, Ted, and The Tipsy Parrot that brought genuine tears to her eyes – El hopped into a second-hand Toyota Camry, with Frankie in the passenger seat.

She drove that thing, like it was stolen, all the way to West Hollywood.

Chapter Twenty-Four

'Oh my God! What the hell is *Fernet-Branca*?' Frankie hissed, pointing at the item on the menu.

It was their first shift at The Avalon – and their first moment alone together. She looked so plaintive that El couldn't help but let out a quick burst of laughter.

'Don't laugh!' Frankie said. 'This is serious! I'm going to get fired!'

'You are not,' El replied. 'I'm going to tell you the biggest secret of high-class bartending right now, okay?'

Frankie looked at her expectantly. 'Okay.'

'Listen closely. *This is not rocket science*,' El said. 'You have to sort of pretend like it is – my guess is some people here are going to pretend that harder than others. And actually, at the very top level, there *is* a lot involved. If you want to be the best in the world, it's fucking hard work. But fundamentally? It's not that different from what you were doing in Anaheim. Tonight, we'll go to the supermarket – the *grocery store* – to get supplies, and we'll practise everything on this menu at home, and it's all going to be absolutely fine.'

Opposite her, Frankie nodded. El had to say, even to her own ears, she'd sounded very comforting, very convincing. Nobody would have suspected that she was nervous, too.

And not in quite the way Frankie was. Not just because she

needed a job. Rather, it was because she *wanted* this *particular* job.

The Avalon was everything it had looked like in the pictures. It was *more* beautiful, even, than it had looked in the pictures. For El, though, there was a pleasure much greater than the surroundings. Here were real drinks again, real ingredients, maybe even – the thought occurred to her – some scope for invention. It was funny, she thought, how things changed and then changed back again. Evidently, all those hand-juiced lemons and limes were going to be back in her life with a vengeance, and she downright relished the thought. Who would have believed it?

She desperately did not want to screw this one up. For the first few weeks, she was permanently conscious of making sure she didn't. She wasn't sure how much goodwill she could rely on here, after all. There was something ruthless about Los Angeles, just beneath its easy-breezy veneer.

One of the oddest ways her overall uncertainty manifested, in those early days, was in a sudden, unprecedented, and distracting level of concern about her appearance. The simple fact of the matter was that she looked a little different now to how she'd always been used to seeing herself. She wondered if it was turning 25 – her metabolism finally slowing down, precisely as old people said it would. Her mother had offered a different explanation: 'the Disneyland diet', she'd called it cheerfully. El was heavier than she'd ever been and was now surrounded by more thin people than she ever had been, to boot.

On the plus side, her accent turned out to be a huge asset. Customers and co-workers alike adored it.

Of course, it had drawn attention back at The Tipsy Parrott, too. Paul Daly had been far from the only one to query how on earth she'd ended up working at Disneyland. She'd often felt like a bit of an oddity. In LA, there was very quickly no room for doubt: she was an *attraction*. People were all too ready to see a certain sophistication in her. Or, they imagined a prim and proper existence, now exchanged for the California dream; they delighted in the idea that she was, in some sense, breaking free by being here.

If their vision of her was never quite an accurate one, then El found she didn't much care. What had she learned in Disneyland if not that a person could make their own reality? That happiness, whatever which way you came by it, was a fucking good thing.

The first real mistake she made at The Avalon, she ended up smoothing over with one easy sentence: 'Oh! Sorry! I suppose we just do it differently in London!'

Immediately, in response, all her new co-workers ranged somewhere from intrigued to deferential. Otto's voice came back to El in a flash. She still couldn't seem to stop that happening – not altogether – no matter how hard she tried. She'd asked him, once, why he'd moved to London, and he'd said something predictably vague in response: *Always go where you're a novelty, kid.*

Standing on a rooftop in WeHo, with the sun shining down on her, it occurred to El that maybe he hadn't been being deliberately evasive at all. Maybe he'd been right on the money.

As for the extra ten pounds, she realized, then and there: she could decide to care about an extra ten pounds. She could let them multiply inside her brain, let her whole existence warp around them. Or she could decide, quite definitively, to simply not give a shit about them. This very basic choice wasn't always available to a person, in response to the full range of life's problems. But where it *was* available? The correct response seemed like a no-brainer.

In the end, those extra ten pounds stayed with El the whole time she lived in California and didn't make a single bit of difference to anything, ever.

*

Within three months, Frankie was snapped up by an agent. Jared Kostecki. El disliked him from the start. She disliked his slicked-back hair and his sinister white grin and the sheer volume of famous people whom he professed to know and referred to, vaguely, as having 'great energy'.

However, he did appear to be legitimate in at least the basic sense of bringing potential job opportunities to Frankie's attention. Not too long after joining Jared's roster, she burst into the apartment with a breathless clatter.

El and Frankie's place on Gardner and Sunset was a one-bedroom – for that matter, it was a one-*bed*. It had a coin-operated washing machine and tumble dryer, located in a communal outbuilding, and allowed for absolutely every moment of their downstairs neighbour's existence to be overheard. That man could not so much as flip on an episode of *30 Rock* without El and Frankie knowing about it.

However, it was relatively cheap and relatively cheerful. Most importantly, it was close to work.

'I got it!' Frankie shouted, slamming the door behind her. 'Ellie! Oh my God, oh my God! Are you home? Can you believe it? I got it!'

El leaped up from bed and took the four steps from their bedroom to their everything-else room. 'Oh my God! Amazing!' she replied, her friend's enthusiasm proving contagious. 'Which one?'

Frankie had been going to around ten auditions a week, and El had spent hours in the afternoons reading scenes with her. It was always more about line-learning than about Frankie giving a full-out performance, though. Privately, El still had no idea whether Frankie was or wasn't a good actress. It really didn't matter to her one way or another.

'The vampire movie!' Frankie replied.

El's expression froze slightly. 'Amazing!' she repeated brightly.

'Somebody got pregnant and had to drop out! Sucker! So,

anyway, they were kind of under the gun to recast the part. Shoots right here in LA, so it's perfect. I'm getting paid scale, but I also get a per diem *and* a back end. Can you believe it? We could probably even get another apartment if you wanted. We could get a two-bedroom!'

'Well, let's not rush into anything right away,' El replied, with uncharacteristic caution. She just wasn't sure she wanted to bet her whole domestic life on the success of this thing. It was hard to imagine vampires as anything but a fairly niche interest.

In one hand, Frankie brandished a yellow cardboard box. 'I got us guava pastries from Porto's, to celebrate.'

El grinned. Truthfully, it wasn't much to do with the snacks or even the movie news. It was that she had a best friend. And together, in this brand-new city, they had a favourite thing at a favourite Cuban bakery. She could think of no better causes for celebration.

The culture, in the US, was very much for servers to make themselves a part of a customer's drinking (or dining or shopping) experience. They'd done more of that at Love and Death than El thought was usual at other bars in the UK – but still, it didn't come close to The Avalon.

'I'm El, I'll be your bartender for this evening,' she was supposed to say to people. 'I'll get you started with some water, and just let me know if you have any questions about the menu.'

Bizarrely, American customers proceeded to do exactly that.

'What do *you* think is good?' they'd ask her.

'Hey, El, could we get another round of French Martinis? Perfect suggestion.'

'So would that be, like, *very* sweet? I don't want anything too sweet.'

They had particular specifications; they asked for things off-menu; they wanted her to know that they knew what they were talking about. Thus, El didn't bat an eyelid when a woman sidled up to the bar one evening in early spring.

'Hey, so I have kind of a weird question for you,' she began.

El just looked up at her, smile on her face, eyebrows raised attentively.

'Have you ever heard of a Citi Slicker?'

Midway through a task, her hands moving automatically, El quite literally stopped in her tracks.

'This is gonna sound so dumb, but I saw it on this show, *BST* – do you know it?'

Feeling her heart rate rising, worked very hard to keep her face the same as it always was. 'I've heard of it. I, uh, didn't know it had aired in the US.'

Truthfully, she barely thought about it airing *anywhere*. The filming of that episode felt so long ago now; it had taken on such a surreal quality in her mind. Also, the show – from what she could gather – had seemed like it was going to be pretty terrible. She wouldn't have ruled out the idea that it had simply died a death, been cancelled before it even really began.

Before her, though, her customer seemed to know better.

'It's on HBO. You've only missed the first episode, so you can totally still catch up. It's like real guilty-pleasure stuff, you know? Anyhow, it's set in London, and that's what the characters ordered. A Citi Slicker. Apparently it's all the rage over there right now, but I googled it and nothing came up. I just thought, with you being British and all . . . do you know what's in it?'

El swallowed. 'As a matter of fact, I do.'

Chapter Twenty-Five

When *BST* aired, the difference was felt at Love and Death almost immediately.

Two days later, there was an article in the *Evening Standard*: 'Inside the *BST* Gang's Favourite London Hotspot', the headline read. *For those who can brave the unknown (and the Northern Line) an unparalleled delight awaits.*

Read by thousands of Londoners as they killed time on their commutes, it was the type of publicity you couldn't pay for (and, indeed, Otto hadn't paid a penny for it).

A shrewd businessperson would have raised the price of everything on the menu right away. They would have made Citi Slickers from morning until night, while the appetite was there. They would have installed a photograph of the *BST* cast, pointed out the exact seats the actors had sat on, and allowed people to pose in similar fashion.

Otto didn't do any of that.

He did the opposite.

'We won't be serving the Citi Slicker here,' he told the whole staff, the night after the article was published.

Robbie's eyes just about popped out of his head. 'What?'

'It's not on the menu. Not now, not ever. And remember, no photographs inside the bar. You see anyone with a camera, and they better be out of here within sixty seconds. I mean it.'

Over by the door, Cormac peeked outside, then withdrew. 'Lot of people out there, boss. More than last night, even.'

Hearing that news, Robbie swore he could see a flicker of excitement, a flicker of pride in Otto. He loved nothing more than a full house.

'What are we supposed to tell them, if they ask for a Citi Slicker?' Robbie ventured.

Otto just shrugged. 'Maybe they won't ask for it,' he replied mildly.

But they did.

Practically every single customer did, that night.

'I'm afraid we don't quite have the secret ingredients for that one right now,' Otto told them, all ease. 'But how about a Sidecar instead?' Or, 'How about a Gimlet?' 'How about a Blue Murder?'

People were disappointed to begin with, no doubt – confused, sometimes, or plain irritated. However, all the things that had already made Love and Death a cult spot – the cocktail lover's cocktail bar – remained true. Somehow, even without the thing they originally came for, a lot of the newcomers still left having had the most glorious night out they could remember.

Maybe it was ultimately to Otto's credit, then, that people kept coming, that the phone kept ringing.

In fact, once word got around that the Citi Slicker was *not available* at Love and Death, that of itself became a subject of interest. Robbie had truly no idea whether this constituted egg on Otto's face or was part of some grand plan. One way or another, for a reclusive owner, there suddenly seemed to be a flurry of articles telling the public just how reclusive he was.

'We've had another few calls from journalists,' Robbie said, almost a month after the first episode of *BST* was broadcast. 'They don't seem to be taking no for an answer. It's like this thing's just taken on a life of its own. I think at this point, even if we're not making the drink, we should probably tell people the recipe for it.'

Otto looked nothing short of aghast. 'That's the *last* thing I plan to do. I can tell you that for nothing.'

'There are other bars doing versions of it now, though, apparently – or their best guess. That seems . . . not ideal. I mean, who knows what they're putting in it. Not to put too fine a point on it, but it could be minging.'

Otto seemed to take that in. He sighed heavily. '*You* talk to people then,' he said.

'Talk to who?'

'I don't know. Whoever.'

And so, Robbie did.

He gave some off-the-record quotes. He accepted a few invitations.

Swiftly, it became apparent that within the industry, all sorts of stories were getting around, about the provenance of the Citi Slicker – and, specifically, about *his* relationship to it:

Robbie had created the drink (and El Tippett – remember her? – had practically gone mad with jealousy, hence her mysterious disappearance).

Otto had created the drink, inspired by Robbie (and El Tippett – remember her? – had practically gone mad with jealousy, hence her mysterious disappearance).

Actress Kate Carroll had created the drink, then had asked Robbie to come up with a good name for it right before filming started (and El Tippett – remember her? – had practically gone mad with jealousy, hence her mysterious disappearance).

Overall, whether Robbie was dealing with journalists, customers, or his peers, everyone seemed to enjoy the idea that his personal background as a would-be finance guy, this television programme set in the Square Mile, and the Citi Slicker must all have overlapped in some quite deliberate way.

To start with, he did his best to correct the record where he could. Doing so did somewhat take the air out of an interaction, though. It felt like stopping to correct someone's grammar in the middle of a party. He wouldn't have ruled out the possibility that he *had* done exactly that as a teenager, and it likely hadn't won him many friends.

What kind of an idiot would he be, to make the same mistake again?

It was so much easier, instead, to let himself get carried along. He might have done a few demos here and there. He might have given out the recipe, when people asked for it. That recipe might have ended up online, and then on the menus of one cocktail bar after another . . .

Truthfully, at this stage, Robbie just didn't see the point in being unduly proprietary about the whole thing. After all, it wasn't like he could direct people towards El for the information they wanted. By now, for all he knew, she could have been in the wilds of Africa or the edges of the Arctic.

The result was that it was his name, instead of hers, that became better and better known around town. He even managed to get a pay rise out of it, and quickly figured out some new ways to spend the extra cash.

'Looking *sharp*, Robbie!' Marcus exclaimed, jostling against his shoulder good-naturedly. 'Time to ditch the M&S specials at last, was it?'

Robbie made a great show of shrugging him off, but he was smiling. A person could absorb so much by osmosis, in a city like London, about what looked and didn't look right.

And he couldn't deny that he enjoyed it – showing up at any number of places and having the head bartender rush to greet him.

'Your usual?' they asked him.

Or: 'Try this new one; let me know what you think of it.'

It felt good to be asked to talk about the subjects he cared about, to be valued for the skills he'd worked so hard to acquire. It felt good, at last, to find himself at the very centre of everything.

Anna-Claire began to come to Love and Death more frequently, usually with various configurations of her teacher friends. They got to skip the queue and sit at the best table in the house. Otto wasn't there, the first time they visited, and without his watchful gaze, Robbie surreptitiously whipped up Citi Slickers all round.

He wasn't sure any of the women present were the greatest fans of whiskey, if truth be told. Nonetheless, they were full of praise for the drinks, the surroundings, the exclusivity of this experience.

By now, it felt like Love and Death was the name on absolutely every Londoner's lips – the hottest new place (that had been open for eight years). There was a cachet associated even with making it in the door. Celebrities had their PRs call ahead, though Otto rejected (almost) all but those with pre-existing loyalty.

Robbie could still well remember his in-laws' visit to London, just six months ago.

'The demon drink, eh?' Anna-Claire's father had said, when Robbie mentioned something innocuous about work. 'That stuff'll kill you.'

Robbie had frowned. It was the type of thing he would once have let lie. 'Too much of anything can kill you, though,' he'd replied evenly. 'Too much *water* will kill you.'

Mike – incidentally, a solicitor by profession – had looked unconvinced. 'In all seriousness, son. What kind of a job is it for a grown man? "Evil company corrupts good habits." First Corinthians.'

Just a few feet away from them – they were, at the time, in one of the pods on the London Eye – Anna-Claire had seemed not to hear that.

Now, though, here she was – basking in the reflected glow of Love and Death's success.

'This is the life, ladies,' one of her pals proclaimed, as they all drained their glasses and Robbie got to work on something they might actually enjoy. 'What it is to have friends in high places, eh!'

'What can I say?' Anna-Claire murmured, reaching across the bar to cup Robbie's cheek affectionately. 'I'm really good at picking husbands.'

Chapter Twenty-Six

Robbie's own parents' visit, when it rolled around at the beginning of summer, brought different complications.

He and Anna-Claire hosted them for dinner – one of the last they'd be having in their lovely flat, as it happened. The owner of the place had picked the wrong bank many years prior, and Robbie and Anna-Claire were now enduring the consequences.

'Screw Northern Rock!' Robbie said, after every viewing.

'Screw Northern Rock,' his wife would agree vociferously.

And somehow, it didn't seem quite so bleak. Buying a place themselves had begun to seem an ever more distant dream, and the London rental market was definitely not for sissies. However, they were, at least, in it together.

How the whole subject of Robbie's social life came up during that dinner with his parents, he wasn't entirely sure. Already, they'd covered the subjects of his new contact lenses, what every single person he'd been to school with was now up to back in Belfast, and the extortionate ticket prices for West End shows.

Conversation then turned towards preparations for the upcoming move. They were bound for a smaller place, south of the river, and Anna-Claire described the organizational blitz she'd begun just the previous evening.

'And where were you during all this, Robbie?' his mother interjected teasingly. 'Keeping a low profile, were you?'

'Oh,' Anna-Claire replied lightly. 'Robbie was out with his GAA friends, weren't you?'

'What?' his father asked sharply.

Robbie bit back his irritation – of course Anna-Claire hadn't meant to put her foot in it like that. Had she? In any case, she had.

'Ah, it's just a bunch of mates,' he told his father. 'The actual . . . *sports* aspect of things didn't last. A few practices, and we just realized we were all a bit shite, really.' He chuckled. 'A few of us just went for something to eat yesterday – that was all.'

Even as he said it, Robbie realized that his father had likely never once in his life gone to PizzaExpress with a group of other men. The very suggestion of it would surely have prompted something homophobic in response, something Robbie would have known his father didn't really mean at all.

As things were, he knew what was coming: something either vaguely or explicitly sectarian that Philip Saunders very much did mean.

'But they're Fenians, are they, these lads?'

Robbie winced internally at the term. 'Some of them. It's kind of a mix really. North and South, different religions, no religion. Some people are second generation so, I mean, technically, they're actually English,' he added, in case that might help.

As a group, they definitely didn't sit around singing 'Kumbaya' together. Early on, there'd been moments when Robbie had undeniably felt a little awkward, a little out of the loop. His total lack of any relevant sporting knowledge perhaps hadn't helped there. He was a natural, though, when it came to asking questions. He found it so *interesting*, being around these people whose life experiences had both orbited and intersected with his own. Differences, where they existed, certainly weren't ignored or denied. However, the process of unpacking them – almost exclusively in raucous and philosophical pub sessions – eventually seemed only to provide fodder for comedy. What seemed to matter more were the endless shared references, the shared sense of humour, the broad agreement that, notwithstanding the many things everyone missed desperately about the island of Ireland, they certainly didn't want to go back and live there any time soon. Very quickly, Robbie had known that here were friendships destined to endure much longer than any he'd formed in an Oxford quad. Here, in short, were people with whom he could have *the craic*.

To his father, he offered up none of this.

'You want to watch yourself, boy,' his father continued gruffly. 'It's all well and good 'til the shit hits the fan, I'll tell you. Then you'll not be long seeing what side your bread's buttered on. These IRA bastards stick to their own, and you'd be a damn sight better off doing the same.'

His mother tutted. 'That's enough of that, Phil. It's different for the young ones nowadays.'

His father let out a disbelieving, mirthless laugh. An uncomfortable pause followed, then was swiftly filled.

Anna-Claire's voice was all brightness and normality. 'More salad, anyone?'

Robbie thought about it all evening, after his parents had gone back to their hotel. He thought about the stories he'd grown up on from his father. War stories, quite literally. He knew that his dad was fundamentally a decent, kind, hard-working man, that he'd had a tough go of it in his youth and beyond.

Robbie thought about his *own* youth, growing up in Northern Ireland. For a long time, he'd been so keen to defend the place. He'd told people it was all very normal, actually – it was a shame how it was always portrayed on the news; the reality had been so much less dramatic.

And it was true that Robbie's childhood and adolescence had

had plenty in common with what he imagined of his peers in Glasgow or Manchester or Dublin.

He'd pleaded for fish and chips on a Friday and watched *Top of the Pops*. He'd cleaned the car for pocket money and spent summers in a caravan on the coast. He'd worried about small fallings out with friends and about whether his mock exam results were an accurate predictor of the real thing.

Nothing very bad had ever happened to him.

None of his direct relatives had been murdered or had murdered anyone. What a thing, though, to be raised in a place where that felt like something to be actively grateful for – where anything short of that felt fairly insignificant.

Bomb scares, almost every Saturday in town for as long as he could remember . . .

Greysteel, Drumcree, Omagh – people who sounded just like him crying on the news. Robbie never heard his own accent on the national news, actually, except in the context of an atrocity.

What else?

Brits Out scrawled on gable walls, and the phrase being shouted at him sometimes, by the lads from the other school . . .

Bonfires every summer, larger than houses, with signs atop them reading *Kill All Taigs* . . .

Realizing who the taigs were, seeing everyone he knew actively celebrating the sentiment. Knowing, in his heart, that *he'd* probably celebrated it, too, a little bit . . .

A feeling that Irishness wasn't his – that it couldn't make room for him and that he shouldn't want it to, that it was a threat and a poison . . .

Mentally categorizing every single person he ever met, within minutes of meeting them. Feeling guilty, feeling wronged, choosing what way he walked home . . .

On reflection, Robbie supposed he wouldn't describe any of these things as *normal*, per se. But he didn't necessarily consider them *traumatizing* either. He didn't consider them the most important things about him. He outright refused to let them be.

Sitting on the couch with Anna-Caire, flipping channels, he couldn't get any of it out of his head, though. And he felt the need to apologize for what his father had said earlier.

She just shrugged. 'Well, I mean . . .'

'What?' he prodded.

'I mean . . . he's sort of right, though, isn't he? Whether it's the Irish language or the sports or whatever. Sure, it's all part of the bigger picture to them.'

'What do you mean?'

'A United Ireland. I know we're allegedly in the "post-conflict situation" now at home and all, and that's all very well. But their lot don't want Northern Ireland to work, do they? Not long-term. They want to destroy the Union, and then where will we be? All *our* culture and traditions – do you reckon the Irish are going to be making room for that? Not a chance. Sad to say it, but your daddy's right. We need to be looking after our own.'

Robbie practically felt the breath sucked from his chest.

He really did not want to live the rest of his life dictated by such a mindset; by the *us and them* of it all. That Anna-Claire – a person he could not excuse on the grounds of her generation – *did* seem inclined to . . . he simply had no clue where to go with that.

It was different from the faith she'd proven to be a bit more fervent about than he'd realized. Different, yet undeniably part of the same issue.

And so, he said nothing, stared at the television, his heart beating fast the whole time. *Location, Location, Location* was on.

'Oh, I've invited Lucy round for dinner tomorrow,' Anna-Claire mentioned idly, a few minutes later. 'You know, my friend from work, the Spanish teacher? She's had such a rubbish time with that guy, and I know school's been so stressful, too. I think she just deserves a bit of spoiling. I might make a strawberry cheesecake for afters.'

It was a lovely, thoughtful thing to say. It was his wife in her best possible light.

Meanwhile, Robbie barely knew Lucy. He had no idea what faith or political persuasion she was. He would bet Anna-Claire didn't either. That was the thing. It was possible, here, not to care.

Chapter Twenty-Seven

In LA, Katy Perry's 'I Kissed a Girl' was the song of the summer. Suddenly, it seemed that a lot of girls were indeed kissing girls – although El wasn't entirely sure how much they liked it. She suspected that what they liked, more so, was the sense of themselves as outliers: as a little bit edgy, but in an open-minded, chilled sort of way.

It was hard not to wonder whether she, herself, was such a girl. Kat had certainly seemed to think so.

By way of investigation, El set about dating as many people in LA as she possibly could.

That turned out to be a lot of people. It was easy. People asked her out all the time.

Or rather, men asked her out all the time. At The Avalon, in coffee shops – one guy asked her out in the cheese aisle of a Trader Joe's. For real. It was the sort of thing that would simply never, ever have happened in the Hackney Road Tesco Express.

With women, things were more akin to how they'd been in the UK. In other words, El had to make a little more effort to find potential dates – she had to make it a little more clear she was interested in *that way*. But it was nothing a quick drive to The Palms bar and a notoriously flirtatious natural manner couldn't sort.

It felt fun, leaning into that part of life again. It felt fun just to be *on the lookout*, just to have someone to fancy.

With Sandy Bowen, an aspiring dermatologist from Michigan, she toured the Hollywood Forever cemetery.

'I really think this is what Judy Garland would have wanted for us,' Sandy assured her, as they kissed furiously by Judy's final resting place.

With Eleanor Perry, a model from the Czech Republic, El went out to Santa Monica and rode the Ferris wheel.

'Do you think it is a problem that your name is El and my name is *also* El?' asked Eleanor, when they got to the top and should have been taking in the view of the Pacific.

El curled one hand gently around the other girl's thigh. 'I suppose that depends. If I said, "Hey, El, do you mind if I put my tongue in your mouth?" would you know who I was talking to?'

With Nate Garcia, a guy she met at The Comedy Store and about whom she knew literally nothing beyond that he made her laugh much more than the comic on stage, El drove up into the Canyons after midnight, both of them stripping off their clothes and diving straight into the infinity pool in Nate's backyard.

The whole endeavour was, overall, a fantastic way to see the city. And it confirmed for El something she'd already known, deep down: that whether the other party was male or female wasn't a determining factor for her. It was irrelevant, really, when it came to the key questions of how much she enjoyed their company or how much she might want to see them naked.

Maybe, overall, there were more women in the mix than men. That wasn't a matter of policy, though. It was just the natural consequence of the overall landscape. Could she help it if women, generally, tended to be more beautiful, less annoying?

In any case, nobody, whether male or female, stuck around for too long. El kept things loose. Breezy. LA's low-stakes, high-volume dating culture – the same one she sympathized about with other girls in The Avalon on a nightly basis – actually suited her down to the ground.

Of course, on a purely practical level, there was never a question of bringing someone she was dating back to her own bed, on account of Frankie already being in it.

One night, she and Frankie had been out at the Troubadour to hear Imogen Heap playing. They returned home on foot afterwards, having their usual congratulatory conversation about the unparalleled walkability of their apartment. It was, they agreed, practically European.

When they got in, El made short work of brushing her teeth and putting on her pyjamas. Meanwhile, Frankie stood at the sink in their en-suite bathroom and painstakingly removed every scrap of make-up from her face. She wore make-up now. A series of various serums and creams followed.

From bed, in the yellowy glow of their night lights, El watched the whole routine in silence. There was something soothing about it, but something sad about it at the same time. Gone were the days of Frankie's Nivea and ChapStick.

'Gotta take care of the money-maker, you know?' Frankie said, by way of explanation, when eventually she climbed into bed herself.

El sighed, as though the whole thing were a great inconvenience to her. 'I suppose so. Will you remember me when you're a big-time actress?'

'No.'

El stretched out a foot to jab sharply at Frankie's calf.

She yelped in response. 'Kidding! Kidding. Of course I will.' Something in her softened. 'I wouldn't even be here if it weren't for you.'

'Of course you would. You told me the day I met you that you wanted to come to LA.'

'Wanting something and *doing it*, though – I know you think those two things are the same, but they aren't for everybody.'

'Well, you can thank me in your Oscars speech – either first or last, please, so it makes an impact – and we'll call it even.'

'I'll do you one better. If I get nominated for an Oscar, you'll be my date, and we'll walk the red carpet together and rate all the other actresses on a one-to-ten scale. In terms of their skin, not their acting ability.'

El laughed out loud. They were lying facing each other, which was unusual. Nightly pillow talk wasn't part of their set-up. With Frankie's new filming schedule, they barely even had to share the bed at the same time anymore.

'I'm so happy I met you,' Frankie said, and with that, she surged forwards to press a kiss to El's lips.

El kissed her back, because why not? It was a sweet, fun thing. They were tipsy, they loved each other.

When Frankie pulled away, she regarded El for a moment.

She scrunched up her face, not in disgust or embarrassment or anything close. It was just goofy. It was Frankie.

'No,' she said, with a little laugh.

El smiled, too. 'No,' she agreed – the beginning and end of the discussion.

'At least we can say we tried it, eh?' El continued.

'Right. And to be clear, you're very good,' Frankie said. 'I mean, *excellent*. I would recommend you to a friend.'

Shortly afterwards, by the craft services table on the set of *Bitten: Part 1*, Frankie did just that.

Chapter Twenty-Eight

Robbie and Otto stood together on Epworth Street, with the first chill of autumn in the air, and watched the artist at work. Once he was gone, they lingered a little longer, taking in the results. On the door of Love and Death, in white paint, half a heart now melted into half a skull.

'I really like it,' Robbie exclaimed.

Otto said nothing.

It had taken some time to convince him of the merits of a sign. Not an explicit one, of course. Robbie was pretty sure that were he ever to see the words *Love and Death* pasted above the door of 45 Epworth Street, Otto would simply evaporate, explode, or otherwise cease to exist. He could agree to some kind of insignia, though. A small one.

And really, it had to be done. So many more people now knew about this once-secret bar. They'd told their friends about it; they'd described in broad and often inaccurate terms how to get there. People were coming from other countries, even – deliberately making it a part of their trip to London. In turn, the complaints from the neighbours had become too frequent to ignore. Prospective customers were apparently nearly banging the doors of nearby properties down. When they received no response, they assumed it was all part of the hazing process and banged all the harder.

'You'll have to talk to him,' Cormac told Robbie eventually.

As an interlocutor, an Otto-whisperer, Robbie sometimes

feared he was still nowhere near as good as El had been in the role. Nonetheless, of the remaining staff, he was the clear candidate.

'Honestly,' Robbie tried again now. 'It looks great.'

Otto just sighed, shaking his head a little. 'Fucking television,' he muttered, and walked inside.

Everything changed when Lehman Brothers went bankrupt. Northern Rock – what had seemed like one badly managed bank – was suddenly the tip of the iceberg. In one fell swoop, the entire world banking system was apparently on the brink of collapse.

That sounded dramatic, but somehow it seemed to be true. On the evening news, experts were ashen-faced. Robbie watched people queueing up outside cash machines all over London and felt the panic wash over him like a wave. It was almost surreal.

For the first time, when he imagined his alternate Citibank self, the notion didn't conjure images of certainty and success. He could, he realized, very easily be one of those guys he now saw on the tube – the ones carrying tell-tale cardboard boxes.

Not that bar work was exactly recession-proof, of course.

Frighteningly quickly, those queues snaking all the way down Epworth Street became a thing of the past.

But week after week, month after month, the doors at Love and Death did at least stay open.

'We'll just . . . ride it out,' Otto told the staff, even as costs rose and interest rates were cut to the bone – even as, all across the country, the spectre of bankruptcy and redundancy loomed ever larger. The 'credit crunch' seemed like vastly too cute a term for what was happening.

According to the papers, in the first half of 2009, the UK had seen fifty-two pub closures a week.

'There's a guy at the *Guardian* who's writing an article on hospitality businesses that have managed to survive the recession,' Robbie told Otto. *So far,* he added in his own mind.

He would never have uttered that bit aloud, though. It still felt like everyone at Love and Death was just holding their breath, afraid to tempt fate.

'Oh?' Otto replied, slightly absently.

'Actually, he also mentioned this other thing – sounded kind of interesting. It's like a new ranking system that's being started for cocktail bars, globally. Part of helping the industry get back on its feet and all.'

Otto's ears seemed to prick up. '*Globally*?' he said. 'Who's running it? As in, who's doing the ranking?'

'I don't know. I could find out?' Robbie offered. 'Anyway, the *Guardian* guy was wondering if you could give a comment for the article. Anonymously, if you want, of course.'

'Comment on what? Give me a specific question.'

'Well, I think it's basically: "How have you guys stayed open when loads of other places have closed? What's the secret?"'

Frankly, Robbie had wondered that himself. He wouldn't have entirely ruled out that they were actually in very deep shit and Otto had decided to simply ignore it, like those musicians on the *Titanic* who played jigs and reels until the very end.

Across from him, Otto cocked an eyebrow. 'Thank God for television,' he said grimly.

Meanwhile, across the Atlantic, El felt richer than she'd ever been. By the standards of many people in West Hollywood, she knew her earnings would still seem like a pittance. But she was bringing in more than she ever had – $500 a night in tips, easy. She and Frankie had at last swapped their tiny apartment for a bigger place.

Little more than a mile away from it, the Chateau Marmont sat tucked into a corner plot of Sunset Boulevard, its white facade and grey turrets rising above lush surrounding greenery. Originally an apartment building, it had been converted to a hotel in the aftermath of the Great Depression, with a series of bungalows, swimming pools, and terraces springing up around the main structure. The place was described frequently as 'discreet', notwithstanding its grandeur, its styling as a literal castle, and the fact that everyone seemed to know so much about the drama and hijinks that had gone down there over the years.

F. Scott Fitzgerald had apparently had a heart attack on the premises back in the 1930s. In the Forties, Howard Hughes held notorious 'viewing parties' from the penthouse, binoculars whipped out to spy on girls sunbathing by the pool below.

1958 saw Bette Davis almost burn the whole place down, and by the Sixties, members of Led Zeppelin were riding their motorcycles through the lobby. Much more recently, Brittany Spears had been spectacularly evicted from the restaurant – El was devastated to have only just missed that one playing out.

She adored the place.

People who said LA didn't have any history . . . as far as El was concerned, it was packed full of the only sort of history she really cared about. Surely the only sort *anybody* really cared about, deep down. She felt it all around her, and nowhere more than at the Chateau – that sense of glamour and danger, of all the madness and mistake-making that this town had sanctified.

By the tail end of 2009, she was a Chateau regular. The bartenders there gave her what she always tried to give her own customers – in other words, exactly what the energy and context of an evening required. At times, that meant comfort, familiarity, some sameness in a world that could otherwise feel constantly in flux. Other times, it was about a sense of excitement and unpredictability, a sense of *possibility*.

One particular possibility, El always managed to decline, even on her wildest LA nights. It was sometimes very, very difficult to do, now that opportunities were so plentiful.

And the thing was, El knew that she'd so easily be able to get it back: the exciting, recreational aspect of drugs – the aspect that for her, to begin with, hadn't been about being sad or anxious or exhausted or plain pissed off. It had just been fun.

She wasn't so confident she'd be able to *keep* things that way, though. And she didn't want to risk it. She didn't want to end up back on her mother's couch.

That was nothing against Anaheim. It really wasn't.

One night, at the Chateau, El looked around at her new group of friends – maybe eight people in all – and thought specifically of her mother in Anaheim: of Darleen's sense of achievement, her pride in having built her life there from scratch. El understood that completely now.

From the squishy sofa she was all but sinking into, she called out above the surrounding chatter. 'Alright, everybody tell me your orders! I'm going to go to the bar.'

Beside her, Jason frowned. 'Isn't it table service?'

'No, I know, but if I—'

On her other side, Frankie interrupted, all amusement. 'If El goes to the bar, she'll be sure to order from *Kacey*, because *Kacey* always gives her drinks for free, is what she was going to say.'

'I see,' said Jason, in such a way as to make clear that he didn't mind that idea – the free drinks, but also the larger intimation – one bit. He liked it, if anything.

El just rolled her eyes a little in response, then went around the group to take everyone's orders.

When she was done, Jason tugged her back down towards him, brushing a kiss against her lips. He was great at that.

'Say hi from me, won't you?' he called after her as she went.

El turned, with a little laugh. 'I don't even know if she's on tonight!'

In fact, she barely knew what night it was. At last, she'd achieved what had always felt, to her, like the most aspirational possible lifestyle – one in which she had very little concept of a weekend. Rather, her whole existence – seven days a week – seemed now to be comprised of opportunities to stay out late or try a new taco place or go see a movie. She said that these days – *go see a movie*. After two years in the city, she'd learned the rules of tipping (double the first digit) and often heard herself ask friends whether they wanted to *grab a bite*. She complained about the traffic, she never went to the beach, and she was on nodding terms with Mischa Barton, having seen her twice at The Avalon and at least twelve times at the Kitson boutique on Robertson Boulevard.

She couldn't help but wonder whether this was just the way she was really supposed to have been, all along: an American girl. Everywhere she looked, there seemed to be points of difference between London and Los Angeles. It was the warren of Soho streets, navigating by mnemonic – *Going For Dinner With Billie Piper* – versus zooming down the 405, swinging onto her exit when the TomTom told her to. It was the teal-velvet intimacy of Love and Death versus The Avalon, all space and light.

Most of the time, London seemed to come out of the comparison looking a little restrained and stuffy – like old money. And new money was just more fun – everyone knew that really.

Now, when El got to the bar, she looked around for Kacey – or, for that matter, Jonathan. He also comped her a lot, in return for drinks on the house at The Avalon and someone with whom he could discuss his new favourite TV show, *The Real Housewives of Orange County*, in his desired level of detail.

She couldn't see either of them, though. There were two guys with their backs to her, both of them busy scooping, shaking, slicing – all the usual choreography of bartending.

Then, they turned.

And El would have sworn she felt her heart stop in her chest. The prospect of a round of free drinks evaporated in a flash.

Because before her were indeed two faces she recognized. They just weren't at all the ones she'd expected.

Chapter Twenty-Nine

'Oh my God! What are you doing here?' El exclaimed.

For a moment, there was only silence.

'We're doing a "pop-up",' Robbie replied then.

El had never heard the term before. However, when she looked to the side of the bar, she could see a roller banner. It read:

Chateaux Marmont x Love and Death
One night only
Mixologists from London's premier cocktail bar
Inventors of the Citi Slicker, as featured on hit TV show BST

That last sentence hit her like a physical blow. El tried to ignore it, tried to ignore the hurt and anger that was coursing through her, suddenly every bit as potent as it had ever been.

If there was any satisfaction to be had, it was perhaps that – on the other side of the bar – Otto and Robbie looked every bit as shocked to see her as she was to see them. And ultimately, this was her turf. She at least got to choose her own exit this time.

'Cool. Well. Great,' she chirped. 'Nice to see you.'

And with that, she turned on her heel to go. Much more than being what she actually wanted to do, it felt like a power move in the moment.

'Wait!' Otto called out after her.

She turned around once more. She felt something stir inside her, suddenly sure that this was it: the conversation she'd imagined in her head during the worst weeks in Anaheim was about to materialize. He was going to say he was sorry – or something else ridiculous, like that he loved her and he'd missed her.

For what felt like a long moment, the two of them just looked at each other. She could feel tears threatening, just at the thought of what was to come.

And then, at last, Otto spoke. 'Didn't you want to order something?' he asked her. 'What can I get you?'

Just like that. As if she were any other customer.

Years later, El would wonder if it had been an olive branch. She would learn the term 'love language' and think that maybe this was Otto's. At the time, the thought didn't occur to her. She felt only the coldness, the callousness of his words. Swiftly, she blinked back her tears before they could be seen.

There was, she knew, another bar just upstairs. It was for residents, really, and other VIPS, but in the circumstances, she was inclined to take her chances. If there was one thing she'd always felt great about, it was her wangling capabilities.

'No,' she said softly, looking Otto directly in the eye. 'I don't want anything from you anymore.'

Afterwards, El wished she was cool enough to go about her evening without giving Otto and Robbie a second thought. She was certainly cool enough to look like that was what she was doing, which was something.

Even as she let herself fold back into her group, though – even as she distributed a tray of drinks and laughed and chatted – the annoying thing was that she still wanted to talk to Otto. Desperately. The way he'd just treated her – *again* – did nothing to dampen that urge. She wanted to talk to him about LA, about the various similarities and differences she'd discovered between

American and British drinks culture. That was, after all, one of his very favourite topics, too. She wanted to tell him all the ways she'd found him to be right and all the ways she'd found him to be dead wrong.

She wanted to talk to him, especially, about this very place – the Chateau Marmont. She knew that Otto would love it here as much as she did. Love and Death struck her as its little sister in spirit – someday, she suspected it might have something of the same longevity, the same mythology, that the Chateau had. It would occupy a similar place in individual memory and collective imagination.

In another world, it was her and Otto behind the bar right now, not Robbie and Otto: Otto's eyes were alight with enthusiasm, and he was saying, 'Look around you, kid. Like I said, LA is a cesspit, but this right here is a jewel in the midst of it. You know why? This place is about good drinks, sure – fucking excellent, world-class drinks. But it's also about good stories.'

It was agonizing to find herself so very close to that, to almost feel the warm glow of it, and yet be so far away from it. Suddenly, her place among her friends – which had started off feeling completely right, this evening – now felt altogether wrong.

As for Robbie, the truth was that El wanted to talk to him, too. Much as she hated to admit it, there were few people she'd ever found more intriguing than the one who, she knew, had never spent a single second of his life trying to pique her interest.

'Is it me, or is that bartender, like, very hot?' Frankie asked her.

And El had no choice but to turn back towards the bar, watch surreptitiously as Robbie shook a drink. The particular way he was doing it was startling to her. He used to always keep his elbows close to his body, his expression steady, as though he might perhaps have been counting in his head. There'd been no performance to it. She could see now that in the time they'd been apart, he'd become a little looser about the whole thing.

Sexier. That wasn't a subjective judgement; it was just an objective fact.

He had also let his hair grow out a little. He'd lost the glasses. It was almost comedic, the difference those things seemed to make. He was suddenly the nerdy main character in every teen movie El had ever seen, the same ones she'd mocked mercilessly for their lack of realism. And yet, here was Robbie Saunders, very evidently in his second act. A bona fide babe. She wondered if he knew it. He must have done – at least a little, even if he pretended not to.

In any case, she turned to Frankie, draining her glass. She wasn't sure, at this point, how many glasses she'd had already tonight. Whatever the number was, it suddenly didn't feel like close to enough.

'Bad news. He's married.'

'Like, very married?' Frankie asked.

El chuckled wryly. 'The most married.'

'Do you think she's living here now, then?' Robbie asked Otto. He was a live wire, his mind and body all nervous energy. Being here – in *Hollywood*, in a place with *paparazzi* outside – was crazy enough, never mind El Tippett turning up in the middle of it all. Immediately, the three years since she'd walked out of Love and Death felt like it might as well have been three days.

Meanwhile, Otto was lifting crystallized rose petals from a jar with a pair of tiny tongs. 'I don't know,' he replied, placing a few of the petals gingerly onto a pale-pink drink. 'I gotta say, I'm not a hundred per cent confident these have been dried properly. I hope they don't just wilt in the glass.'

Robbie barely glanced at them. 'I suppose she could be just on holiday,' he continued.

'It's possible.'

'I don't know, though – I think it kind of looks like she lives here. Don't you think so?'

Beside him, this time, Otto sighed audibly. 'I don't know, Robbie. I'm *working*. As are you, I might add.'

Robbie didn't buy that for a second. Hadn't he just watched as Otto muddled a handful of mint within an inch of its life? He'd have released the bitter-tasting chlorophyll – a rookie error – but he hadn't seemed to notice. Before that, he'd sent out two Cynar Juleps that, in Robbie's humble opinion, looked positively over-diluted.

The sight of El had clearly left him reeling. He'd seemed utterly shell-shocked throughout the entire course of that brief conversation with her. After she'd turned to go, for a moment Robbie had actually thought Otto might leap over the bar and chase after her.

He hadn't, though. Instead, with a quiet, deep breath, he'd recomposed himself, turned away. Since then, he'd all-too-deliberately avoided so much as a glance in her direction.

Robbie felt no such reluctance. He let himself stare across the room, studying her once more. Alas, all he had to go on was the back of her head – her side profile, sometimes, as she moved.

The room they were in was a large, Spanish-style space – more comfortable and less glossy than he might have imagined a hotspot like the Chateau Marmont would be. In a huddle of three plush couches, El was surrounded by people. The man and woman between whom she was sandwiched were both angled towards her, evidently entirely engaged in whatever story she was telling. The woman let out a squeal of laughter. The man put his hand casually on El's knee, and she didn't move it away. Robbie felt slightly sorry for the poor sod. Almost certainly, he was currently ascribing a meaning to this gesture that El wasn't remotely intending.

In any case, yes. As far as Robbie could tell, she certainly seemed pretty well established here. It prompted a peculiar pang of sadness in him, to see her having moved on so thoroughly, when she was still so much missed at Love and Death. Though Robbie had no real experience in the matter, he imagined the sensation might be akin to seeing one's ex, now happily coupled up with a different guy.

At the same time, though, who knew? This was El, after all. It was equally possible she was just passing through here. She might well have met this whole group of people mere hours previously. Making friends with everyone that wasn't him had always been one of her special skills.

Chapter Thirty

It was late – the middle of the night, really, though it didn't feel like it in the Chateau Marmont's courtyard. Candles were twinkling; cicadas were buzzing. The whole place was relaxed chatter and warm night air. Robbie was on his break, and he didn't know what El was doing out there, what had taken her away from her friends. He'd watched her step out the French doors, though, and he was following before he knew it.

Leaving tonight without talking to her again, he'd decided, was simply out of the question. That was all there was to it.

She stopped when she saw him, and for a second, she just looked at him, as though she, too, felt a sense of inevitability about this meeting. 'Hey, Robbie.'

'How are you, El?' he replied. 'Poured any drinks over anybody recently?'

She cocked an eyebrow. 'Every night at midnight. It's my party piece.'

He smiled a little. 'And there I thought I was special.'

She smiled a little, too. He took her in, up close. She wasn't as thin as she'd been the last time he saw her, and she looked a million times better for it. She still had the long hair. She was in a dress he'd seen before, although in London she'd always worn it with – he remembered this – an insane amount of jumpers: at least three thin layers on top of one another, when it had always seemed to him that just one proper winter woolly would surely have done the job. Underneath, that dress turned out to have delicate straps at the shoulder, its floaty material falling almost to the ground. She was barefoot.

'Seriously, you look well,' he continued. 'Are you well?'

She rolled her eyes. 'Well, you know me, Robbie. As soon as things wrap up here, I'll head on down to Skid Row, shoot up whatever's lying around.'

He didn't laugh, didn't respond at all.

'I'm . . . not doing that stuff anymore,' she muttered then, like a child forced into honesty.

Something Robbie could only characterize as relief flooded through him. 'Do you feel better for it?' he asked.

'Sometimes I feel a lot worse,' she retorted.

He took that as a *yes*.

'So, I see you stayed then,' she said, after a moment. 'At Love and Death. I knew you would.'

'*I* didn't know I would,' he countered.

'So, why are you here – really? Last I remember, international field trips weren't part of the gig.'

'Have you heard they're starting this list? The World's 50 Best Bars. It's going to be like an annual ranking. Getting on it would be like getting a Michelin star apparently.'

'Who votes for it?'

'This thing called "the Academy". I think there are like five hundred members from around the world, all hand-picked. Otto's been selected for it, obviously. Anyway, who knows if the whole thing'll take off. But if you want to be highly ranked, there seems to be a bit of winning friends and influencing people involved. That's why we're here, really. We're going to a place in San Francisco after this, plus Amsterdam and Copenhagen. Just a few nights each.'

El took that in, raised an eyebrow. 'Looks like it's good to be *inventors of the Citi Slicker, as featured on BST*, eh?' she said coolly.

Robbie wasn't sure what to say in response. Thus, he said nothing. Instead, he let his eyes drift back through the glass doors, towards where she'd been sitting. From this angle, he could see her friends more clearly. He could see their faces.

'Oh my God!' he exclaimed. 'Is that . . . ?'

Following his gaze, El smiled proudly. She couldn't seem to help it, her irritation all but forgotten. 'Yeah.'

'As in, from . . .'

'Yeah.'

Suddenly, the presence of the paparazzi Robbie had spotted on the way into the Chateau began to make a lot more sense. Still, some part of his brain struggled to compute. It was incredibly bizarre to see the features he'd seen on so many buses suddenly show up in front of him, human-sized.

Francesca Magliano was in the biggest movie of the year. People were obsessed by *Bitten: Part 1*. They were going to see it in their droves, and multiple times at that. Even Otto – a man who'd once told Robbie that his favourite film was *Les Quatre Cents Coups* by François Truffaut – seemed to be quite taken with it. He'd recently added a new cocktail – the Bloodsucker – to the menu in tribute.

As Robbie stared, he saw that Francesca's wasn't the only familiar face in this group. Her co-star from the film, Jason Parker, was in the mix, too. They were, he realized, the man and woman who'd surrounded El all evening, practically competing for her attention.

He almost chuckled out loud, putting those pieces together. Francesca Magliano was a literal film star. On screen, Jason Parker (himself a literal film star) had looked at Francesca like the sun shone from her, like all he wanted was to be near her, like he would, if the plot demanded it, risk everything he'd ever loved in order to touch her.

And yet, in real life, it seemed that neither of them would give each other a second glance if El was in the vicinity.

'I wouldn't have thought you'd be into vampires,' El said then.

'Anna-Claire is,' he replied. And now that he thought about it, yes, that did seem a little surprising. He wondered if she considered it a guilty pleasure or just a pleasure. He wondered what, precisely, was pleasurable to his wife about the concept of an eternally young high-school student wanting to suck a girl's blood. There seemed a fair bit to unpack there, though somehow, he doubted they would ever be unpacking it together.

El's expression shifted, became something warmer. 'Anna-Claire's so great. How *is* she?'

'She's fine,' Robbie replied. He didn't particularly want to talk about her right now. 'So, how long have you been living in LA?'

'A while.'

'And you're still in the industry?'

She nodded. 'I work at a bar near here. It's pretty amazing, actually. Just great drinks, no drama. I mean, who knows where we'll rank on . . . what did you say it was called? The World's 50 Best Bars? I don't think we've entered. But in any case, there are far fewer people taking credit for my ideas on an international scale, you know?'

This time, there was nothing – no more celebrity sightings – to distract from the issue.

'Can I just ask you something?' she continued. 'This might be the last time we ever see each other, so I have to at least ask. Don't you ever feel guilty? For taking the credit?'

'I've never taken the credit,' he replied. Even as he said it, some part of him wondered if it was completely true. It had certainly started off being true. He just wasn't entirely sure it had stayed that way. Hadn't his own star risen – not merely the bar's, but *his* – thanks to the association with El's drink? Hadn't he let that happen, one demo and PR invitation after another? Still, he shrugged off the discomfort, stuck to his guns. 'If you want to have this conversation with Otto, then go ahead and have it,' he said. 'It's obvious he's the one you're actually angry with.'

'Well, Otto's not here, is he?'

'He's pretty close to here, El. He's *steps away from here*. My God, the pair of you really are as bad as each other.'

All at once, El was done with chit-chat, done with civility. 'As bad as each other?' she repeated, aghast. 'I came up with the thing you two are now hawking round the world! I worked on it for months! Not inspired in any way by you, I might add! And now I have to serve it ten times a night, and I never even get to clai—'

She was just finding her flow when he interrupted her, his whole face springing into animation. Even in her fury, she was somewhat satisfied to see it. Something in her had always liked provoking Robbie Saunders, and she still had no idea why.

'For Christ's sake, El, it's an Old Fashioned!' he exclaimed. 'The Citi Slicker, I mean. It's a version of an Old Fashioned – a drink that, okay, is a lot less popular than it used to be, but that's been around since 1895. Which you would know if you'd ever read so much as one book on the thing you've decided to make your whole life's work.' He paused for breath, but evidently he was nowhere near finished. 'You added a bit of maple syrup, essentially, and called it something else, and that's grand. Guess what, that's the name of this whole fucking game. That's what we're pretty much all doing, generation after generation. That's cocktails. But spare us any more of this self-righteous bullshit, will you?'

El was stunned. Again, though, there remained that thread of simultaneous delight. She loved hearing him swear.

'Also! Just as an FYI, there's no *owning* a drink,' he continued. 'Or there's no money in owning it, at least. You can't copyright a recipe – the only money you can make is from making it and serving it to a paying customer, same as you could with any other drink you *didn't* invent.'

'Don't you think that's unfair?' El asked.

Robbie shrugged. 'I think that's how it is. And does it even really matter who came up with something? Or, like, does it matter if we know their name? Surely the whole point of creating something is for it to speak for itself. I mean, who designed the Empire State Building? I have no idea. Does that mean I like it any less than the Eiffel Tower?'

In another discussion, at another time, El might have reflected upon that – might have considered that it was quite an interesting point. But in the moment, she wasn't keen to apply the principle to her personal situation.

'Well, if you're asking me whether I'd rather be Gustave Eiffel or that other guy, then I know which one I'd choose! Why don't *you* come up with something, watch all the credit get stolen from you, and then see how you feel about it.'

'Honestly, El – and I swear to you I mean this – I don't think I'd care.'

She looked at him for a moment, then sighed. 'I don't understand how you can be so . . . passive,' she said, more quietly now.

'I'm not passive. I'm just . . . I don't know. Maybe it's the way I grew up. Maybe keeping the peace matters a bit more to me than it does to other people. Maybe . . . and to be honest, I think this might be it . . . maybe I just have a slightly more developed sense of what an *actual* problem is.'

At once, she was irritated anew. 'Oh, okay, Robbie. I forgot for seven seconds that you're from Northern Ireland,' she scoffed. 'Talk about self-righteousness! And, by the way, of *course* there's money in being the creator of a drink that takes off. I mean, maybe not directly – but what do you think makes the top places phone you up and offer you a job? What do you think influences what they want to pay you? Why do you think the Chateau Marmont wants to parade you and Otto in front of its customers tonight? All of that is about reputation. It's about influence. And if you don't think those things equate to money, in one way or another, then I don't know what to tell you. For a smart person, you can be a complete idiot sometimes.'

It seemed like a good moment to take her leave. As she swept past him, though, he reached out to stop her.

And of course, they used to touch all the time. There was a certain familiarity, behind a bar. All night long, people reached over each other and squeezed past one another. Touch was not charged.

El looked down at Robbie's hand, curled around her wrist now, and he looked down, too. He seemed to take in her tattoo, that tiny cluster of birds she'd kept everyone guessing about, back when she'd first got it. For a few seconds too long, neither of them said a word.

El didn't know how to characterize the sensation that had suddenly zipped through her. She certainly didn't know how to explain it.

'We've missed you, you know. *I've* missed you,' Robbie said, as their eyes darted back up towards one another's.

Suddenly, El wasn't at all sure what was happening here. From his wide-eyed expression, like a deer in the headlights, Robbie wasn't either. He cleared his throat and released her wrist.

Then, with something that felt much more like panic than she would have liked it to, El was gone.

Part Four

Chapter Thirty-One

El created a Facebook account because it got to a point where everyone she knew had Facebook. In what seemed like no time at all, the website had swiftly become the place where plans were made and memories were logged. She had no choice but to get involved.

One morning, she was lying in bed with her laptop, sun streaming in through the windows, when she spotted Robbie's name under *People You May Know*.

It had been months since that night in the Chateau, after which they'd immediately reverted to having zero contact. Now, though, she found herself feeling spontaneous. And she was curious. That was probably the greater truth of why she clicked on the button beside his name. *Add Friend*. It would come, eventually, to seem like one of the most consequential decisions of her life.

Within an hour, Robbie accepted her request. Perhaps he saw it as some sort of an olive branch – El wasn't yet familiar with the politics, the inferences of these things – because almost immediately, his name also popped up in her 'private messages' inbox.

Feb 17, 2010

Robbie: Hey – thanks for the add. I'm sorry about LA. I know we left things kind of weirdly. I've been

> thinking a lot about it – and, actually, you have every right to be upset about the Citi Slicker. I don't know why I didn't just say that at the Chateau. It's your drink. We all know that, and we could have done a lot more to make sure other people did, too. The whole thing just exploded in ways none of us expected, but we could have handled it better. I know I could have. Anyway, I'm happy you seem to be doing so well out in America. If I'm ever back, I'll call into The Avalon. That Pisco Sour you made me the second time I came to L&D (I'm sure you don't even remember it) is probably still the best drink I've ever had in my life.

El reached the end of the message, staring at her screen dumbly for a moment. Then, with a jolt, she got typing. It was as though her fingers were moving of their own accord, the words flowing in one long paragraph. She laid it all out there. She re-litigated various details, fired off a barrage of questions, dotted in exclamation marks liberally. The whole thing took her thirty-five minutes.

When she was finished, she reread her own words back. And suddenly, hearing them aloud, the reality was so clear to her: if she wanted to create an impression of herself as *breezy and unbothered*, this was certainly not the way to do it. If she wanted to actually, properly, move on with her life – imagine that – then her tirade probably wouldn't be of much help there either. Hadn't Robbie apologized? Wasn't she happy now, in LA? Hadn't things, in the end, worked out more or less for the best? In any case, the past could not be changed.

She deleted her paragraph and started again.

Feb 17, 2010

> El: I remember it. And I'm sorry about LA, too.

*

216

Bartending friends! El posted on her Facebook Wall, a few weeks later. *For reasons we don't need to get into, I'm now in possession of a lot more Applejack than I thought I would be (like . . . a lot more). What can I make with this other than Pink Ladies?*

Underneath an array of other comments (most conveying a mixture of amusement, mockery, and sympathy) came Robbie's response.

Of course, he had some actual ideas. *Brandy Sangaree? Calvados Sidecar? Harvest Sour?*

El clicked the *like* button. It was only polite. A month or so later, she was back in his PMs.

Mar 12, 2010

> **El:** Success on the Calvados Sidecars btw! We're selling them like they're going out of fashion! Or, coming back into fashion, maybe?

Mar 13, 2010

> **Robbie:** Amazing!

Mar 14, 2010

> **El:** PS Congrats on the World's 50 Best Bars thing. (I saw the link Jamie posted a week or so back.)

> **Robbie:** Number 14's not bad, eh? Otto's obviously devastated.

> **El:** ahahahahaah

Robbie: I mean, we're the highest rated UK entry. I've personally almost killed myself to help make this happen. And he's acting like we should be holding a wake! Sorry. I probably shouldn't be complaining to you about this.

El: It's fine. In a way, I might be the best possible person for you to complain to about it.

Robbie: Actually, yeah. You could be right there.

El wasn't quite sure what to say in response to that. But as soon as she closed her laptop, she reached for her phone and called her line manager. She wanted to step things up, she told him, in terms of her contribution at The Avalon. Once upon a time, people had said she had a real knack for invention. And had he ever considered entering some competitions?

Magnanimity was one thing, she thought – halfway across the world, watching the sun set from the terrace of her boyfriend's Malibu beach house, El could manage a bit of magnanimity.

But if there was a game here – if Otto was playing it, if he was watching the participants, if he really cared about the outcome – then suddenly, she wanted to play, too.

April 27, 2010

Robbie: Hey have you seen this? Quite funny!

Next, he pasted the link to an online article entitled: 'Reasons Your Bartender Hates You'. El clicked on it with a chuckle. Her personal bugbear – people snapping their fingers at her – got a mention, along with various others she'd commiserated with friends and co-workers about for years.

Apr 28, 2010

El: Lol! I wonder who they interviewed for this piece? I can think of a few names.

May 7, 2010

Robbie: Do you remember Pierre-Alain and Mark? They're still regulars. Last night Pierre-Alain said to Sam – Sam's new – 'You are top; it is no offence to you, Sam, but still I hold El in my heart. I miss her as the bee misses the flower.'

May 10, 2010

El: Omg so French! He is the best. Actually, he would love the Cold Hot Chocolate. Have you heard of that? Came out of this bar in Chicago and now it just seems to be everywhere.

May 11, 2010

Robbie: I'll look forward to it being everywhere in London in about six months to a year in that case ;)

Things stayed in that realm, for a while. Work-related. Sporadic. It was the type of communication that would have never happened by text. After all, texting was expensive, especially internationally. It felt so much more deliberate, more intimate somehow.

On Facebook, a few weeks or a month could easily pass without contact between Robbie and El. They didn't even see one another's messages until the next time they happened to sit down at a laptop.

But then, every so often – increasingly often – a tidbit demanded to be shared. They could spend weeks tossing back and forth the merits and demerits of various methods of making some new drink (to double-strain, or not to? To flame the orange peel, or not to?). They certainly didn't always agree.

However, it turned out to be kind of nice: having someone to talk to – someone who cared every bit as much as they did. When it came to their shared passion, hadn't they always met and matched each other, in a way few others were able to? And without the heat of direct competition, it felt easier to be open, easier to be generous. Though neither Robbie nor El could have ever seen this coming, it seemed that outside of one another's physical presence, they were able to show their true selves. Or, their better selves, at least. Who was to say whether those were one and the same?

Chapter Thirty-Two

Aug 10, 2010

El: So, Robbie. You're a man of God. What's an appropriate gift for a child's baptism?

Robbie: Idk. I think a card is fine. Depends how well you know this baby.

El: Not well. I'm a mere plus one.

Robbie: Oh! Cool!

Are you seeing someone then?

El: I might be.

Robbie: That's great

Well who is it?

El: Do you know Jason Parker?

Robbie: The major film star? Yes I do.

You're not going out with him though, are you?

El: What's wrong with him?

Robbie: Well nothing. It's just he's . . . a man.

El: Yeah, and so?

Robbie: Nothing, I just thought . . .

El: Oh, I see what you thought!! You thought I was a LESBIAN . . .

Let's just say I'm all about the equal opportunities, Robbie.

Sitting in Starbucks on Shoreditch High Street, for the free Wi-Fi, Robbie read each sentence as it appeared – live – and felt the immediate drop in his stomach. It was irrational but undeniable. His eyes darted around self-consciously, as though other patrons would surely see the difference in him – would know that he was no longer just a guy killing time before the beginning of his shift. Instead, he was a guy frantically recalibrating, heat rising in his whole body.

He cast his mind back to seeing El and Jason together at the Chateau Marmont, to what he'd thought was Jason's unrequited crush. He couldn't explain why it was making him feel so foolish, so non-specifically *terrible*, to discover his mistake.

Because of course – *of course* – El Tippett was no more a person Robbie might date, or kiss, or have sex with than she ever had been. He was married. She lived all the way across the Atlantic, and then some. Most of their in-person relationship had involved uncovering new ways in which they were incompatible.

Maybe it was true, though, that human beings were just animals, really. Because in some unwanted, instinctive sort of way, this new information about El *did* make him see her slightly differently. There was a minuscule, entirely theoretical sliver of possibility, where previously there had been none. Another message popped up.

> **El:** I was in *People* magazine last week. Do you read that?

> **Robbie:** I don't. Should I start?

> **El:** I mean if you want to see pictures of me and Jason in Mexico, then yes.

For reasons he chose not to psychoanalyse any further, Robbie found that he did not.

After that, it felt like some sort of door had been cracked open – the door to a different, more personal, sort of interaction. By

2011, in a quick three-sentence exchange, they took things to the next level. WhatsApp.

Suddenly, Robbie and El each had data plans on their phones. Suddenly, they were in one another's pockets. Time zone wise, it worked. They were both pulling shifts at weird enough hours to make it extremely convenient, knowing someone on the other side of the world. When El was starting her shift at The Avalon, Robbie was hopping on a Boris bike after finishing up at Love and Death. By the time she was headed home for the night, he was pottering around an empty flat, fixing himself breakfast at lunchtime.

Jan 26, 2011

> **El:** So I had a great night in the end! Like, just one of those shifts where everything *glides* you know? Glorious. Collapsing in a heap now.

Feb 12, 2011

> **Robbie:** I've just got off the Central line, ten stops, without 'being held at a red signal' at any point. I've actually arrived at the predicted time. Is this a first?

Feb 18, 2011

> **El:** Have driven all the way to this shop in Eagle Rock because someone told me they had Maltesers in there, and now I'm here and THEY DON'T!

Feb 21, 2011

> **Robbie:** I think I'm getting the cold again. I swear I wish we could give people some kind of quick health check before they come in and just breathe all over us every night.

As with all their industry chat, there was nothing inherently private or scandalous about any of it. There was an argument that much of their communication was actually quite boring. The very mundanity of it, though – the minutiae, the degree of narration . . . in some ways, that was what was most important. Inside jokes were established; they came up with little games they liked to play.

Apr 3, 2011

> **El:** Bruce Willis. Century City Mall, coming out of an AllSaints. Held the door open for me – no eye contact, but I suppose that's understandable, he doesn't want to be mobbed by normies. 6/10.

May 15, 2011

> **Robbie:** Tulisa Contostavlos. Love and Death. Ordered a Cheeky Vimto, and I thought Otto was going to implode but actually he seemed to sort of respect it on a level. Like it was so bad it was almost good again kind of thing? 8/10.

> **El:** . . . Who the fuck is Tulisa Contostavlos?

Jun 7, 2011

> **El:** Johnny Depp. The Avalon. Seemed to want a degree of worship I could really only provide to Lady Gaga or a surviving Beatle. Or Kristin Scott Thomas. Good tipper though. 4/10.

There was something about staying in touch that simply became a question of habit. At a certain point, neither Robbie nor El could help it if, on the occasions their minds wandered, there was a certain place it went.

Jul 23, 2011

> **El:** Omg did you hear about Amy Winehouse? So sad. I'm honestly in shock.

> **Robbie:** I know. It's horrendous.

> **El:** Alcohol poisoning, apparently.

> **Robbie:** I used to see her around a lot.

> **El:** Did she come into Love and Death? I never saw her.

> **Robbie:** It was after you'd gone.

Reading that one, while she awaited Frankie outside a Pilates studio on Santa Monica Boulevard, El couldn't deny she felt slightly sucker-punched. There were times it still hurt – sometimes a lot – to think of Love and Death, of its continued existence without her. There were times she wanted nothing more than a grey sky and a rummage round Camden Market, before hopping on the tube to Epworth Street.

It made her wonder what on earth she and Robbie were doing. She wondered if their communication was, on her part, some sort of masochism. When Jason told her, entirely casually over brunch, that according to his therapist, she – *El* – was still living partially in the past, El had disagreed vociferously. Out loud, at least.

For his part, Robbie, too, often wondered what exactly was happening between him and El. It could just be so hard to reconcile the relationship they'd previously had with the one that seemed now to have developed. He wondered why he'd never told Otto about any of their communication. He wondered about the urge he felt, whenever Anna-Claire came into a room, to shove his phone back in his pocket and deny everything.

Thus, there were sometimes periods of silence.

There were times when Robbie and El each brushed against each other's sore spots, caught each other at the wrong moment, in the wrong mood. How surprising it was to learn that even a text relationship, across a long period, had its ups and downs like that. Tiny ones. Unspoken ones.

Always, though, they had the space to retreat, to course-correct. After a few days, they could return anew, ready to dance a while longer around the core questions: what do we owe each other, here? Is this a real thing? A significant thing? It was so difficult to know, with all the stuff that now happened on phones – difficult to know whether any of it was happening in real life.

Chapter Thirty-Three

Aug 23, 2011

> **El:** So you're in Belfast?

She'd seen the photos uploaded on Facebook, WhatsApped Robbie in response. There was some strange sense of kudos, merely in having that dual means of communication with a person – the one that was for everyone else, too, and the one that was private.

In all the pictures, Robbie and Anna-Claire were grinning happily, surrounded by a cross-generational bunch of friends and relatives. It was a version of family life – of community – that El had never had, and thus found herself fascinated by. Filming on *Bitten: Part 3* had recently been moved to Wyoming. Now deprived of both Frankie and Jason in Los Angeles, she was feeling plaintive.

Scrolling through one snapshot after another, she stared at Robbie, trying to put her finger on the ways he looked different from all the guys around him. Trendier, somehow. To hear him talk (and frankly, El could well believe it), as a kid he'd faced the exact opposite scenario. It was funny how things turned out.

Robbie: Yep. Just for a week. We're at my parents.' I think I might be about to totally lose my mind. I don't know how you lived with your mother for a year.

El: Well I was in the middle of a complete emotional breakdown, Robbie, plus a mid-level drug detox, so I didn't have a whole lot of options available to me.

Halfway through boiling the kettle in his mum and dad's little scullery kitchen, Robbie had his phone in one hand and snorted a laugh. He knew El well enough now to know that this was said tongue-in-cheek. She wasn't annoyed at him, and nor had she chosen this moment to confide her deepest emotional truths. She just wanted to amuse him.

Robbie: Ha! Fair enough, yes. The problem is there's no space. Anna-Claire's parents' place is better from that point of view, but there are other issues there.

El: Nice to be back in Belfast though? Domestic quibbles aside.

Robbie: Yeah, Anna-Claire loves it.

El: What about you? Do you love it?

Robbie hesitated. He enjoyed so much about being around his family. He loved that his wife was happy, that aspects of the . . .

strain he sometimes felt between them in London had all but dissipated. He wasn't sure how to say that, though. Talking too much about Anna-Claire, to El in particular, always felt wrong.

Instead, he strode the few paces towards the front of the house. Opening the camera on his phone, he snapped a quick picture out the window.

El raised an eyebrow when the image reached her. It was of a street bedecked in Union Jacks. She had honestly never *seen* so many Union Jacks. They were strung up between lampposts, emblazoned on the hats and T-shirts of people clustered around. Even the kerbstones were painted in red, white and blue. Down the middle of the street, what looked like a brass band was parading. They hadn't got the memo about the colours, though – they were in black, with orange sashes.

> **El:** Intense!

> **Robbie:** Marching season. We've actually missed the main parades etc (they were last month) so this is actually semi low-key by comparison.

El just waited. Though there was nothing on the app to confirm it, she suspected he was still typing away. She'd acquired a sense of when he wasn't finished.

> **Robbie:** I dunno. When I was a kid, all this was the highlight of my year. And even now, there are definitely really nice bits of it. But tbh, it also just feels like . . . is this all kind of mental? Plus then I feel massively disloyal for even thinking that. . .

Robbie: Anyway. New subject? How are you getting on without Frankie in the apartment? How's Jason?

El: Mmm. New subject?

Aug 29, 2011

El: I'm at the hospital

Robbie: What?! El. What happened? Are you okay?

El: Fender-bender.

Robbie: ARE YOU OKAY?

El: Fractured wrist. A few cuts and scratches. I think I'm going to move to Berlin.

Robbie: Berlin? Why?

El: Really good public transport ;)

That was how they did it, a lot of the time. They sidestepped the big stuff – or they approached it with the lightest of touches.

Little more than a month later, El was touching down at Schönefeld Airport.

Oct 1, 2011

> **El:** It's so cold !!! I really think if any born-and-bred Californian came here, they would just have to leave.

> **Robbie:** I take it Jason hasn't moved with you then?

> **El:** Why do you say that? You don't think he'd want to ditch his movie career and experience a German winter with me instead?

> (No. He hasn't.)

Every single person that El had ever slept with, she'd greeted effusively if she ever ran into them afterwards. *No harm, no foul*, she'd always thought. However, she doubted she'd feel the same about Jason, going forwards. It was a brand-new experience for her. Frankie said it was a human one – that even if it hurt, it would add to her 'emotional toolbox'.

On a break from filming, Frankie was presently two days into an 'immersive retreat' with a spiritual leader named Wren. El suspected she herself would literally rather check in to Wormwood Scrubs than spend a week with Wren.

Gradually, gaps like that had opened up between her and her friend.

The Pilates, El could get on board with. The macrobiotic diet, the coconut water, the cupping therapy . . . those things were just about okay, too.

But running a crystal – *dry* – across her underarms, ostensibly as a deodorant?

El sometimes thought back to the Frankie she'd met at The Tipsy Parrot, with her jean shorts and fresh face, and knew that girl would never even have entertained any of this bullshit. People changed, of course. Such was life. It was just a little sad, sometimes.

Hauling two suitcases into her Berlin apartment – a sparsely furnished, industrial-style loft she'd found online – El *let herself* be sad about that. And she let herself be a bit sad about Jason, too. Sad that he'd shagged his therapist and told her it was part of his *journey*. Sad that he'd specifically chosen to reveal this while she was driving down the 101. In her shock, she'd taken her foot off the pedal and swiftly found herself meeting the rear end of a delivery truck. The resulting medical bill was the icing on the cake. Really, was it any wonder she'd decided she'd had her fill of Los Angeles?

A few hours later, almost entirely unpacked now, she glanced down at her phone again.

Robbie: He was too good-looking anyway.

El: Too good-looking for me, you mean?

Charming!

Robbie: No, just too good-looking generally. He looked like he'd been put together in a lab – like, as if he was made up of bits of other men. Keanu Reeves's eyes, Brad Pitt's chin, etc. It was weird.

El: Lol!

In her new apartment, El truly did laugh out loud. It felt like a release, like a burst of hope. Things were going to be fine here, she decided. They were going to be *great*.

Nov 4, 2011

Robbie: I'm so desperate for a coffee, honestly, I don't know how much longer I can do this.

El: So don't! Just go back on it! Caffeine is not a vice, Robbie.

Robbie: I can't.

El: Why not?

Robbie: Just want to get a bit healthier, you know . . .

Anna-Claire and I are trying

El: !!!!

Also, too much information. Why must you *constantly* foist the details of your sex life on me?

I jest, I jest. That's great.

You'll be the best dad ever.

After that, any time his name flashed up on her phone, El was half-expecting the news: Baby Saunders, coming on such and such a date. Maybe there'd be a pair of booties or an ultrasound scan. She'd drafted the whole announcement in her head, composed her own response to it.

All through those first months in Berlin – even as she was diving headfirst into this new city, dancing, drinking, dating – some part of her was also *waiting*.

November became December became January, though. And . . . nothing.

Then came a night in February 2012. El was in Incognito. Her new workplace, located in a basement in Mitte, was aptly named. She often thought it would be a perfect place to have an affair or to otherwise go unrecognized. Every night, before her eyes adjusted, she could barely see a fucking thing.

It was a little grimy, but deliberately so. And the darkness – that was certainly deliberate, too. What little light there was came only in the form of discreet strips, tucked under other things – the metal artwork mounted on the walls, or the black skirting board that lined the perimeter of the space. The whole effect was tough, sleek, achingly cool.

Shortly after 4.30 a.m. on the night in question, El was still there, still serving. That was Berlin. When she saw Robbie's name flash up on her phone, it was no surprise at all. He was, by then, entirely part of the punctuation of her days and nights.

The message, though. The message almost made her drop her phone right into someone's Negroni.

Feb 6, 2012

Robbie: Can I ring you?

Chapter Thirty-Four

Robbie and Anna-Claire's place in Bermondsey, the one they could afford at market rate, was a lot less nice than their previous flat. By now, though, it was home. When Robbie got in the door that night, Anna-Claire was in her pyjamas, mug of tea in hand, the television playing on mute. It was after 3 a.m. Robbie could thus only conclude that his wife had been sitting there, with her own thoughts, for some time.

Given the way things had been lately, it was impossible to perceive this as anything but bad news. She looked over at him, her eyes seeming to scan every bit of him from head to toe.

'Hi,' she said simply.

'Hi,' he replied.

He'd had a couple of drinks, just to be sociable, after work. He wasn't drunk. However, as compared to her – a sober person – he suddenly felt like he was. He knew he'd smell of booze. She was fresh and clean and cosy, and he was the opposite of all that. It made him feel suddenly disgusting.

'You didn't have to wait up,' he said, though of course Anna-Claire knew that.

She never usually did anymore. Not even on Fridays or Saturdays when – it sometimes occurred to Robbie – maybe she *could*, even once in a while, for fun. In any case, this was a Tuesday night. His wife had school tomorrow and netball club after it.

The girls on wing attack were struggling, and the rest of the team was on the verge of staging a mutiny against them if they didn't shape up soon. It was all, Robbie knew, extremely fraught. Anna-Claire often needed two glasses of white wine on a Wednesday evening.

However, she seemed, for the moment, to have put all such concerns on the back burner. She had identified some bigger problems, perhaps.

'I thought this might be the only time I'd get to talk to you all week,' she said. 'You know, I never would have believed it, before you took the job at Love and Death . . .'

Robbie didn't interject, just awaited whatever was coming next.

'. . . how little it's possible to see someone and yet still be in relationship with them.'

He sighed heavily. 'I know. I'm sorry.'

'Did you ask about Saturday?'

Robbie winced. They were headed to Guildford for a friend's thirtieth in the afternoon. The prospect of staying overnight, making a weekend of it, had been mooted.

'Yeah. It's just tricky because Marcus is already out with – well, we don't know, some sort of gastro thing, and Otto sa—'

Anna-Claire held her hand up to stop him. 'It's fine,' she said tiredly. 'It was just a thought.'

'I'm sorry,' he repeated.

'Aren't you getting tired of saying that?'

'Aren't you getting tired of making me?'

The words just slipped out, and when they did, Robbie didn't even try to take them back.

'Can I ask you something?' he continued instead. 'I mean, since you're up.'

She gestured vaguely: *be my guest.*

'Do you actually want to live your life with me? *This* me.

237

'Cause this is the only one there is, Anna-Claire. There *is* no other Robbie. Or Robert. For years, I've imagined there was, too – some other version of me that went and became a banker. Or even a third or a fourth version – one who never went to Oxford, who stayed in Belfast or who fucking joined the circus or whatever.'

His wife balked at his language, but still Robbie didn't stop.

'That's all bullshit, though, in the end. None of those people actually exist. It's just me. Do you want to spend the next fifty years with *me*?'

Perhaps in a bid for parity, Anna-Claire leaped to her feet. 'We're married, Robert,' she replied, aghast. 'Of course that's what I want.'

If we weren't, though . . . would you still want it then?

The question was on the very tip of Robbie's tongue. But even in his current frame of mind, it felt like one question too many. He just wasn't sure what her answer would be, or where they could possibly go – together – from there.

'Okay. Well, then we have to figure out a way to make this work, don't we? Because sniping at each other or shuffling around in silence, not saying what we really mean . . . I'm not sure how well that's going.'

For a beat, Anna-Claire took that in. She offered a little nod. 'I want you to quit,' she said then.

Instinctively, Robbie chuckled a little, not in amusement but in confusion. 'What?'

'You're right: I can't expect you to be a mind-reader. So, I'm making it really clear to you – right here, right now. That's what I want. For you to find some other job as soon as humanly possible – I don't even care what it is, at this point. Just something that doesn't have you getting home in the middle of the night stinking of booze.'

'Oh, so Starbucks then? What about that? Or Debenhams?'

Anna-Claire huffed impatiently. 'Don't be ridiculous!'

'What's ridiculous about that?'

His wife was quiet.

'No, come on,' he prodded. 'If you're going to be a snob, you have to at least be prepared to be one out loud.'

'You have a first-class honours degree from Oxford. *Yes*, I think it would be ridiculous for you to work in a Starbucks. I'm sorry if you think that makes me an awful person, but that's what 99 per cent of the population would think.'

'What about working in a bar?'

'What do you mean?'

'Do you think *that's* ridiculous? Do you think that's beneath me? Beneath *you*? Let's talk about what this is really about, eh? Because I think your ma and da probably factor into all this somehow – as ever. I think all the people we'll see at the barbecue on Saturday probably do, too.'

By now, so many of their mutual friends had risen through the ranks at work, got on the property ladder, begun to collect Le Creuset. 'So, you're still at the bar, are you? As in . . . *full time*?' they'd ask Robbie, as though the subject required extreme discretion.

'I might point out that teaching doesn't exactly earn mega bucks either, you know!' Robbie told Anna-Claire now. 'What was the idea – I'd make the money so you wouldn't really have to?'

'Actually, yes! Yes! That was exactly the plan! And you knew it!' she exclaimed. Her voice was rising with every word, almost hysterically. He'd never seen her this way. 'If you're asking me whether I think you're capable of more than bar work,' she continued, 'then of course I do! If you're asking did I *expect* this turn of events, when we got together and you were talking to me all day long about Immanuel Kant . . . no, I didn't, *Robbie*.'

'So, what? I have to stay the exact same as I was when I was 18? That's not how life works, Anna-Claire! I don't think it's supposed to be how marriage works . . . is it? I love my job.'

She seemed to soften a little. 'I know you do,' she quietly. 'I know that. I just really think I've been more than supportive, and—'

'Oh, you're a real saint, yeah!' he interjected. 'Come on – you can't say there haven't been bits of this whole thing that you've enjoyed, too! You thought it was great, when I first decided to do that extra year at Love and Death. You *loved* that I was a bit different from every other Hooray Henry you could have picked. You told people like it was the best thing ever! And then when *BST* came out, when you used to come in with your teacher friends and they'd spend the whole night ogling the drinks – not to mention ogling the bartenders, let's be honest – you got a kick out of that. You liked feeling, for once in your life, a little bit cool.'

'*I* did? Or *you* did?'

'I *did*, yes!' he exclaimed. 'I'm not denying that I did. But I'm just saying that you did, too.'

'Okay, so I made the best of things! I tried to have a bit of fun with it, where I could. But fun can't last forever, can it? At some point, we have to get serious. I can't believe I have to say this to you, of all people! You were practically buying stocks and shares with your student loan! And now, when I actually need you to be a grown-up? I mean, for fuck's sake, how's it going to work once we're parents?'

Robbie was shocked.

Anna-Claire raised an eyebrow, slightly defiantly. 'What? We can all say some swear words, darling. Grow up.'

For a long moment, there was silence between them. The TV continued to play on mute in Robbie's peripheral vision, and he wanted to swat the images away like flies. He sat down on the sofa and leaned forwards, resting his elbows on his knees, his face in his hands. When he looked back up again, he exhaled a big breath through puffed out cheeks.

Anna-Claire sat down beside him, her knees against his. She

was, despite everything, so familiar to him. Her physical presence still felt so normal.

'I know you probably wish I'd never asked you to quit. That's fair enough,' she said. 'I wish I hadn't even had to ask.'

Robbie nodded. 'That's fair enough, too,' he replied.

He really didn't know where that left them, though. She didn't seem to, either.

'I'm going to go for a walk,' he said, sometime later. He couldn't have guessed at how long it had been, specifically. They might have sat there together for two minutes or twenty.

'Now?'

'Yeah, I just . . . need a minute, with all this. Is that fine?'

Anna-Claire shrugged, like she had no real choice in the matter. Robbie supposed she was probably correct on that one. Suddenly, he needed – with some urgency – to get out of this flat.

'Sure,' she replied. 'I'm . . . going to bed, I suppose.'

Robbie rose, grabbed his coat. He didn't slam the door as he went – even at their worst (and he was certain this evening was the low point of their entire relationship), he and Anna-Claire weren't door-slammers. Still, he felt the urge to do *something*. Something to get him out of his brain or out of his body. Sex, drugs, violence, rock and roll . . . all of these were unavailable to him. Instead, he settled for marching along Rotherhithe New Road, letting the wind whip at him. With no clear idea of where he was going, he sped up his pace until he was practically breathless. Then, he slowed right down, forced himself to take measured inhales and exhales. He didn't feel any better either way.

The fact remained that he was now facing a decision he had no idea how to make: to stay at Love and Death or to go?

Truthfully, he and Anna-Claire had probably been circling the issue for some time. The conversation they'd just had was one he'd begun to have in his own head with increasing frequency. He had it when he looked at his pay cheque. He had it every time he spoke with Anna-Claire's parents, underneath the brief chit-chat before he passed the phone over. Was he a failure? That was the fundamental question. So much of his young life had been geared towards never having to wonder. People who got A-stars in their exams were not failures.

These days, nobody was grading him any longer. It was probably just as well. Robbie suspected that, in more areas than one, he might fall very far short of an A-star.

He was almost at Southwark Park when he noticed he still had his coat in hand, and he was shivering. He pulled it on, looking up at the gates to the park. It was closed, of course. A dead end. All was quiet around him. London at night was often so much quieter than people expected.

Robbie didn't know what to do, either next or in general. What he needed, he realized in a flash, was to talk to someone. And yes, it was true that El Tippett was probably one of the only people he knew who would definitely be awake at this hour. But that had nothing to do with it, really.

Six hundred miles away, in Incognito, El stared at the message on her phone.

Robbie: Can I ring you?

Another one followed ten seconds later:

Robbie: It's about work.

She didn't know if that made things better or worse.

In any case, her phone started to ring immediately. Among all the normal noise and debauchery of her working night, she looked at the device as though it was an unexploded bomb. In their entire history of digital correspondence, she and Robbie had never spoken on the phone. Once, she had accidentally called him – she'd hit cancel before he could pick up, but something about explaining the simple truth afterwards, by text, had still felt like a lie. Or rather, like *he* might have thought it was a lie. The mortification had lingered for days.

This wasn't a butt dial, though, was it? He'd explicitly told her as much. She had no choice but to pick up.

Abandoning the White Russian she was midway through assembling, El ran out of the bar without so much as a word to any of her colleagues. She bounded up the stairs towards street level, then around the corner and into the back alleyway. With a last deep breath, she clicked the green button.

'Hello?' she said uncertainly, lifting the phone to her ear.

'Hi,' came Robbie's voice on the other end of the line. It was really him. Just him. The immediate familiarity of it was somehow startling and soothing at once. 'I'm sorry to ring.'

'No, it's fine. It's fine. Uh . . . what's up?'

'I suppose I just needed someone to talk to. About . . .'

'About work,' she prompted.

He cleared his throat. 'Yeah. I just . . . it's not about Love and Death exactly. Or it is, but it's also about the whole industry.' He paused again, sighed again. 'Do you ever wonder if you've wasted all this time on a pointless thing?'

This time, El exhaled heavily herself.

She was almost 30. So many of the people she had worked with over the years were doing other jobs now. Better paid, more grown-up seeming jobs – the jobs they'd really wanted to do all along, perhaps. There was something strange about doing, for the long term, something that many others viewed as merely a temporary stopgap. It could result, inevitably, in a slight feeling of being left behind. It could result in some irrational resentment of those who'd thrown in the towel. She got it.

'Sometimes,' El admitted.

Robbie let out a little chuckle. 'What? No. You're supposed to tell me that there's value in making something beautiful and in giving people pleasure, and that it's creative and skilled and it's going to outlast us. You're supposed to tell me this matters.'

'I can tell you all that,' El replied evenly. 'I believe all that. But I'm just saying that the other thing, the fear – there are nights I understand that, too.'

She didn't know if it was the most helpful thing to have offered him. But it was the truth. For good or for bad, they had never told each other anything else.

Chapter Thirty-Five

Berlin wasn't Robbie's sort of city, really. It was all hard edges. Of course, he could see the appeal – if he were a different sort of person, if he had a greater appreciation for, say, dance music or graffiti art or various forms of cutting edge technology . . . in those scenarios, he was sure this place would feel like heaven.

As things were, what he'd primarily observed around him, in the course of an admittedly short visit, were cloudy skies, stark buildings, and the remnants of violence and division. It reminded him, in certain ways, of Belfast.

None of that mattered, though, as he descended the steps to a particular basement, made his way into a particular cocktail bar. In that moment, he could have been in any city, in any town or country backwater in the world. All the sightseeing activities he'd failed to tick off his list were rendered entirely irrelevant. There was really only one sight he wanted to see.

Inside, his eyes darted around, struggling to adjust to the low lighting. This place had the slight sense of a dungeon, albeit one that was about to cost you a lot of money.

The very second he spotted El, Robbie had a sudden, terrible change of heart. Immediately, he wished that he'd never come here at all. What had he been thinking? What if she didn't want to see him? It struck him that there was an unfairness about this – about a meeting he had planned for and that she was about to be entirely blindsided by.

More than that, he was – undeniably and overwhelmingly – just plain afraid. Of what, he didn't exactly know.

He was about to turn right around and leave again, unseen, when of course she clocked him, too.

'Robbie?' she said, squinting over at him. She was on her way back from a table, empty tray in hand, and she seemed truly to be unsure of what her eyes were seeing. An occupational hazard in this place, presumably.

'. . . Yeah,' he replied, like a man who'd been caught red-handed. 'Hi.'

'Oh my God!' she exclaimed. 'It's really you! Oh my God!'

She walked closer to him, and there was a strange, hokey-cokey situation as they decided whether to hug, not quite in sync with one another. They got there eventually, in a manner of speaking – a quick embrace that, for both parties, seemed mainly to be about getting it done. Her tray whacked him lightly on the back as they pulled apart.

'Sorry,' she mumbled.

And, for a moment, they just stared at one another.

El exhaled a little. 'What are you doing here?' she asked.

'I'm here for a conference,' he said, and immediately regretted it. Hadn't he set himself up for the very thing El asked next?

'Oh! What conference? Have I totally dropped the ball? Things have just been so hectic here.'

Robbie hesitated.

Her assumption was a fair one. After all, there seemed to be so many cocktail conferences popping up – all sorts of new competitions and awards ceremonies, new ways to get noticed. More and more, *craft cocktails* were becoming a mainstream interest. The term seemed to roll off the tongue these days. It was like *street food, small plates, no reservations*. It equated to *big business*.

It just wasn't Robbie's business anymore. He felt what he could only describe as a full-body wince.

'Uh, no. The conference was about . . . well, it was about young Europeans in management consultancy.'

El frowned. Before his very eyes, he watched her expression change, watched her put two and two together. Confusion turned to understanding turned to something else. 'You've left Love and Death,' she said softly.

He nodded.

'You didn't tell me.'

Hurt. That was the other thing Robbie could see in her now. After all, they'd texted just yesterday, about Barack Obama and the litany of non-political things the US president had either already proven himself to be great at (placating babies, singing) or that Robbie and El imagined he would be great at (El: kissing. Robbie: poker – and, yes, he agreed probably also kissing).

They'd texted the day before that, about a disappointing lunch Robbie had ordered, and about El's latest invention – did Robbie think Cruzan Black Strap or Goslings rum would work best for it, she'd wondered.

In other words, there were plenty of occasions on which he could have mentioned his new job – plenty of occasions within the last week, never mind in the weeks (and months) preceding it.

Even in the semi-darkness, Robbie could see all of that written plainly on El's face now. It pleased him, in a perverse sort of way, to know that he could read her in person as well as he'd learned to read her ellipses and emojis, her reply times and word choices.

Perhaps she could read him pretty well, too. Perhaps she'd decided to make it easy on him, at least right now. Or was it something else? Was it that same urge she always used to have, to behave so frustratingly *casually* about things?

Either way, she cracked a small smile. 'So, Citibank got you at last, did they?'

Robbie breathed out a laugh, too. 'They didn't want me, if you can believe it. Deloitte.'

'Wow.'

'Yeah. Business and Financial Advisory. I think I'm probably the oldest person in a graduate role in the whole place. I don't know quite what they made of my post-uni CV, to be honest, but I suppose I must have managed to spin it into something positive.'

El seemed to take that in. He heard his own inference right along with her – that the way he'd spent those seven years *wasn't* anything very positive, really – and he cursed it.

'When did you start?' El asked next.

And this was the very worst bit. The duration of his deception.

He gulped, said it fast. 'Five months ago.'

He watched her count the time back in her head, put the pieces together. She looked at him, her eyes narrowing, and suddenly, he knew she had the measure of him. Whether he wanted her to or not.

'Did you quit before or after you spoke to me? That night.'

'After.'

The very next day, in fact, Robbie had walked into Love and Death and handed in his notice. He hadn't been sure Otto would ever forgive him.

El cocked an eyebrow. 'Okay, so, note to self: maybe *not* a sideline in motivational speaking for me.'

Abruptly, she turned to nab her passing colleague. 'Hey, any chance you could make a Penicillin and a Dark 'n' Stormy for the couple in the corner? And could you also see if table four want anything else?'

In response, El got nothing but an incredibly severe expression and a single nod. She seemed to take that as a win, though, turning back to Robbie once the other woman had disappeared.

'That was my colleague Prune,' she offered.

'. . . Prune?' Robbie repeated.

'Prune,' El confirmed solemnly. There was, somewhere hidden under a neutral expression, amusement flickering. Just the fact that he could see it – that she *knew* he could, that she *wanted* him to – felt significant. It felt like proof that they were friends now. Friends *or something*, after all this time.

'Do you have . . . anything else to say on that?' he prodded.

'Not here I don't.' El lowered her voice. 'She's okay. She's just a bit fucked off because she's worked here for like four years, and then I landed in from LA and leapfrogged her.'

'Mmm. The thing is, that's not your fault though, is it, El? It's not your fault at all.'

His tone was ever so sincere, and it took El a minute to catch his meaning. When she did, she rolled her eyes. She couldn't seem to help but crack a smile, though. Who would have ever imagined that?

'How long are you here? In Berlin, I mean.'

'Flight's about nine a.m. tomorrow morning.'

'Oh!' she said. She looked a little taken aback. 'Okay. Well, I can't leave Prune on her own so . . .'

Instantly, Robbie felt foolish. He tried to ignore the sting of rejection. 'Absolutely! Of course, yeah. I just wanted to say hello, but I . . . I'll leave you to it.'

He'd already turned to go when El spoke again. 'No. I mean' – he stopped in his tracks – 'I can find someone to cover for me. I just need to make a few calls. It'll probably take an hour before someone gets in. That's if . . . I mean, do *you* have time?'

'I have time,' Robbie said.

He and El looked at each other, and in those few seconds, it felt like they were – at last – on exactly the same page here. They had tonight.

'Cool,' she replied quietly.

Another beat of silence followed before he spoke again.

'So, that's how it works around here, is it?' he asked, more loftily this time. 'You say *jump* and people say *how high?*'

A smile tugged at her lips. 'That's how it's worked everywhere, Robbie. You remember.' She nodded towards the bar. 'Pull up a stool. What can I get you?'

Chapter Thirty-Six

'Alright. Will I do the honours?'

The midnight air was mild as they left the bar and climbed the steps up towards Brunnenstraße. El had swiped a bottle of Champagne on the way out.

'Go for it,' Robbie replied, and El popped the cork. Instinctively, she emitted a little squeal as some of the liquid bubbled over her fist.

'Happiest sound in the world, eh?' he said.

She grinned in response, sweeping up the spillage with her tongue. 'So much nicer than Prosecco. I will die on this hill. I know everyone's crazy about Prosecco these days, and don't get me wrong, I love the *price* of Prosecco myself. But there's still just something about Champagne, isn't there?' She passed the bottle his way.

'What are we celebrating?' Robbie asked.

El didn't know how to respond to that. By now, the shock had just about subsided, but she still had no clue what Robbie was doing here. It was taking absolutely everything in her to let him get to that in his own time. How long more could she wait, though? Time was the one thing they didn't have much of tonight.

'You tell me,' she said.

Before answering, he took a glug from the Champagne bottle. El found herself watching his mouth, where her own had been just seconds previously. She watched his hand close easily around the neck of the bottle, his Adam's apple bobbing as he swallowed, and the feeling that fizzed inside her had nothing to do with the Champagne. She only knew one way to characterize it.

What the realization prompted, more than anything, was disbelief. A sense of total panic that she remembered, suddenly, from that night in LA.

'Hmm. Your move to Berlin?' Robbie offered then. 'Belatedly, I know. How's everything going at work?'

El bit back an exclamation. Because the thing was, he *knew* how it was going. Didn't she tell him, in increments and anecdotes, all the time?

But then, as was becoming all too clear, there were limitations to a text relationship. She had never lied to Robbie, in all the time they'd existed in the palm of one another's hands. But she hadn't told him everything, either. She'd chosen, always, how to frame things. She'd chosen what to omit altogether. That he was, naturally, doing the exact same thing, had never particularly occurred to her. Confronted with the reality of it, she felt just plain lied to.

How could she say that aloud, though? It was too vulnerable.

'Good,' she replied instead. 'I like Berlin. You can definitely get a nicer flat here, for less money, than anywhere I've ever lived. And the whole industry scene is incredibly cool, obviously. I've been entering loads of competitions and all that stuff. People seem to love inventiveness here. It's just a bit tricky, you know? At Incognito. I want them to like me, but I'm a manager now. I'm kind of there to tell them what to do.'

'Age-old question, eh? Can you be someone's boss and also be their friend?'

'Yep.'

'Is the language barrier part of it?'

'Mmm, maybe a bit. I'm trying to learn German. I just really don't want to be one of those English people who doesn't bother, you know?'

El's nationality – what it actually was, and whether those around her perceived it as a good or a bad thing – seemed to be an ever-evolving theme in her life. She suspected Robbie might understand that one.

She'd been thinking about it a lot during the past week or so, actually. The Olympics were happening in London, and she'd been watching along on television. There was just something about the sunshine and the spirit, about the bunting and all those majestic drone shots. Ordinarily, El genuinely believed that Prince William and Kate Middleton were just reasonably good-looking grifters who wouldn't last a fortnight in a real job. And yet, the sight of them cheering in the stands had prompted in her something that she could only call a pang. Something she could only call patriotism.

'You must be the only person trying to get *out* of London right now, anyway,' she said to Robbie.

'Yeah, it's been mental. Everyone thought it would be a disaster, but actually it's turned out to be quite good. People have been getting enthused about really weird sports. Otto's done a bunch of Olympic-themed specials.'

'Oh, so you . . . you've stayed in touch?'

'Yeah. I call in when I can. You'd be amazed how cool it's getting around there now. Who knew so many people wanted to come to East London and play ping-pong?'

El managed a smile. She tried to ignore the twinge she felt, knowing that Otto and Robbie had managed to maintain a post-working relationship. Certain pain she carried like an old injury, at this point. It lay dormant a lot of the time, but it could flare up at any moment.

'Are they doing the jam jars at Love and Death?' she asked, by way of distraction.

'Nope. Feels like everyone's doing that now, doesn't it? Or fish bowls with a bunch of straws. Anything but a regular glass. But definitely not on Otto's watch.'

'Yeah. Come to think of it, I can't see him going for that.'

In her Tipsy Parrot years, El had derided his stringent standards, but she had come back around to grudgingly respecting them while at The Avalon.

These days, it wasn't even really about respect or the lack of it. It was about understanding. At Incognito, she was often the most senior member of staff on shift. Her standards had to be high, or else nobody else's would be. Her taste had to be, if not good – who was to say what was good, really? – then at least *specific*. It was no use to anyone if she wasn't sure.

She wondered what Otto thought about whether it was possible to truly be someone's friend when you were above them in the hierarchy. He'd certainly managed it for a long time, with her – until he hadn't.

Robbie passed the Champagne back her way, nudging his shoulder against hers a little. 'Call me crazy, but it seems as though you'd like to talk to him . . .' he prodded. It was as though he were reading her mind. 'I think he'd like to talk to you.'

El just shrugged. 'My number's still the same.'

She'd kept it, even to her own huge financial detriment, all this time. She found herself strangely attached to it. It was about the only thing in her life that had stayed consistent. She took another luxurious sip from the bottle, and when she was finished, she didn't even have to glance over at Robbie to predict the aggravated expression that would be on his face.

She turned towards him anyway. She let herself take him in, from head to toe, in the comparative brightness of a street-lit night. What she remembered from LA was evidently not a fluke or a figment. When she hadn't been looking, he'd somehow gone and become the kind of man she couldn't look away from.

'It's weird to see you,' she offered then. 'I feel like this is our first meeting, sort of.'

He nodded. 'I know.'

'But then, at the same time, it's like . . .'

She wasn't sure of the ending to that sentence, but he didn't seem to need one.

'Yeah,' he said. 'I know.'

For a moment, a certain intensity flickered between them again, the same as it had back at the bar.

Their pace, by now, had slowed, and Robbie cracked a smile. 'So, can we work on the basis that you no longer think I'm an anally retentive virgin, then?'

El cringed. 'Well. It's only *half* true, I'll give you that. I suppose it was only half true even when I said it. You know I haven't always been massive on factual accuracy.' She chuckled, gave him back the bottle. 'And what was it you said? Coked-up mess with daddy issues? Or something like that. That one's definitely still half true.'

'I take it your old man hasn't been clamouring to visit then? Now that you're back in Europe and all.'

'He extremely hasn't, no.'

'Feels like so long ago, doesn't it? That night when they filmed *BST*?'

El nodded. 'Another lifetime.'

Just recently, after five seasons on the air, *BST* had been cancelled. The Citi Slicker was kind of old news by now. People did still order it sometimes – it hadn't been entirely forgotten. But it wasn't the new thing, the trendy thing, any longer. It was just another drink. Among certain groups, at least here in Berlin, El was sure it would be considered downright passé. She found she didn't mind. Everything about it, even to her, now seemed so much less important than it once had.

'Where are we going, anyway?' Robbie asked, after they'd been walking a little while, just the sounds of the city around them.

'I was thinking Berghain?' El suggested.

There was a time Robbie would not have so much as heard of

the place. Now, he snorted out a laugh. 'Amazing, yeah. I'm not really dressed for it, but I'm sure you know at least one of the doormen.'

El chuckled too, looking down at herself. 'I do, yeah. But I suppose, ultimately, I'm not really dressed for it either.'

It was as good a reason as Robbie imagined he'd ever get to look at her again – properly, openly. She was wearing, to put the matter in its most basic form, a pair of trousers and a top. Her hair still fell to waist-length; her eyelids were still smudged with black liner. She looked fundamentally exactly the same as she always had, but a little bit different, too. That, he was learning, seemed to be her way. This time, she'd traded the beachy barefoot look for more muted colours, more unusual shapes. Robbie could say no more on the subject. He knew only that the outfit before him seemed to be baggy in places he wouldn't have expected, and equally, to have cutouts in places that entirely boggled his mind. She looked incredible.

'You look like a pagan priestess,' he said, instead of that, to make her laugh. It worked.

He noticed the sliver of her clavicles that her shirt left visible, the flashes of her sternum sometimes as she moved, and he bet she fitted right into Berlin. How did she manage to do that wherever she went? He still didn't always feel like London was exactly his city, even if he could fake it a lot better these days. But if Belfast wasn't his either, he wasn't sure where that left him, short of throwing darts at a map. And of course, he couldn't just take off, in any case. He had more than only himself to think about.

'How about I just give you a little tour,' she offered then. 'Or . . . I don't know – what did you want to do tonight?'

It felt traitorous, the way his heartbeat seemed to accelerate in his chest as she looked over at him. Traitorous and insane. It was a simple question, after all.

Still, he couldn't help shifting his eyes from hers. 'Uh . . . I don't know,' he mumbled.

With that, she seemed to snap into decisiveness, into hostess mode – the way he remembered her behind the bar, when *somebody* needed to take control of a situation.

'Well, then, let's walk. Don't worry – I'll skip anything historically significant. It'll be purely the stuff that's significant to me. *Here's where I almost fell in the Spree; here's where I come for breakfast sometimes* – that type of thing.'

Robbie could only grin. 'Sounds perfect,' he said.

Chapter Thirty-Seven

They walked for hours, in the end. All through the night. Around Mitte and towards the river, then across the Tiergarten and past the Brandenburg Gate. They peered into bookshop windows (one of Robbie's core passions in life) and predicted the interpersonal dynamics existing between various drunken passersby (one of El's core passions in life).

Robbie couldn't remember what he'd disliked about Berlin as recently as six hours previously. Now, it struck him as beautiful – magical. There was something romantic about seeing a city this way, by streetlight. That was simply an objective fact.

'You know, I once had a customer tell me that nothing good happens after 2 a.m.,' El remarked as they meandered along cobbled streets, passing the Champagne back and forth until it was done. 'Do you think that's true?'

Robbie glanced down at his watch. They were well past the hour now. 'No,' he murmured.

'Me neither,' she agreed.

And, when she offered him a small smile, he felt a lightness in himself that he hadn't known in such a long time. He got a bit of it any time he saw El's name flash up on his phone. However, he could see now how diluted a sensation that was, really. It was nothing compared to physical proximity.

The source of his hesitation, when he'd first walked into

Incognito earlier, was suddenly all too obvious to him. He had been afraid that he'd see her again, in real life, and it would not go well. He had been *more* afraid that he'd see her and it *would* go well. Because how to go back from this feeling?

He remembered those old ads: *this is your brain on drugs.*

This is your brain on Eloise Tippett, he thought to himself.

When the sun was just beginning to rise, they chose a bench in the Gendarmenmarkt to sit on. Around the square stood two cathedrals and a concert hall – they were the types of grand, medieval buildings that Robbie barely gave a second glance as he marched through London. Now, however, he found himself staring upwards in awe.

'So that's called splitterbrötchen,' El said, ripping open the paper bag that lay between them on the bench. 'And that's franzbrötchen, I think. And then hörnchen. All just sweet bread, essentially.'

'That'll do me,' Robbie replied.

A nearby bakery, although still technically closed, had taken pity on them and sold them some pastries and coffee. For a few minutes, they ate in easy silence. El was still wearing his jacket, he realized. He'd given it to her crossing the Luther Bridge, and she hadn't given it back.

Once again, there was the shot of pleasure, then the resulting chaser of shame.

'How's Frankie?' he asked. He was sincerely interested, even though he'd never actually met Frankie. He knew her only through El's stories.

'She's alright, yeah. It's been a bit of a weird time. With *Bitten*, I think she was just so happy to get an acting job – as in, any acting job, you know? I don't think it would have occurred to her to ask herself whether she really wanted *that* job. She went on *Ellen* to promote the third film a few months ago, and she said something a bit . . . well, it was fine, really. By any normal standards, it was fine. But the fans kind of lost their minds.'

'Eek.'

'Yeah. I mean, personally I thought what she said was great. For a while there, it was starting to seem like *I* was the more down to earth one in the relationship, which was obviously a *huge* red flag.' El rolled her eyes self-deprecatingly. 'But then she went on this retreat that was meant to provide healing and connection and whatever – just all that LA stuff. For the first few days, she was loving it. I think by the end, though, it was just one sound bath too far. She came back, and she had this whole new "no bullshit" attitude. Or her old attitude was back again, maybe. Either way, she was ready to kill dead things, as you would say.'

Robbie smiled. That *was* one of his favourite phrases. He'd told it to her over WhatsApp. She'd remembered.

'Anyway, Frankie's employability's taken a bit of a dip, given how many people she pissed off with that interview. And her agent is just . . .'

'What?'

'I don't know. She still won't hear a bad word said against him. But he acts like he made her career when, if you ask me, she made his.'

Robbie took a sip from his coffee, let his eyes scan the square. The sun was almost all the way up now. Some early commuters were dotted around the streets, there was the sense of a new day beginning. Between him and El, though, he had a sudden panic that time was running out.

'Would you ever come back to London?' he asked her.

She made a face, apparently unenthused by the idea.

'Why not?'

His enquiry came out a bit less casual, a bit more pressing, than he'd intended.

This time, El smiled – a deflection. 'Come on. I thought I'd converted you to the Vaterland.'

'You have. It's great. But . . .' He trailed off. What was wrong with saying it, really? What was wrong with telling a friend that you'd love them to come back and live in the same place that you also lived?

Robbie went a different way. 'If you ask me, Otto would be delighted to have you back at Love an—'

'Oh my God! I don't want to talk about Otto or Love and Death!' El exploded. The force of it surprised him.

'You do!' he replied, and in a flash, his aggravation matched every bit of hers. 'It's so obvious that you do! I just don't understand why you're here, in this random city by yourself, when you could just come home and be with the people who love you!'

For a moment, she just looked at him. 'Like who?'

He felt flustered. 'Lots of people!'

She said nothing. The silence seemed to stretch out between them, filled with all the things they hadn't said to each other, even as they'd talked all night. Even as they'd typed back and forth for months and years.

'Why didn't you tell me you'd left Love and Death?' she asked then.

Robbie sucked in a breath. They were finally getting to it. Inevitably. 'I thought you would be . . .' He halted, gave a little shrug. The truth, he supposed, was as good as anything. 'I thought you'd think less of me,' he said quietly.

Again, she offered nothing in response. He couldn't even read her expression. Her inscrutability turned out to be more unnerving than anything she could have said aloud.

'Well, *do* you?' he prompted. 'Come on, El, don't hold back. You never did think I could hack it long-term, did you? What do you reckon, eh? Am I just another guy who got within spitting distance of 30 and threw in the towel?'

She cocked an eyebrow. 'You said it.'

'So, what? You can move on – you can take off halfway round the world, twice, and it's all just part of your *evolution* or whatever? But I'm a sell-out?'

'Well, first of all, you might remember I got the sack from Love and Death. It wasn't my choice to go. And I didn't leave the industry altogether, so it's a bit different. Why are you picking this fight with me? What does it even matter what I think? What do *you* think, Robbie? Are you happy? Because you could have fooled me.'

'What?! I told you: Deloitte has actually been great! Who doesn't like being invited to European conferences? And the work's interesting and—'

She cut him off. 'I'm not talking about the job!'

On the bench, their pastries and coffees sat all but forgotten now.

Robbie swallowed. 'You're asking me about my marriage? Come on.' He shook his head a little. 'I'm not talking to you about that.'

'Why not?'

'Because it's none of your business!'

It felt like a shitty thing to say to her, but he said it anyway.

She greeted it with more pragmatism than he might have expected. 'Okay. Yeah. Maybe not. You could still tell me, though. In fact, I think if you're going to come all the way to Berlin to see me and *not* mention it, that seems a bit weird.'

'I told you: I'm here for a conference.'

El rolled her eyes. 'Fine, yeah. Let's go with that.'

'Sorry, what? Are you saying you don't believe there's a conference at the Marriott on the economic landscape in the aftermath of the recession? I must have imagined yesterday morning's session on intermediary asset pricing. Or the afternoon one on disembodied unilaterali—'

'Ugh, stop! I think there's such a thing as a pretext, Robbie! I think there's such a thing as creating a little bit of a safety net, and you've always been a master at it. And by the way, I don't appreciate the insinuation that my life here is somehow empty. You don't know anything about my life!'

Robbie leaped to his feet, for no particular reason than that he felt the urge to be moving. 'Well, back at you!' he said, and when he started to walk, he had no idea where he was going. In any case, he didn't get very far.

'Is Anna-Claire pregnant?' she called out after him. 'Is that what this is all about? You're going to be a dad and you're freaking out?'

When he turned, El was standing now, too, and she suddenly looked about as fearful as he'd ever seen her.

'For fuck's sake, just go ahead and tell me,' she said. 'As a matter of fact, I wish you'd just told me on WhatsApp, but whatever.'

Robbie felt a stab in his chest – the pain of a different failure altogether. 'No,' he replied quietly. 'Anna-Claire's definitely not pregnant.'

'Oh!' El appeared thrown off by the response, her brow furrowing as she processed it. 'So, did you . . . decide to wait?'

'Well, we've been waiting. That's for sure. But we didn't *decide* to wait, no.'

She nodded. Just like that, all the heat seemed utterly gone from their interaction. 'Got it. Have you had tests, or . . . ?'

'We're having them now. For ages, we just assumed it would happen, you know? Even when we'd been trying for a while, we still talked about it like it was a dead cert. We'd say "when we have a baby" or whatever. Then we stopped doing that, but I think we were still too afraid to actually go to the GP. Once you medicalize it . . . you can't deny you're worried at that point, can you? Anyway. We went last month.'

Anna-Claire, Robbie knew, talked to her friends about this all the time. He, on the other hand, had never told a single soul. He waited for some version of the responses Anna-Claire apparently received on the regular – the ones that, by turns, encouraged and agonized her:

Have you tried . . . – insert food or activity.

My cousin Sandra had the same issue, and she said . . . – insert crackpot theory or Bible reference.

Plus, the classic:

It'll probably happen right when you stop thinking about it.

From El, Robbie got none of the above. 'That's so shit,' she said quietly. 'I'm sorry.'

Instantly, it felt like the only response he needed. It made emotion rise up in him, catch unexpectedly in his throat.

'And how are things . . . outside of that?' she continued carefully. 'Or is there no outside of that?'

Robbie swallowed. 'I thought that leaving Love and Death would help,' he said. 'Which it has, in some ways. But in others . . .' He couldn't face continuing. It felt too disloyal.

El just nodded. 'Sometimes I *am* a bit lonely here,' she offered, a moment later. 'I mean, I like it mostly, but sometimes, it's so hard. I cried on the phone to my electricity provider. Twice.'

It took Robbie a second to calibrate this information, to connect the dots. Then, suddenly, he understood what was happening.

'Sometimes I *do* feel like it was a terrible mistake, going to work at Deloitte,' he returned. 'Some days – a lot of days, actually – it just feels like an endurance test.'

'I'm incredibly jealous of you, sometimes,' she said.

He smiled wryly. 'Believe me, *same*.'

'I'm very worried that somewhere inside me, there's a manic depressive just waiting to get out.'

That one was a surprise to Robbie, but he didn't stop to question or to analyse. That wasn't what they were doing here, was it? This was confessions only. No solutions.

'I don't think I'd go to church anymore if it was just up to me,' he offered.

She raised an eyebrow there, too, before moving right along. 'I shouldn't have said you don't know anything about my life. At this point, sometimes I actually think you might know me better than anyone on earth, which is a big problem.'

'Why?'

'Because you're married!' El exclaimed. 'And it just feels so pathetic for me to say that about a married man. I can't believe it. I'm actually furious about it – and mortified – but I think it's true.'

Robbie took that in for a moment, before he spoke again. 'I came to Berlin to see you,' he said softly. 'I mean, I did also go to a conference, but I came here to see you. You should know, at a minimum, that you were completely correct about that.'

They looked at each other, all out of secrets now. They seemed to have ended up closer together than they had been before, their bodies all but touching.

As for what happened next, from El's point of view, the crucial thing was that he started it.

She would never have started it, but once Robbie's lips were on hers, she didn't stop it either.

Not by a long shot.

And the truth was that she'd kissed quite a lot of people in her life. She would admit that. She'd always thought of a kiss as a fundamentally pretty low-stakes situation. Yet, like skinny-dipping or downing a shot of tequila, it could also feel like an essential part of being alive – almost no matter what the specifics. El hadn't always been massively fussy about the specifics. In the past, there'd been times she'd just found herself happily carried along with a general atmosphere. Or she'd wanted to liven things up, or she'd been curious. She'd been bored. She'd been horny. She'd wanted to prove something, to herself or to the person in front of her or to some third party altogether. There had been a wide range of circumstances, essentially.

But El had never kissed anyone, ever, and had it feel like this did.

Of course, that didn't make it the right thing to do.

Once she and Robbie pulled apart for air, reality reasserted itself, fast and frigid as an ice bucket.

'Oh my God. I'm so sorry!' she exclaimed.

Opposite her, Robbie blinked. He looked entirely shell-shocked. 'I . . .' He paused, his voice coming out hoarse. 'Wow. I don't know if *I* am.'

It created in El an immediate sense of alarm. She didn't know how she felt, and she didn't want to be forced into figuring it out right here and now. Her instinct was to back away from this. Perhaps she should have known he wouldn't be keen to let her.

'Of course you are!' she insisted. 'But don't worry. It was just . . . it was an impulse. These things happen.'

Robbie frowned. 'And so, what now? We just pretend that it *didn't* happen?'

'Exactly.'

'I don't think that generally works out, El.'

'I mean, on *TV* it doesn't, no. In real life? I think it happens all the time.'

Robbie didn't seem convinced. 'Either way, I think it's safe to say my marriage is over,' he murmured. He sounded a little dazed, almost as though speaking to himself.

'Oh my God! Do *not* leave your wife!' El found herself yelping in response. Some physical space seemed like it would be wise, and she took a few steps backwards. 'I'm so serious, Robbie. Don't leave her; don't tell her about this, just . . .' She trailed off helplessly. 'We are not in love!' she spluttered.

For a beat, Robbie looked at her like he wasn't sure that was true. For a beat, she suddenly wasn't sure either.

She took some deep breaths, in and out. What a turn-up for the books, that of the pair of them, she was having to be the logical one.

'Look, Robbie, you're having a crisis. I mean, no judgement from me – I'm practically permanently in some kind of minor crisis, as you know. But this is new for you. You hate your job, and you might be infertile – I'm sorry, but it sounds like you might be – and you're in Berlin for the weekend. The fact is, people who come here for the weekend do all kinds of out-of-character shit. I don't know what it is about the place.'

He said nothing, looking over at her searchingly. Then, El imagined she could almost *see* the moment that he came to his senses. She'd known it would happen eventually – maybe, on some level, she'd merely wanted to get in there first.

'You're right,' he said quietly. 'I should go. Flight to catch and all.'

She just nodded.

'I think you and I should probably . . . I mean, I know texts are just texts, but . . .' He trailed off, anguish writ large on his face.

'Yeah,' she replied, feeling something settle like lead in the pit of her stomach.

They both knew. Their one night together was over. And now, everything else between them was, too.

Chapter Thirty-Eight

Perhaps everybody got to a certain point in their life and wondered whether they'd done absolutely everything wrong – whether even the decisions they'd been sure about, at the time of making, had been huge mistakes. To say nothing, of course, of the decisions they had *never* been truly sure about – the ones they'd privately agonized over and then taken a punt.

For Otto, this moment arrived on the 12th of September, 2014 – the day of his fiftieth birthday.

The cliché of it displeased him, but there was nothing to be done.

Undoubtedly, there were things in his life that he could be proud of. Didn't he own what was now, apparently, one of the premier cocktail bars in the world? The Museum of the American Cocktail, in New Orleans, had recently asked him to come and give a series of seminars there. Bartenders, when they met him, were very often quite starstruck. Even the average Joe, who wouldn't recognize him in the street, had likely downed a Cecilia at some point or another. Over the years, he'd come up with so many other drinks, too – drinks that were beautiful, surprising, complicated, drinks he knew were something special.

And yet.

As Otto walked around the V&A – normally one of his very favourite places in London – he found himself dissatisfied. Rec-ollecting his many achievements didn't help; attempting to lose himself in the art proved impossible. He could think only of the first time he'd ever come here.

That was the day he'd met El on the way home. She'd barrelled into his life and, out of nowhere, the two of them had become a pair. He hadn't planned it or wanted it. However, she had turned out to be a difficult person to keep at a distance.

Sometimes, looking back, Otto wished he had never agreed to let that goddamn TV crew anywhere near Love and Death. Sometimes, he regretted every single bit of it: everything it created, and everything it destroyed.

But then, hadn't he needed the cash? In those days, Love and Death had relied on private investors. The money from *BST* had got the Volkov Brothers off Otto's back for good. The bump in custom thereafter had helped him weather the financial crash, when so many other bars hadn't.

Of course, by then, he'd had his secret weapon, too.

Robbie Saunders was another one who came out of nowhere and managed to worm his way into Otto's heart.

What a pleasure it was, to teach someone like him – someone who was so very ready to learn. Added to that, across his tenure at Love and Death, Robbie had probably done more than anyone to make sure that somehow the books were always balanced.

Without him – it had now been over two years since Robbie's departure – Otto knew he might have let things slip a little, when it came to the finances. But it was that or let standards slip. He knew which he preferred.

Business acumen aside, he found he still missed Robbie desperately behind the bar. There was nobody else out there with his level of knowledge, with his sheer consistency and exactitude.

The whole thing might have been easier to accept if Robbie *himself* now seemed happier about the change.

Instead, Otto couldn't help but think that tension practically radiated off Robbie, even as he announced one promotion after another.

Should he have fought harder, then, to keep Robbie at Love and Death? Otto turned the question over in his mind as he drifted from one of the V&A's galleries into the next.

It was true that he'd accepted the resignation without too much protest. What he'd wanted, even more than to keep Robbie at the bar, was simply to keep Robbie in his life. Hadn't he learned his lesson from the way things ended with El?

Otto looked vacantly at the painting before him and – at last – gave up entirely, sinking into a nearby bench.

So much, as always, seemed to come back to El.

Needless to say, he'd kept an eye on her, where he could.

He'd clocked it, when The Avalon had appeared in the World's 50 Best Bars, the year after Love and Death's first entry. *Stand-outs include the Punch-Drunk Darling, with its homemade pineapple and almond soda*, the piece read. *Creator El Tippett trained under famed mixologist Otto Kettinger and has evidently inherited every bit of his panache.*

Reading that, Otto had felt a glow of pride the likes of which he'd never experienced before – not for himself, not for his business, never.

Next, El had had a bevy of competition successes. He'd seen them reported on the internet: finalist in the Diageo World Class competition for her Bloomsbury Martini; winner of a Spirited Award; listed in *Difford's Guide* as 'one to watch'; it went on and on . . .

His girl, quite clearly, was working her butt off out there. She'd even made it into some non-industry press.

An article in *Time Out* magazine – 'The 100 Best Things We Ate and Drank in 2013' – included the Hackney Whore, at Insignia Berlin: *If we could, we'd have head bartender El Tippett whip up this mescal/agave nectar delight every night of our lives.*

Then, earlier this year, she'd been mentioned in an article in *The Atlantic*, too. '5 Must-Try Cocktails For Summer': *At Butter-Scotch, Berlin's first 'ice cream and cocktail bar', El Tippett's Brixton Breeze is what all the cool kids are drinking.*

It struck Otto as interesting, the way that El often seemed – at least in recent years – to have been working around a London theme. When he got home from the V&A, on the afternoon of his birthday, he said as much in a letter to Cece.

Oh my Lord, Otto, you know where she works – just call her already, Cece wrote back, a few weeks later.

Sitting in Hyde Park – he often took her letters out and about, in order to really *enjoy* them – Otto just rolled his eyes affectionately. He'd always thought Cece was like Robbie in a lot of ways. She was the calm to his chaos.

I actually don't know where she works at this point. She seems to like to move around, he replied. In that regard, he thought, with some measure of satisfaction, it was precisely as he'd once told El's girlfriend Kat that it would be.

Overall, though, even *he* could hear the feebleness of the excuse. In truth, his reluctance to reach out to El was for the same reasons it had always been.

Even after all this time, he felt profoundly uneasy about the Citi Slicker.

He'd replayed that moment – taking the credit for it – over and over in his mind, wondering how he could possibly have breached his own code of honour so egregiously. Yes, there were some extenuating circumstances at play. He could never have predicted what those few seconds – that one little white lie – could have spun out into. And El had been in such a state, that night. She was barely fit to be there at all, much less be representing the bar. Otto had been forced to finally admit that everything he'd tried to foster in her – commitment, focus, professionalism – seemed to have been on the decline for some time. He'd been hurt, let down, *pissed the fuck off*.

Still.

Looking back, he regretted letting her go more than he could, or would, ever say. Not because of the success she'd known elsewhere, not because she'd proven to be every bit as talented as he'd always suspected she was. No. He shouldn't have fired her for one very simple reason: you didn't *fire* family.

He still remembered the disgust in El's expression, that time they crossed paths in LA. In his worst moments, he wondered if she now scorned any lingering association with him.

Added to, and apart from, all of that, Otto remained a man who refused to allow photography inside his cocktail bar. A man who'd never worn a pair of jeans since the day and hour he left Pennsylvania, who'd maintained a decades-long written correspondence with his best friend. The idea of calling El up on the telephone, all business, just didn't appeal to him. Not after such a long estrangement. There should be an element of romance to any reunion, he thought.

Cece knew all that, without him having to tell her.

Alright, I'll ignore how easy it would be to find out where El works, came her response, in due course. *If you want some other way to get her attention . . . I don't know. Maybe think about the ways she manages to get yours?*

Otto hadn't the first clue what she meant by that. He stared at the letter – this time, he was at his favourite table in The Wolseley – with his brow furrowed. And then, slowly, the cogs started turning in his brain.

No matter the explosion he'd seen in the cocktail industry across his career, there were times it still felt like an incredibly small world. One way or another, news had a way of getting around. It didn't seem too egotistical to note that the things *he* did certainly got around. In a flash, Otto knew just what he was going to do next.

'Alright, gang,' he said, when he went into Love and Death the following day. 'We're going to add a new special to our menu – for the foreseeable.'

Before him, in a Collins glass, the cocktail was charcoal black and garnished with three Luxardo cherries.

'Allow me to introduce you to the Hackney Whore.'

Chapter Thirty-Nine

By summer 2015, El was in Japan, conjuring things out of absinthe and sake that very few punters had a taste for. That was fine, though. She didn't need very many punters. Lab Eight in Tokyo could accommodate a total of eight patrons at any one time. It was the most chilled, most autonomous job El had ever had. And the more bizarre and outlandish her concoctions, the more that industry aficionados seemed to enjoy them. She created pearls of Cointreau-infused caviar that burst in the mouth; she conjured a twist on a Bloody Mary with hot sauce and stout, serving it alongside a grilled cheese sandwich. In many ways – twirling jiggers one-handed, lifting domes from glasses to reveal plumes of smoke, playing Kate Bush and Sinéad O'Connor on repeat because nobody could stop her – she was in her element.

Undeniably, she'd had a good couple of years. Everything, at least on the work front, seemed to have somewhat come together. She'd thrown herself into it and hit her stride.

Of course, none of her drinks had had anything like the reach of the Citi Slicker – they hadn't been beamed onto television screens around the world. Nonetheless, by the time El felt she'd wrung everything she possibly could out of the Berlin scene, she'd practically walked into the first job she applied for. In fact, she'd walked into the first two. One was in Paris and the other in

Tokyo. She'd plumped for the option that seemed most exotic – that seemed it would make a better story later.

Increasingly, this seemed like a questionable life strategy for a 32-year-old woman.

El hated Tokyo. That was the reality. People were unfailingly respectful, and the trains ran on time, and eating out was cheap. The whole city was leaps and bounds ahead of any place she'd ever lived in terms of cleanliness, technological advancement, and storage solutions. She adored the fashion, spent weekends wandering around Harajuku in search of bold geometric prints. The cherry blossoms in Ueno Park, this past spring, had been one of the most beautiful sights she'd ever seen.

And yet, still, she hated it here.

Every day, she felt her own foreignness keenly. She'd struggled to make friends – what a humbling experience *that* had been. Inside her tiny apartment ('the coffin', Frankie called it), El now spent more hours on the internet than seemed likely to be ideal. There was a time – she remembered this time; it really wasn't that long ago – when she used the internet only if she had a particular purpose already in mind. These days, more often than not, it was *lack* of purpose that sent her reaching for her laptop. YouTube knew what she liked and served it to her endlessly. Deaf babies being fitted with hearing aids for the first time. People in the aftermath of dental surgery, drugged up on painkillers. Newscasters being caught unawares by bad weather. It all filled the hours that El might previously have spent dancing, drinking, bed-hopping.

Nowadays, though, she was *tired* after work. And, ever since a particular early morning in Berlin, she'd begun to feel like less was more when it came to sex, too. Or maybe less was just less. If so, she found herself fine with that.

'Why don't you just come on home, sugar?' her mother implored on the phone. 'Ted and I would love to have you!'

El appreciated the offer.

Darleen was a supervisor at Disneyland now, and was living with El's one-time driving instructor. They both posted some absolutely undeniably batshit-crazy stuff on Facebook, but they were happy. They were harming nobody. It made El glad to think of them together.

Anaheim wasn't her home, though. Not really.

Instead – and even before her arrival in Tokyo – her thoughts had been turning more and more towards London. She'd expressed that the only way she knew how.

She just couldn't seem to help it if – sitting at a street-side counter with a plate of delicious yakitori before her – she found herself fantasizing about being able to cook a different sort of meal entirely. Not a fancy one. Nothing offbeat or exotic. Something the opposite of that, actually. Something traditional and hearty, like a roast dinner.

The type of thing, she was sure, that Robbie sat down to every Sunday. There could even be a toddler running around by now. Who knew? She hadn't seen or spoken to him since that morning he'd walked away from her in Gendarmenmarkt. It had been almost three years.

Would El have been able to better embrace Tokyo life if she didn't, in the back of her mind, have an out? She really couldn't say, because she *did* have an out. She had a standing offer from the place she'd turned down in Paris.

When the list of The World's 50 Best Bars 2015 was published, El was in her apartment, at a little table sandwiched between her bed and her kitchen sink. Scanning the website, she barely even looked for her current place of employment. Of itself, that was likely telling.

Lulu White Drinking Club in Paris, though, was rated number 8. She saw the name immediately, smiling to herself. *Yes*, she thought. That would do her just fine.

Nevertheless, she didn't hang around to read the review – she'd do that later. Right now, she had other priorities. As ever, there was one bar she found herself more interested in than any other. This year, Love and Death came in at number 27:

Otto Kettinger, unquestionably the godfather of London's cocktail scene, needs no introduction. This Shoreditch venue was once a true speakeasy – legend has it that American-transplant Kettinger operated without a liquor licence for his whole first year of business. Secrets are made to be shared, though. These days, there can be few Londoners who haven't heard of Love and Death. Standards remain unimpeachably high – it's one of the few establishments, globally, to stick around in our Top 50 year after year.

As ever, fresh ingredients are key in this dimly lit jewel of a spot. Standouts include Kettinger's own Pimmlet – a Gimlet made with British classic Pimm's No.1 Cup (so simple we wonder how no one's come up with it 'til now) – and the Hackney Whore, from Kettinger's one-time protégée El Tippett.

'It's a perfect drink,' Kettinger says. 'I couldn't have done any better myself – and I mean that literally. Nothing gives me greater pleasure to serve.'

There's a delightful sense of circularity here. After fifteen years and counting, Love and Death continues to influence the wider industry, but – in turn – is now being influenced by it, too. Are there newer, hotter spots in East London these days? Sure. For those of a certain vintage, though, Love and Death has still got it.

In her tiny apartment in Tokyo, El felt almost breathless. That quote. Otto may as well have reached through the screen and spoken to her directly, such was its potency to her.

She knew what it meant . . . the fact that Otto was even aware of her drink, the fact that he was serving it in Love and Death, the fact that he'd lauded it in print. To her recollection, he didn't do or say anything by accident. What it meant was that he still felt it, too – the connection between them that El had never quite been able to sever.

For example, his quote aside, she knew it would be *killing him* that Love and Death was rated number 27 this year; that, after a few years of getting closer to top billing (its highest ever ranking had been number 3) it was now getting further away. As for the implication that it was something of an old dog's boozer? No matter the positive tenor of the piece overall, El could easily imagine Otto taking to bed for three days straight.

She read and reread the piece that afternoon, and as she did, she could hardly stop a vision from taking shape in her mind.

She'd been in Tokyo for nine months. If it truly was inevitable that she'd be leaving for Paris just as soon as she could face the practicalities of actually doing it, could she perhaps . . . stop off in London en route? Could she perhaps even . . . stay in London? Might there be a job for her there, too?

'I mean, that's a *come and get me* plea from Otto if ever I saw one,' Frankie declared, via Skype. She was in Croatia, working on an indie film for which she'd had to actively try to become less attractive.

'You think?' El replied. *She* thought so. She just wanted to hear someone else say it.

'Ellie. Come on. *Absolutely.* Any time I mention a director in an interview, you think I'm just doing it for shits and giggles?' Frankie shifted in her seat, her elbow briefly obscuring the whole webcam. 'Are you still pissed with him, though? Otto. Would you even want to go back there?'

El exhaled heavily. For the first time in years, she allowed herself to sincerely consider the prospect.

In truth, the anger of how everything ended . . . that had burned off long ago, like ethanol. What had remained was the hurt.

Now, though, when she imagined herself walking into Love and Death . . . the thing she felt wasn't trepidation or pain. It was, she realized, something altogether different. It was anticipation. She could feel it fizzing, deliciously, just below the surface. She had the sudden ever-familiar urge to begin perusing some airline websites.

'And what about the Robbie of it all?' Frankie prompted then.

Immediately, El felt the same unease she always felt when Frankie brought him up.

Every single day that El hadn't contacted Robbie Saunders, across the time they'd been apart, she *could* have contacted him. That was the hardest bit.

In the early days, she'd found herself doing pathetic things that she despised in herself. Typing messages only to delete them. Looking at the word *online* below his name on WhatsApp, knowing he was *right there*, out there, somewhere.

For longer than she would have liked – and for reasons she hadn't overly wanted to delve into, even in her own mind – it had all felt almost impossibly hard. Then, eventually, it got easier. That was the prosaic truth of the matter.

These days, she didn't know what to think, how to categorize the relationship.

One view of the whole thing, between him and her, was that they were meant to be together and they always had been – that theirs was some sort of a tragic romance. They'd simply met a tiny bit too late, when he was already promised to another. Every bit of their previous conflict could be repackaged, made a part of that story. There was a thin line between love and hate. They were opposite sides of the same coin. Love was friendship set on fire, and so on.

In certain moments – generally drunken ones – El entertained all that.

Another view: they were two people who related to one another in a very particular way. They'd shared a passion, a lifestyle, that few others could understand. They'd had, from the beginning, a capacity for honesty with one another, and there was something intoxicating about that – about being seen so clearly by another person, and having that person, for whatever reason, only want to keep on looking. Added to which, the remote nature of much of their relationship had allowed for a level of projection on each of their parts, a level of interpretation. They'd been able to see, in one another, what they wanted to see. Gradually, they'd become more invested than was sensible – more invested than the situation really merited. They had each, for the other, become a far-off field. And, at such a distance, they each looked very green indeed.

Mostly, in her saner moments, that was what El thought.

She really didn't believe that she was, currently, in love with Robbie Saunders. Nevertheless, maybe she wouldn't mind seeing him again, she thought. It couldn't hurt to double-check.

When she got the call, less than a week later, El was walking through Shinjuku Golden Gai after work. Its six narrow alleyways housed almost two hundred bars and eateries, she'd been told. It was like a life-size version of a neighbourhood designed by children out of shoeboxes, held together with string and glue. Eclectic and chaotic, sure, but delightful.

Lab Eight closed relatively early, at 2.30 a.m. Plenty of other nearby places stayed open until 5, though, and as El made her way through the streets, she took in the sepia glow, the hum of conversation, coming from one little hideaway after another.

No matter where in the world it appeared, there was something about that type of environment that – still, despite her exhaustion – felt magical to her. Sacred.

When her phone buzzed, it was already in her hand. El looked down at the screen, let out an involuntary gasp when she saw the name on it.

He hadn't changed his number either, then. She'd wondered about that, from time to time – asked herself whether she could get back in touch with him by phone, even if she wanted to. She took a single deep breath in and out, then lifted the phone to her ear.

Immediately, the surrounding noise seemed to fade to nothing.

'It's me,' came that familiar accent on the other end of the line. Then a mangled sound, half a squawk, half a gulp, like an animal in pain. 'I . . . fuck, I don't know how to say this. He's gone, El.'

Chapter Forty

Robbie planned the whole funeral. He'd never known Otto to have any particular faith, and no instructions were left, so he had to wing it. He considered all sorts of weird and wonderful options. He looked up humanist ceremonies, Buddhist ones – things that felt *cool*. In the end – and with nobody to tell him otherwise – he did what he would do for his own family. He couldn't figure out anything that felt more right than that.

On the way to the ceremony, in the back of a taxi, he and Anna-Claire were silent.

Then, eventually, his wife spoke. 'I don't know how much longer I can do this,' she murmured. 'I know today's not the time to talk about it, but somehow, I . . .'

Robbie understood. In a strange way, it felt like this was exactly the time. There was nothing like death to make a person confront their life.

'Let's just go home,' she implored. 'Now that Otto's gone, what's keeping us here, really?'

Robbie sighed. They'd had this fight over and over. That they were having it now, within earshot of a cabbie, would – he knew – only be one more thing in his wife's arsenal. In Belfast, they could have a car; they could have a four-bedroom house with garden. Robbie just wasn't sure what they'd do with those things, in the circumstances. He certainly wasn't convinced he and Anna-Claire would derive any more joy merely from each other – there – than they managed to here. That thought struck him as incredibly, irredeemably sad.

Those early evenings walking across Christ Church Meadow when they were students, or the weekend mornings at Borough Market as newlyweds, all seemed like a very long time ago now.

'I think it'll feel worse in Belfast,' he said. 'Emptier, like. At least in London, most people aren't even married yet. In Belfast, all the people we know' – all the people *you* know, he amended in his own mind – 'are already knee-deep in nappies and soft play.'

'But it might happen when we're there!' Anna-Claire replied, her voice breaking a little. 'When we're more relaxed.'

It killed him, to hear the desperation in her voice. Unexplained infertility was an especially brutal one to come to terms with.

Ever since that trip to Berlin, some secret and irrational part of Robbie had half-feared that there *was* an explanation for it. Wracked by guilt, he imagined that perhaps Anna-Claire hadn't got pregnant since then because of what he'd done. Was it so crazy to imagine that breaking the vows one made before God might incur the wrath of God? It was, after all, the type of messaging he'd been around since childhood – less within his own family than in the overall culture he'd been a part of.

Robbie knew for sure that he would *not* be more relaxed in Belfast. All that dogmatism and whataboutery. He suspected that, thrust back into the midst of it, he and his wife might only uncover yet more issues about which they no longer felt the same. Moreover, some ungenerous part of him couldn't help but feel that he'd already made one big change – a huge and permanent sacrifice – in the interests of Anna-Claire's happiness. Hadn't he quit Love and Death for her? Wasn't he in the suit and tie now, bringing home the bacon, just like she'd wanted?

He was doing well at Deloitte. He liked the intellectual challenge of it, and he liked his colleagues. Though they hadn't become in any way involved in one another's personal lives, he was always happy to chat to them in the queue for Pret at lunchtime. In short, it was very normal, very even-keeled. He certainly didn't hate it. But still, both he and Anna-Claire knew he wouldn't have *chosen* it.

It was all a lot of hard, sad, unsaid stuff. Robbie knew all too well that his wife had her own accumulating pile of unspoken truths, too. It grew between them by the day, even as they did their best to hold onto one another.

The church, described as being in East London, was in fact halfway to Romford. Robbie peeked his head inside, his eyes darting around to make sure all the details were as he'd hastily planned them: the flowers, the orders of service, the black bows on the pews. Whether Otto would have cared for any of it, he still had no idea. The thought made him feel almost sick.

They were here now, though. The organ was beginning to play the opening hymn.

Alongside five others, including Marcus and Cormac, Robbie carried the coffin down the aisle. With every step, he felt the weight on his shoulders, felt the eyes of the congregation upon him. Making a similar journey on his wedding day, he'd thought he was leaving childhood behind. He could see now how wrong he'd been there. Absolutely nothing in his life before today had demanded quite this sort of adulthood.

One after another, he took in familiar faces: people from the trade, people he hadn't seen in years, all looking more solemn than he could ever remember them. Briefly, his eyes landed on a woman he didn't recognize. She looked about 50, this stranger, with striking red hair curled neatly under her chin. Robbie watched as, all of a sudden, she moved to dart out the church's side door, her face crumpled with emotion. He might have paid it more attention, had he not been busy seeking out another face in the crowd.

There was no El in sight.

Their phone conversation, ten days previously, felt like a lifetime ago. It had been short and dazed, on both their parts. Afterwards, he had WhatsApped her the funeral details, as she'd asked – the first message on their chain for such a long time – and she hadn't responded.

Her call, he supposed. He was going to have to figure out how he felt about that one later, because he was approaching the altar now. Once the coffin was settled there, Robbie took his seat beside Anna-Claire. He focused his gaze resolutely in front of him, as though trying to steel himself for what was ahead.

Then, just as the organ music came to a close, Robbie swore he could somehow sense it – the slight change in atmosphere. Sure enough, when he turned to look around, there she was. Head to toe in black, El looked almost *too* good for a funeral. She looked like a mob wife in a film, one who'd secretly killed the man she was mourning. The turban – a huge, unwieldy wraparound thing with streaks of gold cutting through the black – added particularly to the drama.

Watching her walk down the central aisle and settle into a pew, Robbie fought the inappropriate urge to laugh out loud. Instantly, he knew for certain: there was at least one thing in this church that Otto would have absolutely adored.

Afterwards, at the cemetery, she avoided him. She exchanged hugs and condolences with others she knew, she rallied in order to tell some funny stories about Otto. Then, as others began to drift away, one by one, El lingered alone at the graveside.

There was no headstone yet. Contrary to anything Robbie had ever seen on television, apparently that part didn't happen fast. The ground could take up to six months to properly settle. For now, it was just a mound of raised earth, flowers placed all the way along it. El stared at it, her face pale and expressionless, for ten minutes, then fifteen minutes. She seemed in no hurry to go anywhere.

When Robbie and Anna-Claire shuffled towards her – they were the only others remaining, by that point – El looked up.

A brief, polite exchange between El and Anna-Claire followed. Then – at last – El met Robbie's eyes, and something wordless passed between them. It was as though they'd both known that this moment would come – that after all the sympathy and cere-mony to be endured, it would, in the end, be just the two of them here.

The inevitability of that seemed to strike Anna-Claire, too. With a last, reluctant glance in their direction – Robbie barely registered the specifics – she was gone.

After that . . . nothing.

He and El just stood there together, in total silence, for another long while. Around them, it seemed like the sort of day that should be raining – it seemed like the heavens should have opened and the whole of London should have come to a standstill to mark the tragedy of Otto's death.

Instead, the sky was blue and cloudless. Out there, beyond this graveyard, other people were going about their days. They were on coffee dates and in traffic jams; they were sniping at their colleagues in office buildings, worrying about their silly little deadlines.

'I think maybe he would have preferred to be cremated,' Robbie said eventually. Suddenly, that made so much more sense to him, the idea of scattering Otto's ashes in all the places he'd loved best.

'Mmm,' El replied noncommittally. 'Maybe.'

'He would, wouldn't he? *You* would have known that.' He could hear the way it came out sounding strangely accusatorial.

She just shrugged, like she couldn't deny it aloud, didn't under-stand why he wanted to make her.

'You weren't here,' he continued brusquely – another blow.

It was an unusual experience, having only his own side of the fight. This time, El flinched a little at his words. But still, when she looked at him, there was compassion in her expression. It was as though she could see, in him, exactly what she felt in herself. Emptiness. Agony.

'It was a nice service,' she offered instead. 'It was nice how the minister . . . you know. Seemed to think there was some kind of point to it all. I can actually see the appeal of the whole thing.'

She meant religion, Robbie knew. Or did she mean faith? He wasn't sure whether they were one and the same. However, this didn't seem the time to get into it. Again, he and El lapsed into silence.

'Were there any warning signs?' she asked, after a moment. 'Health-wise, I mean?'

Robbie shook his head. 'That's aneurysms for you, I suppose. The doctors said it just came out of nowhere.'

It was so stark, said aloud that way, in the silence of the cemetery. Feeling a fresh wave of grief threaten to overwhelm him, Robbie cast around for a distraction.

'So, how's Berlin?'

'Oh, I'm in Tokyo now,' El replied vaguely. It was as if she were telling him she'd updated her car or changed hairdressers.

In response, Robbie had to work very, very hard to stop the shock from registering on his face. The displeasure. Of course, he knew he had no inherent right to this information, or to any other information about El. But in the privacy of his own brain, he had a right to think about her, surely – to occasionally imagine the life she was out there living. To know that he had been, for God knew how long, placing her in the wrong country entirely . . . it felt like a betrayal.

'I thought you liked Berlin,' he said evenly.

'I did. Just . . . best to keep it moving, you know?'

Robbie couldn't help but huff out a little laugh. It was all cynicism. 'Right, yeah. I know you don't like to get too attached, El.'

She grimaced. 'So, what do you want to do about the bar?' she asked then.

'What *about* the bar?'

She squinted across at him in the sunlight. 'Well, about the fact that he's left it to us.'

Robbie froze. He tried to reconcile the ordinary meaning of what El had just said with some alternative truth. He couldn't think what that might be, though. He could barely get the words out to ask. 'What do you mean, left it to us?'

'What do you *think* I mean, Robbie?' She was impatient now. 'In his will, apparently.'

'And when you say "us", that's as in . . . ?'

'As in, me and you – Christ!' She took a breath, her eyes narrowing again as she studied him. For the first time, she seemed to consider that perhaps he wasn't being deliberately obtuse here. 'Didn't the solicitor phone you?'

Robbie felt a little faint. 'I've had a few missed calls these past few days,' he managed weakly.

He'd had all manner of them, in fact, from grief-stricken friends and grief-adjacent service providers alike. It had been hard to keep track.

He cast both hands over his face and down his neck, his mouth agape. 'You're serious. Are you serious? We *own* Love and Death? The two of us?'

He was enunciating each syllable carefully, and of course, something about that only made El extra nonchalant.

'Yep. We own it,' she replied. 'So, the question is, what are we going to do with it?'

Chapter Forty-One

For at least a full thirty seconds, Robbie said nothing at all. He looked utterly stunned. 'I don't understand. Why did he leave it to us?'

'How should I know? He didn't mention it, then, in all your little heart-to-hearts?' El snapped.

There was a beat of silence.

'Sorry,' she said. 'That was . . . sorry. I just . . .'

'It's fine,' he replied.

He sounded like he'd barely registered her petulance, actually. Maybe he felt it was par for the course, by now, that the two of them would irritate each other and lash out at each other; that they would, in many ways, display the worst versions of themselves to one another; that they might even go years without seeing or speaking to one another. And that, ultimately, none of those things would matter very much at all.

'I mean, I was pretty shocked, too, when I heard, if it helps,' she offered. 'Anyway, the way I see it, this is pretty simple. We either keep the place, or we sell it. Lease runs for another five years apparently.'

Robbie nodded. Slowly, his practical, problem-solving brain seemed to be rebooting. 'And did the solicitor tell you anything else about . . . well, about Love and Death?' he asked.

'What do you mean?'

'Well, you know. Just about its status or . . . anything.'

El had no idea what that meant. She looked across at Robbie blankly, waiting for more.

What she got from him was no less vague.

'Things have changed a bit since you left.'

No shit, El felt like replying. After all, in her day, Love and Death had been a new-ish hole-in-the-wall spot – revered by a small subset of drinkers and drinks-makers, but broadly unknown, and inconveniently located. These days, it was world renowned. It was in the coolest part of town. It was an established mainstay, associated with celebrities and accolades.

The thought that returning to the bar, as its owner, would be yet another step forwards for her career . . . of course that thought had occurred to El in recent days. It would, she knew, be perceived as a full-circle moment – as a triumph. Evidently Otto had wanted to give her that – in death, if not in life. Once her own shock had subsided, it had been impossible not to be moved by the notion.

Across from her now, in the cemetery, Robbie cleared his throat. 'There's no money,' he said.

El practically did a double-take. 'What?'

'The place is drowning in debt,' he continued. 'No one in their right mind would take it on. Or . . . I suppose that's not true. We probably both know who would buy it.'

'We definitely *don't* both know,' she countered.

'Well, a competitor. Someone who could buy it cheap, and either they keep the brand but completely bastardize it, or they wait a few months and all of a sudden Love and Death is the newest branch of Nightjar or Mr Fogg's or wherever.'

'Wow. Okay.' Now El was the one struggling to process. 'So, you're saying essentially it's us or . . . what? The bar as we know it just disappears?'

'I mean, I don't know. But if I'm looking at this from a purely practical, economic perspective . . . I think that's about the size of it, yeah.'

El exhaled loudly. She felt like she'd been sucker-punched. It had already been an emotional day – an emotional couple of weeks.

'I need to sit down,' she murmured. For lack of any other option, and with not a moment's thought for her silk skirt, she plonked herself right down on the ground.

She looked again at the mound of earth that was now Otto's permanent home.

So, he hadn't given her a golden ticket, after all; she wasn't going to swoop in here for a victory lap. Instead, he'd given her something else entirely – he'd given her a challenge. She couldn't help the little laugh that escaped her.

'I want us to do it,' she said, looking up at Robbie. 'Take it over. What about you?'

Much later, it would occur to El that perhaps she and Robbie never needed to remain the *us* that Otto had suddenly rendered them. One of them could have bought the other out, perhaps, or been a silent partner. Of course, such options might have ultimately proven impossible, for some legal or financial reason. It would strike her, though, that neither she nor Robbie even floated the suggestion. From the off, it was either going to be both of them or neither of them.

Robbie crouched down on his hunkers beside her. 'We can't kid ourselves, El. This would be a rescue mission. Plus, if Brexit ends up happening, who knows how that's going to affect the whole landscape in terms of small businesses, importing goods, people's disposable income . . .'

It was one concern El could very easily wave away. 'Brexit's not going to happen.'

He looked less convinced.

She forced herself to think briefly about the practicalities as she *did* accept them. She lived in Japan. She couldn't distinguish her profits from her losses on a spreadsheet, and she had no desire to try to. Meanwhile, Robbie worked . . . wherever he worked now. Quite possibly, he hadn't so much as set foot behind a bar in years. He had a whole different life.

On top of all that, there was also the issue of the two of them. They hadn't always got along. To say nothing of the point at which, if anything, they'd suddenly had the very opposite problem.

Ultimately, though, for El, none of that mattered.

She couldn't bear the thought of Love and Death swiftly shuttered or otherwise destroyed. She couldn't bear to have Otto's legacy tarnished in that way.

She also still remembered those first miserable months in Anaheim, the last time she'd lost Otto. She could probably call that a kind of depression, looking back on it. Given how she felt right now, she feared it might be very bad for her to return to Tokyo and that tiny coffin-like apartment.

'I still want to do it,' she said, not a hint of doubt in her voice. 'Do you?'

Beside her, Robbie hesitated. He knew there was no universe in which Anna-Claire would see this as anything but a regression – not to mention a renewed commitment to the city she wanted to leave.

They were making each other so unhappy, though. The slow death of their marriage often felt, by now, like nothing short of agony. Robbie suddenly felt that as well as being quicker, it might be kinder to just explode it once and for all. Or maybe that was bullshit – the selfish excuse of a weak man.

In the end, he, too, pushed logic aside, fell back instead on pure feeling. When he looked across at El, his answer came quick and urgent, like she'd thrown him a lifeline and he could not have it float out of reach.

'I do,' he replied.

She didn't smile, and he didn't either. They just stared at one another, wide-eyed, each taking in the magnitude of the moment.

'So, what next? I mean, how does this work?' El asked eventually.

'I don't know,' Robbie replied. 'Are we really supposed to show back up at Love and Death on Monday and just . . . start running it?'

'Maybe not next Monday. Maybe we give ourselves 'til . . . I don't know.' She cracked a smile. 'The Monday after that?'

He grinned, too. It faded quickly, though, all his natural caution kicking back into high gear. 'This feels fast,' he said. 'It could be such a bad decision.'

'Yeah, well. I'm pretty sure I'll have made worse decisions in my life. Slower.'

And, when he really thought about it, Robbie realized he could probably say the same.

Part Five

Chapter Forty-Two

Certain things hadn't changed a bit – there was the record player El remembered; there was the framed photograph of the street that had once been Otto's on the Lower East Side of Manhattan. In a lot of ways, stepping into Love and Death was like going back in time – a sensory overload, memories coming at El everywhere she looked.

Then, as she wandered around, the differences in the place began to strike her, too. Behind the bar, there were spirits and bitters that hadn't even existed when she was here last, but that now felt like staples of the trade. When her eyes landed on one of the corner booths – the same one in which she and Robbie had once sat together, before his wedding – she noticed that the velvet on the seats was aged and worn.

'I suggested we give them a bit of a refresh once, and Otto wasn't having it,' Robbie replied, when El offered that last observation aloud. 'He said, "Don't you think there's something to be said for faded elegance, Robbie? It's the only sort you can't buy, after all."'

El let out a laugh. 'Sometimes, I really do think he was like a member of the British landed gentry, reincarnated.'

'I know. But then, other times . . . like, the week before he died, he asked to meet me at this new place, Pop Brixton? It's another one of those repurposed shipping container situations, you know with all the different vendors? Anyway, so everyone there was like half his age, it's communal seating, they're blasting Flo Rida. But there was this one place he was dying to go to because he said they did authentic deep-fried cheesesteak. I've barely ever seen him so happy.'

El's smile faltered a little. It was hard to think about all the extra time that Robbie had got with Otto – all the extra memories that were now his to keep. It was hard knowing that if she'd booked a flight from Tokyo the very day she saw that quote from Otto about her drink, she'd probably have seen him again before he died.

Maybe Robbie could intuit all of that, because he reached for commonality again. 'Do you remember the time he told us that if someone ordered a Martini, we asked them if they wanted it wet or dry and they didn't know the difference, then we weren't allowed to serve them either?'

El let herself laugh once more. 'He could be unbelievably arsey, couldn't he?'

'Mmm. Unyielding,' Robbie agreed.

'Self-righteous.'

'Moody.'

'Elusive.'

'. . . God, I miss him, though,' Robbie said.

It was an understatement.

Suddenly, El felt tears spring to her eyes all over again. 'I just can't believe he's gone,' she replied hoarsely. 'I know that's such a cliché to say, but . . .'

It had been a few months since the funeral – enough time for her to pack up her life in Tokyo, for Robbie to serve his notice at Deloitte, and for the legal formalities to be concluded. Yet still, it all felt so raw. Any time El pictured Otto being lowered into the ground, at barely more than 50 years old – there forever now, cold and alone – it was almost too much to bear.

She blinked furiously, tried to pull herself together. 'So, how bad is it, then? Money-wise?'

She sat down at a table, and Robbie joined her. Though the bar was as dimly lit and cosy as ever, it was only the early afternoon. They had the time.

'I'm going to dig into the books today,' Robbie replied. 'Go through everything properly. I know he'd been overspending, though. I tried to talk to him about it a million times.'

'But there are still *customers*?' El prompted. 'The place is still busy?'

Robbie shrugged. 'I haven't really been here either, you know. I think you might be overestimating how feasible it was for me to just pop in of a Saturday night.' There was a sudden tightness in his voice, and he cleared his throat, started over. 'Marcus has been keeping me up to speed these last few months, though. According to him, there's been a pretty steady trade. I mean, it's not exactly the post-*BST* heyday . . .'

Another sore subject, moved past quickly.

'To be honest, I think it's just that there's so much more competition these days,' Robbie continued. 'Love and Death hasn't got worse; it's just other bars have got way better. Ironically, in a lot of ways, they've got better *because* of Love and Death.'

'What do you mean?'

'Well, so many of Otto's ideas have been replicated now. Even down to the *unmarked door* thing. Seems like every other bar in town these days involves going down to the basement of a barber's or crawling through a washing machine in a launderette or whatever.'

El snorted.

'Plus, so many places have at least one bartender who trained under him. And now they're out there, still making his drinks, still with his voice in their head every night. He set the standard for all of us, really.'

El found that somewhat comforting – the notion that Otto's legacy was all over this city, that it didn't rest entirely upon her and Robbie.

Realistically, though, she still felt like it was mostly on them.

'So, what should our plan be?' she asked. 'I still can't fully grasp that we actually own the place. We could reupholster all the seats and nobody could do a thing to stop us.'

'We could make every one of them wipe-down vinyl,' Robbie agreed.

She chuckled, but it felt bittersweet.

'I actually don't want to change anything in here,' Robbie said. 'Not the menu, not the decor – nothing.'

'Me neither.'

'I don't think we need any gimmicks. Just good drinks, well made – that's what I want us to do here.'

El wasn't entirely sure she agreed with that one. However, she let it go. That was what they were doing, today – letting things go. Keeping the peace, being gentle with one another. It was already such a hard, strange day. It already felt overwhelming to be back here. And it was a little exciting, too, in a way that felt utterly wrong. The only thing harder than managing all those emotions would have been doing it alone.

'But what about the money? The debt, I mean,' El continued.

'We'll go to the bank. We'll get a loan,' Robbie said.

It was far from the alarm he'd expressed at Otto's funeral. Now, instead, he made it sound easy – as though, if he said it decisively, it could only be true.

She cocked an eyebrow. 'Will that work?'

His response came in paragraphs, and El let it wash over her. She could suddenly see how truly excellent he must have been in the corporate world. She absorbed certain phrases here and there – *business case, fiscal responsibility, lender discretion.* And she certainly caught the last bit:

'I'll *make* it work,' he said.

From the tone of his voice, the expression on his face, she was inclined to believe him.

Robbie only wished he had the same confidence – or even the ability to project it – in all areas.

'I wonder if I even still remember how to do this,' he couldn't help mumbling, later that afternoon. They were in the stockroom, divvying up jobs.

'Inventory?'

'All of it. It feels like forever since I've had to make a drink at speed.'

'Oh, it'll all come flooding back to you,' El said easily. She kneeled down, reaching in under the bottom of the shelves to haul out several crates jammed full of miscellany. 'Give me a hand with this, will you? God, it looks like some of these things have been here for years.'

'I think that must have just been his stash for playing around with, yeah.'

Robbie sat down beside El, and they swiftly fell into a rhythm. She checked the date on each bottle, passing any non-expired item his way to be noted down on his clipboard.

There was something about the task that proved soothing to the emotionally overloaded brain. Here was something absorbing but repetitive and unchallenging – here was a goal they could visibly achieve, little by little.

'And how are you about . . . you know. Everything else?' El enquired carefully, after some time had passed. Now that they were in the swing of it, they didn't even need to verbalize the ongoing process as their hands moved.

Robbie swallowed. 'I feel a bit shell-shocked. But I don't . . . I don't wish it wasn't happening. Or . . . I wish things were different and so it didn't *have* to happen, but as things are, I—'

'I get it,' El interrupted him gently. 'You don't have to explain. I'm just . . . glad you're doing okay.'

Robbie looked across at her. Hunkered down in here, in this windowless room, he suddenly realized how close they were to one another. It felt like no time had passed since they were last here, together, and yet everything was different, too.

Anna-Claire was back in Belfast now, living with her parents. He was in their Bermondsey flat alone. When he'd told his wife that he'd agreed to take on the bar, almost everything about that conversation had gone precisely as he'd thought it would. He couldn't say he hadn't been aware of what was at stake. There had just been one surprising part of the whole thing.

'Has anything ever happened between you and her?' Anna-Claire had asked him, standing opposite him in their bedroom.

Robbie had felt his blood pumping. 'Me and who?' he'd replied. It was probably the worst, most insulting thing he could have said. At least that was the impression he got, from his wife's face.

'You and El Tippett.'

To his shame, instead of an answer, Robbie had taken a coward's way out. 'We haven't even been on the same land mass for years,' he'd said.

Anna-Claire had frowned, like she just couldn't tally that objective fact with her own instinct. 'I don't like the way she looks at you.'

And Robbie had considered asking what she meant by that, or when she'd even noticed El looking at him at all. But really, at that stage, what did it matter?

In the stockroom now, with El's eyes on his, all Robbie could think was that he *did* like the way she looked at him. Moments seemed to flash in his memory, like a montage. Her bare feet, beside him in a booth in this very bar, on his stag night. Her wrist in his hand in the Chateau Marmont. Her lips on his, one early morning in Berlin.

Suddenly, his mouth was dry, his brain fuzzy with grief and tiredness and a strong sense of what he could only categorize, broadly, as *risk*.

Before he had even fully processed any of it, he seemed to be speaking. 'What happened in Berlin . . . we're business partners, now. You know that, right? We're people's bosses. Nothing like that can ever happen again.'

El held his gaze for a moment. Then, there was a slight shift of her body away from his, a slight tilt of her chin. 'Nothing like what?'

Chapter Forty-Three

In the end, they only made it two months before their first real fight.

Looked at another way, they held out a whole two months.

'This isn't working!' El practically shouted across the bar.

Could she have chosen a better time, a better scenario, than in front of three of their employees, midway through a shift? Possibly. But in the circumstances, she felt she deserved a pass. It had been a challenging day. And a worse night. There were, at least, no customers around to witness her outburst.

Robbie turned to stare at El. Marcus, Adam, and Johnny all did the same. Marcus was the only one of the old crew still in the picture. He was a manager now and the others were newer recruits, working behind the bar and on the door, respectively.

'Alright,' Marcus said. 'Let's make ourselves scarce, eh, kids? Mum and Dad need to have a grown-up conversation now.'

El and Robbie each shot him a glance that was half exasperation, half gratitude. Without having to ask, Marcus seemed to know that nobody would be coming back tonight. He directed Adam and Johnny to grab their coats as they all filed out the door.

'Well, *that* was unprofessional,' Robbie said, the second they were alone.

El reached for the needle on the record player and the music – a last clinging attempt at positivity – was switched off.

'Do you feel like you were professional with Carl today?' she fired back.

Robbie grimaced.

They'd been to the bank together that afternoon. Robbie had done most of the talking, and he'd seemed incredibly convincing to El. Alas, not so to Carl, the manager at NatWest on Islington High Street. Carl had told them in no uncertain terms that – after a long process of reviewing all the many documents Robbie had provided – he could not extend their line of credit even an inch further. Moreover, if they didn't begin to make repayments within three months, they'd have to file for bankruptcy. El had wondered why he couldn't have just told them that over the phone.

She'd been anxious in response to the news – intimidated in a way that manifested in occasional dashes of inappropriate comedy.

Robbie, conversely, had been priggish and combative. There had been a lot of *I think you'll find*.

At one point, he had threatened to report Carl to some sort of financial ombudsman. Between both men, the volume had reached levels that El imagined might be common in the Gherkin but that she found frankly mortifying inside a little glass booth in a high street bank. Mortifying and pointless.

Evidently, they were on the losing end of this one, plain and simple, and El hadn't seen the harm in building in some levity, just a little layer of self-preservation, along the way.

Outside on the pavement, after the appointment, Robbie had disagreed.

Then came this evening's shift. It was mid-week, and a quiet one. On a night they really needed the magic of a full house – or merely the *distraction* of it – they didn't get it. Instead, for almost the full hour prior to El's big declaration, the place had been empty. The resulting idleness had offered nothing but dangerous amounts of time for contemplation.

In truth, even with a busier crowd, Love and Death just wasn't the same without Otto. That was the reality.

Robbie and El both knew it, and it sometimes seemed like every single customer did, too. No matter their efforts to keep everything exactly as it had always been, it felt like the spirit of the place was gone.

Part of El was furious with Otto for putting them in this position. For going and dying on them and leaving them with the aftermath. Part of her wanted to just throw in the towel right now, admit defeat and have some dignity about it. On to the next thing.

Another part of her, though . . .

That part of her looked over at Robbie now.

'So, if we need to make more money, then we probably need to start charging a bit more, and we need some more bums on seats. I mean, I know I don't have an *economics degree*,' she told him – that one had been cast up to Carl earlier – 'but it seems pretty basic to me.'

He huffed a little in response. 'So, what?'

She shrugged. She wasn't claiming to have any real answers here.

'No, come on, you're the expert,' Robbie continued tersely. 'You're the one who's been off bar-hopping round the world. You must have some international insights to share. How do you suggest we actually do those things, El? And not in terms of vibes. In terms of *plans*.'

She almost chuckled blackly. They were going to get into all of it then, were they?

As it happened, that suited her fine.

'Alright, don't get shirty with me just because Carl didn't like your sums,' she tossed back. 'And it's not my fault you didn't know what a Purple Maize was when that woman asked for it last night.'

A newly invented concoction, the Purple Maize comprised of Japanese shōchū, Dolin Blanc, and St-Germain. The customer had tried it, apparently, on a visit to the New York bar that originated it. El had come across it in Tokyo. Robbie had been at a loss.

'Well, it's not my fault you don't know who any of the suppliers are!' Robbie exclaimed. 'Or what the keys on that hook by the freezer do, or where people even go out in London anymore!'

Petty as they were, El felt the injury of each of those accusations, too. They were all true.

'I don't want to put a sign above the door,' Robbie continued. 'I'm sorry. I just . . . that's one thing I don't want to do.'

El wasn't sure where that had come from. 'And you think I do?' she replied, all incredulity.

'What *do* you want to do, then?'

She thought about it for a moment. It might have been good, she realized, to have thought about it *before* starting this conversation. 'For one thing, I think we need to start serving food.'

She saw his lips part, could almost hear the protest about their kitchen's capacity before it arrived.

'Calm down, I'm not talking full dinners,' she added. 'But *something*. How many times a night did people used to ask us for even a bag of cheese and onion in here? Seventeen zillion. Hungry people go home. I'm telling you – we need to start feeding them.'

A pause. They both knew Otto would be turning in his grave at the very idea. Nonetheless:

'Fine,' Robbie replied.

El ignored the flatness of his delivery and took it as a victory, going straight for another. 'And we need to change up the drinks menu.'

This time, Robbie looked vastly more apprehensive. 'Oh God . . .'

'"Oh God" what?'

'Oh God, I dread to think what you want to serve in here, El.'

'Probably the same sorts of things I've been serving for years – to international acclaim, since you mentioned it – while you've been off sending emails.'

His face contorted with annoyance. 'We need drinks that are replicable, though: drinks that can be made relatively quickly, and not just by you – by anyone who happens to be on shift. Frankly, at this point, we probably need drinks that are sort of cheap. And there's also the question of integrity.'

El raised an eyebrow, letting that last bit settle between them. 'The question of integrity?' she repeated slowly.

'Yes. Love and Death isn't some off-radar, experimental place anymore—'

'Maybe it should be,' she interjected, but he wasn't finished.

'Well, it isn't! It's one of the most established cocktail bars in London, even if it's not one of the splashiest right now. There are certain standards people have come to expect, and rightly so. To put it bluntly, we have to keep this place classy, El. We can't let it turn into one big nonsense performance art piece.'

'Oh, fuck off, Robbie.'

They stared at each other, animosity pulsing between them, and then suddenly, she laughed out loud.

El didn't expect it from herself, and she certainly didn't expect that he'd join her – just a sharp, staccato burst, the tension not quite gone but punctured somewhat.

She let herself sink into a seat at a table. 'Can you believe we're back here?' she asked wryly. 'Having this same fight we had a *decade* ago?'

'I know.' Robbie came to join her. 'We had a good run somewhere in the middle, though, didn't we? Things were quite harmonious there for a while.'

'You mean when we didn't work together? When we didn't even live in the same country?'

It was a good point, and Robbie cocked his head in concession.

El sighed heavily. She tried to think of a way she and Robbie could come up with a new drinks roster for Love and Death, while also maintaining any level of harmony. What would be exciting to the modern customer, and cost-effective to produce, and pleasing to both her and Robbie's sensibilities?

She didn't know if even one such cocktail existed, much less a whole menu's worth.

'Why don't we just . . . ask people what they're in the mood for?' she suggested instead.

Robbie frowned. 'What, you mean like no menu at all?'

El nodded. 'Why not? I don't know if you've noticed, but it's not like the old days. Customers have way more knowledge now. They've travelled more, or they've got cocktail recipe books at home. A lot of people come into a cocktail bar and already know exactly what they want. And if they don't, we can help them figure it out. I'm talking really basic questions. *Do you like rum? Would you prefer a long drink or a short one? Are you in the mood for something sweet?* That actually sounds fun. Don't you think? It'd be like one of those magazine flow-chart quizzes.'

Robbie looked across at her blankly, like a man who'd never read *Cosmo*, never wondered which member of a pop band was his perfect match.

'Just think of it, Robbie,' she continued. 'By stealth, you could fill this whole place with drinks from the eighteenth century if you wanted. Meanwhile, obviously I'll be over at the other end of the bar, setting things on fire.'

He cracked a smile. 'I suppose we could try it. Maybe it's kind of a good selling point of itself. The bar with no menu.'

She raised one eyebrow slyly. 'A gimmick, you could say.'

He ignored that, pointedly.

After a moment, he spoke again, his voice little more than a murmur. 'I really thought we'd get the loan. You know? I really thought I could make it happen.'

'I know you did,' El replied, her own tone gentler now, too.

'The thing is: I'm not sure any of these changes will actually solve our problems – not really. We don't just need cashflow to stay afloat. We need to start reducing the debt.'

El took that in. Without the assistance of a bank, then, what they needed was a backer. Hadn't Otto himself started off with private investment, in the early days? But who could be prevailed upon to donate to two first-time business owners, to a business whose financial history Carl had today called 'volatile'?

Only one name, however unlikely, sprung to El's mind.

'I might have an idea there,' she found herself saying, before she could think better of it.

Robbie looked dubious. 'A legal one?'

'Yes, legal one!'

'I need more details.'

'Mmm. I'll tell you the details if it ends up happening.' She let her gaze drift towards the bar itself, towards all the work they'd effectively just excused their employees from doing. 'Shall we clear up? Call it a night for tonight?'

He nodded, and they rose.

'Also, I think we probably need to get an Instagram account,' Robbie said. 'All the bars have them now – have you noticed that?'

El hadn't particularly.

'Well, if we're changing stuff . . .' he added, a little defensively.

El just nodded. She could give him this one, she thought. She had no strong thoughts on Instagram either way. 'I'll set it up.'

When they were finished, it was not yet midnight, and they walked to the tube together. Somewhere in the distance, they could hear fireworks going off, and El realized with a start that tonight was Guy Fawkes Night. November had really crept up on her.

'So, how are Niall and Nigel working out?' she asked, as they made their way into Old Street station.

Niall was one of Robbie's mates (job unknown, at least to El), and Nigel was a biochemist whom Niall had found on the internet. El found the similarity in their names much more amusing than the situation likely merited. Robbie had recently moved into their house-share in Finsbury Park.

'Alright, yeah. I sort of can't believe I have flatmates now.'

'I can't believe I *don't*,' El replied.

It had felt like a miracle when she'd found her little one-bedroom place near Kennington. Everyone said how lucky she was, and despite the dodgy street and dodgy electrics, despite the windowless bathroom and noisy neighbours, El *felt* lucky.

'I'm glad of the company, to be honest,' Robbie continued, as they passed through the barriers. 'And it's actually quite nice being in a new area. New coffee shops, all that.'

Whether he meant it or was just trying to mean it, El couldn't tell. She'd been disinclined to pry too much into the details of his personal life, ever since he'd made clear his feelings on that Berlin blip.

Evidently, if he'd once seen her briefly in a certain light, he no longer did.

It was not in her nature – she'd reminded herself repeatedly, as required, that it absolutely was not in her nature – to dwell on such matters. Instead, since her return to London, she'd thrown herself into rejuvenating old friendships, and had cast the net wide in terms of potential romantic partners.

Anything else, like grief or confusion or *exhaustion*? She simply ignored it.

In any case, the point was that she and Robbie lived on opposite sides of the city now, on different tube lines. They'd reached the escalators, where they went their separate ways.

'Oh, one more thing,' she added. 'About Love and Death, I

mean. We need to get some girls in there. Not as customers – as bartenders. I don't know what Otto had against them.'

Robbie pointed out the obvious. 'You being the exception.'

'I suppose so.'

Some part of her still liked the thought of that – of having been the exception, the special one. She was only human. Equally, based on the evidence before her, it seemed possible that Otto – for all his good qualities – may have harboured some type of latent misogyny. El really didn't know. Either way, she needed some female company around the place.

'We can't afford to take on anybody new, though,' Robbie said. 'Are you saying you want to sack a man just to hire a woman?'

She stepped onto her escalator. 'I'm saying I want to sack at least *two* men and hire at least *two* women,' she replied, beginning her descent.

'That might be gender discrimination!' he called after her.

'I'll google it!' She grinned, and as he watched her disappear, Robbie could only laugh.

Chapter Forty-Four

El invited her father into the bar because it made sense (for him to see the place in which he'd theoretically be investing) and also because she did not want to go to his house. It had once been her house too, of course, but it had never much felt that way.

The last time she'd laid eyes on Daniel Tippett, she'd been in her early twenties, and in the fifteen minutes prior to their reunion, it occurred to her that she might not recognize him. The moment he walked into Love and Death, however, that concern evaporated. He looked exactly as he ever had.

His drink of choice, when she asked for it, was still the same one it had always been: whiskey on the rocks, with a twist.

He still had that strange, slightly removed way of speaking – that weird transatlantic twang.

'What an . . . *unusual* ensemble,' he said to her, almost right away, looking her up and down.

El tugged a little at her dress. It was a short pinafore she'd made, inexpertly but enjoyably, across a few of those long afternoons in Tokyo.

Yep, she thought grimly. *Same old Dad.*

Once they'd handled the business side of things – that was done in a trice; all it really required was her own total prostration – they had to find some way to fill the time it would take for her father to finish the rest of his drink. Thankfully, El had anticipated exactly this. She'd prepared any number of neutral subjects about which she could enquire at length.

'So, how's—'

'You have always been such a disappointment to me Eloise,' he interrupted.

El closed her mouth abruptly.

It wasn't nice to hear, but neither was it a surprise. She took a sip from her own drink. She'd gone for a gin and tonic, generous on the gin. The freshness of the fizz, the bite of the alcohol cutting through, felt like just what she needed as it slid down her throat.

She was sitting opposite her father, at his table, and she was conscious of Robbie's occasional curious glances towards them from behind the bar. While she prided herself on giving her customers a lot of personal attention, sometimes at the expense of efficiency, this was another level.

'Wow,' she said dryly. 'Don't hold back, Dad. This is great; it's like 1999 all over again.'

He continued as though she hadn't spoken. He looked pained now, genuinely confused. 'You know, when I left Arkansas, I had fifty bucks in my pocket. I was always pushing, pushing, pushing – for the next promotion, the next pay rise. Didn't matter where I had to go, what it took from me. I just wanted you to have the best of everything. And you did, Eloise. I gave you all the opportunities you could have wished for. But for what? For you to squander them, waste your time and your talents?'

'I don't think I've done either of those things,' El replied, keeping her voice light. And then – this wasn't part of the plan – she kept on talking. She couldn't seem to stop herself, even if it was doubtless going to be to her own detriment. Maybe it really *was* like 1999 all over again. 'I mean, yeah. The drinks I make here are just drinks. Same as my clothes are just clothes. Or the movies my mate Frankie is in are just movies, just made-up stories. What do they matter? And I suppose none of that stuff *does* matter, insofar as we'll all be dead someday, and nothing matters. But what kind of a way is that to live?'

Her father said nothing.

'I'm actually asking you here, Dad,' she pressed. Perhaps that was some kind of growth, she thought – to find herself sincerely interested in his response. Certainly, it was a big change from her adolescent self. 'Do you think there can be no value in something that's transitory?' she continued. 'Or do you just think there's no value in beauty at all? In something that's fun and frivolous, like a cocktail? I don't understand that. Because life is hard, okay? The whole "fifty bucks in your pocket" thing and the schlepping all over the world – schlepping Mum and me along, too, with no consultation, by the way – but anyway . . . the point is, I get it. That's not easy. Life can sometimes feel like a fucking *obstacle course*. So, don't you think it's nice if we can try – just here and there, in whatever stupid, tiny ways we can – to make it a bit more *bearable* for each other? Don't you think there's some sliver of nobility in that?'

Unbidden, her voice seemed to have risen, become a little shaky with emotion. She swallowed, tried to ignore the warm feeling in her cheeks.

Again, her father said absolutely nothing. He just looked at her for a long moment, his expression entirely inscrutable. Then, he downed his drink, placed the glass decisively back on the table – right alongside the cheque he'd written her – and stood up.

'You'll want to lodge that within twenty-four hours,' he said.

And, before she could so much as reply, he was gone.

Left alone, El let out a long, slow exhale, followed by a long, slow sip of her G&T.

How many years had she avoided precisely this scenario? The predictability of it – little rich girl goes running to Daddy in the end. But she'd done it now. She knew she'd never, ever do it again.

And so, she thought, this one time – this one exception, for Otto, for Robbie, for the greater good – had better be worth it.

'Well? Who was he?'

Robbie had forced himself to wait until after closing to ask her. They were side by side, just the two of them that night, unloading clean glasses from the dishwasher, putting the dirty ones in.

El didn't cease her movements. 'That was my father,' she replied.

Robbie's lips parted slightly in surprise. 'Oh wow. I mean, I remember I did see him, that one time . . . I didn't recognize him tonight, though. I actually didn't even realize your dad lived here full time.'

'Yep. He's an American man, living in London, who's never really seemed to think I was good enough. Remind you of anyone? Do you think I need a trained psychiatrist to figure this one out, or would any drunk in the bar do?'

It was barked out, like a joke, and Robbie duly smiled in response.

'He did give me this, though,' El continued. From her pocket, she produced a slip of paper and passed it to him.

As distractions went, it was a good one. Robbie's eyebrows shot up when he took in the number on the cheque. 'What's this?' he asked, idiotically.

'For the bar, obviously. Small change to him, honestly.'

'Oh my God! El! That's . . . that's huge.'

'It's a loan, not a gift, obviously. But still. Is that a kind of love, do you think? Investing in a business you believe is a total waste of your daughter's time and talents?'

Robbie grimaced. 'He said that?'

'Yep.'

Robbie wasn't sure what he could offer, by way of reply, that wouldn't seem horribly trite. So, he bided his time.

El began polishing each clean glass, passing it across to him to be placed back on the correct shelf. Certain choreography seemed to have stayed with both of them, after all this time – like it was embedded into muscle memory.

'You know, it's funny,' he offered, after a moment. 'With *my* mum and dad, the bar thing is fine. If anything, I think they probably just wish it was more of a "pints" sort of pub. Less of this poser-y shit, you know? But at a basic level, they're probably more comfortable with the idea of me as a barman than they were when I was 20 and it seemed like I was going to be a "fat cat banker", as they called it.'

El met his eyes, and it felt like a bit of a triumph – that he'd unlocked a smidge of curiosity in her, found the way into a real conversation with her.

'There's a lot you don't agree with them on though, right?' she ventured.

'Oh yeah.'

'So, how do you . . . manage that?'

'Three words. The Irish Sea.'

They both chuckled. There was undoubtedly some truth in the joke, though. Hadn't recent events in Robbie's life been a classic example?

His separation from Anna-Claire certainly hadn't been easy.

Everything about the architecture of his life felt different now. He had gone from his childhood home to a university in which he'd had a private bedroom and bathroom, with meals served by staff in the dining hall. From there, it was straight to his marital abode. In his 30s, and for the first time in his life, Robbie was now negotiating a cleaning schedule, an ongoing debate about how frequently to put the heating on.

There were moments when the change was so hard. Moments when, especially given the grief of Otto's death, all he wanted was familiarity, sameness.

He had come to understand why people sometimes returned

over and over again to a relationship, even if it wasn't the right one. And undoubtedly, he'd lately acquired a brand-new appreciation for all the things, both practical and aesthetic, that Anna-Claire had done to make both their lives more pleasant.

On the other hand, there was a simplicity to certain aspects of his new existence. It was actually a *relief*, he'd found, to no longer be trying and failing at something all the time.

Some evenings now, Niall or Nigel might say, 'Are you on for a bit of *Assassin's Creed* tonight?'

Or: 'I'm just ordering a burrito on Deliveroo if you fancy one.'

And Robbie honestly could whoop with joy at the low stakes of it all.

This nuance was lost on his mum and dad. They were just plain devastated. Not *by* him, necessarily. After all, unlike Anna-Claire's parents, they were culturally Protestant, more than anything. They didn't genuinely lie awake at night worrying that divorce was a sin against God. Even the social embarrassment, while certainly present, seemed to be manageable.

No. What Robbie had realized quickly was that his parents were, instead, devastated *for* him.

Quite simply, they considered that with Anna-Claire, Robbie had always been – as his younger brother put it – *punching*. The fact that he hadn't been on the first easyJet over to Belfast, doing everything he could to win her back, was a continued source of amazement to his family.

'I've said it before, and I'll say it again: you would want to catch yourself on, son,' his mother had told him briskly on the phone, just last week.

This week, though, she'd sent him a Tesco delivery, lest he was 'wasting away over there'.

Behind the bar at Love and Death, in the wee hours of the morning, Robbie smiled a little at the memory.

'I think they're basically good parents, you know?' he said.

'Not right about everything – not by a long shot. But they love me and . . . they're not *bad* people. And so there are certain areas of my life, certain topics of conversation, that I choose to just . . . sidestep, with them, as best I can. Maybe that's wrong. I mean, I'm pretty sure they're going to vote for Brexit, against their own best interests in every possible way, just because the DUP will tell them to. So, I don't know. I go back and forth on it.'

El seemed to take that in. 'Sounds a bit like me with my mum.'

'What was *she* like, when you were a kid?'

El hesitated. 'Mmm. That's probably a story for another day,' she said.

And just like that, Robbie could tell, the window for exchanging confidences was closed.

'Point is, I think my dad might be a different kettle of fish,' she continued, a new efficiency about her tone. 'But at least we can pay the bank now. The money's enough, yeah? It'll make a difference?'

'Absolutely. I mean, this . . . saves our bacon, basically. It's amazing, El.'

She just nodded, satisfied.

Robbie found, however, that there remained one thing he couldn't let lie. 'Otto *did* think you were good enough, by the way,' he said. 'I mean, just for the record.'

'Not as good as you,' El replied simply.

Robbie was staggered. The notion was so insane to him that he accidentally laughed out loud. Hadn't she been the shadow he'd chased, the shoes he'd tried to fill, for years after she'd left?

'What? That wasn't remotely it. El! Are you joking? If anything, it was the opposite.'

This time, she said nothing to contradict him. But he really didn't think she believed him, either.

Chapter Forty-Five

Bit by bit, after that, things shifted at Love and Death.

An array of bar snacks became available for peckish drinkers.

On Instagram, buoyed by photographs of El's most dramatic creations, the bar's follower count grew steadily each month. One thousand, then three thousand, then six thousand . . .

The staff roster had a bit of a shake-up.

Tameka Owens was tall, self-possessed, 24 years old.

'I like the idea of hosting a party but in someone else's house,' she said, when asked about her interest in cocktail bartending.

El liked that.

'Also, I trained as a chef at The River Café for two years.'

Robbie liked *that*.

At a certain point, it only made sense that Robbie and El would start to take alternate shifts. That way, at least one of them was present to keep an eye on things, while the other could have a night off. Even on the evenings an extra pair of hands was needed and they were there together, they often lacked the time for in-depth discussion.

What they got, instead, were snatches of conversation here and there. Or, sometimes, information gleaned second-hand from one of their employees.

El knew, for example, when Robbie and his housemates became briefly obsessed with Pokémon GO, almost causing an accident on the Strand in their search for Charizard.

Robbie became aware, vaguely, that El was seeing a Scottish woman named Laura. Equally, it came to his attention when that was no longer, as El called it, *a thing*.

Together, they talked business; they talked news and gossip; they weaved their lives and schedules in and around each other's, by necessity.

'Frankie's coming to do a show in the West End!' El said, one afternoon as they were doing payroll. *He* was doing payroll; she was also present.

'Oh wow! That's amazing,' Robbie replied, a little distractedly.

'Yep. Who would have thunk, eh? One minute she's prancing about in a hula skirt with me . . . the next she's on stage with Tom Hiddleston.'

Somehow, Robbie's attention seemed to have been caught.

'I really wish I'd seen you in the hula skirt . . .' he said.

'I bet you do,' she replied.

That seemed to happen, every once in a while. They'd flirt with each other and pretend they hadn't, then eventually do it again.

Of course, they irked each other very regularly, too.

From him: 'Could you maybe *not* keep scooping ice with the glasses? Loads of them are chipped already.'

From her, later the very same night: 'Could you maybe *not* hover round me like a serial killer?' She dusted parmesan onto the top of an Espresso Martini, crouching down to look at it at eye level, just like Otto used to. 'I promise you, the very second I am done with this, you can have it. I can feel you breathing down my neck.'

'In a good way, or . . . ?'

'*Not* in a good way!' she seethed.

What they didn't do, in the midst of all these interactions, was socialize much together. Whether that was a matter of practicability or choice – and if the latter, whose – was unclear. Then came Robbie's suggestion, once they'd been in business a year:

319

'I think we should go out,' he proclaimed.

They were standing outside NatWest in Islington, having just met with bank manager Carl. Relations had been much less combative on this visit.

El's expression froze. 'What?'

Robbie felt suddenly panicked, embarrassed. 'To celebrate,' he clarified hurriedly. 'And, you know, reflect. What are we doing well, what could we be doing better, et cetera.'

Before him, El seemed to visibly return to her usual self. 'Sure,' she replied easily. 'Great. Let's do it.'

They went to a wine bar in Clerkenwell – all high ceilings and calming tones, Scandi-chic. Robbie let his gaze drift around, wondering idly whether he'd like to work in a place like this. There was something airy and appealing about it, no doubt. But then, this time of year especially, he wasn't sure Love and Death could be beaten on cosiness, on that twinkling, sumptuous, cocoon-like thing. Dotted around the wine bar, the Christmas decorations were sparse and tasteful – in his opinion, a little *too* much so.

'Stop analysing,' El scolded.

He smiled sheepishly. Hadn't they chosen somewhere with no cocktails on the menu precisely to try and avoid this issue? Robbie just could never seem to stop the questions and comparisons occurring to him, the taking of mental notes.

The waiter arrived with a bottle of Champagne and poured two glasses.

'Well, happy one year!' El proclaimed, as they clinked their flutes together.

'Fifteen months in!' Robbie replied, and they exchanged a wry look. Somehow, that was how long it had taken to successfully schedule this evening – months, after he'd first mentioned the idea, for each of them to be free of other social obligations, for neither of them to be hijacked by some last-minute issue at work.

'We haven't burned the place down,' El said.

'We haven't killed each other,' Robbie returned.

For him, the shift back to bartending had proven exhausting and all-consuming – and the best possible distraction he could have asked for.

On the days he'd most needed something to get him out of his house, out of his own head, Love and Death had been that thing.

Their new menu-less approach, in fact, he'd turned out to especially enjoy. Maybe more so than El, even.

He supposed there was more novelty in it for him. She'd mostly seen the menu as a set of loose suggestions, in any case. By contrast, he'd always liked a clear brief. The first time he found himself freewheeling it – telling a customer what *he* thought they'd like, rather than the other way around – he'd panicked all the while.

His suggestion had seemed to go down well, though – that night and all the nights that followed.

'Leave it with me,' he would hear himself say. 'If you like a Marg, I think you'll love a Scoville Sipper.'

Or, 'I promise, made right, a classic Daiquiri is the best thing you'll ever drink. None of this "grown-up Slush Puppie" stuff.'

In work, as in life, it slowly began to feel quite fun – being the one who made all the decisions, being the person who sized up a situation and declared what should happen next. It began to feel a bit like freedom.

'And hey, God bless Daniel Tippett,' Robbie said now, looking across at El in the wine bar.

'Cheers to that,' she agreed dryly, with a large gulp from her glass.

Because of course, no amount of creativity, strategic thinking, or hard graft would have mattered without her father's money. Robbie had spent so much of his own life trying to wish away, or work around, precisely this kind of economic reality. There'd been times when it really seemed like he could – times when he'd wholeheartedly bought in to the notion of *upward mobility*. These days, less so. After all, most of what he'd earned at Deloitte had now disappeared on lawyers' fees, on the expensive business of carving two lives from one. Financially, he was all but back where he started.

'Have you seen him lately? Your dad, I mean. I know he likes to be updated on his investment.'

El grimaced. 'I don't know why he insists on doing that with me in person, when you offered to just email him the reports. Anyway, no. Haven't seen him in a few months, so our next meeting'll be coming for me fast. We do what we've got to do, I suppose.'

Robbie nodded. 'Wow, it's run the gamut, hasn't it? What we've had to do since we took over?'

They'd spent weeks, for example, trying to figure out how *exactly* Otto had made his chai-infused Vermouth. They'd broken up a fight, that one time a wife had walked in and found her cheating husband wrapped around his girlfriend. They'd hired people, fired people . . . in many ways, serving drinks felt like the least of it.

However, there turned out to be something unifying about having been in the trenches together. By now, they'd amassed at least a whole glass of Champagne's worth of shared triumphs and mortifications. And after that, another one.

Chapter Forty-Six

'Do you remember what you said to me, on our first shift together?' Robbie asked idly when they were on to their third glass.

'Mmm. First shift back or first shift ever?'

'First shift ever.'

El had no idea, just waited. She felt warm and loose.

'"I've been in this game a long time,"' he quoted.

El cringed. 'Christ. Spoken like a 22-year-old, eh? The thing is: I'm sure I genuinely thought that was true. But I thought all sorts of things were true back then. I reckon I probably called a lot of stuff fascism that definitely wasn't fascism.'

'You were amazing,' he countered, and the affection in his voice caught her off-guard. 'You were the most *yourself* person I'd ever met.'

'That's so funny,' she replied lightly. 'I'd have said the exact same thing about you. I remember I used to find it so unnerving sometimes.'

'What? Why?'

She shrugged. 'I know I was the one getting tattoos and doing coke and all . . . but let's face it, so were a lot of people. What do they call it now, the whole "indie sleaze" thing? Point is, it wasn't the 1950s, was it? I don't think I was particularly counter-cultural, really. Broadly speaking, I was getting a pretty positive response from people.'

'Not always, in terms of you and Kat . . .' Robbie pointed out.

'No, that's true,' El conceded.

It didn't take much to remember some of those instances. The fear and injustice of them. Briefly, El considered the possibility – genuinely brand new to her – that maybe she didn't give her younger self enough credit.

'Whatever *happened* to Kat?' Robbie asked then, dragging her back to the present moment. 'Do you ever hear from her?'

'I see her on the internet. She's living in Brighton now, by the looks of things. I don't know what she does work-wise. Something civil service-y. She still makes the jewellery on the side. She has one of those Etsy shops.'

Robbie offered a slight raise of his eyebrows, a slight tilt of his head – the sort of mild interest a person could retain in a past acquaintance.

'I was actually talking about *you*, though,' she continued. 'Can I get back to that?'

'If you must.'

'I just – I've thought about this – and looking back, I reckon it was probably way harder to do what you did. To say out loud "I believe in God" or "I want to meet one person and wait for them". I mean, I know you weren't trying to be punk, but for the record, I always thought that was pretty punk of you.'

Immediately, El wished she hadn't brought up Anna-Claire, however tacitly. They rarely talked about her. That was as true in the aftermath of Robbie's separation as it had ever been before.

On the other side of the table now, though, Robbie's mood seemed unaltered. 'What do you reckon to a divorce?' he asked loftily.

She took her cue from him. 'That's not punk. But it *is* chic. You know it's my dream to be thrice divorced.'

'I don't think I did know that,' he replied. And there was that warmth in his voice again – that sense of indulgence in the way he looked at her. Frankly, it wasn't uncommon for her to elicit that sort of response, from men especially. She seemed to like it all the more from Robbie, though, for getting it less. She wondered how often, over the years they'd known each other, it had featured alongside the smudge of alcohol – that slight dip in sense and defences.

'Oh absolutely, yeah,' she replied. 'I want to wear a big hat and say, "I shall never marry again."'

He laughed out loud, his eyes crinkling at the corners, and El was overcome with such a rush of reciprocal affection for him that she barely knew what to do with it. At this point, she'd just *known* him so long. Was this what sibling love felt like? The ups and the downs of it, the aggravation and protectiveness and immutability of it? She had no way to tell.

'Final papers came last week, actually,' Robbie continued, and she ceased thinking about herself.

'How do you feel?'

'You know what?' He drained the last sip of Champagne from his glass. 'I don't know if it's the done thing to say so, but honestly? I feel absolutely fine.'

Looking across at him now, his whole countenance as open and easy as she'd ever seen it, El was inclined to believe him.

They ordered another bottle, at his urging.

'My God, Robbie, is this an AGM or is it a piss-up?' she said, but offered no other protest.

They were, by then, in the midst of a serious conversation about streamlining, delegation, whether there were ways to achieve the exact same results at Love and Death but with far less stress and expense. (There weren't.)

'I do think we could probably lean on Marcus more, though,' Robbie suggested. 'I can't believe how lucky we are to still have him.'

El nodded in agreement. '*Here's* a fun fact about Marcus,' she added, after a beat. 'He asked me out!'

And, deep down, maybe she didn't *really* think Robbie would receive this news in the way she presented it – casually, as though it were gossip, a turn-up for the books. If she wanted that reaction, she could have gone to Frankie.

Why, then, did she mention it to Robbie at all?

She supposed it was simple. She mentioned it because, at some level, she wanted him to know. She wanted to see what he'd have to say about it.

For a few seconds, he didn't say anything at all, just looked horror-struck. Then: 'You haven't said yes, have you?'

'I've said I'd think about it.'

'What? I thought you were back on women!'

'I'm not *back on women*, Robbie. I'm bisexual.'

She was trying to practise saying it that way: neutrally, without adornment. Of course, she wasn't aiming for *pride* – that seemed entirely ludicrous to El. She no more needed to feel proud of being bisexual than she did of being a brunette or a Sagittarius. The explanations, though, the half-jokes . . . she had long since begun to tire of hearing them come out of her own mouth.

'I've never completely understood that, if I'm honest,' Robbie said.

'Me being bisexual?'

'Yeah. Like, just the *thought* that I might start going out with men now . . . I can't even imagine it.'

'Then you probably shouldn't do it,' she replied. 'Is it the idea of a penis?' Her tone was conversational – disarming, maybe, because Robbie laughed.

'Honestly, yes. No interest. It surprises me *anyone* has any interest, really.'

'Fair,' she said, with a smile. 'For me . . . I don't know. It's just not about the anatomy, necessarily. Or, it *is* – of course it is – but that's not the main thing.'

'Let me guess. You're attracted to the spirit and all that, are you?'

She didn't take the bait. 'I'm attracted to what I'm attracted to. Same as everybody.'

'And you're attracted to . . . Marcus. All of a sudden.'

She shrugged. 'Maybe, yeah. I mean, Marcus is great. He's nice-looking. You're the one who's always on at me to get serious with someone.'

Robbie's whole face sprung into animation. 'When have I ever said that?!'

'A few months ago, in the bar. When Laura went back to Glasgow and we broke up. You said, "Don't you ever want to get serious with anyone, El?"'

'Well, I didn't mean you should get serious with Marcus!'

'Then what *did* you mean?'

For a moment, he said nothing. 'I just . . . if you really want to know, I suppose I just don't think it's appropriate for you to be dating one of our staff,' he offered then.

'Is that right?'

'Don't shit where you eat, El.'

'Where *you* eat, more like.'

'Well, that's the same thing, isn't it? That's exactly my point. I don't want everyone at Love and Death to end up dragged into one of your melodramas.'

El huffed out a little laugh, through her nose. 'That's the reason? That's the reason you don't want me shagging Marcus?'

He winced briefly at the term, at the image it presumably conjured. 'Yes.'

She let his response linger between them for a moment, holding his gaze as she picked up her glass.

'Cool,' she said. 'Well, I will bear that in mind, Robbie.'

With that, she downed the rest of her Champagne in one. When she looked across the table, Robbie was doing the very same.

Chapter Forty-Seven

Christmas came and went.

It was always an intense time in the trade. First, all the energy and exhilaration of the festive season, bar staff running on fumes night after night. And then the inevitable crash – the prospect of lean months ahead while most of the population hibernated, dieted, counted the pennies.

Robbie got away for a few days, just after New Year's. Galway with Cormac, Niall, and a few of the other lads meant gale force winds on the beach, pints of Guinness in Naughton's.

'Well, what d'you reckon, Robster – any possibilities here?' Cormac asked, casting his eyes around the pub, no subtlety about it whatsoever. They were six pints in. 'You need to get out there.'

'Strike while the iron's hot, and all that,' Niall added sagely.

'Do you actually know what that phrase means, Niall?' Cormac replied. 'You know it's not some kind of advice for dealing with blue balls? Not that Robbie couldn't use that, let's be honest.'

Robbie just rolled his eyes good-naturedly as the others sniggered. He'd been having a version of this conversation with Cormac for six months or more. Now, though, it was a new year, and he was starting to think his friend might be right. For the zillionth time, El's revelation before Christmas floated back into his brain. He pushed it out again, reaching for another sip of his pint.

Meanwhile, Niall shook his head. 'I'm talking *Fifty Shades*, lads. The Nordie accent. It's the Jamie Dornan effect, isn't it?' He gestured towards Robbie. 'I'm telling you, the girls'll be only too delighted to get trussed up like a roast chicken for this fella.'

Cormac exploded with laughter. 'Alright, steady on.'

'Apart from anything else, Jamie doesn't even use his own accent in those movies, does he?' Robbie added. 'He does an American one.'

His two friends stared across at him now, drunk and delighted. 'How do you know that, Robbie?'

He didn't live it down all night.

Once Robbie was back in London to relieve her, El's respite came in a different form. Frankie had a suite at The Savoy, with a bed three times the size of the one she and El had once shared in West Hollywood. It felt like they'd each lived so many different versions of themselves since then. But through every iteration – every country, every job – they'd managed, in some sense, to remain alongside one another.

Holed up in the suite together, room service on speed dial, the two women talked and ate and then talked some more.

On the first night, they covered the state of the world. On the second, the state of their respective industries.

'Is it wrong to say I'm just finding it all . . . a lot?' El admitted. 'Sometimes, I honestly feel like I never leave the place. I mean, I used to feel that way at the beginning, too. But somehow it felt more like a good thing, back then.'

It was the sort of confession she'd have felt far too guilty to dump on Robbie. It felt so discombobulating, even to acknowledge in her own mind.

'*Also*,' she continued, mouth half full of tiramisu, 'it's like, yes, we've managed to keep the doors open, but I suppose I'm just not sure what we're *aiming for*, at this point. Like, when will we have officially *succeeded*? What does that even mean? It used to just mean making rent and having a good time.'

'Hollywood's so fucked up,' Frankie proclaimed, once the conversation had wound around to her work. 'Sorry, I know you've heard me say that seven million times. But it's just so *aggravating*. Everyone *knows* who the creeps are. We all know. And yet if we want to stay employed, we still have to sit right there next to 'em at awards ceremonies. *Smiling*.'

By their third evening together, they were clear to move on to simpler matters. Or *were* they simpler? Certainly, they were more timeworn.

'Where are all the men?!' Frankie lamented, her voice filling The Savoy's 'aroma grotto'. As far as El could see (and she really couldn't see much), it was a steam room. 'I mean, seriously. At this point, do I accept that I'm just meant to be single? Why have I barely dated *anyone* my entire adult life? Am I the problem? Is my job the problem? Is fame the problem?'

'I don't know,' El replied. It was merely her opening gambit. She was all set to discuss this for a further two hours when Frankie took a left turn.

'What about you?' she asked. 'What about Robbie?'

El prevaricated. 'You two are always so interested in each other, given you've never met.'

Frankie's foot prodded the side of her hip.

'I don't know,' El continued. 'I think at this point we're just . . . us.'

'Am I supposed to know what that means?'

El chuckled wryly. For more than a decade, she'd barely been able to understand what it meant. She certainly wouldn't expect anyone else to.

El left The Savoy late on the fourth night, having had more sleep than she'd had in a year. Outside, when the cold air hit her spa-fresh face, there was something invigorating about it. She marched across Waterloo Bridge, well dressed for the weather in her big faux-fur coat, feeling purposeful and optimistic.

Across the river, she could see the London Eye all lit up, and the Houses of Parliament too. On the other side, the ornate dome of St Paul's Cathedral stood out against the newer buildings, their harder edges. Then, right in front of her, another familiar sight appeared:

Striding towards El, wrapped up in pea coat and scarf, was Robbie.

'Oh, hi! What are you doing here?' she asked, as they each came to a halt.

'I could ask you the same thing. I thought you were with Frankie until tomorrow?'

'Turns out she has to be up at an ungodly hour to do *BBC Breakfast*. I could have stayed another night, but the thought of her hair and make-up people arriving at four o'clock in the morning just wasn't massively appealing.'

Robbie nodded. 'Bet she's glad to be out of the US at the moment, eh?'

It was a fair assumption. A known predator was about to be president.

'Mmm, kinda. There's this Women's March thing planned for later in the month, though. I think she'd like to go but she won't make it.'

'Will her play have started by then?'

'Yep. Opening night's on Friday. Oh my God, Robbie, you'll never believe who else is in this play. Kate Carroll!'

'The girl from *BST*? No way!' Robbie replied. Without discussing it, they shuffled to the side to let other walkers get around them. 'Isn't she, like, old news at this point?'

El shrugged. She let the railings on the side of the bridge take her weight. 'She's having a resurgence. I suppose 40's the new 30. Or at least I fucking hope it is. Apparently, she remembers me *very* well.'

Robbie raised both his hands, as if in surrender. 'I'm saying nothing!'

She just grinned. 'So, what have you been up to?' she asked. As much as Waterloo was an unusual place for her to be at this time of night, it seemed all the more so for him.

Robbie hesitated. And there was something about the expression on his face.

Immediately, El got the picture. She tried to ignore the peculiar way her stomach dropped in response. Instead, she pounced, all jubilance. 'Robbie! Have you been on a date?! You have! What was she like? Where did you go? What's her name?'

'Her name was Suzanne,' Robbie replied. Very evidently, he was parting with this information reluctantly. 'We had dinner at a place in Southwark – her choice.'

'Very nice. Bit of a way away from here, though.'

'I fancied a walk along the South Bank,' he said, a little defensively.

'And what about Suzanne? Did you fancy her?' El tossed back.

'She was . . . nice.'

El searched his face for clues, found nothing. 'Nice is good,' she replied carefully.

Then, all at once, Robbie's guard seemed to drop. 'Oh, El! It was awful! Seriously, I think it might have been the worst evening of my life. She ordered salmon and then sent it back because it was too fishy. At one point, she told me she wouldn't rule out the idea that Princess Diana might still be alive. And I could tell she thought it was going *well* – that was the worst bit. She ordered a dessert *plus coffee*. And she invited me back to her place.'

El snorted a laugh. 'Well, that was very hospitable of her. How'd you meet this woman anyway?'

A pause.

'Online,' Robbie admitted. 'Tinder. Do you think I'm a sad case?'

'No! There's this one woman I know – she's my downstairs neighbour – and she actually met her husband on the internet, if you can believe that! He was a stranger on a website, and now they're married. I mean, who knows. Maybe someday soon, that'll just be how we're all doing it.'

'Christ, I hope not,' Robbie replied. 'Anyway, let's just say I don't think me and Suzanne are destined to go the distance.'

'Good!'

The response tumbled out of El's mouth before she could analyse it. Meanwhile, Robbie was distracted enough not to analyse it either.

'So, not only have I not found someone I want to go out with,' he continued, as if she hadn't spoken, 'but now I've also got to figure out how to ditch this woman. I'm worse off than I was to begin with! I don't know how people do this, El. How do you do it?'

'Do what?'

'Dating. I'm seriously asking. Give me your expert opinion.'

'I don't go on that many dates!'

He laughed, as if in disbelief.

'I don't! You know, there's something about me, Robbie,' she continued conversationally. 'People have always seemed to think I'm kind of a hussy. It's probably the way I dress. How prosaic. But true.'

He said nothing, and she exhaled. She shifted her body a little, looking out at the inky black expanse of the Thames and all those iconic buildings. It was a magical sight – easily ignored, in the rush of daily life, but spectacular when you stopped to really take it in.

'I don't know,' she offered then. 'Maybe – and I know this is probably a ludicrous thing to say to *you* – but try not to put too much pressure on it? Sometimes, the thing is just to get your sea legs, isn't it? To just . . . entertain the possibility.'

Robbie moved to mirror her, leaning his forearms on the railings.

'And as for ending things with Suzanne,' El continued, 'I'd just try to be honest. If you're not feeling it, you're not feeling it. That's just part of life, isn't it? I mean, it's not the *most* fun to hear, but it happens to everybody.'

Robbie raised an eyebrow, all scepticism. 'When has that ever happened to you?'

'Plenty of times! Jason Parker – that's right, People's Sexiest Man Alive 2010 – dumped me for his therapist! I was so shocked when he told me, I drove my car right into a Walmart delivery truck. Any time I saw a Walmart after that, the whole thing just came rushing back to me. I had to flee *the entire United States* to escape the humiliation! Did I ever tell you that?'

He held her gaze for a second. 'You know you didn't.'

'Whatever. The point is, I'm under no illusion that I'm every-one's cup of tea. I've just tried not to pay it too much attention, when I haven't been. Also, what a question, coming from you.'

'What do you mean?'

El sighed. There was evidently nothing for this but directness. 'You're a babe, Robbie. It's weird that I need to tell you that. But you are, and you're nice – I mean, for the most part, when you're not being incredibly annoying. You co-own quite a cool cocktail bar in quite a cool part of town. Women come into Love and Death all the time who are just *waiting* for you to look twice at them. You must know that.'

Robbie frowned. Was that really true? If it was, it was brand-new information to him. He supposed that when he and El were in the bar, his attention was just always . . . elsewhere. On the drinks.

Yes, that was it, he told himself. His attention was firmly, firmly on the drinks.

For a moment, neither he nor El said a word. All the while,

something fizzed inside Robbie, bubbling up until he could no longer ignore it.

'Did you go out with Marcus?' he asked urgently.

He braced for impact.

To his huge surprise, though, El shook her head. 'I told him I didn't think it was the best idea. You were right. I'm his boss, after all.'

Silent relief flooded through Robbie. He swore he could physically sense it. 'How did he take it?'

'Incredibly well. He really is a great guy.'

Robbie nodded. His mouth felt dry. Before he could second-guess himself, he let his next question tumble out. 'Is that, uh . . . is that the only reason you didn't want to go out with him?'

Suddenly, El seemed profoundly aggravated, the impatience radiating off her. 'Well, obviously *not*, Robbie. You know that. But I'm happy to ignore it if you are. I'm happy to advise you on dating random women.'

Her snappiness made him snappy.

'I have *no interest* in dating random women,' he fired back.

After that: silence, their eyes locked on each other's.

How similar it felt, really, to all their other little flare-ups in the bar. And yet this wasn't the same at all. Robbie found himself totally unprepared for the moment, no matter the argument that it had been a long time coming. It had just always felt so outlandish, to imagine that someone like El would really go for someone like him. He could still remember that early morning in Berlin, her telling him in no uncertain terms: *we are not in love.*

Nonetheless, he and El each seemed to have angled towards each other now, all the surrounding traffic and pedestrians fading to nothing. His heart was pounding. They stared at one another as the seconds stretched out, possibility pulsing inside every single one.

'I mean, this is bound to end in tears, isn't it?' he murmured.

335

His voice came out low and scratchy, like he'd never heard it before.

'Absolutely,' she replied, her own voice barely above a whisper. 'How do you reckon, specifically?'

He moved ever closer to her, and the relief of just letting his body – at last – do what it wanted was profound.

'Well, that's the thing – I don't know,' he said.

'I think I just . . . don't care.'

Her face was inches from his now, and for a moment, he took in every eyelash and freckle, felt every breath in her chest like it was his own. One single truth surged through him.

'I don't either,' he said, and then he grabbed her face in his hands. He kissed her with everything he had, like he meant it. Like he'd been waiting his whole life to do it.

Chapter Forty-Eight

The cab journey, and racing up the stairs to El's flat, and fumbling with the key in the lock – it was all a blur. Making their way blindly towards her bedroom, coats and scarves discarded along the way – that was hazy, too.

All the while, hands moved frantically. Mouths returned greedily to each other's over and over again. Some instinctive, insistent force had been unleashed, the entire world suddenly reduced and expanded at once.

'I can't believe this is happening,' Robbie mumbled, when El shimmied out of her top and stood before him. Unabashedly, he took in the newly bared skin, swallowing thickly.

A shiver darted through her, though it hadn't much to do with the cold. 'Tonight or in general?' she asked.

'Tonight *and* in general.'

'I know. Me neither.'

She reached a hand towards his neck again, then hesitated. Her brow furrowed. 'Do you want to stop?' she asked.

How peculiar, to have been in this scenario – or one ostensibly very like it – so many times before in her life. And yet here, she found herself more nervous than she could ever remember being.

Meanwhile, Robbie felt as though there was a person inside of him that he had never met. He kissed El again fiercely, walking her backwards towards the bed. When they reached it, she let herself topple, and he crawled to hover over her, barely breaking contact with her lips. He looked down at her.

'No,' he replied firmly.

She let out a little sound he could only describe as a moan, from the back of her throat, and he'd never heard anything more glorious in his life.

After that, he could feel her heel on his calf, her tongue in his mouth, her hands in his hair. Too many sensations to distinguish from one another, and no need to distinguish them, anyway.

'I don't think this is really what business partners do, though,' she offered, as she reached down towards the buckle on his jeans. She kept her eyes on his all the while, a familiar hint of mischief dancing in her expression now. 'That's the only thing.'

Robbie just breathed out a laugh. 'Let's be business partners in the morning.'

The next morning, though . . .

The next week, the next month . . .

They couldn't seem to go back to the way they were before. Or they simply didn't want to. One night was all it took for their entire lives to be reframed. Everything, suddenly, became part of the *before* or the *after*. Every day became about the opportunities they could find to be alone together. When they were apart, or around other people, they were each susceptible to an occasional panic about *the whole thing* – but, somehow, that always dissipated the moment they were back in her bed, back in his shower, anywhere alone together.

Robbie had never felt euphoria like it.

Within his marriage, sex had been planned and practical for years. A means to an end that never came.

Even before he and Anna-Claire had started capital-T *Trying*, there'd been an element of small-t *trying* between them – wanting it to be good, wanting it to be better, unsure of what the other might be up for, of what might be weird or embarrassing or too much.

Of course, Robbie didn't want to entirely rewrite history. There'd been times, especially in the early days, that he'd been very happy with his sex life as he knew it.

It was just that he hadn't known *this* back then.

He hadn't known about weakness like this. A lot of the bad decisions he'd watched other people make over the years suddenly made total sense to him. Because wouldn't he, too, now do pretty much anything – sacrifice any other aspect of his life – so long as he got to keep this one aspect?

On the flipside, he'd also never felt power like this either. How mind-blowing it was, to know that he could have El wet and wanting – that he could tease her, torment her, unmake and remake her – that he could apparently do all of it just by being desperately attracted to her, just by following every natural instinct in his own body, following all the cues of hers.

Nothing in his life had ever felt more fun, more intense, more right. The closest he'd ever come might have been a handful of his best nights behind the bar. Part of Robbie started to wonder if in fact they'd always been one and the same, for him – El and the cocktails. If, all this time, he'd just been chasing the feeling of her wherever he could find it.

'So, I know you have a lot more experience with this type of thing than I do,' Robbie said one morning, fingers pressing into her hips. 'But don't you think that this is kind of . . . completely incredible?'

El was on top of him, her breath ragged, her skin flushed. His flatmates had, blessedly, left for work already.

'Yeah,' she managed, collapsing onto his chest. 'I do.'

And the truth was, she hadn't seen it coming.

If she'd had to guess – if, theoretically, she'd ever previously imagined having sex with Robbie Saunders – she might have imagined herself as the one taking charge, the one with the upper hand.

Now that it was happening – for two months and counting,

it had been happening all the time – sometimes she *was* the one who took charge. But the notion of truly having *the upper hand* had begun to seem ridiculous. Somehow, he could now say the most basic things to her . . .

He could say *do you like that?* and *can I touch you here?* and *I want you so much* . . .

All of it made El feel like she was lit from the inside out. It made her feel – when he brushed up against her behind the bar, whispered something fast and gruff in her ear – like she was losing her mind.

Some nights, they lingered at Love and Death long after closing, exchanging drinks until the sun came up. It was a bit like cocktail jam, back in the day, but with fewer clothes.

The first time, she mixed him a cocktail of her choosing then flopped down on an adjacent chair in the middle of the bar. Her bare feet were in his lap, his fingers tracing patterns along her calves.

'You're just so *messy*, though,' he tutted, taking in the carnage she'd left behind, the lids off bottles, the ice melting on the bar, dripping onto the floor.

'You're just so *uptight*,' she replied, shifting her feet strategically, wondering if this was the happiest she'd ever been, wondering if so many of her historic arguments with Robbie might have been vastly more enjoyably resolved.

In the daylight hours, she continued to try desperately to rationalize it. She tried to understand on precisely what basis sex seemed suddenly better than she'd ever known it to be – whether with men, women, or her own imagination.

Maybe, she thought, there was something about knowing a person well, trusting them completely. Or something about being a little older now. Something about a build-up that perhaps couldn't be precisely defined in its duration but that could reasonably be called *lengthy*.

Maybe, she thought, there was just something about her and Robbie Saunders, together. Maybe it defied analysis entirely. Wasn't that a terrifying thought?

'It's pretty crazy nobody's cottoned on at work, don't you think?' Robbie said, once another month had passed.

The two of them lay tangled in El's bedsheets, spent and staring at the ceiling, sunlight streaming in through the windows. It had become a common feature of their afternoons – to sneak away like this, to snatch the time together wherever they could.

'Mmm.'

He turned onto his side, looking over at her. 'Niall was telling me the other day – and do bear in mind that Niall is full of shit – that he reckons he can *always* tell when two people have "embarked upon a sexual relationship". His words.'

El snorted, shifting onto her side, too. 'Obviously not a single person at Love and Death shares that gift. Although, I suppose there's an argument that pretty much the whole time we've owned the bar, we've had *kind of* a sexual relationship.'

'What? No, we haven't.'

'Yes, we have. We just haven't been having sex.' She clocked his scepticism, spoke again. 'What? You don't reckon thinking about it counts? If you ask me, sometimes thinking about it counts the most.'

Robbie raised an eyebrow. 'If thinking about it counts the most, I'm going to hell.'

It was delivered easily, some combination of flirtation and a joke. Still, it stoked a certain fear in El, one she'd been trying for a while to ignore.

'Do you feel badly about this? Us. From a "going to hell" point of view, I mean. You could tell me. I wouldn't mind. Or I'd try not to mind. I'd know it wasn't personal, is what I'm saying.'

Robbie traced his finger along the dip in her waist. 'Well, it *is* personal, though, isn't it? That's the whole point. Everything that happens between you, personally, and me, personally . . .' He shrugged. 'I don't believe any part of that is wrong. I can't believe in any God that does, either.'

It felt like a huge thing to hear. El laughed with what a *relief* it was to hear, embarrassed to feel her cheeks flushing. He smiled, too, dropping to kiss her shoulder, her elbow, her forearm. He lifted her wrist, ran his tongue along the three little birds tattooed there.

'Why'd you get these – really?' he asked then.

'Mmm. Father, Son, Holy Spirit?' she joked.

He smiled.

'You, me, and Otto?' she tried again.

Actually, she kind of liked that idea, when she said it aloud. It wasn't the truth, though.

'Honestly, they don't mean anything. They mean it was 2005 and I'd probably had two lines of coke and an Aftershock.'

'Well, that's beautiful, El,' he said, his voice just as gentle and sincere as it had been previously. 'I want to thank you for sharing that.'

Immediately, they both felt apart with laughter.

No matter the ways they inched ever closer to each other, who could say how long it might have taken them to go public, if they'd been left entirely to their own devices.

There was, after all, something sexy about having a secret, about sneaking around a little.

All the nights at Love and Death that Robbie had contorted himself into awkward shapes, odd places, to avoid touching El . . .

All the nights he'd averted his eyes, wished it was acceptable to ask her to *wear something else* . . .

They felt like another lifetime ago.

Now, he let his hands linger a little on her waist any time he slid past her, his thumbs grazing the bare skin between her top and her skirt.

She let herself watch him, just for a few seconds, as he twirled a dash bottle or spun a cocktail shaker in his hand. She took in the flicks of his wrists, the tension in his biceps, her lips parting a little, and when their eyes met – just briefly – it was with the certain knowledge that she wanted him and he wanted her right back.

That nobody else knew could feel like a turn-on. It could feel like the low lighting and lush furnishings of Love and Death – the intimacy and intensity that had always been part of the space – existed only to provide Robbie and El with a solid six hours of foreplay.

'You know, you really should use your powers for good, not evil,' Robbie murmured, right into the shell of her ear, one night in the spring.

She'd been teasing him, in their usual subtle ways, all shift.

Now, at last, they'd just watched their staff troop out the door. A nearby place would be hosting the industry crowd after hours tonight, apparently – more and more, there seemed to be no need to go into Soho.

El turned, raised an eyebrow. 'I can think of a time or two I've used them for good.'

Within seconds, Robbie was lifting her onto the bar, urging her knees apart as he stepped in between them, hands on her thighs.

He dropped his head to her clavicles, and El moaned, her hands working their way into his hair.

Then, suddenly, there was the creak of a door opening, a familiar figure breezing through the curtain.

'Sorry, I forgot my—' Tameka's voice fell silent as she took in the scene before her.

El and Robbie froze.

'Tameka! Hi! This, uh . . .' El began to laugh, evidently barely even able to take herself seriously as she attempted a denial. 'This isn't what it looks like.'

'I bloody hope it *is*,' Tameka countered, delighted. 'I've just won seventy quid.'

'What?'

'We've all had a pool going for, like, three months. First one to catch the pair of you at it wins the jackpot.'

Robbie and El just looked at each other, unable to stop the grins from spreading across their faces.

Perhaps they had not been *quite* as subtle as they'd imagined.

Chapter Forty-Nine

Without ever discussing or defining it, they became a couple.

In a certain way, working together actually made things easier, to begin with.

In Love and Death, Robbie and El had a huge shared priority. They didn't have to apologize for it or explain it or compartmentalize it, as they'd often had to with others in their lives.

By then, things were ticking over nicely at the bar. They were steadily repaying El's father; they could work the schedule to suit themselves.

How strange it was, to realize that for all the many hours Robbie and El had spent in one another's company, there was still so much to discover.

They'd never gone out for lunch together, until they did. They'd never chosen a film to watch, or debated the quickest *and best* route from A to B across the city.

Robbie, as it turned out, took a disgusting amount of milk in his tea. It pained El even to make it for him. 'Tea-flavoured milk,' she called it.

Meanwhile, El was learning to knit. Robbie took in that fact with some surprise. He noted the whole corner of her living room piled high with materials, watched as she happily spent hours 'messing around' with her sewing machine. She was, in certain ways, so much less the thrill-seeker, the bringer of chaos, than he remembered meeting back when he was 21 and she was 22.

Across the summer, they picnicked on Primrose Hill; they went out dancing; they repainted the walls of a flat that El would never own, just for kicks. Lots of evenings, they met Frankie after her play and went for a nightcap.

Robbie still liked to check out the competition, still found himself obsessed with how other people did things.

'So, the watermelon and jalapeño infusion – are you doing that sous vide or what?' he asked, at a new spot in Dalston.

His and El's one-time colleague Aziz was the head bartender there now. He had a few silver strands in his beard but otherwise looked just the same as ever.

'Yeah. Honestly, mate, game-changer. I can do in about four hours what would have taken us half the week back in the day.'

'No shop talk!' El proclaimed good-naturedly.

'Give us a *little* shop talk?' Robbie countered. He reached idly for her hand, sliding his thumb along her palm. 'It's different for you – you've worked in so many places . . . I'm playing catch-up here.'

Some part of him really felt that was true. After all, save for a short stint at that hotel back in Oxford, he'd worked at a total of one bar across his career. As ever, he imagined that what he lacked in direct insight, he could surely make up for in research.

'Oh my God, do you remember that place you worked in Colombia?' Frankie chimed in. 'And the one in Puerto Rico?'

Robbie looked between the two women, out of the loop.

'After El finished in Berlin, and before she started in Tokyo, she had these three months to spare, right?' Frankie explained. 'So, she came on my movie shoot with me and just picked up work along the way.'

'Picked it up, then dropped it just as fast,' El said, pulling a face. As ever, she could make her own culpability so charming.

'You really have been everywhere,' Robbie said.

'Even if I can't ever go back to a number of those places,' she joked. 'I'm pretty sure there's a bar owner in Cartagena who'd happily have me killed.'

Robbie grinned. It was a version of her he'd always been dazzled by. If he found himself, this time, a tiny bit jealous, it was only a tiny bit.

Shortly afterwards, and fresh from the latest meeting with her father, El called into Love and Death to see Robbie. They'd started opening earlier on Saturday afternoons.

All the seats surrounding the bar were free, so she hopped up onto one, as if she were a customer.

'How was it?' he asked, leaning across to kiss her. 'You look amazing.'

She just smiled her thanks. 'Yeah. It was okay. He . . . actually does ask some quite good questions, sometimes.'

'About the accounts?'

Robbie was distracted, putting the finishing touches on a cocktail. El watched him for a moment, enjoying the look of sheer concentration on his face.

'No, just generally,' she replied.

In fact, she and her father rarely discussed the specifics of Love and Death's financial affairs. Robbie prepared the spreadsheets plus various other reports, she passed it all across to her father, and – with little input from her – it appeared that the two men were able to reach a common understanding. It always made El feel juvenile and useless. But at the same time, did she have any natural desire to try get to grips with the finer business details? She did not. To her secret embarrassment, she didn't even really believe herself capable of it.

'That looks great,' she added, as Robbie straightened, regarded his finished creation. It was the palest yellow in colour, garnished with a delicate slice of pear, a long vanilla bean, and a single star anise pod. 'Hang on, let me just take a quick pic for Instagram.'

She clicked with her phone a few times, capturing the drink from various different angles, before he disappeared with it.

Idly, she swiped back through her shots, deleting the duds. When she had first set up the Instagram account, photography had remained prohibited for customers. El had taken photographs and uploaded them, but no one else was allowed to.

Then, somewhere along the way, that rule was relaxed; certain exceptions were made. 'It's a losing battle,' Tameka had proclaimed breezily.

And, indeed, it seemed they had lost it. Customers now openly used their phones in Love and Death, whether for photography or otherwise.

'Would Otto like all this, do you think?' El asked, when Robbie returned to the bar.

From his look, she could tell this was a deeper topic than he'd been expecting. Silently, he awaited more context.

'My dad asked me, today, what we wanted to do next. And I suppose I didn't really know. It's weird, isn't it, the constant pressure to be *generating*? I don't think anyone asks, like, hairdressers or heart surgeons what they're planning to do next. It's like, "Well, I suppose I'll just keep cutting hair, keep saving lives."'

Robbie chuckled.

'It reminded me of this conversation I had with Frankie once,' El continued. 'About, like, what success is. You know what she said?'

'What?'

'She said, "Maybe it's just knowing Otto would be proud of you."'

'Wow.'

'Yeah. But so, *would* he be?'

El twisted in her chair, let herself scan the space. At this very moment, four people at the table closest to her were diving into a platter of olives and cured meats.

Sacrilege! Otto would have said. She could just hear him.

Robbie seemed less concerned. 'Every single change we've made, even if Otto wasn't initially into it, I'm a hundred per cent confident you could have talked him into it.'

She just exhaled a little laugh.

'I mean it,' Robbie continued. 'He could be a moody bugger. It was a proper skill, the way you could bring him round – God knows we missed it when you'd gone.'

This time, El tried to properly absorb the compliment.

'My mum was a bit like that, growing up,' she said. 'Moody. So maybe I'd got some practice in, there.'

Immediately, she realized she was doing the exact thing she always hated when her parents did it: minimizing what she'd had to navigate as a kid – wholly mischaracterizing the situation, in fact.

'Actually, not really,' she amended. 'Otto was just a creative person with a creative person's brain – and, as you say, a moody bugger sometimes. My mum was . . . different.'

Robbie was quiet for a moment. 'You don't have to talk about it,' he offered then. 'But I want to listen, if you do want to.'

And for the very first time in her life, El found that she did.

A few months later, they were in her flat, doing nothing in particular, when El checked her phone. She frowned. 'I think there's something wrong with Instagram,' she said.

'Hmm?' Opposite her, Robbie looked up briefly from his book.

'It's saying we have way more followers than we actually do,' she continued. 'For the Love and Death account, I mean.'

'How many more?' he asked. Still, he sounded only vaguely engaged in the topic.

'Uh . . . about 70,000 more?' El said.

Robbie put down his book.

Chapter Fifty

After they went Instagram Famous, everything was different.

The drink that did it was one of Robbie's – or maybe it was both of theirs. Beforehand, El had been making sorbets, as an experiment. She'd tried a whole array of flavours: peach, almond, and marigold; damson and gin; mixed berries and Cabernet Sauvignon.

'I'm sure we'll find something to do with it,' she said, packing it all into the freezer.

The next time a customer asked Robbie for something 'light and refreshing', it was a hectic service; he was under time pressure.

Thus, out came the sorbet, topped with an English sparkling wine he'd lately been raving about to all who'd listen. As ever, it was the little touches that made the difference: the delicate, ice-cold glass, the perfect roundness of the scoop of sorbet, the edible gold glitter dusted liberally atop the finished product.

'Oh wow,' said his customer, reaching reflexively for her phone. 'It's so sparkly! What's it called?'

'Uh . . . a Spark Plug,' Robbie improvised. 'If it's to your liking, we can do a variety of different flavours on the sorbet.'

'*Ohmygod* I love it already,' the customer declared, snapping away.

Robbie didn't recognize her at the time, and nor did her name ring any sort of bell when he heard it later. But for literally millions of other people, she was a big deal. Millie Jade posted make-up tutorials on the internet. An 'influencer', *The New York Times* had lately labelled her and her ilk. What had begun with Millie Jade recommending merely the lipsticks and mascaras she liked had expanded, now, into a much wider remit. For the benefit of her many fans, she recommended all manner of other things that she happened to like, too.

Love and Death turned out to be one of those things.

She gave it a rave review on Instagram, calling it one of her 'secret spots' in London. Within a sentence, she made the bar into something exclusive again, instead of something established. Something exciting, instead of merely beloved.

To begin with, Robbie and El doubted that all the new followers Millie Jade had driven to their account would actually manifest in a longer line out the door. At their advanced years (namely their mid-30s), they instinctively assumed some level of disconnect between the online and offline worlds.

What a shock it was, to discover that there didn't seem to be one. The first day that they showed up to work at 5.30 p.m. – ninety minutes before doors opened to the public – and saw a small crowd already gathered on Epworth Street, they could hardly believe their eyes.

'I haven't seen this since just after *BST* first came out,' Robbie said, then slightly wished he hadn't. Because of course, El had missed that. It could still, sometimes, be a bit of a sore spot.

On this occasion, however, she seemed disinclined to dwell on it.

'This is the dream!' she told him breathlessly, as she moved like a whirlwind during service – powered, much as he was himself, by pure adrenaline. The place was packed; it felt alive with energy.

He grabbed her as she passed, taking a moment away from his own creation to kiss her. 'I couldn't agree more,' he said.

A month later, looking at their bank balance, he *really* couldn't.

*

At some level, they assumed the interest wouldn't last. They thought they were riding a wave. They didn't try to hold back the tide, as Otto had once done. Instead, they welcomed it. And there was a lot to love about being loved. Every day, pinging right to their phones, were gushing reviews and five-star ratings, a new deluge of media requests and PR invites.

'There's this writer for *The Sunday Times Magazine*,' Robbie told El over lunch. They'd once ironically referred to such meetings as 'business lunches', but now that seemed to be what they actually were. 'He's going to put Love and Death in their "going up" section this weekend. You know how they do a little "going up" and a "going down" bit?'

El frowned. 'Did that come into the Gmail?'

Admittedly, she did not monitor the account as closely as Robbie did, but she tried to keep an eye.

Across from her, Robbie looked faintly embarrassed. 'No. The journalist's my friend Pete from uni. He's always said he was happy to do me a favour, and I thought it might be time to let him.'

Immediately, El rolled her eyes.

'Oh, here we go,' Robbie said, with a bit of a chuckle. El wasn't sure he really meant the chuckle.

'What?'

'You say you're not a snob, but you *are* a snob when it comes to this! You're a *reverse* snob, which is just as bad! Pete's a great guy. He's smart and nice and normal. Some people who went to university – yeah, even the fancy ones – are just smart and nice and normal, El.'

There was, suddenly, a slight undercurrent of tension – a thread that, if they chose to pull at it, could unravel this lunch altogether.

'I suppose so,' she mumbled. She reached for another bite of her avocado toast. 'I've always wondered how they come up with those things, in magazines,' she added then. 'What's hot and what's not, et cetera. Turns out they really do just ask their mates.'

Several weeks later, it was on page two of the magazine.

Love and Death, the snippet read. *With cocktail maestro Robbie Saunders at the helm, London's OG underground bar is back in a big way. No menu (iykyk) just vibes. And is that Andrew Garfield in the corner?*

When El saw it, she rolled her eyes again. 'Robbie Saunders at the helm, eh?' she said.

In bed beside her, Robbie winced. 'He's an idiot, I know. Like I said, we've known each other a long time. He probably just had a limited word count and was trying to be nice.'

El said nothing.

Robbie dropped a kiss on her bare shoulder. 'Don't be annoyed with me,' he murmured, moving in towards her neck. He nipped gently on that spot beneath her earlobe, the one that always drove her crazy, before moving to soothe the skin with his tongue.

She let out an involuntary exhale, admitting defeat of a sort.

'All publicity is good publicity, I suppose,' she said.

Of course, that wasn't true at all. They just didn't know it yet.

By the autumn of 2018, their new popularity was something to be managed, more than to be enjoyed.

They only had so much space in Love and Death. True, turnover was faster now – their new clientele tended to stay for a drink or two rather than for a whole evening. They'd also begun opening even longer hours to accommodate demand – seven days a week, one shift blurring into the next.

Still, there was no let-up in the pace of things. Every night, there were many more people lined up outside than they could ever seat or serve. By then, the bar had 200,000 followers online.

'We could set a new password,' El suggested. 'Everyone and their mother knows the old one by now. At least that'll thin the herd.'

'Or it'll just piss people right off,' Robbie countered.

It did both.

But neither for long.

Somehow, treating people mean did indeed seem only to keep 'em keen.

When El arrived to work and saw the queue of people already snaking all the way down Epworth Street every night, it was increasingly hard to feel excited about that. Oh, she still played the part alright. She whipped up the drinks that people asked her for, the ones that they'd seen a hundred photos of before they'd even stepped through the door. But it had been a long time since she'd created anything new or even had much desire to.

What she *did* have was an intermittent ache between her shoulder blades. She'd begun to be irrationally, silently jealous of the years that Robbie had spent out of the industry, merely because he'd given his body a break.

'We're like that bookshop in Paris that has to do one in, one out,' Marcus declared. 'Or the cupcake bakery in New York. You know the one I mean? There's certain places people want to go to now, just to have been to them. Y'know? Get a snap for the grid, tick it off the list.'

There was something incredibly depressing about that thought. El sometimes got the sense that it bothered her more than it did Robbie. Or at least, she felt he was coping with it all much better than she was.

'I know this probably sounds insane, but do you think there's any way to just . . . stop people coming altogether?' she found herself asking him eventually, a little desperately.

Robbie just shrugged – in this moment, she acknowledged that even he looked somewhat overwhelmed. It was five in the morning, after all. They had both been at work for eighteen hours.

In the circumstances, an impromptu trip to New York was the very last thing El needed. It required finding extra cover at work – during the lead up to Christmas, of all times – then taking a long flight to a city even more hectic than the one she was leaving. However, it was a mercy mission.

'I just . . . I think I need you,' Frankie had said on the phone, and was there any way to say no to that?

Her agent had been MeToo'd. MeToo'd was a verb these days. Jared Kostecki had never sexually assaulted Frankie – he needed her too much – but a litany of other victims had come forwards. Frankie was devastated.

'When all the allegations started coming out last year, I never even *considered* that Jared . . . how is it possible that I didn't know?' she implored El, over and over, in the living room of her Tribeca apartment. It was a question lots of news outlets had also seen fit to ask. There was truly no crime committed by a man that a woman couldn't end up at least partly blamed for.

El was glad to be with her friend, glad to offer all the support she could. Still, Bloomingdale's and a Broadway show, it wasn't. She felt utterly drained.

'Absolute fucking *sea monster* of a man – I've always said so,' she said on the phone to Robbie.

'You *have* always said so,' Robbie agreed dutifully. 'Listen, I'd better go, okay? I've got this meeting with the accountant to prep for tomorrow.'

At his kitchen table in Finsbury Park, Robbie's brain was foggy with percentages and exchange rates, with thoughts of dividends and diversifying. Not having any money had been a problem, of course, but having it turned out to require no small amount of work either.

With the best will in the world, even when she *hadn't* flitted off to Manhattan, El was of little help to him there. Sitting at a laptop for hours on end, his eyes gritty with fatigue, he tried not to hold it against her.

Chapter Fifty-One

Among all the challenges that came with going viral, there were some very good days, too. The day El met her father to give him his final cheque was undeniably one of those.

Of course, it made absolutely no sense to do the repayments this way – in 2019? It was all but unheard of. Online was faster, but offline was what her father wanted. In a way, El found she quite liked the tangibility of it, too. There was a sense of achievement in handing over that last cheque, a sense of calm in knowing she was back where she'd always wanted to be – owing this man nothing.

'Thank you,' he said, taking the cheque from her. They were at a café in Chelsea – his choice.

'Thank *you*,' she replied.

Her father looked across the table at her for what felt like a long moment.

'You are most welcome, Eloise,' he said quietly.

El felt some unexpected, undefined emotion rise up in her. Blinking fast, she cast her eyes around for a distraction – and very quickly found one. Underneath his jacket, two of the buttons on her father's shirt were incorrectly buttoned. The whole shirt was left slightly misaligned, in fact. El frowned. She'd never seen this man anything but pristinely turned out. How could he not have noticed those buttons? She had a long history of vociferously protesting *his* comments on *her* personal appearance, though. She didn't fancy giving up that moral high ground. Thus, in the moment, she elected not to mention it.

She thought about it afterwards, though. She thought about the ways her father seemed so much older, frailer now, even than when he'd first made the investment in the bar. She thought of him all alone in a big house.

All of it kept coming back to her, every couple of weeks, like a recurrent itch – the type of thing that was probably fine. Or alternatively, was not fine at all.

In Love and Death, they hired more staff. They continued to offer a world-class experience. They killed themselves to make sure that every person who managed to get through the door experienced something they'd remember for a long time.

Undeniably, the atmosphere was different than it used to be. At this stage, there seemed no way to undo the change in their customer base. Influencers, tourists, professional reviewers . . . one-time visitors, all of them. There wasn't much of a community any longer. Those who had once been regulars had tired of the invaders.

Nobody prepared a person for this, Robbie thought – for the problem of *too much* success, for a level of demand that was overwhelming, for what almost felt like the public's *entitlement* to access. It was like a runaway train. They couldn't get off it now, even if they wanted to.

Along the way, arguments had crept in between him and El. Petty ones, unoriginal ones. It became harder and harder to know whether the problem was that they had an excess of time together, or not enough. But either way, their points of friction were probably normal. Weren't they?

After all, Cormac was a new dad – reportedly, he and his fiancée now communicated almost exclusively in terms of who was more tired. They, too, apparently often lacked the time and energy to have sex. It didn't mean anything, long-term.

That Robbie had ended up in a comparable position without even having the kid was not lost on him.

El had asked him about that once. They'd been in a PizzaExpress that appeared to be functioning, on the evening in question, as a semi-creche.

'I mean, when you were with Anna-Claire . . . I know you wanted a baby a lot,' El had said. 'Do you still think about it?'

Robbie had glanced around pointedly, jokingly. There were dough balls being fired in all directions. A vision of familial bliss this was not.

'I don't know,' he'd replied, when it appeared she was still awaiting a proper answer. 'With Anna-Claire, it just became so hard to disentangle what she wanted – or, I suppose, what we had collectively declared we wanted – from what I actually wanted. You know? I can tell you I'm incredibly glad now – for obvious reasons – that it never happened for us. What about you? Would you want to be a mum?'

Given what he knew of El – and what he now knew of her childhood to boot – he wouldn't have been at all surprised if the notion daunted her.

Indeed, sitting across from him and considering the question, she'd looked something close to terrified. 'I feel like probably not,' she'd concluded slowly. 'Or at least not any time soon.'

The obvious went unsaid. She was 36 years old. If it wasn't any time soon, it might not be any time ever.

'That's fine by me,' he'd replied, reaching for her hand across the table. 'I wouldn't want one unless you did, too.'

He'd barely thought about the response before he offered it, but he really had meant it. Of course he wanted what El wanted, of course he didn't want what she did not. If, perhaps, it wasn't a million miles from the dynamic that had characterized his failed marriage, that didn't occur to him in the least.

*

'So there's this podcast. Startender,' Robbie mentioned, halfway through a busy shift. Speed was more of the essence these days than it had ever been.

'Eugh. I kind of hate that term.' With one hand, El placed the final sprig of basil on a Kale Pineapple Smash. With her other hand, simultaneously, she reached towards the edible glitter for a Spark Plug.

'I know, it's the worst,' he agreed. He was pouring blue Curaçao down the long spiral handle of a bar spoon. 'But in this case, we'd be the startenders in question. The guy wants to interview us.'

'About what?'

'About our wisdom, obviously.'

El snorted.

'Nah. Well, maybe a bit. Just our careers, the drinks we've created, this whole social media explosion and so on.'

It was the type of opportunity El would have given anything for in the aftermath of the Citi Slicker, or even in that year leading up to its creation. Back then, what she'd wanted more than anything was to be loved and lauded, to be in demand.

Funnily enough, those things didn't feel quite how she'd thought they would, now that she had them. She didn't wake up every morning euphoric. Instead, the pain between her shoulder blades had become almost constant. She was so tired all the time, and yet when her head hit the pillow, she often barely slept a wink all night.

'So, do you want to do it then?' Robbie pressed, a few minutes later. She'd delivered her round of drinks, moved swiftly on to the next, and the next, and the next.

'Uh . . . sure,' she said. 'Whatever, yeah.'

And she did *plan* to attend the podcast recording. She really did.

It was just that when the day in question came around, a month or so later, she awoke with that familiar sensation, that mental itch. Robbie was already out – gone to New Covent Garden Market to meet a potential fruit supplier – so she sent him a quick text.

Can't do this afternoon actually – soz. Am sure you'll all get on fine without me. Tell them your fun fact about the Tom Collins!

With that, she was on her way to Chelsea.

'I just thought I'd . . . see how you're doing,' she said, at her father's front door.

He wasn't necessarily gushing with warmth, which she took as a good sign. In other words, he seemed like himself.

Nonetheless, in his usual aloof fashion, he did invite her inside and offer her a cup of tea. He had all the proper gear – the loose leaves, the strainer, and the caddy spoon. Perched on a wingback chair in the living room, he executed the whole process as well as any native Englishman, and with more enjoyment than most.

El duly sipped her Earl Grey and kept up the sort of faltering, intermittent chit-chat that she and her father could manage.

It was unbelievably odd, to be back in this house – to see all the things that had changed and all the things that hadn't. There was still a photo of her in her school uniform on the dresser in the corner.

Bizarrely, El had the sudden urge to go upstairs and crawl into her old single bed – the same one she'd spent half her youth sneaking out of – and just sleep for a week.

Needless to say, she ignored that. She was getting up to leave – certain, now that her visit had been entirely unnecessary – when her father spoke again: 'It's a shame you missed your mother – she's just out with her acupuncturist.'

El frowned in confusion. 'What? Mum's in Anaheim, Dad. My guess is she's sandwiched between Anna and Elsa as we speak, belting out "Let It Go" just for the hell of it.'

This time, her father was the one who looked confused. And,

when the expression on his face turned to sudden fear, El felt a shot of the very same thing dart through her, too.

As quickly as the moment came, it passed.

'Of course,' her father said – not entirely smoothly, but fairly close to it. 'Just a joke. Those were the bad old days, huh? Trying every hippy-dippy therapy known to man.'

She smiled along politely. It was just about enough to convince a person (who wanted to be convinced) that everything was A-okay here.

Somehow, though, El wasn't quite sure.

A few weeks later, on a rare day off, she was bound for some retail therapy on Portobello Road. As ever, El enjoyed nothing more than rifling through the clothes that other people had discarded. She loved finding the monstrosities as much as, if not more than, the gems. Letting her mind wander, imagining how she might be able to transform an item if she had the energy . . . these days, it was the closest she came to a creative buzz.

What possessed her even to think about Startenders, much less download it for her journey, she didn't know. She barely kept up with all the noise about Love and Death any longer. She'd passed over the running of the Instagram account to one of the new hires.

In the aftermath of the podcast episode's recording – in the aftermath of her no-show – Robbie had seemed a bit irked, but it had blown over.

As such, nothing about El was set on edge when she pressed play. She was expecting a fairly standard discussion – questions she could lightly mock with Robbie later, ones she already knew his answers to.

However, that wasn't what she got.

Barrelling through the London underground, with Robbie's voice in her ears, that wasn't what she got at all.

Chapter Fifty-Two

El got to Love and Death ready for a fight. It was so much easier to lead with anger than with the alternatives: confusion, hurt, vulnerability.

Of course, when she arrived, the place was packed. Most people already had their phones within arm's reach; they'd be all but conditioned to immediately start filming any unexpected drama. It really wasn't like the old days. You couldn't even have a semi-private screaming match in here anymore.

Robbie was delivering a tray to a table when she approached him. She brandished her phone, the podcast's logo visible.

'Oh, you listened to it,' he said. His voice was neutral.

'Yes, I listened to it!' she replied. Her voice was not neutral. 'Stockroom. Now.'

'What's up?' he asked, once he'd dealt with his customers, followed her past the bar and into relative privacy.

El hardly knew where to begin. Instead, she hit play on the podcast, let the host's opening gambit ring out between them.

'So, Robbie, you first came to prominence when you created the Citi Slicker,' he began. 'We know it; we love it. It's a classic at this point. More recently, of course, you're also the man behind the Spark Plug. For listeners outside the London bubble, this is what all the cool kids are clamouring for. It's pretty simple – all

362

the best ones are, eh? English sparkling wine – who knew, right? – poured over a surprise sorbet. They've got all kinds of weird and wonderful flavours going on at Love and Death. All you Instagrammers out there will know that's a whole craze in itself – what flavour are you going to get? Pistachio, rosewater, and saffron, I think it was, the night I managed to sneak in. So, tell us, Robbie, where do you get your inspiration from?'

El stopped the audio, stared at Robbie. 'Do you remember what you said in response to that?' she demanded.

Robbie offered up nothing. Could he even see where she was going with this? El genuinely couldn't tell.

'I'll tell you what you didn't say,' she continued. 'You didn't say the words "El Tippett" at any point. You didn't say, "Oh, actually, it was my business partner *El* who invented the Citi Slicker." "Actually, El personally shelled a zillion pistachios for your sorbet; actually, she comes up with the recipes for every single one of them." What the fuck, Robbie?'

Again, he was quiet. He looked caught in the headlights, like his mind was reeling, looking for a way to correct her. *I think you'll find . . .*

On this occasion, though, he came up with nothing.

'You spoke to that guy for an *hour*, and you barely mentioned my name once,' she said, cursing the way her voice broke a little, betrayed her a little. She could hear how pathetic, how juvenile and self-important the complaint might sound to an outside observer. Nonetheless, she readied herself for battle once more.

'And that might be fine,' she continued, 'if it was the first time. But it isn't, is it? How many times can you claim it's an oversight? "Oh, my mate who writes for a national newspaper, what's he like?" and all that. Well, I have to tell you, I'm starting to think it's *deliberate*, Robbie. Don't think I haven't heard about how you were dining out on being the man behind the Citi Slicker back in the day!'

This time, Robbie's face sprung to life. 'Hang on, *that's* what we're talking about now? One sentence in the paper from more than a year ago? Or stuff from more than a *decade* ago? Are you ever going to move on from that?'

'Well, it would be a lot easier if you didn't keep pretending that you do everything around here!'

'I *do* do everything!' he exclaimed. Even he looked a little surprised by the force in his voice, but he continued nonetheless. 'A lot of the time, lately, that's what it feels like, El! I do the cashflow and the payroll and the VAT return, and the meetings with our tax adviser, and the research on corporate investments, and the worrying about all of it! If you're asking me why I didn't exactly feel like talking about you during that podcast, maybe it was because you'd just bailed on me! Again! Forgive me if I didn't fancy getting into a whole soliloquy about your creative prowess. And, look, you're tired – I get it. But don't you think *I'm* tired? Don't you think maybe that day, with the podcast, might have been a day I could have used *your* support? You knew I was nervous about doing it!'

El was silent, taken aback.

She *hadn't* known that. She'd missed it, somehow, even as they'd seen each other literally day and night, even as they'd shared a bed, made each other cups of coffee, checked in with one another by necessity about a million other practical details.

But then, Robbie hadn't known how worried she'd been about her dad. And she still didn't think he understood – truly – how physically exhausted she was to her bones, how much her own procrastination, her own dip in focus and creativity, was troubling to her, too.

She swept all of that aside.

'Even if I'd been there, I doubt that guy – the host – would have been a single bit interested in me anyway,' she continued. 'A lot of these cocktail guys can be real arseholes. Have you noticed that? Misogynistic.'

He sighed. 'Come on, El.'

'No, it's true. They see you as a *mixologist* and me as a *barmaid*.'

'That's completely unfair!'

'Isn't it!' she fired back pointedly.

On this, as on various topics, they seemed to be missing each other.

'What about the other thing?' she asked then, able to avoid it no longer, her mouth suddenly dry. 'The moving thing.'

'So let's talk about the future,' the podcast host had said, towards the end of the interview. 'You're riding high right now, at Love and Death. Any plans for expansion?'

'Well, there's definitely a precedent for it,' Robbie had replied. 'Somewhere like the Experimental Cocktail Club is a big inspiration there, obviously. Or Please Don't Tell. These are bars that started off as hole-in-the-wall joints and now have multiple out-postings. Both American, of course. I can't think of a British – British or Irish – cocktail bar that's had that kind of replicable success.'

'Is Love and Death going to be the first?'

'You never know. I hope so.'

'Where have you got your eye on, then? Can we get an exclusive here on the pod?'

'Oh wow, I don't know about that. Definitely nothing official to confirm yet. Paris might be cool, eh? Or New York? Who knows. Bear in mind I'm a boy from East Belfast, so any of these feel like pretty lofty goals. And don't get me wrong, London's great. But I'm like a lot of people in that I *ended up* here more than I ever actually *chose* to live here. So, yeah. Definitely excited, over the next year or two, to do a bit of travelling. Or even relocate for a while, as the case may be. Personally and professionally, that probably feels like the next natural step.'

'Watch this space, then, for Love and Death 2.0?'

El had been able to hear the smile in Robbie's voice as she'd listened along, her heart beating faster by the second.

'Absolutely. Watch this space.'

Standing opposite her now, Robbie shrugged.

'I mean, I didn't commit us to anything. I know we'd want to think about the details of what's next, once we have a bit more brain space.'

'But *expanding*?' she pressed. 'Moving? You'd want to do that?'

He looked genuinely nonplussed. 'Well, yeah. Don't you? To be honest, I've been expecting you to get itchy feet for a while.'

'What do you mean?'

'Come on, El. You told me you don't want kids; you've spent your whole adult life going from place to place . . . I just assumed that would be in our future.'

Put that way, it didn't seem an unreasonable assumption.

'I thought we'd kind of . . . settled in London, though,' she said, hearing how her own voice came out sounding a little pitiful. 'And, well . . . it's a madhouse out there.' She nodded towards the door. 'We're overwhelmed running the bar we currently have. Not waving but drowning and all that. And you're saying you actually want *more*?'

'I want *different*.'

'Different how?'

He shrugged. 'For starters, I suppose I'd like to try just *being* somewhere different. Honestly, I can't believe we're not on the same page there. Like, you of all people. And in terms of another bar . . . I don't know, exactly. Maybe we wouldn't even have to call it Love and Death. Maybe it's not in Paris or New York or wherever. Maybe it's somewhere totally random. No hype, no pressure. Just great chats, great drinks . . .'

'More like this place used to be, you mean?'

Robbie didn't reply.

'No, come on. I'm going to say it, even if you won't. Otto would *despise* it here, now.'

The assessment was bald, brutal, maybe the worst thing she could possibly have said to him. Part of El expected him to deny it – needed him to, even if she wouldn't have fully believed him.

Instead, he just looked at her. When he spoke again, his voice was quiet and measured. 'Do you think I don't know that?'

And there it was: the reality. What they had on their hands – by the only metric that really mattered – was a profound failure. El had to live with that, clinging to her daily. Robbie did, too. Perhaps worst of all, they might never be able to disassociate it from one another.

'At least I'm trying,' Robbie added then. 'At least I'm trying to figure out *some* kind of strategy!'

His voice was accusatory, and it put her hackles back up.

'Oh, well, you be sure to let me know how I can help. When you've decided. Maybe go back on the podcast.'

Instinctively, she moved to leave – she just couldn't handle any more of this – and Robbie called after her as she went.

'Storm out, yes. Brilliant!' he said. 'Do that. Just don't be too pissed off when I don't follow you, eh? I have to work.'

El hardly knew how she passed the rest of the day. Walking, lingering over a single latte in a coffee shop, walking some more.

When she turned the key in her front door at 7 p.m., she could tell immediately that Robbie was already there. The coat and rucksack in the hallway, the music playing softly from the living room . . . He must have got cover, at Love and Death, in the end.

Should they have discussed it – explicitly – before he all but moved into her flat? Perhaps. It was starting to feel like there were any number of subjects they should have discussed, explicitly.

Wearily, she made her way towards the living room. In an ideal scenario, she'd have spent this evening entirely alone – she'd have had a bath to soothe her back and gone straight to bed. It had been a long fucking day.

As it was, she knew she needed to execute at least a brief greeting. Her only goal was to get in and get out, without another argument they'd never be able to take all the way back.

As soon as she laid eyes on Robbie, though, her jaw dropped.

The living room was half-covered in lit candles. Robbie seemed to be in a bit of a scramble, as though caught unawares by her return. He took her in for a moment, with a slightly panicked expression on his face. Then, without preamble, he dropped to one knee.

'Marry me,' he said simply.

The whole experience – from first seeing him through to those two little words – might have lasted ten seconds. Fifteen, tops. Yet El felt as though she heard it all, saw every bit of it, in slow motion. She was stunned. Not in a good way. She was stunned *and horrified*.

Perhaps because she couldn't get a single word out, he kept speaking.

'I'm so sorry about earlier,' he said, his voice strained with emotion. 'All that stuff with the podcast. You were right. And I don't want to lose you, El. I can't picture my life without you. *Of course* I just want to be where you are. So, let's go all in. Will you marry me?'

'Oh my God!' she exclaimed. 'No!'

Before her, Robbie's face fell. She cursed herself and her own lack of tact.

He got to his feet, his cheeks flushing.

'Sorry,' she added. 'But . . . fuck. What are you thinking, Robbie?'

For another long moment, they just looked at each other, each of them panicking in their own way, each at an utter loss as to where to go from here. Then, with his head down and a few mumbled words she couldn't hear, he was striding out the door. Going, going, gone.

After that, they didn't see or speak to each other at all for three weeks.

Chapter Fifty-Three

Robbie had never felt humiliation like it – that was the main thing, he thought.

Or was heartbreak the main thing? The two were inevitably intertwined, when you asked a person to spend the rest of their life with you and they said, *no thanks*.

Or in El's case, just *no*.

Then, on top of all that, there was the guilt.

That fucking podcast, and all the things he'd either said or failed to say. He thought about listening to the whole thing back and couldn't bear to. He suspected it might turn out that El was exactly right. He'd gone into the recording pissed off – infuriated, suddenly, by the exact same flightiness he'd seen in El at 22 years old. Didn't she know things were different now, though? Didn't she know she had to show up, even when she didn't especially fancy it? Didn't she *want* to show up? For the bar, for Otto, for *him*? If she didn't, what did *that* mean?

In the circumstances, of course it was easier, once the recording light was on, to wax lyrical on the renaissance of English sparkling wines. In many ways, Robbie found it steadying, soothing, to do so. That felt like his happy place.

As the interview had gone on, he hadn't deliberately sought to deprive El of the credit she deserved, for the Spark Plug, the Citi Slicker, or anything else. The truth was much simpler. He was a boyfriend who was annoyed at his girlfriend, who didn't much want to delve into the details of their relationship on that particular afternoon – not when he was supposed to be projecting professionalism, confidence, enthusiasm. And so, he'd referred to her only cursorily; he hadn't gone out of his way to actively bring her up when the host chose not to.

It was a bad mistake, though. He could see that now. It would have been the wrong thing to do to any colleague and collaborator.

And with El, it was so much worse.

It was worse because she'd grown up with so little in the way of genuine acknowledgement from either of her parents, worse because he knew she'd carried certain secret insecurities all the way since school, worse because she *had* been sidelined at times, in her career.

More than any of that, of course, it was worse because El wasn't merely his partner in business. She was his partner in every other possible way, too. Across these past couple of years, he'd wrapped his whole life around her, and she'd done the same for him. He'd treasured every small way she'd made herself softer and more vulnerable with him, clocked every bit of the long-prized independence she'd ceded to him. Yet somehow, he'd ended up treating it all so carelessly. He'd hit her where it hurt.

No wonder she didn't want to marry him. That's what he thought some nights, as he lay in bed awake, seized with regret.

Other nights, he wondered whether she'd ever loved him, *really*, the way that he loved her. Where was the forgiveness, if so? Where was the benefit of the doubt? Did she even really *want* to build a life together – a proper one, for keeps?

Occasionally, he let himself segue into a kind of scorn for her: doubtless she found the entire institution of marriage hopelessly bourgeoisie, etc. Of course, she'd be vastly too cool for something as basic as a roomful of candles and man on one knee. That was what the kids said now, pejoratively: *basic*.

In light of her rejection – *rejection*; that word still stung so painfully – Robbie felt it wasn't his place to reach out to El again. If she wanted to avoid him for the rest of time, he was happy to let her try.

Then, one evening, both Adam and Tameka called in sick. At such short notice, it was difficult enough to find one replacement. Two proved entirely impossible. Thus, what began as Robbie's shift suddenly became El's, too. It was bound to happen sooner or later.

'Hi,' she said quietly, when she walked in.

'Hi,' he replied.

She took a step towards him. 'I'm so sor—' she began, and he felt the embarrassment-hurt-shame swirl in him anew.

He cut her off, holding his hand up, as if to call a halt to things. 'We don't have to talk about it,' he told her quietly. 'Honestly. Let's not talk about it, eh? Not here. I got the message the first time.'

It was one of the longest shifts El could remember, in twenty years of bartending.

To make matters worse, as usual, she and Robbie were the last two out of the place. They tiptoed around each other, doing their best to avoid one another's eyes, communicating only the brief information that was absolutely required.

Robbie was in the back, and El was in the bar itself when she heard the front door open. She felt a slight flicker of irritation, directed inwards. She was supposed to have locked that door. Why couldn't she seem to stay on top of her responsibilities? Perhaps Robbie had been right about her.

Now, a woman popped her head through the velvet curtain.

'We're closed,' El said.

Undeterred, the woman stepped fully through the curtain,

looking apologetic. 'Of course,' she said. 'I just . . . wanted to see the place.'

She spoke softly, with an American accent, and absolutely nothing about her seemed like she should be here at this hour. She was somewhere between 50 and 60, her striking red hair styled in a neat bob. In jeans and a twinset, with flat loafers on her feet, she had a youthful, sprightly look. But it was neither cocktail nor club attire.

El had a sudden, unbidden thought of her father. She wondered if this lady, too, might be feeling a little unsure of herself.

'You do know it's . . .' She glanced down at her watch. 'Ten past three in the morning,' she said gently.

'Oh, I don't sleep,' the woman replied, like that was a given. 'And I knew it would take you a good hour after closing to actually get out of here. I just figured . . . no time like the present, huh?' She laughed, a little nervously. It was if she were realizing, right then and there, that this was perhaps a slightly insane thing for her to have done.

El frowned. 'Are you in the trade? Or were you?'

The woman shook her head. 'Oh no. I'm a librarian. Or I was. Retired now. But I'm familiar with the ins and outs of the industry. I'm a friend of Otto's. Or – again – I *was*. I can't get used to saying these things.'

El's expression, her entire frame of reference for this interaction, shifted immediately. 'Oh wow,' she said. She made her way out from behind the bar, gestured towards a table. 'Please – have a seat. Uh . . . can I get you anything?'

She found herself at a loss for what else to say. She had so many questions that she hardly knew where to start.

'I'm fine,' the woman replied. She made no move to sit, but she nodded towards the headpiece El was wearing. 'That's so beautiful.'

'Oh.' El reached up and touched it instinctively. It was a vibrant floral material, the only splash of colour in an otherwise all black outfit. 'Thank you,' she said. 'I actually made this myself.'

She had a little collection of the headpieces now. They were easily made – just a long rectangle of fabric, with some wire inside. But once complete, they were versatile. They could be sculpted into everything from a tight turban to a dramatic bow.

The first one she'd ever made had been for Otto's funeral.

'He always said you were so creative,' the woman murmured, and El was agog.

'Who are y—' she started, but suddenly Robbie's voice sounded over the top of hers.

'Right, that's everything, I think,' he was saying. 'Look . . . I know what I said before, but should we maybe go som—'

He emerged from the back and silenced himself immediately once he realized they had company.

'This is . . . a friend of Otto's,' El offered, by way of explanation.

'Oh.'

For a moment, they all stood in silence.

'You were at his funeral,' Robbie said then. His brow was furrowed, as though he was putting the pieces together in his own mind. 'I think I saw you leaving the church, just before the service started. Was that you?'

The woman nodded. 'That's right. I'm sorry. I just couldn't stay. But that was very rude of me. I didn't even introduce myself.' With that, she extended her hand to both Robbie and El in turn. 'I'm Cecilia.'

Chapter Fifty-Four

'So . . . do you live in London?' Robbie asked, once they were all settled together at a table.

Cecilia had walked around the space for a few minutes beforehand, taking in the details of it, blinking back tears. All the while, she'd been silent, and Robbie and El had been, too. They were in their own bar, but El had felt oddly like their mere presence was a kind of intrusion.

'No,' Cecilia replied. 'The first time I came here was for the funeral. But lately, I've just . . . I've just been missing him, I guess. I thought maybe it would help to be here, so I booked a flight.'

'And has it? Helped?'

'Yes and no.'

'So, you knew Otto from . . . New York? Or from Pennsylvania?' El asked.

'From New York,' Cecilia said. 'Although actually, we were only there together for about eighteen months. I moved to Connecticut after that, and we didn't see each other in person.'

'What, like *at all*?'

'Nope. But we wrote letters for . . . more than twenty years. Do you think you can really know a person that way?'

El thought of the years that she and Robbie had spent in a similar fashion. By necessity, so much of her relationship with Frankie had been conducted that way, too, and with her mother.

It was less romantic – pixels instead of ink, waiting for the two ticks or the three dots instead of the postman's footsteps, the letter on the mat. However, the fundamental principle struck her as the same.

'Yes,' she replied. 'I do.'

'I do, too,' Cecilia said.

'Were the two of you . . . ?' El trailed off, unsure if the enquiry was too personal. But when had that ever stopped her before? 'Were you in love?'

It didn't seem like the sort of question a person would need to consider, but Cecilia did pause to consider it. 'I don't know. We loved each other. I do know that. Or . . . I think I do. I loved him, at least.'

'He loved you, too,' El found herself replying. How could she say anything else to this lovely woman, who'd travelled across the ocean to be here, whose grief was written so plainly on her face?

'Did he talk about me?' Cecilia asked hopefully.

Robbie and El exchanged a sidelong glance. Despite their current estrangement, they'd had so much practice in this sort of wordless communication by now. How, and whether, to tell Cecilia that they hadn't even known of her existence until fifteen minutes ago – that was the question.

'You know Otto,' Robbie said kindly. 'He was so private, especially when it came to the things he cared most about. But I can tell you one thing: he served the Cecilia every day of his life, with a smile.'

'And that's from a man who – from what I hear – once entirely outlawed the Citi Slicker,' El joked.

It got a small chuckle out of Cecilia, too.

'Pretty cool, to have a drink named after you,' El continued.

Cecilia nodded. 'My little legacy. Sometimes, I like to think of us in a sort of secret club – all the people who've had recipes created for them or songs written about them or a portrait painted of them. It's funny, isn't it? So many of the things we think of as public property started off being for just one single person.'

El had never thought about that. In her life, she'd reflected a lot on creators – on the extent to which they were valued, on the inherent value (if any) of creation. She'd thought a lot less about all the many unknown people who inspired creators. But what, she wondered now, would have ever been produced without them?

'He used to tell me about cocktail jam – do you remember that? Before your shifts started, everyone in here together?' Cecilia seemed to be enjoying reminiscing, almost as though she'd been part of it herself. 'If you ask me – and this, I must confess, is pure conjecture on my part – I think he came up with the whole exercise mostly to motivate *you*, El. To help you realize your own talent. He always saw so much of himself in you.'

For El, the pleasure in hearing that didn't last long.

'But then why did he let me go?' she found herself asking plaintively. It was almost pathetic, how much she still cared about the answer to that question. 'And why didn't he ever reach out to me when I'd gone?'

Cecilia didn't seem to find the enquiry pathetic. 'He was obstinate, I suppose. Afraid. Embarrassed. I don't know. I mean, I think he *did* try to reach out to you, in his way – with the drinks? Practically everything you ever invented, if he could find out about it, I think he was serving it in here before he died.'

El just nodded, swallowing the emotion that had caught in her throat. To know that she hadn't imagined that overture from him, that she hadn't been seeing only what she wanted to . . . it was something.

'And why didn't *you* reach out to him, might I ask?' Cecilia continued. 'If there was a problem, between the two of you, he always seemed to think it was that you were just too similar.'

'Really?' El asked.

'Really.'

'Well, I could have told you that!' Robbie exclaimed suddenly, all aggravation. 'As a matter of fact, I'm pretty sure I *have* told you that. You and Otto were peas in a pod! I don't know if he ever really did "pick" me over you, the way you thought he did, El. But if he did, it was because he needed a lackey! He needed someone who could just serve up the same drink, the same way, all night long if that's what a customer wanted – which let's face it, they very often did! Otto didn't always have it in him to do that himself. And you didn't either.'

El blinked, tried to take in both what Robbie was actually saying to her and the fact that they seemed to be back speaking to one another in general.

'Oh, I think you do yourself a disservice, Robbie,' Cecilia interjected gently. 'I don't think it was about being a "lackey", as you call it, at all. It was about being *complementary*. He was awe of all your knowledge, your skill. He said you were just about the most remarkable young man he'd ever met.'

A slight flush of pleasure rose in Robbie's cheeks. 'What do you think he wanted from us? With this place?' he asked, after a moment. 'It's . . . a little different now, from how it was.'

Cecilia shrugged. 'I don't know.'

Robbie's face fell. He seemed to feel the same puncture of disappointment that El felt herself, no matter how foolish it was. After all, Cecilia hadn't come here with a crystal ball or a magic wand. She, too, was only human.

'What I can tell you is this,' she offered, after a moment. 'Otto Kettinger was a lot of things. He was probably the most fun, most frustrating, most fragile person I've ever met. He could be tricky to figure out . . . and didn't he know it, huh? But when it came to this bar? He didn't do much accidentally. If there was something specific he'd wanted, or not wanted, from you guys . . . don't you think he would have made it his business to let you know?'

She let the question hang for a moment, before she continued. 'What he wanted was you two. Simple as that. He picked you – *both* of you – to take over Love and Death for a reason. Whatever decisions you had to make from there, I figure the only thing he really wanted was for you to go ahead and just make the hell out of 'em. You know?'

Something about the turn of phrase, the force of it, was delightful, coming from this woman in her twinset. Both Robbie and El smiled.

Cecilia wasn't finished. 'If you ask me, that could have meant closing the place the very day you inherited it, if you'd thought that was the best thing to do. Things change; times change. Who knows how Otto would have changed, too, if he were still here.' She paused, swallowed thickly. 'But he's not. And you *are* still here. Otto trusted you. He loved you. You're both still so *young*. If you ask me, at a certain point, you have to stop wondering what he would have wanted. You each have to think about what *you* really want.'

Hanging on her every word, neither El nor Robbie could seem to summon a single thing in response. When she'd stopped speaking, the silence lingered, not uncomfortably.

Cecilia took another, expansive look around Love and Death. 'Well! I'm sure I've taken up enough of your time. Thank you,' she said, to both of them in turn. 'Sincerely. I'm so glad I got to see the place. I'm glad I got to see both of you.'

'Wait!' Robbie blurted out, instinctively. 'We'd love to talk more . . . hear some more about you. Are you married? Kids?'

As soon as he asked the questions, he knew they were probably *normative* in some kind of negative way. Or were they really? Perhaps they were just *normal*. Nice. He couldn't tell anymore.

'Oh yes,' Cecilia replied, as she got up from her seat. 'Sure.' Her eyes twinkled. 'You know, it's funny. A librarian from Connecticut can have a much more interesting life – on the inside – than it might sometimes seem from the outside.'

With that, she was gone. They didn't even get to thank her.

Afterwards, Robbie and El just stared at each other, both of them digesting what had just happened.

'Do you ever wish people could still smoke in here?' El asked eventually. She hadn't lost the capacity to surprise him, even after all this time.

'Not really,' he replied, but he was smiling a little. 'That was pretty gross.'

'I know it was *mostly* gross. But it was kind of fun, too, no? Kind of sexy.'

There was a glint in her eye that he hadn't seen in a while, a quick flash of familiar energy. It felt so good, even briefly, to remember a time when anything and everything – merely by virtue of being between him and her – had the potential to be charged.

Robbie cleared his throat. 'So, we should probably talk,' he ventured.

He wouldn't have blamed her for some cutting reply. He could almost hear it: *you've changed your tune,* or similar. After all, hadn't he rebuffed her efforts when she'd first arrived this evening?

Instead, El just nodded. Somewhere in the last twenty minutes, they'd softened towards one another.

'Now? Tonight?'

He hesitated. She looked about as exhausted as he felt – or more so.

'It's late. Maybe we meet tomorrow afternoon?' he suggested instead. 'I just . . . I think maybe we should have this conversation in the daylight.'

Chapter Fifty-Five

They met in Soho Square in the late afternoon and had no trouble finding an empty bench. All around them, the trees were bare, the ground a carpet of golden-brown mulch. Already, the light was fading – at this time of year, in their line of work, it was possible to barely catch any daylight at all. They were in the last weeks of autumn.

They managed some pleasantries to begin with, recapping the surprise of last night's events. Eventually, though, there was no way to avoid it any longer – any of it.

'So, I think it might have been . . . ill-timed,' Robbie offered. 'The . . . proposal. I think maybe you felt a bit blindsided.'

El quirked an eyebrow: *I'll say.*

'I'm sorry.'

She nodded. 'I'm sorry, too. I'm sorry I couldn't . . . respond better.'

Not *I'm sorry I didn't respond differently*, Robbie noted. At this point, he wasn't truly surprised. It had been weeks, after all. Still, it somewhat took the wind out of him, to know for sure that she hadn't changed her mind.

'Why'd you do it?' she asked, after a moment.

Robbie couldn't help the defensiveness that sprung up in him. 'Why does *anybody* propose, El?' he bit back. 'I proposed because I fucking love you!'

'I love you, too!' she cried, the emotion in her voice suddenly matching his. There was nothing of the Hollywood ending in their declaration, though. They were like two wounded animals.

Robbie forced himself to take a deep breath. 'I suppose I . . . I just wanted to *fix* things between us,' he said. 'Which I can see now probably isn't . . . well, it probably isn't a very good reason.'

El didn't disagree.

'And I'm so sorry about the podcast,' he continued, leaning in towards her a little. 'That was beyond shitty of me. If I could take it back and do it differently, I would. You've no idea how much I wish I could. But if you think it means that I was deliberately trying to sabotage you . . . I mean, honestly, after everything we've been through together, I just don't how you could think that, El.'

'I don't,' she replied quietly. 'I was . . . exhausted. And hurt. And pissed *off*. Actually I still am all those things, a bit. But I don't think that.'

'Okay. Good.'

'And *I'm* sorry I wasn't there,' she offered. 'At the podcast recording. I'm sorry I wasn't there when you needed me to be.'

'It's okay,' Robbie replied.

With that, theoretically, they'd reached the end of their dispute. Apologies duly exchanged, they were ready to move on, put it behind them. Somehow, though, it didn't quite feel that way.

He reached for some levity. 'Of all the fights we've ever had, do you think this might be our worst?' he joked.

She exhaled a little laugh in response, but the sound soon petered out. 'How many is too many, do you reckon?' she murmured, squinting over at him. 'Like, too many to come back from?'

He didn't answer that.

They each let their gazes drift around, staving off the inevitable. They'd crossed this square on so many nights when they were younger – they'd treated all the surrounding streets like a playground, one made just for them and their friends at 4 a.m. in the morning.

They'd had so much *fun* together. It was easier to see that now than it had been at the time, to remember that in among all the drama – all the misunderstanding and competitiveness that had characterized their early relationship – there had been so much fun, too. Sitting here now, it felt like yesterday, and it felt like another lifetime.

El looked back over at Robbie. 'I don't think I want to work at Love and Death anymore,' she said. Just like that – simple and unadorned. 'As a matter of fact, I don't think I want to work in any cocktail bar anywhere.'

Right away, Robbie felt the breath sucked from his lungs. 'What?' he all but gasped. 'What are you talking about? You love your job!'

'I . . . I don't know if I do anymore,' she replied. Her eyes widened with the admission, her voice faltering. 'It's all I've ever really done since I was a teenager. I mean, I know I've worn that like a badge of honour, but lately . . . I'm not so sure it's a good thing.'

She paused for breath, her cheeks flushed with colour now. 'I know I'm supposed to be "the creative one" and all,' she continued, 'but at this point, I feel like I don't have a drop of creativity left in me. I'm just . . . empty. And I *hate* feeling that way. I honestly don't know how much longer I can bear it. Maybe it took last night – talking to Cecilia – for me to finally let myself really admit it.'

Beside her, Robbie could hardly find the words to respond. He felt punch-drunk, dazed. 'What about a break from the bar?' he suggested weakly. 'A few weeks. Or a few months, even?'

She just shook her head. 'I don't think so.'

Robbie cast his mind back to their shift just last night. He'd watched El smile brightly, expertly mix one drink after another, grab a few seconds of chat with the customers where time allowed. He – the person who was supposed to know her best – had had no idea she was struggling to the extent she was now describing. The realization hit him like a full-body blow.

Almost of its own accord, a certain conclusion began to take shape in his brain, pieces slotting into place whether he wanted them to or not.

It seemed horribly avoidable – surely, by some different sequence of events, some different set of priorities that he and El would each have needed to commit to long ago, they could have avoided this. As things were, however, it also felt entirely inevitable.

'So . . . we close the place then,' Robbie said quietly.

El sucked in a breath. 'Or you could keep going with it.'

Without me – that part went unsaid.

'I can't do that.'

'You can,' she countered.

'Okay, so I just don't want to, then,' he replied, a bit snappily. And, after a second, 'Sorry.'

'*I'm* sorry,' she said, emotion swelling in her voice. 'I know I'm . . . I know I'm letting you down here. Believe me, I know that. But I think I've been doing that anyway, haven't I? In certain ways, I think you've probably been carrying my weight ever since we took over the place. I honestly just . . . thought you liked all that stuff. The finances and all.'

Robbie didn't have it in him to explain that he *had* liked it, at one point – that somewhere along the way, however, he'd stopped liking it, had come to slightly resent bearing such responsibility alone.

In any case, it felt inconsequential now.

'What about us, though?' he asked searchingly. 'Us without the bar. *Is* there an us without the bar?'

It utterly terrified him, voicing the question aloud. Worse, when he looked into El's eyes, he could see nothing but that very same terror reflected right back at him.

'Can I ask you something?' she murmured after a while. By then, they'd been silent so long that it was almost a shock to hear her voice. 'What did *you* think about last night . . . when Cecilia asked us what we really wanted?'

Unprepared for the question, Robbie's mind was a complete blank.

'You know what *I* think,' she continued, when he offered no response. 'I think you haven't had anywhere near enough time in your life to think about just you. What do *you* want, Robbie, in an ideal world? You. Not your parents, not Anna-Claire, not Otto or me.'

He opened his mouth to speak, but she stopped him.

'No, don't answer yet. I'm asking you to really think about it.'

And so, Robbie did. Or at least, he tried to. But what came to him – or more to the point, what didn't – only prompted a whole new wave of panic. Instinctively, and for the first time in a very long time, he found himself silently praying to God. For inspiration, certainty, *something*.

Maybe he didn't exactly get any of that, bestowed from on high – at least not right then and there. But the simple act itself did serve to calm him somewhat. It seemed to halt the spiral in his brain, just a little. How odd – when he'd really thought he'd closed the door on all that, committed himself to atheism at long last.

'Do you *want* to be married and have kids?' she prodded. 'Deep down?'

'I don't know. Maybe?' he replied falteringly. 'I think I might just still have a certain version of success in my head, you know? Or of happiness, even. Of being a grown-up. Marriage, 2.4 kids, all that.'

'Those aren't bad things to want, though,' El said. 'They're actually very normal, good things. I mean, yeah, sometimes it's all bullshit social conditioning and whatever, but a lot of times, it's really not. I just don't think that *I* want . . .' She trailed off. 'Or I'm not sure I would even know *how* to . . .'

She couldn't quite seem to find the right verb. Robbie, entirely at a loss himself, supposed he wasn't in much of a position to judge.

'But you *do* want to stay in London?' he prompted. 'As in, for the foreseeable?'

Beside him, El worried at her lower lip – he had never seen her do that before. 'I . . . I don't know. I mean, I heard how excited you sounded on the podcast, when you talked about giving somewhere else a go . . .'

'If it wasn't for me, though?'

This time, she said nothing. She worked both hands underneath her thighs, and they lapsed once more into thick silence. Around them, the wind whistled gently, and Robbie felt like a vision of his future – yet another one – was disintegrating before his eyes.

'Travelling . . . it doesn't actually *make* a person interesting, you know,' she offered then. 'Sometimes you go somewhere new, and it turns out you're just . . . elsewhere. It doesn't necessarily make you more empathetic or more informed or any of that.' She cocked an eyebrow wryly. 'Trust me. Some of the worst people I've ever met in my life have been to Machu Picchu.'

Even as he managed a chuckle, Robbie suspected they both knew all that was easy for her to say – she, who'd lived in three continents, who'd skipped from one city, one job, to the next, and now had all the scars and the skills to show for it.

The idea that she'd done it, and now she might be *done* with it, still left Robbie slightly reeling. And yet suddenly, even in his anguish, he could see the source of their difficulty so clearly.

He and El had such a long history together. There was an ease to that; there was something incredibly precious and beautiful about it, something intoxicating at times. But it had a flipside, too.

In certain ways, perhaps they'd each stayed stuck in the other's mind: her still the flighty good-time girl, him still the bookish homebird.

'We don't have to decide anything right now,' El said. It was as if she was trying to convince herself as much as him. He could see her blinking back the tears that had sprung to her eyes.

He nodded, swallowing the emotion that rose up within him too.

Just then, in his pocket, his phone pinged. From her handbag, El's did the same.

When they each pulled out their phones, looked down at the email that had arrived in their inboxes, they couldn't help it. They turned to one another and laughed out loud at the instinctive joy and the pride of it, the irony of it.

Before them was the sort of news that could change absolutely everything, going forwards. Or it could change nothing at all.

The heading read: *The World's 50 Best Bars – London's Love and Death clinches top spot at last.*

Chapter Fifty-Six

New Year's Eve 2019 was a big one: twenty years to the day since Otto first opened the doors on Epworth Street. Every 'end of year' round-up in the papers said that the second iteration of the Roaring Twenties was just up ahead. And Love and Death was the number one bar in the world.

Robbie and El invited everyone to the party they threw in celebration – as many people as could conceivably fit into the place, once all the tables and chairs had been removed, plus a few dozen more just for fun.

An 11 p.m. start meant nobody had to wait too long to get to the main event. Together, they all counted down the last ten seconds of the year, and when the clock struck midnight, confetti released in bursts from somewhere overhead.

Robbie looked across at El in surprise.

'EBay,' she said.

He smiled.

Around them, people in party clothes hugged and kissed, broke into impromptu renditions of 'Auld Lang Syne'. It seemed like everyone who'd ever worked at Love and Death was present, plus an assortment of others. There might even have been some famous faces in the mix, resting easy in the knowledge that here was a crowd in which everyone else would pretend not to recognize them. Robbie's mates, taking up one whole corner of the bar, very likely *didn't* recognize them.

For the first time since she'd fled the UK all those years ago, El's mother had made the long trip back across the Atlantic, accompanied by Ted Tarrent. When El sought them out, shortly after the hubbub of midnight had passed, they were happily chatting with Frankie, giving her their detailed thoughts on an animated movie she'd just done, then their equally detailed updates on local Anaheim happenings.

Cecilia had flown back to London for the occasion, too. 'Please, call me Cece,' she said. By the bar, Marcus was keeping her drink filled and introducing her to all the people who'd known Otto.

For one night only, all the old rules applied: no star-fucking, no guitar-based music, no food, no jeans, no cameras.

It seemed a shame, in some ways, to interrupt proceedings with a speech. Nonetheless, El tapped a fork against her Champagne glass, glancing over at Robbie as the noise gradually faded to a hush.

Robbie gave her a little nod as though to say: *you start.*

'Happy New Year!' she yelled. 'Here's to 2020, eh? Thank you all so much for coming – Robbie and I are so pleased to have you with us to celebrate. And it turns out there is *literally no better place in the world to be* than right here.'

She gestured towards the bar, to the gold plaque that was now in pride of place, surrounded by spirits and liqueurs. Whoops and hollers rose up in response, and she paused to let it happen, take it in. She grinned right along with everyone else. Discreetly, she gestured to Tameka, who was now poised behind the bar. From somewhere, two trays with great brass domes covering them were produced.

'Now to mark the occasion, Robbie and I have each prepared something a little bit special . . .' El continued.

'We actually haven't even seen each other's yet – can you

believe it?' Robbie chimed in. He cleared his throat, took on a mock-officiousness. He looked towards Tameka, who was brandishing the first tray aloft now. 'Okay. What we have here is a gin cucumber cocktail – it's light and refreshing, with just a little extra something in the mix. I *will* be taking guesses all evening as to what. Behold . . . the Debutant!'

Everyone cheered as Tameka unveiled the drink. From three feet away, El could hardly believe what she was seeing or hearing. There was a time, undoubtedly, that she would have felt usurped right now – furious. As it was, she felt nothing of the sort. All she felt was amazement.

When the noise died down, and Robbie looked over at her expectantly, she raised her voice again.

'And up next! This is one for all of you who have a sweet tooth when it comes to cocktails. I know you're out there – there's really no shame in it! We have Vermouth, we have vanilla, we have lilac syrup! Behold' – she couldn't help shooting Robbie a quick sidelong glance – 'the Dilettante!'

'They match!' someone shouted from the crowd as soon as her offering was uncovered. And who could deny it? Both drinks were served in a coupe glass, El's a vibrant violet in colour and Robbie's a very pale green. In both appearance and in name, they seemed like a pair. Robbie and El stared across at each other, slightly agog.

Their public awaited, though. Robbie was the one to jolt back to awareness first.

'And hey, you know what else? They're both on the house all night!' he shouted, and the place erupted anew into cheers. As ever, there was absolutely no drink on earth that tasted as good as a free one.

Hours passed in a blur of chatter and laughter, old friends and new cocktails. For once, the door to Love and Death was opened and the curtain pushed right back. Light and life poured out onto the street, despite the freezing temperatures. If the neighbours complained about the noise, they complained. Tonight, Robbie and El had decided not to care.

Eventually, in search of a breather, El pulled on her coat and stepped outside, moving past the spillover crowd. She meandered further along Epworth Street, on the side opposite the bar, her cocktail glass resting between two fingers. When she got to the end of the street, she stopped in her tracks. There, lingering on the pavement, was Robbie. Some part of her wasn't in the least bit surprised.

She glanced down at her watch. Morning was beckoning, though it was still pitch dark on account of the season. They had a little more time.

For a minute or two, neither she nor Robbie said a word. Instead, they just stood together, watched all manner of drunken antics unfolding up ahead of them. Marcus had Cecilia in what looked more like a death grip than a dance hold, and was twirling her halfway down the street.

El smiled at the sight, drained the end of her cocktail. 'So, the Debutant,' she offered, tipping her empty glass in Robbie's direction. 'I might have had myself a few of these tonight. It's a fucking good drink, Robbie. And I like the name.'

'Back at you,' he replied.

The Debutant and the Dilettante. It seemed incredible that they'd both chosen – at the end – some manifestation of who they'd been at the very beginning. A crude interpretation, of course. But that was okay. Sometimes you couldn't get the full range of nuance into one single drink. You could get a hell of a lot, though.

'What do you see, when you look at a cocktail these days?' El found herself asking.

Robbie thought about it for a moment. 'Art,' he replied.

'Commerce,' she countered.

He smiled, understanding this game immediately. 'Science,' he said next.

'Beauty.'

'Effort.'

'Instinct.'

'History.'

'The future.'

Robbie paused. He was all out of responses, it seemed. Or, perhaps not quite.

'You,' he said.

El swallowed. 'Yeah. I see you, too. I always will.'

And suddenly, she just couldn't stop herself: she surged towards him, pulling his lips down to meet hers. It was a real kiss, frantic and fierce. El flung her empty cocktail glass aside, and when it smashed into a thousand pieces on the pavement, neither she nor Robbie paid it the slightest heed.

Instead, they made this moment last, their bodies wrapped around each other's in the cold night air.

'Oh God. Why are we doing this?' Robbie asked, when eventually they pulled apart, both gasping for breath. There was an urgency to his voice. 'El, please. Come to Paris with me. I mean it.'

El sucked in another sharp breath. This was, of course, a conversation they'd had more than once already. Since that afternoon in Soho Square, they'd wrung themselves dry having it.

Right now, though, with the taste of him still on her lips, she felt herself wavering. It wouldn't take much for her to say *fuck it*, flit off and start from scratch once again.

Staying put – that was the thing she had no practice in.

That was the thing she knew she most needed to do.

Thus, she shook her head. 'I can't. My dad's here, and I—'

'But you don't even really like your dad!' Robbie exclaimed, aggravation flaring back up again suddenly.

'Well, that's beside the point! How many times have I told you? I just have this weird feeling there's something not right with him, and I can't . . .' She trailed off, with a heavy sigh. The frustration between them seemed to dissipate as quickly as it arose.

'You could stay,' she tried instead, even though she knew he wouldn't. She knew he *didn't want to*, at this point. What gluttons for punishment they both were, rehashing all of it again.

He had a job lined up in Paris. Lulu White Drinking Club in Pigalle, the very same place that had once wanted El, now wanted none other than Robbie Saunders. And he was excited about it. She knew that – she'd seen flashes of it in him, along with all the uncertainty and the pain.

In her best moments, she was excited for him, too.

Some part of her actually didn't want him here, in London, while she figured out whatever the hell came next for her. She didn't want him to witness her floundering, didn't want him in some other bar job around town, resenting her for all the ways it felt like a step down, a step backwards.

Another part of her just couldn't believe that he – the man who professed to love her – was ultimately choosing to leave her.

She imagined Robbie must feel some similar mix of emotions. Hadn't he told her over and over that he didn't want her to continue with something her heart was no longer in? He'd told her that he agreed with her – the whole industry had changed, not just Love and Death. A cocktail culture that comprised of chasing likes on the internet, or of 'corporate' cocktails – the ones invented and promoted by drinks companies – *did* feel a bit less exciting, a bit less creative, than the job they'd started off doing. He'd told her he understood all that.

Nevertheless, El knew that Robbie must look at her now, at least sometimes, and see only the woman who quit on him. How could he not?

She stepped away from him, forced herself to create some

distance from the heat and the smell of him. For a moment, there was quiet between them. Again, they took in their friends a little further up the street, every one of them blissfully ignorant, still causing a joyful ruckus.

'I was the happiest I've ever been in my whole life here,' El murmured. 'With you. I just want to say that for the record.'

Robbie reached for her hand, grasping it tightly. 'Me too,' he replied. His mouth was a fixed line, as though he couldn't trust himself to say anything more without entirely falling apart.

For the millionth time, El wished that she could hate him and have him hate her right back. She'd know what to do with that, at least.

As it was, they'd both been hurt. They'd neither of them got quite the ending they wanted – if they even knew what that was. They each now felt raw in one another's presence, like a layer of skin had been stripped away.

'I think this has to be it, though, doesn't it?' Robbie continued softly, solemnly. 'Whatever's next for the both of us, it's not going to work unless we can . . . disentangle. And not, like, halfway. I think this time, it has to be all the way, El.'

She nodded. Even if it struck her as awful, impossible – a life without Robbie in it, in any capacity – she knew he was right.

'Trying to go back's always a disaster anyway, isn't it?' she said, aiming for briskness, for pragmatism in her voice. 'You can only go forwards.'

'What else has this place taught us, if not that?' Robbie agreed, nodding towards the bar.

El followed his gaze. 'I haven't always known what Otto would have wanted from us, here,' she said. 'But I know he would have wanted to go out on a high. And I know he would have wanted it to be creative until the end.'

It was the reason they'd agreed to concoct two brand-new cocktails for the evening – to give them something of an unveiling, to put on a bit of a show, even if they'd never be served again. Hadn't Otto always relished a sense of occasion? Hadn't he loved nothing more than freshness, surprise, the next new thing?

Although nobody inside realized it, when the sun rose this morning, Love and Death would close its doors and never open them again. Together, Robbie and El stood on the street and regarded the place for a moment more. They looked at the last fifteen years of their lives – their entire adulthoods.

El snuck a final sidelong glance at Robbie, then took a deep breath, her face brightening. They were not going to cry tonight. That was one promise they'd made to each other that they could keep.

'Come on then,' Robbie said. He dropped her hand, put a smile on his face, too. 'Let's go and serve the good people in there some drinks, shall we? It's a party, after all. The night's young.'

Epilogue

1 January 2025

On Epworth Street, the air was still ice-cold, the wind still bracing. But morning had broken, now, and five years had passed. To the very day.

Slowly, Robbie and El took a few steps towards one another, halting once they were within speaking distance. They squinted across at each other in the winter sunshine.

'You changed your hair,' Robbie said. He heard the words come out of his own mouth, as if uttered by someone else.

El reached upwards, running a hand through her dark pixie cut distractedly. 'Oh yeah,' she replied. 'A couple of years ago.'

Robbie's brain was bursting with all the things he wanted to say to her – all the things he'd imagined he might say, if fate ever brought them together again. But none of it came out. As the seconds ticked by, it seemed that all they could do was stare at each other, practically open-mouthed.

'Hi,' she offered then, with a bit of a shrug. It sliced through the awkwardness somehow.

'Hi,' he replied.

When she let out a little laugh, he could do nothing but smile in return.

El nodded towards Love and Death. 'It's weird the landlords haven't done anything with the place, eh? I think that's part of why I've never come back. I didn't want to see it turned into an Itsu or something.'

'It's my first time back, as well,' Robbie said.

'Did you speak to that journalist, for the article?'

'Yep.'

El just nodded, which he took to mean that she had done the same.

Robbie would never have predicted, five years ago, that anyone would even still *want* to write about Love and Death in 2025.

It had caused a huge stir, when he and El announced the end of the place. Their online statement had been four sentences in total – enough to convey gratitude and a goodbye, but no explanation. In a world of so much ready disclosure of information, there'd been no shortage of fury and confusion in the comments.

Time passed, though. Somehow, the closure of Love and Death – how it happened, when it happened – had only fed into its mythology. Even now, years later, people still talked about the legendary Otto Kettinger, about a tiny speakeasy on Epworth Street. Somewhere along the way, the periods of financial instability, the unpopular decisions, maybe even some pretty weird drinks . . . all of that had been forgotten by the public at large.

What people remembered, instead, was an overall impression. A *feeling* about the place that long outlived the facts.

'Do you think we should . . . buy the paper?' Robbie suggested. 'Read the article?'

El seemed to consider the idea. 'I don't know. Maybe. I could use a coffee before that, though.'

It was an invitation if ever Robbie had heard one. He felt his heart rate spike, but worked hard to keep his tone comparable to hers. 'I could have a coffee,' he agreed. Like this was normal, *casual.*

A smile broke across her face. 'Great then. Let's have a coffee.'

*

They walked along Scrutton Street, up Curtain Road and on to Great Eastern Street. The whole place was yoga studios and TV production companies, cateries and co-working spaces. All the rundown buildings and burned-out cars that Robbie could remember from his earliest days here were a thing of the past now. They popped into a Tesco Express and picked up two copies of the paper. At the self-checkout, Robbie could hardly stop himself sneaking a few more sidelong glances at El. Her new haircut was sharp and stylish, and she was as bold as ever in her bright-pink coat. There was something softer looking about her, too, though. He couldn't quite put his finger on what it was.

She still smelled the same.

Afterwards, the café they plumped for was exactly like all the others on the street: smooth, matt surfaces, save for the aluminium shine of a monstrous coffee machine. A young man and women were behind the counter.

'Two flat whites, please,' Robbie said.

'Colombian, Kenyan, or Ethiopian?'

'What was that?' he replied absentmindedly.

'As in, the beans.'

Robbie looked blankly at El, and she looked back at him equally blankly.

'Why don't you just give us whatever you reckon we'll like?' Robbie suggested.

'Absolutely! No problem at all,' the barista chirped, and for a moment or two, she openly sized them up. Then, she got moving. It was a highly complicated process, involving various buttons and levers and the sort of scales once associated exclusively with drug dealers. What was presented, at the end of it all, were two perfectly formed ceramic cups (neither with a handle), each of them appearing to contain around five good-sized sips of coffee. Together, Robbie and El paid ten pounds.

'I suppose there's probably more to the whole thing than we realize,' Robbie said wryly.

A smirk pulled at El's lips. 'I suppose there probably is,' she agreed.

They settled themselves in a table by the window, sunlight in their eyes be damned. They were the only two customers in the place.

'So you're back in London,' she declared.

'Yep. I am.'

'I was thinking about you a lot, when the pandemic hit. Did you stay in Paris, or . . . ?'

'Nope. Not for long anyway. It started to feel a bit dangerous, as well as being depressing. I actually ended up going back to Belfast for a year or so.'

'Oh wow. How was that?'

'It was good. I wouldn't have chosen it but, actually, I think I might have needed to do that even more than I needed to be off "finding myself" all around the world. I'd just developed this weird . . . *block* around it. I mean, *you* know that.'

El nodded. She had indeed known that.

'It's different now, though – Belfast. I mean, it's not perfect. I think all that stuff about generational trauma and whatever . . . it feels like bullshit, but I think it's probably all true. Most people are just so dead on, though. There comes a point in life where you realize that counts for a lot. And there's so much energy there . . . definitely more than I stuck around to see when I was 18. I mean, not that I can take any of the credit for it, but parts of East Belfast I honestly would hardly recognize now. There's even a pretty great cocktail scene.'

El smiled, happy for no other reason than that Robbie was. 'Is Anna-Claire still there?'

He nodded. 'We did a few socially distant walks. She has a little girl now, and another one on the way. New husband, obviously. Met him at church.'

'Wow,' El said again. Some part of her braced for what was surely coming next. She decided just to get it over with. 'And for you? Is there a new Mrs Saunders? Or any mini-Saunders knocking about?'

'No. Just me,' Robbie said lightly.

For a second, silence.

'Me too,' El replied then, her tone matching his – like the fact was nothing, as throwaway as it might have been to be single at 20 or at 25. She took a sip from her coffee.

'So did they manage to get *you* back in church?' she continued. 'When you were home? Or in Belfast, I should say.'

If Robbie thought it an intense topic for such an early hour of the morning, from a person he hadn't laid eyes on in years, he didn't show it one bit.

'Kind of. The unfortunate thing is, turns out I believe in God. I think I just *do*, even though sometimes it would be much handier not to. I just don't much believe in religion anymore.' He rolled his eyes self-deprecatingly. 'Yeah. I'm one of those guys now.'

'You're *spiritual*.'

He chuckled. 'Something like that. I go to a Sunday service every now and again. Or sometimes – I know this probably sounds a bit mental – I'll go to one in Polish or Romanian or whatever, just to sit there and not understand a word of it. I do *feel* something, though, sometimes. Apart from anything else, it's pretty much the only place on earth at this point that forces me not to be on my phone.'

El understood that appeal entirely. She thought, often, about the explosion of interest in astrology and crystals and mindfulness and affirmations and supper clubs and talking cafés and running and yoga and wild swimming. There was clearly some value in what churches had provided for generations, she figured. Why else would people be trying so hard, now, to find it in other places?

'Anyway, once travel opened up again, I did go back to Paris for a bit,' Robbie continued. 'Paris and then a bunch of other cities, actually. I got a job consulting for a big hotel chain – so, designing their menus but also looking at their costs and seeing where the bars could be more efficient and so on. Way less stressful when it's not my money, I can tell you that.'

'That sounds like the perfect thing for you.'

Robbie just smiled. 'So, what about you then, eh? I saw you at the Oscars.'

It was El's turn to smile at the recollection. 'Oh yeah.'

Frankie had been nominated for Best Actress in 2024.

'Who else would I go with?' she'd asked El, when she'd called to invite her to the ceremony.

'Uh, Trent?' El had replied. Trent was an emergency room paediatrician.

'Are you kidding me, Ellie? When we've only been dating for four short years? No way. You and me have been in this for the long-haul, babe. And a promise is a promise.'

It had been a glamorous week for El, among lots of much less glamorous weeks. She said as much to Robbie, and he leaned back in his chair a little, awaiting more explanation.

'My dad's not great. Stage 6 Alzheimer's now,' she said.

'Fuck.'

'Yeah.'

'I'm so sorry.'

'He's out in Richmond these days, so I essentially moved out there for a couple of years, to help look after him.'

'Wow.'

'I know! Can you believe it? Me, in the countryside!'

Robbie cocked his head. 'I don't know if we'd call Richmond the countryside, would we?'

'Well, I've seen a lot of deer there.'

'Have you also seen an overground station and a full-sized Waitrose?'

El chuckled. Busted.

'So, the two of you've made up properly then, have you?' Robbie prompted.

'I don't know. He was kind of a shit for most of his life. I don't think I have to forgive him for that, exactly. But I think of Otto and how I never . . .' El trailed off, emotion catching unexpectedly in her throat. 'Sometimes, there's just a right thing to do, you know? Even if it's a hard thing. And, don't get me wrong, there are times it's so sad – seeing the way Dad is now. I spent so much of my life trying to keep any sort of sadness at bay, and these days, sometimes there's no choice but to just *feel* it. At other times, weirdly, these past few years have been some of the nicest times I've ever had with him.'

'I get that,' Robbie said. 'God. Time has been so weird since Covid, hasn't it? Like as if it's sort of expanded in places and contracted in other places.'

'I know.'

'I'm so, *so* glad we got to finish at Love and Death on our own terms.'

'Me too,' El replied vehemently.

The Chateau Marmont had closed during the pandemic. Shortly after it, Lulu White did, too. There had been a while when El had thought that life – *society* – was fundamentally changed. She'd thought that people would never again be in a bar and cram into a booth with strangers, only to strike up a conversation, become friends or enemies for life. She'd thought the days of *try mine*, of Martini glasses exchanged, were gone for good.

In fact, things had soon reverted more or less to normal. Fewer people than she'd imagined had left their husbands or quit their jobs. She herself bought about as many clothes as she ever did, wasted just as much time assessing them online. She pressed the germ-ridden pedestrian crossing button without thinking, no matter that she'd once sworn she never would again.

'We had a good run,' she said to Robbie now.

'An *excellent* run, I'd say.'

He held her gaze, and it was the strangest thing. He'd aged, but in a good way, she thought, the way men seemed to – just a few extra, lived-in lines on his forehead, a few salt-and-pepper strands in his hair. With his artful stubble, his maroon jumper, he was all ease and assurance. A real proper grown-up now, at last. Somewhere inside him, though, El swore she could still see that earnest boy, barely more than 20, pushing his glasses up his nose.

'You know, it's funny,' she began. 'I see these kids on TikTok or wherever, and they look so good. Cool drinks and cool hair and cool holidays. I don't think they're going to look back on their photographs and just be mortified at the state of themselves, the way that we do. But to be honest, I don't know if they're having anywhere near as much fun as we did.' El paused. 'Did I just basically say *it's not like it was in our day*? Jesus.'

They both laughed.

'I'm grateful, that's all. That I got to be unfiltered when I was young.'

Robbie took her in, a smirk tugging at his lips. 'You were definitely that,' he said.

And it was a bit of a shock, to remember the sensation that his tone of voice – his particular brand of *attention* – could evidently still prompt in her. El did her best to hold onto her train of thought.

In truth, as well as feeling sorry for young people these days, she also frequently found herself incredibly irritated by them. On buses and tubes, she asked them insincerely whether they'd like to borrow her earphones. Recently, she'd seen a bunch of 19-year-old girls ordering Hackney Whores in a bar. It had given her a little thrill, to watch them all delightedly clinking glasses when their drinks arrived. They'd had no idea they owed her anything. In fact, she suspected that, in one way or another, it wouldn't have taken long for every one of them to denounce her as a Karen.

'You know what else makes me glad to be 40?' she continued. 'Well, 40-*something*, I suppose I should say. Escape rooms. Absolutely delighted I've never had to do one of those and act like it was a good time.'

Robbie laughed. 'See also: shuffleboard. Have you noticed that's a thing now? It's the new ping-pong.'

'Yeah. Another no from me.'

'Fuck the kids,' he proclaimed, and she grinned.

'That's exactly it, yes. In conclusion, fuck 'em.'

If there were also bits of their lives that El wouldn't have minded, that was a topic for another day. She thought sometimes, of her mother – of all the years Darleen had spent without the help she needed, and then ashamed once she'd got it. It amazed El that within such a short time, it had become absolutely fine and normal, for example, to be on Zoloft. It was fine and normal to be bisexual. It was fine and normal not to want to have a baby. Or even to envisage oneself maybe doing it at 40 (something). Women who were, in the grand scheme of things, only slightly younger than El, said those things all the time now. Nobody batted an eyelid.

She looked out the window, letting her gaze span the empty streets. She'd always liked this time of day, albeit for much of her life she only ever saw it having not yet been to bed.

'Do you remember that morning in Berlin?' she asked softly.

Robbie just looked at her. 'Of course I do.'

She smiled. She had nothing specific to say about it. There was just something nice about a memory shared.

'So, after the consulting with the hotels . . . what then?' she asked.

'Well, you're never going to believe this, but I'm writing a book now.'

'Robbie!' El exclaimed. 'Of course I can believe that! Of every-body I have ever met in my life, you're the person I'd *most* believe was writing a book. What's it about?'

'It's about cocktails. What else? It's not a recipe book, though. It's about the history of the cocktail. Remember, on our first shift, I was talking about various different people who'd made influen-tial drinks, and you asked me how many of them were women? Well, turns out loads of them were.'

El cocked an eyebrow. 'Who'd have thunk?' she said dryly. 'That sounds like a book I might actually read, Robbie.'

'High praise! Due to deliver it next week, actually, so it's all been a bit stressful. I have a hot-desk at this place in Holborn, and I've been pretty much living there since Halloween. *Please* will you tell me more about you now, though? I already know all about me.'

She shrugged. 'Well, looking after my dad has honestly been most of it. As I say, that's not always easy, but it does feel right. I've been feeling quite . . . peaceful, if you can believe it. I've also been . . . that is, I *am* . . . doing this course at Central Saint Martins.'

Some part of her still felt oddly embarrassed to say it out loud: *her*, at university – who did she think she was?

Immediately, though, Robbie's whole face seemed to expand with pleasure. 'What?! El! That's amazing!' he said. 'What kind of course is it?'

She felt her cheeks flushing. 'BA in fashion design. So, it's mostly practical, thankfully. But there's been more reading and essays and business-y stuff than . . . well, more than I probably would have signed up for had I known about it at the beginning.'

'It's going well, though?'

nodded. 'Yeah, it's actually going . . . amazingly. On track this summer.'

rt your own brand? I suppose you *do* know at

least one A-list actor who might be willing to wear something from a new designer, eh?'

El smiled. 'Maybe. I don't know. Sometimes, I think the best way to keep on loving something is not to try to make a living at it. But then sometimes I think . . . trying to make a living at it can actually be pretty fucking great, too.'

'Do you miss it?' Robbie asked her then. 'Bartending?'

There it was. The big question.

'To be honest with you? Sometimes, not whatsoever,' she replied. 'And sometimes . . . yeah . . . Sometimes, I miss it so, *so* much.'

There was an intensity to her own voice that she hadn't expected – an intensity, suddenly, to his focus on her.

'Me too. Would you ever . . . ?' Robbie paused, cleared his throat. 'Would you ever want to do it again?'

El just looked across at him. It didn't feel like a casual enquiry.

She wasn't altogether sure that they were even still talking about bartending.

She raised one eyebrow. 'Would you?'

'I . . . wouldn't rule it out,' he replied.

She felt her heart rate quicken, looked away from him.

Her eyes landed instead upon the newspapers that were on the table between them. 'Welcome to Q2', the front-page headline read. It promised a bumper read, a myriad of articles looking back at the first quarter of this century, and looking towards the next twenty-five years.

In the piece about Love and Death, El imagined there'd be comments from Marcus and Tameka – they'd been snapped up immediately, of course, they were riding high now at world-class bars in Manchester and Edinburgh, respectively.

Who else? El was sure a smattering of high-profile customers would feature – the *BST* cast maybe. Cecilia, perhaps, if the journalist had really dug deep. And she knew, now, that there would be an account in there from Robbie, too.

'What did you tell her, anyway? That journalist?' she found herself asking.

Suddenly, it seemed very important indeed.

It seemed like the difference between leaving this café and never seeing one another again, and . . . something else. Something brand new.

'What did I tell her?' Robbie repeated. 'Just the truth.'

'Me too.'

They stared across at one another, the next question asked in silence. What did that *mean*, though?

El found she had absolutely no idea how Robbie might have told their story, to a neutral third-party observer. How had he processed it all, with the benefit of hindsight? As a love story, in its essence? Or as a car crash? It certainly hadn't all been pretty.

For that matter, how might El's own recollections read in black and white? What, she wondered, might they reveal even to herself?

At the exact same moment, realization seemed to dawn on her and Robbie both: there was only one way to find out.

And so, with a deep breath, with a last look at one another, they each braced for whatever was ahead: for the past and the future, somehow rushing towards them all at once.

Coffees in hand, while the rest of Shoreditch slept, they opened their newspapers and began to read.

Acknowledgements

Thank you to my editor Lynne Drew, and to the wider team at HarperFiction, for all the energy and care that has gone into publishing this book. The credits following these acknowledgements underline what a team effort it truly is, and I am indebted to every single person who's been a part of getting this story out into the world.

Equally, thank you to my amazing team at Curtis Brown: Sheila Crowley, Sabhbh Curran, Anna Weguelin, Gemma Craig and Krys Kujawinska – I've so appreciated your expertise, enthusiasm, and wise counsel throughout.

I remain hugely grateful to all the readers, reviewers and booksellers who have supported my writing thus far. Authors just couldn't exist without you, and hearing from you reliably brightens even the toughest writing days. If you've stocked, reviewed, or just picked up and enjoyed *Nothing Good Happens After 2 a.m.*, thank you! Please do come and say hello on social media if you're so inclined!

I also feel so lucky to have incredible friends in my life – people who checked in over and over again about how this book was going, told me it was bound to turn out wonderfully in the end, and offered to go for cocktails with me in the name of vital literary research. Massive thanks to all of you – you know who you are! – for the lols, the reassurance, and the distraction (as required).

A few pals in particular have really taken my made-up characters far more seriously than any writer could reasonably expect:

Thank you, Marie, for still – after all these years – being my first sounding board on almost any thought that happens to cross my mind.

Thank you, Rachel, for the initial brainstorming, for all your amazing insights and plot help, and for finally getting off iMessages and onto WhatsApp just for me.

Thank you, Heather, for letting me talk about this book over so many lunches, even when you had just given birth to a (non-book) baby. Please never stop sending me links for places you'd like us to go and eat.

And thank you, Sophie, for reading my draft and allowing me to read yours, for gorgeous writing retreats, and for generally being *in the arena* with me.

Lastly, my biggest thanks, as ever, are to my family. Here's the truth, as simply as I can put it: your love and support are the bedrock of everything, and I'm forever grateful.

Credits

Together with the author, HarperFiction would like to thank the following staff and contributors for their involvement in making this book a reality:

Editorial
Lynne Drew
Olivia Robertshaw

Sales
Holly Martin
Harriet Williams
Angela Thomson
Ruth Burrow
Bethan Moore
Tony Purdue
Méabh de Courcy Mac Donnell
Laura Daley

Publicity
Libby Haddock
Patricia McVeigh

Marketing
Emily Merrill
Tink Blauth-Muszkowski

Audio
Fionnuala Barrett
Sarah Allen-Sutter

Design
Ellie Game
Claire Ward

Production
Sophie Waeland
Deborah Wilton

Operations
Melissa Okusanya
Hannah Stamp

Copyedit
Katie Lumsden

Proofread
Rhian McKay

Finance
Natassa Hadjinicolaou
Fiona Cooper
Katrina Troy